"Champagne and chocolate in book form. Prepare to be completely swept away."

>—Helen Hoang, *New York Times* bestselling author of
>*The Heart Principle*

"I am deeply in awe of Chloe Liese's spectacular talent for creating
characters that make readers feel seen. *Two Wrongs Make a Right*
is the perfect rom-com: a stunning mix of hilarious tropes, swoony
romance, and lovable, relatable characters. A must-read for every
romance lover!"

>—Ali Hazelwood, *New York Times* bestselling author of
>*Love, Theoretically*

"Absolute romantic perfection! *Two Wrongs Make a Right* is sexy,
and smart, and achingly sweet. I absolutely adored every word."

>—Christina Lauren, *New York Times* bestselling authors of
>*The Unhoneymooners*

"These two wrongs are so very right for each other. Equal parts
smart and steamy, with razor-sharp wit and an elegant, playful
rhythm that would make Shakespeare proud. There's no warmer
hug than a Chloe Liese book."

>—Rachel Lynn Solomon, *New York Times* bestselling author of
>*Business or Pleasure*

"Exquisite tension, hilarious banter, steamy romance, and a hero
and heroine with personalities that burst from the pages. A top
must-read of the year!"

>—Samantha Young, *New York Times* bestselling author of
>*The Love Plot*

"*Two Wrongs Make a Right* is an excellent addition to any contemporary romance lover's keeper shelf! Trope lovers will swoon as Bea and Jamie journey from annoyances fake-dating to unlikely friends who fall in real love! Chloe Liese nails the fast-paced ensemble chemistry of the source material and delivers a sophisticated playfulness of prose that echoes Shakespeare himself."

—Rosie Danan, author of *Do Your Worst*

"*Two Wrongs Make a Right* is a deeply tender romance that plays delightful music upon both the heartstrings and the funny bone. Full of charm, zest, and sensual heat, and with characters who are sure to join the ranks of readers' beloved favorites, it is the perfect book for anyone who loves love."

—India Holton, national bestselling author of
The Secret Service of Tea and Treason

"*Two Wrongs Make a Right* overflows with snappy banter, heartfelt emotion, and delicious swooniness and heat. Bea and Jamie's tenderness and care for one another shine on the page, and Liese's wit and humor undergird the entire story. This book is a true pleasure to read, sure to delight her many current fans even as it earns her many new ones."

—Olivia Dade, national bestselling author of *Ship Wrecked*

"*Two Wrongs Make a Right* is like hot chocolate and a croissant. It's whimsically patterned leggings on an autumn day. It's cozy, soft, sweet, and satisfying—Bea and Jamie are opposites-attract excellence; I loved their banter, and even more than that, how they evolve to become each other's unwavering pillar of support and protection. Jamebea forever!"

—Sarah Hogle, author of
Just Like Magic

THE WILMOT SISTERS SERIES

Two Wrongs Make a Right

Better Hate than Never

Better Hate than Never

CHLOE LIESE

BERKLEY ROMANCE
NEW YORK

BERKLEY ROMANCE
Published by Berkley
An imprint of Penguin Random House LLC
penguinrandomhouse.com

Library of Congress Cataloging-in-Publication Data

Names: Liese, Chloe, author.
Title: Better hate than never / Chloe Liese.
Description: First edition. | New York: Berkley Romance, 2023.
Identifiers: LCCN 2022059136 (print) | LCCN 2022059137 (ebook) |
ISBN 9780593441527 (trade paperback) | ISBN 9780593441534 (ebook)
Subjects: LCGFT: Novels.
Classification: LCC PS3612.I3357 B48 2023 (print) |
LCC PS3612.I3357 (ebook) | DDC 813/.6—dc23/eng/20220118
LC record available at https://lccn.loc.gov/2022059136
LC ebook record available at https://lccn.loc.gov/2022059137

First Edition: October 2023

Printed in the United States of America
1st Printing

Book design by Kristin del Rosario

For every feisty,
outspoken woman who's been called the shrew,
who the world's tried to tame.

And for those who've seen and loved those women
for who they really are:

big hearts, brave voices,
believers in a world that can be better.

And where two raging fires meet together,
they do consume the thing that feeds their fury.

—WILLIAM SHAKESPEARE,
The Taming of the Shrew

Dear Reader,

This story features characters with human realities who I believe deserve to be seen more prominently in romance through positive, authentic representation. As a neurodivergent person with often invisible chronic conditions, I am passionate about writing feel-good romances affirming my belief that every one of us is worthy and capable of happily-ever-after, if that's what our heart desires.

Specifically, this story explores the realities of being neurodivergent (ADHD) and living with a chronic condition (migraines). No two people's experience of any condition or diagnosis will be the same, but through my own lived experience as well as the insight of authenticity readers, I have endeavored to create characters who honor the nuances of their identities. Please be aware that this story also touches on the topic of parental loss in the past and its impact on one's life in the present.

If any of these are sensitive topics for you, I hope you feel comforted in knowing that only affirming, compassionate relationships—with oneself and others—are championed in this narrative.

XO,
Chloe

· PLAYLIST ·

CHAPTER 1: "Beatnik Trip," Gin Wigmore

CHAPTER 2: "Atomized," Andrew Bird

CHAPTER 3: "no friends," mazie

CHAPTER 4: "Doin' Time," Sublime

CHAPTER 5: "Lonely," Mean Lady

CHAPTER 6: "La Cumparsita," Sabicas

CHAPTER 7: "Beautiful Dreamer," Sara Watkins

CHAPTER 8: "Mess Around," Cage The Elephant

CHAPTER 9: "Wishful Drinking," Tessa Violet

CHAPTER 10: "Hallucinogenics," Matt Maeson, Lana Del Rey

CHAPTER 11: "Paper Bag," Fiona Apple

CHAPTER 12: "Medicine," Radio Fluke

CHAPTER 13: "This Is Love," The Hunts

CHAPTER 14: "The Next Time Around," Little Joy

CHAPTER 15: "Between My Teeth," Orla Gartland

CHAPTER 16: "Punchin' Bag—Unpeeled," Cage The Elephant

CHAPTER 17: "Guilt," Mountain Man

CHAPTER 18: "Howlin' for You," The Black Keys

ONE

Kate

My life has come to this: all my worldly possessions shoved into one trusty, albeit three-wheeled and wobbly, suitcase; seven dollars and fifty-nine cents in my bank account; and zero idea of what comes next.

This is what I get for heeding my monthly horoscope.

As the stars align, your path shifts. Change creates new chances. Old wounds offer wisdom. Your future awaits. The question is: Are you brave enough to embrace it?

That damn horoscope.

Starfished on my sister Juliet's bed, I stare at my reflection in the nearby standing mirror and ask it, "What were you thinking?"

My reflection arches an eyebrow as if to say, *You're asking* me?

Groaning, I paw around the mattress until I find my dinged-up but still operational phone, then swipe it open to turn on music. It's too quiet in here and my thoughts are too loud.

Moments later, a song from my aptly named playlist, GET UR SHIT 2GETHER, fills the room. But it doesn't help—not even the most high-octane feminist anthem can change the fact that I am so prone to act first, think later, so easily goaded by a challenge, that one minor family crisis coinciding with a taunting horoscope, and look where I've landed myself.

Home, where I haven't been in nearly two years, or stayed for longer than a week at a time since I graduated from college. Specifically, in my older sister Juliet's room while she flies over the Atlantic, headed for a stay in the quaint Highlands cottage I'd been renting. A cottage, I quickly realized after breaking my shoulder and having to pass on my usual photojournalism gigs, that I couldn't afford (neither budgeting nor saving has ever been my forte).

Since I had a rental cottage I couldn't pay for, and my sister Juliet needed a change of scenery, swapping places was a no-brainer at the time. Now, lying in my sisters' apartment, left alone to contemplate my choices, I'm not so sure.

As if she knows my thoughts are spiraling, my phone lights up with a text from Beatrice, my other older sister and Juliet's twin. I can feel her happiness in a few simple sentences, and a wave of calm crests through me, a reassuring reminder—I made the right decision in coming home. Not only did it enable Jules's much-needed escape, but it freed Bea to reunite with her boyfriend.

> **BEEBEE:** Hey, KitKat. I'm really sry for dashing off so soon after you got here. I know you get why I needed to talk to Jamie right away, but I'll come back tonight & we can spend time together, OK?

I bite my lip, thinking through how to respond. Neither Bea nor Jules knows how much *I* know about the predicament they were in or the solution made possible by my return. That's because my sisters don't know Mom spilled the tea on our monthly phone check-in and told me everything I'd missed:

Juliet and her fiancé had matchmade Bea and Jamie, the fiancé's childhood friend. The fiancé turned out to be a toxic piece of trash, and Jules ended their relationship. Even though Jamie also cut out the piece of trash, Bea brought their relationship to a halt because she knew Jamie would be a painful reminder for Jules of the man who'd hurt her. Until Jules was in a better emotional place, Bea felt that, even though it crushed her, they had to stay apart.

As I listened to my mother explain what a pickle my siblings had gotten themselves into, her voice's speed and pitch escalating in tandem with her worry, I realized for once I *wanted* to come home. The people I loved were hurting, and for once, I actually felt like I could help them, even if only in this small way.

Sure, my method required a few . . . untruths. But they were worth it. Small lies of omission. Harmless, really.

Harmless, huh? Just like that horoscope? My reflection gives me a skeptical glance.

I flip it off, then refocus on my phone, typing a response to Bea.

> **KITKAT:** If you dare show your face tonight here, BeeBee, I will spin you right around & send you back where you came from.
>
> **BEEBEE:** I just don't want you to be alone your first night home. 😞

A sigh leaves me, even as a twinge of affection pinches my chest. Older sisters.

> **KITKAT:** Newsflash, I like being alone. I get to eat all the food Mom stuck in the fridge & dance around naked to Joan Jett.
>
> **BEEBEE:** Newsflash, you'd do that with me around, anyway.

I snort a laugh and roll off the bed, wandering out of Juliet's room into the hallway.

KITKAT: I'll be fine. Seriously.

BEEBEE: You're sure?

KITKAT: Yes! I promise.

BEEBEE: You could always go to Mom & Dad's for some company?

I scowl at my phone, picturing the man who lives next door to my childhood home, who's been a source of misery for as long as I can remember.

I will not be going to my parents' and risk bumping into Christopher Petruchio—long-standing nemesis, bane of my existence, asshole of epic magnitude—because the universe is a jerk and, whenever possible, I always have the misfortune of bumping into Christopher.

KITKAT: I'm good. Now get off the phone & go bang your boyfriend's lights out.

BEEBEE: Done & doner.

BEEBEE: OH! I forgot. Cornelius needs his dinner. Would you mind feeding him? His meal is in a container in the minifridge, labeled for today.

I peer into Bea's bedroom and spy her pet hedgehog waddling around his elaborate screened-in living structure. A smile tugs at my mouth as he perks up and his little nose wiggles, sniffing the air. I'm an animal lover, and while I've never looked after a hedgehog, I'm not worried about being able to handle it.

KITKAT: No problem.

BEEBEE: Thank you so much!!

KITKAT: You're welcome. Now STOP TEXTING &
GET BANGING.

BEEBEE: FINE! IF I MUST!

I shove my phone into my back pocket and slump against the hallway, scrubbing my face. I'm jet-lagged, my system heavy with exhaustion yet humming with energy. I can't stand when I'm tired yet hyped, but such is life. Just because my body's wiped doesn't mean my brain gets the memo.

Moaning pathetically, I traipse through the living room, then flop onto the sofa just as my phone buzzes again. I reach inside my pocket and yank it out.

BEEBEE: Wait, just one more thing!

BEEBEE: In case you change your mind, a reminder
that the Friendsgiving party I told you about is 4–8.
There'll be PUMPKIN PIE.

I roll my eyes as I swipe open the screen, then type my response. Yes, my weakness is pumpkin pie. But my hatred of Christopher, who will be there, is much stronger.

KITKAT: Not a chance in hell, BeeBee. But nice try.

––––––––

Okay, so maybe my dependence on pumpkin pie is a *smidge* stronger than I care to admit.

Not so strong that I've decided to swing by the Friendsgiving party and risk seeing Christopher. Instead, there's Nanette's, a kick-ass bakery that I'm headed to, located a handful of blocks from the apartment. After some slight (read: thirty minutes of) social media scrolling, I discovered Nanette's was having a flash sale this evening on pumpkin pies, buy one, get one half off.

I might have seven dollars and fifty-nine cents in my bank account, but I do have a credit card for extenuating circumstances that I am prepared to use. Thankfully, I don't have to—I found an envelope on the kitchen counter with my name on it in Mom's loopy cursive and five twenty-dollar bills inside it. Not even the prick to my pride, that my mother had both inferred and fussed over my rocky financial status, could stop me from snatching up two twenties and powering out the door.

Clearly, the universe intends me to have some pumpkin pie, after all.

Strolling down the sidewalk toward my destination, I bask in a bracing November wind that whisks dried autumn leaves along the concrete in tumbling, percussive swirls. My WALK IT OFF playlist blasts in my headphones and I feel a swell of joy. Fresh air. Two whole pumpkin pies, all to myself. No Friendsgiving required. No having to face—

Slam.

I collide with someone just as I round the corner of the block, my forehead knocking into what feels like a concrete ledge but is more likely the other person's jaw, followed by their hard sternum jamming my sore shoulder. I hiss in pain as I stumble back.

A hand wraps around my other arm to steady me, and its warmth seeps through my jacket. I glance up, assessing if I'm under threat, but we're caught in a shadowy patch of the sidewalk, late-evening darkness swallowing up our features.

Before I can panic, the strength of their grip eases as if they've sensed I stopped wobbling. As if whoever this is understands something about me that I don't feel anyone ever has: that while I am fiercely independent, sometimes I want nothing more than a caring hand to catch me when I falter and just as freely let me go when I'm steady again.

The rumble of a voice dances across my skin, making every hair on my body stand on end. I yank off my headphones so I can hear them clearly.

". . . so sorry," is what I catch.

Two words. That's all it takes. Even if they're two words I've never heard him say before, they're all I need to recognize a voice that I know as well as my own.

Fiery anger blazes through me. Not because my shoulder's throbbing, though it is. Not because my head feels like a bell that's been rung, though it does. But because the person I've been trying to outrun is the very person I just ran into:

Christopher Petruchio.

"What the *hell*, Christopher?" I wrench my arm out of his grip, stepping back and stumbling into the reach of the streetlamp's glow.

"Kate?" His eyes widen, wind whipping his dark hair, sending his scent my way, a scent I'd give anything to forget. Some criminally expensive cologne evoking the woodsy warmth of a fireside nap, the spiced smoke of just-blown-out candles. Resentment twists my stomach.

Every time I see him, it's a fresh, terrible kick to the gut. All the details that have blurred, carved once again into vivid reality. The striking planes of his face—strong nose, chiseled jaw, sharp cheekbones, that mouth that's genetically designed to make knees weak.

Not mine, of course. And strictly objectively speaking, merely from a professional standpoint. As a photographer, I spend a lot of time analyzing photogenic faces, and Christopher's is unfortunately the epitome. Slightly asymmetrical, the roughness of his severe features smoothed by thick-lashed amber eyes, the lazy sensuality of that dark hair always falling into his face.

God, just looking at him makes my blood boil. "What are you doing here?" I snap.

He rubs a hand along the side of his face, eyes narrowed. "Thank you for asking, Katerina. My jaw is fine, despite your hard head—"

"What a relief," I say with false cheer, cutting him off. I'm too tired and sore to spar with him. "Though if you'd simply been where you're supposed to be, we wouldn't have had this collision in the first place."

He arches an eyebrow. "Where I'm 'supposed to be'?"

A flush creeps up my cheeks. I hate my telltale flush. "The Friendsgiving thing."

Christopher's mouth tips with a smirk that makes my flush darken. "Been keeping tabs on me, have you?"

"Solely to avoid the displeasure of your foul company."

"And there she is." He checks his watch. "Took all of twenty seconds for the Kat to find her claws."

A growl rolls out of me. Hugging my sore arm to my side, I start to walk past him, because he has this infuriating ability to get under my skin with a few well-placed words and that aggravating tilt of his damn eyebrow. If I stay here, I might actually turn as feral as he's always accused me of being.

But then his hand wraps around my good arm at the elbow, stopping me. I glare at him, hating that I have to look up in order to meet his eyes. I'm tall, but Christopher's towering, his body broad and powerful, his arms thicker than I can get two hands around.

Not that I've thought about that. No, if I've thought about wrapping my hands around anything, it's been that neck of his, giving it a good hard squeeze—

"What happened to you?" he says.

I blink, yanked out of my thoughts by the sharp tone in his

question. Feeling defiant, I lift my chin and dare him to look away first.

He doesn't.

My breathing turns unsteady as I realize how close our faces have become. Christopher stares down at me. His breathing sounds a little unsteady, too. "Lots happened while I was gone," I finally manage between clenched teeth. "Sort of unavoidable when you step outside your tiny world. Explore new places. Encounter obstacles."

Such as a bit of rocky Scottish landscape that led to a now-mostly-healed broken shoulder two months ago.

Not that I admit that to him.

Still, his jaw twitches. My dig's landed where I wanted.

For all his sophistication and success, a corporate capitalist's wet dream, Christopher has never left the city. Without stepping so much as a toe outside his kingdom, he's simply crooked his finger and success has come to *him*. His world is contained and controlled, and he knows I judge him for it. Just as he judges me for how carefree—and in his eyes, reckless—I am, for how quickly I walked away from my hometown and family the moment I graduated.

After losing his parents as a teen, he doesn't have a family of his own, besides his grandmother, who acted as guardian until he was eighteen and has since passed. My family is his, and he's protective of them, which is fine, but he doesn't see my perspective. He doesn't understand that I feel like an outsider in my own family, that I know I'm loved, but I don't often feel loved the way I need to. He doesn't get how much easier it is for me to feel close to those I love from a distance.

Finally he glances down, once again frowning at the arm I hold against my side. My shoulder's healed—despite what I told my family—but it's still tender enough that ramming into the brick wall of Christopher's chest has it throbbing.

A notch forms in his brow as he examines how I'm clutching it.

"You do realize," he says, his voice low and rough, "that you don't *actually* have nine lives to burn through."

Before I can answer with some stinging reply, his thumb slips along the inside of my arm, making my breath hitch. My voice dies in my throat.

Releasing me abruptly, he steps back. "I'll walk you home."

My mouth drops open. The audacity!

"Thanks for the daily dose of patriarchal manhandling, but I don't need an escort home. And I'm headed there"—I point toward Nanette's over his shoulder—"to pick up buy one, get one half off pumpkin pies. I did not suffer a head-on collision with you only to be turned around by your high-handed nonsense and sent home without them."

His jaw's twitching again. "Fine. Get your pies. I'll wait."

"Christopher." I stomp my foot. "I'm twenty-seven. I don't need to be babysat."

"Trust me, I'm relieved we've outgrown that. You were a holy terror to keep an eye on."

"Oh, har-har." There's six years between us, but for how condescendingly superior he's always acted, you'd think it was sixteen.

Brushing by him, I storm into Nanette's. The friendliness of the folks behind the counter, the tantalizing scents of pumpkin and vanilla, chocolate and buttercream, that wrap around me as I wait for my pies to be packed up, take the edge off my irritation, but not for long. When I walk back outside, clutching both pie boxes, he's still there.

Plucking the pies from my hands, Christopher nods his chin toward my sisters'—now also my—apartment. "After you."

I try to snatch the pies from him, but he lifts them out of reach.

I glare up at him. "I can walk six blocks to the apartment alone, thank you very much."

"Congratulations. So could the woman who was mugged right here the other night."

"That's terrible," I say sincerely. "But I know how to handle—"

"You have *one* fully functioning arm," he argues. "How would you defend yourself?"

Totally beyond rationality, I swing my arm and wave it around, hating myself as pain pulses in my shoulder socket. I definitely bruised it when I ran into him, if not something worse. "I'm fine, okay? I'm fine."

Or I was, until I crashed into Christopher. I told my family the truth, just not the whole truth: I *did* break my shoulder back in Scotland while working on a long-form piece about adaptation to climate change in the Highlands—it just happened two months ago.

I had to pass on jobs while it healed, then I had to face the weight of my relief and the resulting guilt that I'd been enjoying a reprieve from witnessing and capturing the bleak realities of political instability, global warming, human rights violations, the endless atrocities that were near to my heart just as much as they wore on it.

My finances dwindled, and when it came time to try to pick up work again, I couldn't seem to catch a break. So when Mom told me Jules and Bea's predicament, I had the perfect solution for all of us. I offered to swap places with Jules for a while, conveniently neglected to say *when* I busted my shoulder, only that I had, and made sure to wear the sling when I showed up this morning.

Yes, it's dishonest, and no, I don't like deceiving my family. But I knew without a legitimate injury as an explanation for my uncharacteristic return home, Jules wouldn't take me up on my offer, Mom might get her hopes up that I was home for good, and then where would we be?

Christopher stares at me, eyes narrowed. Suspicious.

Dammit, I had to bump into him while not wearing the sling,

and I just flailed my arm around to show him I'm fine. Now I have to figure out how to keep him quiet about that when everyone else in the family thinks my shoulder's freshly busted.

I'm so tired, so annoyed, so sore, I can't think straight. This conundrum is for Future Kate to solve. Present Kate needs a hot shower, a cozy bed, and a pumpkin pie eaten straight out of the baking tin.

Catching him off guard, I wrench the pies out of Christopher's hands. "Now, if you'll excuse me. I have a walk as well as a couple pies to enjoy *by myself.*"

Breezing by him, I round the corner and stomp the remaining five long blocks leading to the apartment. I don't once look back, but I feel his eyes on me the whole way.

As the foyer door of the building drops shut behind me, I scowl down at the pastry boxes in my hands. "You had better be the best damn pumpkin pies of my life." Wrenching open the inside door, I traipse up the stairs, anger a white-hot inferno burning through me. "Nothing less would make what I just suffered worth it."

TWO

Christopher

Thunder rumbles as the sky darkens to an ominous steely gray. Dashing across the lawn to the Wilmots', I scowl up at the clouds. Thanks to the rapidly changing barometric pressure and the habit my brain has of viewing my rare days off as great times for a migraine, I'm staving one off only by the grace of a strong abortive medication that I downed the second I felt pain sink its claws into my temples and scrape down my skull.

Up until thirty minutes ago, I wasn't sure if the meds would work in time—whether I was spending Thanksgiving buried under the blankets with the curtains drawn, or next door with the Wilmots.

Though, with Kate being home, I'm not sure attending Thanksgiving is going to be any less painful than a migraine.

Taking their porch stairs two at a time, I grit my teeth and mentally prepare myself.

I spend all the holidays with the Wilmots, but I'm not used to sharing them with Kate. The Wilmots' youngest daughter, the always-traveling globe-trotter, she's so rarely home, I can't remember the last holiday she spent here since she graduated from college. Which has been a mercy, because since I've known her—and that would be since she was placed as a newborn in my six-year-old arms, then promptly blew out her diaper and drenched my clothes in shit—she's been a menace to my existence. A sentiment that came naturally when we were kids and that I clung to when we became adults.

Kate despises me, which I've told myself I welcome. Despising means distance. And distance means safety. If you'd watched the people who were your world slip into a car and never come back, if one small choice meant their death and your life irrevocably altered, you'd value safety, too.

As I step up to the front door of the Wilmots', I catch my reflection in its window glass and grimace.

I look as rough as I did an hour ago in the bathroom mirror. It's not just the narrowly avoided migraine that's to blame—I slept like shit last night. I never sleep well, but last night was unsurprisingly worse, after running into Kate.

Angling my face up and to the side, I examine my reflection, the purple-green bruise that's bloomed on my jaw where Kate's hard head knocked into it. I debated shaving the dark stubble that hides it well. If I didn't shave, there would be no questions, no concern that I covet as much as I recoil from.

But if I *did* shave and the bruise was evident, Maureen—Kate, Jules, and Bea's mom, a mother to me, too—would not only see it and fuss over me, but also demand an explanation.

And then I'd just have to tell her Kate was wandering the city at night, all alone, with her headphones on, like a stubborn sitting duck, when she plowed right into me.

Obviously, I decided to shave.

Gripping the handle, I ease open the front door. Like it or not, I have to face Kate again. At least this time I won't be caught off guard.

"Boo!"

"God*dammit*." I spin, heart pounding, and face Kate. Glaring at her, I start to shut the door, but the wind takes over, dragging it out of my grip before it closes with an echoing *thud*.

Kate stands with Puck, the ancient family cat, propped on one shoulder, stroking his long white fur like a conniving villainess. Mahogany hair piled messily on her head, like always. Devious, sparkling blue-gray eyes flecked with sage. She bats her lashes innocently. "Oops."

"*Oops*, my ass." I hike the bag containing my food and wine contributions higher on my shoulder. "Like that was any less intentional than any of your other jump scares."

"Poor Christopher. Did I *scare* you?"

My jaw clenches so hard it creaks. "You didn't *scare* me."

Too much.

Suddenly, she steps closer. I take a step back. Keeping distance between us is second nature.

Kate frowns. "Would you stop? I just need to say something and then we can part miserable ways."

"Say it already, then." My jaw clenches again. I can't take being close to her, seeing the freckles dusting her nose, the fiery flash in her eyes. My gaze drags down her face, disobeying my commands, taking stock of her. The long line of her neck. The stretch of her collarbones—

That's when I realize her right arm is tucked in a sling.

The same arm she was holding tight to her side last night.

I frown, an unwelcome sensation tugging at my chest. We bumped into each other pretty roughly last night—I have the bruised jaw to prove it—but it shouldn't have been bad enough to put her shoulder in a sling. I could tell she was hurting from our collision, but she swung her arm around, showed me it was fine . . .

Then again, I know the games she can play. I came prepared with my bruised jaw. Kate's got her sling. Maybe she's not hurt but instead planning on faking it in front of her mom, casting me as the bad guy.

Then *again*, if she did that, she has to know I'd tell her mom how we ran into each other—Kate wandering the city, unaware and in her own little world with her headphones blocking off any sound, any warning of danger coming. Maureen would lose it.

So, I can only deduce she's actually hurt.

Not that I care.

If I cared about Kate and the risks she takes, pinballing her way around the world—traipsing along cliffs' edges while her thoughts are a thousand miles away, making friends with strangers who could be serial killers for all she knows, sleeping alone and unprotected in hostels, losing her wallet, forgetting to eat, dropping her phone so many times it's deplorably cracked and unreliable—I'd lose my goddamn mind.

So I don't care. I refuse to. It's that simple.

"Christopher."

I blink. I haven't heard a word she's said. Instead, I've been staring at that damn sling pinning her right arm to her body, my thoughts spiraling. My chest feels painfully tight. "Say that again."

"Try actually listening this time," she snaps. Stepping closer, she glances both ways, looking to see if anyone's coming. Voices waft from the kitchen in the back of the house, where Thanksgiving meal prep is in full swing. "I wasn't exactly honest last night," she says. "I did mess up my shoulder."

"When you ran into me."

"*You* ran into *me*, jackass. But no, before that."

I search her eyes. There's something else going on. "Then why wasn't it in a sling last night?"

Shifting on her feet, she sighs impatiently. "It's complicated."

I arch an eyebrow. "Indulge me. I think I can handle a 'complicated' explanation."

"I don't *owe* you an explanation, complicated or otherwise, Petruchio."

"You do if you don't want your parents to know you were

wandering the city alone last night with your noise-canceling headphones on and no sling in sight."

She glares up at me. "Are you *blackmailing* me, you motherfu—"

"Who's there?" Maureen says from the kitchen. It's louder, closer when she calls, "Christopher?"

I smile serenely down at Kate. "You were saying?"

"Fine," she hisses, frantically glancing toward the doorway her mother will walk through at any moment. "I tripped and broke my shoulder a couple months ago. It's healed, just sore still, okay? Now, keep your mouth shut about last night."

Our eyes hold. I fold my arms across my chest. "I'll keep quiet, but it's going to cost you more than an explanation."

She looks like she wants to strangle me.

Shit, I'm smiling. There's something wrong with me.

"What do you want?" she says between gritted teeth.

I stare at her arm, pinned against her body, and try to ignore my twisting insides.

I want to know exactly what she was doing and how endangered she was when she broke her shoulder. But I shouldn't. Because that's not how we work. I don't think about Kate when she's gone. I don't worry or care, and I sure as shit don't need to know how she hurt her shoulder.

Forcing a wide, lazy smile, I tell her, "I'll collect my due when it suits me."

"Great." Sarcasm drips from her voice. "Extortion. Can't wait."

"Happy Thanksgiving!" Maureen says, strolling into the foyer and wrapping me in a lavender-scented hug. Those blue-gray-green eyes that she gave her daughters sparkle as she offers me a distracted smile, her attention drawn toward the kitchen, where an oven timer has started beeping. "What were you doing, dawdling in the hallway like a guest?" she asks.

"I was cornered by the Kat." I jerk my head toward Kate, who glares at me viciously.

Maureen glances between us and puts her hands on her hips. "Is it too much to ask you two to get along for once?"

"Yes," Kate grumbles, spinning on her heel and storming past us toward the kitchen.

"Well." Maureen sighs wearily as we follow in her daughter's wake. "I suppose the holidays are all about tradition."

"Christopher doesn't need a holiday tradition to be an asshole," Kate calls over her shoulder. "He's an asshole every day of the year."

"And you'd know because you've been around so much?" I ask dryly.

Without looking back, Kate flips me a middle finger high in the air.

"Katerina!" Maureen chides. "You've just volunteered for after-dinner dish duty."

Kate has to have whiplash from how violently she glances back. "Mom! I have a busted shoulder."

"And one hand healthy enough to be profane in my hallway, so it's surely healthy enough to clean some plates."

Kate glares daggers at me as I throw her a smug smile.

"And you," Maureen says sternly as Kate stomps off into the kitchen.

My smile dissolves. "Me?"

"You've got enough energy to provoke Kate. You'll have plenty to handle being on dish duty, too."

I gape as she leaves me standing at the threshold.

"You're a true gentleman, West."

Bea's boyfriend—*West* as everyone but Bea calls him—stands beside me at the sink while we tackle dinner dishes. He gives me an *it's nothing* wave of his hand. "I'm happy to help clean up. And I meant it when I said you can call me Jamie. I'd actually prefer it."

I peer his way, noticing how much more relaxed and happier he seems since I first met him earlier in the fall, when we struck up a fast, easy friendship. "You're sure?"

He throws me a wry glance. "I'm sure."

The tight-lipped man, with his starched shirts and serious de- meanor, who introduced himself as West just a few months ago is nowhere to be seen. Now he's Jamie Westenberg—casually rolled-up sleeves and loose-limbed contentment as we share dish duty at the double sink.

His mouth crooks at the corner as he dries a just-rinsed sauce- pan and notices me inspecting him. "What is it?"

"You just seem . . . good. You seem happy."

The crook at the corner of his mouth becomes a full-on smile. "I am. Very glad for a holiday spent with people who actually *feel* like family rather than my family, which most certainly does not. That's what got me thinking about what name I use, what made me say it over dessert—I don't want to use West anymore. It's a name that I got at boarding school, and I've used it like . . . armor, to keep people at a distance. I don't want that armor anymore."

"We all need our armor. There's nothing wrong with needing distance."

"From people who aren't worthy of our closeness," he concedes. "Boundaries are one of my favorite things, trust me. But I don't want this boundary with the people I care about. That's why I want to be Jamie, not just with Bea, but with all the people who matter to me. You're one of them."

"Well, I'm honored, Wes—I mean, Jamie." After a beat, I give him a look, wiggling my eyebrows. "Have we just taken our bro- mance to a whole new level?"

He laughs. "Damn right, we have. It was written in the stars,

Bea says. Not that I put much stock in astrology or the zodiac, but I'll admit the more Bea foists it on me, the more compelling some of it is."

"I'm not very knowledgeable about it. What's the gist?"

"Well," he says, "take the two of us. I'm a Capricorn. You're a Taurus. Those born under those signs have a number of diverging traits but also fundamental compatibilities—both are Earth signs who align along core values such as dependability, stability, and pragmatism."

I chuckle. "I can already hear rebel-child Bea explaining all of this to you and saying that, in short, we're a snoozefest."

Jamie chuckles, too. "We are, in her words, 'inclined to be protective, practical—albeit deeply lovable—stick-in-the-muds.'"

"Well, someone has to have it together and keep things in order."

He nods. "Couldn't agree more. Which is why you're stuck with me and this astrologically ordained bromance. I'm in it for the long haul."

"Makes two of us." With no extended family living remotely close to me and my antipathy for romantic entanglements, friendships are the only kind of long-term relationship I have or allow myself. I value them deeply.

Refocusing on the dishes we're surrounded by, I pick up the pan that the turkey was roasted in and plunge it into the soapy water. "Thanks again for helping out here," I tell him. "You really didn't have to."

"I don't mind helping. Though, judging by how tense things seemed during dinner, I have a hunch you're thanking me less for the dish-duty assistance and more for the fact that my insistence on taking Kate's place means she's out there while you're in here."

I stare down at the greasy, crusted baking pan and focus on

scrubbing the hell out of it. "She's got an arm in a sling. She wouldn't be much help."

"Mm-hmm." He sets down the saucepan he was drying and picks up the next rinsed pot from his side of the double sink.

I peer his way and catch him grinning. "What?"

"You're really scrubbing that pan, Christopher."

"It's greasy!"

His grin deepens. "Mm-hmm."

"Stop saying 'mm-hmm.'"

"Step away from the pan, my friend." He plucks it out of my grip, rinsing it on his side of the sink. "You're going to take the finish right off."

Sighing heavily, I pick up a serving platter too big for the dishwasher and force myself to think only about scrubbing that. But my mind disobeys me, returning once again to dinner.

Seated next to Kate at the table, her long legs bouncing steadily beside mine.

When she reached across me for the bread basket and I breathed in her soft scent—a garden after a long, warm rain.

The moment Maureen asked about my bruised jaw and Kate's bony knee knocked mine, then stayed there, as if she was stunned that I'd kept my word—instead of telling on her, I said I'd been sparring.

To be fair, it *was* sparring when I ran into Kate. Sparring is all we do.

From outside, Kate yells, "Three-pointer!" drawing our gaze to the driveway, where she and Bea are playing one-on-one basketball.

"Bullshit!" Bea yells back. "You landed over the line!" A sports car roars down the road, drowning out whatever she says next.

I tell myself to look away as Kate bends over in hysterics, the only hand she has available braced on one knee as she laughs so hard, a wheezing sound leaves her lungs. Bea throws back her head and cackles.

"Work still stressful?" Jamie asks, taking another saucepan from his side of the double sink and towel drying it.

I tear my gaze away and scrub the platter more. "It always is this time of year."

Jamie stares at me, assessing. "But it's a little more so than in the past, I imagine."

"Yes," I admit. "Nothing I can't manage, though."

I've been managing it for a month already, when my not-large-to-begin-with investment firm lost two team members in the same day—Jean-Claude, whom I fired, and Juliet, his former fiancée, who was reeling from everything that led to him being fired and to her breaking up with him. She's been on leave for a month, taking the time she needs, which I've firmly supported.

I don't say any of this out loud, because Jamie's former friend and roommate, my former employee, Jean-Claude, is a delicate subject. Even though they're unspoken, Jamie's thoughts still follow mine.

He stares down at the pan in his hand, somber quiet settling between us.

There's no getting around the fact that Juliet's been gone from work for a month and she's an ocean away from us now because of Jean-Claude's emotional abuse. His possessive, irrational jealousy of my familial relationship to her led to a fistfight with me during my regular meeting with Jules, whom I retained as a PR consultant.

Jean-Claude's out of all our lives for good. Now that some time has passed, and Jules is on her self-care getaway, it's my hope that the echoes of his damage will finally stop lingering.

My hope seems reasonable, given Friendsgiving last night felt upbeat, albeit with a teary group photo that we texted to Jules, saying we missed her. Even tonight the Wilmot family managed a video with Jules post-dinner that put a smile on everyone's faces. Bea and Kate seem happy outside after talking with her. Maureen and Bill are still content to sit on the front porch with the laptop between them, sipping their coffee as they chat more with Jules.

"It's been a stressful season," I tell him. We both know I'm not just talking about work. "But we'll get through it. I'm confident."

Jamie nods, a small furrow in his brow. After a beat, he peers up at me, an examining intensity in his gaze. "And after you wrap up this busy year, how do you plan to recharge over the holidays?"

I shrug. "I don't have the time."

"Have or won't take?" he asks pointedly.

"I give my team the week leading up to Christmas through the week after New Year, but I don't take it myself. Busy year-end or not, I don't personally have much use for the holidays."

He frowns my way. "No use for the holidays? What kind of blasphemous nonsense is that?"

I groan. "Jamie. Don't tell me you're a holiday fanatic."

"Not a fanatic. But I do love a quiet stroll in the snow, singing Christmas carols around the piano, a glass of eggnog in front of the newly decorated tree, though not the homemade variety made with egg whites—no amount of deliciousness is worth the risk of salmonella." He pauses, then says carefully, "Why aren't the holidays of much use to you? Is it . . . because of your parents? I'm sure that it's hard, that you miss them especially then."

I peer down at the soapy water, mulling over how much I want to share. "I do miss them especially then, yes, and that's certainly part of what makes the holidays less appealing to me now. But mostly it's the aura of self-imposed stress that saturates everything during this time of year. People seem to lose perspective when it comes to all they *do* have, with this pressure to be and do even more. I want to grab them by the shoulders and shake them and say, 'At least you have money to buy presents, to put food on your table and heat your homes and clothe your kids for the cold weather. At least you have loved ones to be stressed about buying presents for. At least they're here.'"

Tipping his head, Jamie says, "Perhaps I'm projecting my despicably entitled father who embodies all of that, but does it happen at work, managing wealth? Do you deal with people who have so much yet who've lost sight of that?"

I shake my head. "Not at all. That's the beauty of how we work. Most hedge funds don't care about how they make their money and their clients don't either, but we care and our clients do, too. The entire point of how we manage and invest money is to pursue perspective, to recognize wealth's privilege and allocate it into reparative, revitalizing, equitable initiatives, companies, and organizations."

"Ethical investments," he summarizes.

"Exactly."

A fresh burst of Kate and Bea's laughter draws our focus again. Kate scoops up the ball at her feet and dribbles toward the hoop, Bea guarding her sister while careful of her right arm in its sling.

Kate flashes a feisty smile that I can't seem to tear my gaze away from. Between dribbles of the ball, she pokes Bea in the armpit, making Bea shriek and stumble away. Taking advantage of her sister's defenses being down, she shoots a layup.

"Dirty move," I mutter.

Jamie huffs a laugh. "She *is* playing one-handed. I think she's allowed to get a little creative."

"Since when are you on Team Kate?"

He grins, eyes locked on Bea as he dries the pan. "Since Kate came home and put that smile on my girlfriend's face."

Bea dribbles toward the basket while Kate does some ridiculous defending that looks more like trippy dance moves. When

Bea starts laughing so hard she can't even dribble, Kate swats the ball away, then runs toward the hoop, making another layup.

As she turns, arm raised in triumph, our eyes meet. Her glare could peel paint off the walls.

"How did you end up faring last night, with the migraine?" Jamie asks.

I blink, glancing his way. "Sorry?"

Jamie taps his temple. "Your migraine that was coming on last night."

"Oh. Uh. It wasn't the worst I've had."

I'm still kicking myself for confiding in Jamie that I get migraines in the first place, let alone that I had one last night. But when I was about to leave early from Friendsgiving last night, just as he and Bea showed up for pumpkin pie and a nightcap, looking like they'd enjoyed a thoroughly satisfying reunion, he seemed so disappointed that I was leaving. The truth just . . . came out. I told him I felt a migraine coming on, and I asked for him to keep it between us.

"How long have you had chronic migraines?" he asks.

"Easy now, the bromance isn't *that* developed."

He clears his throat. "Sorry, I get in doctor mode when I'm concerned about the people who matter to me. It's a bad habit."

"You don't need to be sorry," I tell him, meaning it. "I appreciate you caring, I'm just not used to talking about them with other people."

"Well," he says, "I respect that. But I'm here if you need to vent or if you ever need anything. I promise not to medicalize you or tell you that while lowered stress and more rest, especially around hectic times of the year like the holidays, won't *cure* your chronic condition, it doesn't mean it's a bad idea to take time off and practice self-care."

"Ah, but then who would take my place as local Scrooge, amassing his wealth while everyone else decks the halls?"

He gives me a dry look and sighs.

"Poor Jamie," Kate says. The door bangs shut as she marches in, Bea behind her. Cheeks pink, the scent of cool autumn air lingering around her. "He's badgering you into his capitalist schemes, isn't he? Typical Christopher."

I roll my eyes as she strides purposefully toward the leftovers. "Typical Kate. Misses most of what's happened, then shows up and acts like she's got it all figured out."

Kate glares at me, ripping off the lid to a container with her name scribbled on it in Sharpie.

"Wow," Bea says brightly, clearly trying to move past our tiff. "You two crushed the dishes. Thank you, Christopher." Her voice warms as she wraps her arms around Jamie's torso. "And thank you, Jamie."

Leaning in, he brushes back the hairs stuck to her cheeks. "No trouble at all."

I glance away from the lovefest and redirect my attention to the sudsy water as I fish around for lingering silverware.

"Shit," I mutter, dragging my hand out of the water. I stabbed my thumb on a knife. Inspecting it, I'm relieved to see I'm barely bleeding.

"Mess up your manicure?" Kate says.

I give her an incinerating glare, but she's oblivious or ignoring me, eyes down as she stabs a fork into her food. "And if I did? It's sexist to imply that a man getting a manicure is fodder for humor."

"I implied nothing," she says airily. "I asked a question."

Our eyes meet. I telepathically call bullshit. Kate beams a silent middle finger my way.

I stand at the sink, white-knuckling its edge, while Kate leans one hip against the counter and glares death at me. Raw, electric aggravation crackles in the air between us.

Why, when I can control *everything* else in my life, can't I control this?

As if looking at Kate hard enough will answer my question, I stare at her, hating that I notice every tiny auburn tendril kissing the nape of her neck. My gaze dips to her clothes, the ripped-up jean overalls she's wearing, the gray long-sleeve shirt that's so gossamer light I can see her skin through it.

I spend enough time around wealth to know her wardrobe isn't the purposefully distressed style rich folks drop three, even four figures on. Her clothes are old, sun-bleached, and threadbare. I wonder if she's struggled to find work or keep it, if that's why she looks like this—beaten-up clothes draping on her beanpole-thin frame. If she's home because she's financially strained.

My chest tightens sharply.

Her eyes narrow, still holding mine. "Stop staring at me."

"I'm not staring at you," I lie, rinsing my smarting thumb under cold water. "I'm trying not to gag at the sight of you eating tofurkey and gravy made with vegetable broth."

"Yes, well, at least I can rest easy knowing an animal wasn't slaughtered for me to consume on a holiday commemorating mass genocide of indigenous peoples." She throws me a fake-as-hell smile. "Not that you'd understand, Christopher, but some of us like to sleep with a clear conscience at night."

My jaw clenches. I slap off the water I've been running over my cut, then wrap my thumb in a paper towel. "Of course. Because I'm so morally bankrupt."

She glares at me and stabs another piece of tofurkey. "I'm not sure what else you call someone who makes a living off of widening the wealth gap in this fucked-up country, but—"

"If you remotely understood what I did, Katerina, you'd comprehend that I'm trying to leverage wealth in this country to *close* that gap, to direct capital into initiatives and organizations dedicated to *counteracting* social inequities—"

"Ah, right!" She tosses her fork into the now-empty container on the counter. "How could I forget? 'Ethical investing.'" Her air quotes are made a little less impactful since she only has one hand at her disposal, but it still pisses me off. "That's what you pretend it is."

The door from the dining room swings open as Bill and Maureen enter the kitchen, Bill's laptop tucked under his arm from their video call with Jules, two small coffee cups in Maureen's hands. I'm too livid to acknowledge them.

"*Pretend?*" I ask Kate. "You have no idea what you're talking about, but then again, how would you? You ran off the moment you could and haven't once looked back. You don't know about my life. You don't know about any of our lives. Because guess what happens when you leave, Kate?" I step closer to her, my voice tight and furious. "You *miss* things. Like your dad's retirement party. The launch of your mom's after-school gardening program. Bea's last art show before she stopped painting. Jules's awards ceremony for being one of the city's most promising thirty under thirty."

"And you just *live* to lord that over me, don't you?" she growls, stepping into my space. "Perfect Christopher. Knows-everything Christopher. Christopher who's always there because terrible Kate isn't."

"I didn't say—"

"You didn't have to," she snaps. "It's implied in everything that comes out of your judgmental mouth. I'm not good enough. I'm doing things wrong. I'm a fuckup. But guess what, Petruchio? You don't get to make me feel like shit about who I am or the life I live." She lifts her chin, her voice louder as she points toward her family and says, "They know I love them. They know I care. I call. I email. I send care packages. I'm here when I'm needed."

"You were *always* needed!"

"I'm here now, okay? I'm fucking here!"

"Finally!" I step closer, so close our bodies brush, jolting us both. "It's about goddamn time."

My breath is fast and ragged as heat pulses through my veins. Kate stares up at me, wide-eyed and flushed. I realize that she's ended up pressed back into the counter, that my hands are planted there on either side of her, bracketing her in. I tell them to let go. I tell my body to move away.

But I'm rooted here, resenting Kate for her unique ability to get under my skin and drive me up the fucking wall, loathing myself for not being able to stop myself from responding to her, no matter how hard I try.

And now I'm staring at her mouth, soft, parted; at her throat, working in a swallow. Kate's eyes are on my mouth, too, her breathing harsh. And then her hand settles over my chest, right beside my pounding heart. Air rushes out of me.

Her hand curls into the fabric. With surprising strength, she shoves me back.

"As much of a pleasure as this has been," she says, her voice pinched, her cheeks pink with anger, "I think it's time for me to do what Christopher says I do best."

Without another word, she storms out of the kitchen toward the front of the house, by the sounds of it, struggling with her coat and her bag, thanks to her one-handed state.

When the door slams behind her, it's so hard, the windows rattle.

· THREE ·

Kate

I'm a damn good photographer, but my truly elite skill is avoidance. I've passed the last thirty-six hours in a blur of movie marathons and social media rabbit holes to distract myself from thinking about how badly Christopher's and my familiar antagonistic cycle spun out of control.

We have our ritual. I poke Christopher. He snaps back. Christopher provokes me. I hiss and flex my claws. Wash. Rinse. Repeat.

But this was *more.*

I've never felt him watching me like he did in the kitchen, like his gaze could burn through my clothes, straight down to my skin. I've never sunk my hand into his shirt and felt air rush out of him, as if *I* had the power to make him do that. I've never seen him cage me in, fire burning in that amber gaze.

You were always *needed.*

A shiver slips down my spine as I remember Christopher saying that. I scrunch my eyes shut against the memory of him, close and intense and . . . so . . . *infuriating,* then take a gulp of my coffee.

Which is scalding hot.

"Fucking *hell.*"

"Good morning to you, too, KitKat!" The door shuts behind Bea as she marches into the apartment, cheeks pink from the brisk autumn air, her hair up in a dark ballerina bun swirled with the bleached blond that colors its ends.

She plops beside me on the sofa. I hold away my mug as the coffee inside it swells and dips, nearly sloshing over the edge.

"Sorry about that," she says, setting on the coffee table a paper bag that smells knee-weakening wonderful. "I come bearing doughnuts."

I stare at the bag as guilt curdles in my stomach. Since coming home, I've managed to show up unannounced at my sisters' apartment for an extended stay with no money to put toward rent (yet); I've had a throw-down fight with Christopher that took a giant crap on the Thanksgiving festivities in front of her and her new boyfriend; and from the moment I stormed out of Mom and Dad's house and rode the train back into the city, I've been avoiding my sister entirely.

In other words, I've been a shit sibling. And what's Bea done? Brought me doughnuts.

Sighing, I meet her eyes. "Thanks for this, BeeBee."

"You're welcome." She smiles. Then she digs into the paper bag and pulls out the only thing that outstrips my love of pumpkin pie.

"So many doughnuts," I whisper, peering in.

"Boston cream. Cake with sprinkles. Maple glaze with facon bits—"

"Hell, yes." I wrench a maple and facon bits doughnut from the bag and promptly take a hearty bite that bursts with the perfect balance of salty-sweet. "So good."

Settling back into the sofa, Bea bites into her cake doughnut. After another bite, then swallow, she glances my way. "So. You doing okay? You disappeared on Thanksgiving and haven't surfaced since."

"I'm sorry for being scarce, BeeBee. I needed some time to cool off. And I'm sorry for what happened on Thanksgiving."

She stares down at her doughnut and picks off a sprinkle. "It's no big deal."

"It is." I set down my doughnut and take her hand, my thumb tracing the edge of her beautiful tattoo sleeve, where a leafy vine curls along her wrist. "It's been hard for you and Jamie, and I didn't make it any easier on Thanksgiving. I lost my cool and made things uncomfortable."

Which isn't unheard of for me. I'm aware that I seem to feel things more intensely than most, and I know I have a short fuse, but awareness and knowing don't always translate into preventing a behavior, something I'm grateful Bea understands.

Like me, Bea's neurodivergent, though she's autistic while I have ADHD. And while she doesn't quite have the temper I do, she gets how hard it is to regulate your responses when you're over- or understimulated, when your thoughts are splitting in a hundred directions, and your skin's buzzing, and your brain feels like a Technicolor disco ball. My medication helps with this—it makes my thoughts flow better, allows me to complete multistep tasks that I'd otherwise struggle to stay focused on long enough to see through. Medication for me feels like I spend less time frustrated, spinning my tires, feeling like life happens *to* me rather than being something I actively choose.

But the great irony is that my naturally routine-disinclined, deeply curious, easily redirected brain needs to follow a routine in order to keep track of my medication regimen. On top of that, keeping track of my medication, which is already challenging for me, gets even more challenging with how irregular my work is, when I happen to be on a job somewhere that interrupts my routine and I miss a dose, or we relocate quickly, and I lose track of where my meds even are.

"KitKat," Bea says gently. "Where'd you go?"

I shake my head. "Sorry. I'm here."

Bea turns her hand so our palms meet and gives me a firm squeeze. "I didn't bring up Thanksgiving to make you feel bad. I brought it up because I wanted to check in with you. Are you okay?"

I pull my hand away. "I'm fine."

"You sure? Because what Christopher said really seemed to get to you. And I want you to know he doesn't speak for us. None of us think of your being gone in terms of what you've missed."

Of course they don't. This is the crux of my family. My older sisters are twinny close. My parents are deeply in love. Then there's me, the fifth wheel. They adore me. I know this. But I don't have that connection with them like they have with each other.

I used to feel sad about it when I was younger, when finding people who could vibe with my busy body and brain and never-ending curiosity and always-changing interests was hard and I felt lonely a lot. But now I've found my own way, a life full of new experiences and adventures, fast friends whom I'm content to part ways with and lose touch with even faster. I'm frequently alone, but I'm not lonely anymore.

At least, not often.

And yet what Christopher said struck a nerve, reminding me how deeply I've felt left out. The things I've missed. Now Bea's just confirmed how little that's mattered to them.

"KitKat?"

I blink, forcing a smile my sister's way. "I'm fine. Promise."

Bea's eyes narrow. "No, you're not. And if Jules were here, she'd get it out of you."

"If Jules were here, she'd side with Christopher."

"She would not!"

I arch an eyebrow. "She works with him. She voluntarily socializes with him. She's always sticking up for him."

"Often, but not always. She doesn't agree with everything he does. They have their disagreements, especially since he hired her to PR consult for his firm."

"That firm," I mutter darkly, shoving the rest of the maple glaze and facon bits doughnut into my mouth. "It's probably a front."

"A *front*?"

"An 'ethical investment firm'?" I snort. "Talk about an oxymoron."

Bea literally bites her lip, keeping quiet.

"What?" I ask her. "You haven't considered that it's like the perfect cover for something sinister? Money laundering! Embezzlement! Offshore banking!"

"Of course," Bea says dryly as she takes another bite of her sprinkle doughnut. "Why didn't I think of that? Christopher's got mafioso written all over him."

"He *is* Italian."

She rolls her eyes. "So that's all it takes: Italian heritage, proximity to wealth—boom, he's Don Corleone."

"You witness as much twisted shit as I have on the job, BeeBee, and see if you blame me for being suspicious."

"But it's *Christopher*."

"Precisely!" I tell her.

She sighs. "I know he wasn't on his best behavior the other night, and I'll admit that when you two are together, generally, he's no saint, but is it so impossible to believe he's capable of things like generosity and goodness?"

"Yes!"

She sighs wearily. "I don't think this is just your work talking. I think you've turned into a cynic."

I gape, offended. "I have not. I'm a realist. I always have been."

"Mm-hmm." Bea bites into her doughnut. "Okay."

"Am I perhaps *slightly* jaded, given what my work makes me see? Yeah. But I'm not a *cynic*."

"It's your blessing and burden as an Aquarius, KitKat—you see all the world's possibilities and all the ways it's failing, too."

A groan leaves me. "I deeply resent the zodiac for making me this transparent."

"That, sweet sis, is just another example of how you are a textbook Aquarius. And I love you for it."

Bea sets her hand on my thigh and pats it softly in a steady rhythm, a stim she hasn't done in a long time. I feel a nostalgic pinch in my heart that she's slipped into something she used to do often when we were kids—touch in a way Jules never found comfortable to receive for extended periods of time. Jules was the hard-hug giver. I was the one Bea tap-tap-tapped on, because it made my sensory-seeking body happy.

"I just . . ." She sighs, still steadily tap-tapping. "I just wish you saw the good parts of Christopher."

"I'm sorry, his *what* parts?"

She draws her hand away and dives into the parchment bag for another doughnut. "I'm not saying it right. I meant, I wish he *showed* you his good parts."

"I want to see none of Christopher's parts, thank you very much."

Bea frowns thoughtfully. "That's fair. It's like when you come around, he's his worst self."

The world does a record scratch. I stare at her, surprised. "You've noticed that?"

"Of course I have. I've also noticed that *you* are your worst self with him, too." She slouches on the sofa, doughnut in hand. "What I don't understand is why you two make each other so miserable."

"It started with him! He made me miserable first," I blurt, instantly kicking myself for my honesty as I watch Bea's eyes widen.

My family has never seen Christopher for who he is—someone who's always made me feel like an annoying outsider when I already struggled to find my place in our dynamic. My parents and sisters perceive his behavior as big-brotherly concern, good-natured teasing. Often, it feels like they haven't perceived it at all, how every chance he has, he arches that disapproving eyebrow and says just the thing to piss me off or make me feel like shit.

Bea slips her hand over mine. "What do you mean?"

"Never mind." I desperately want to slap a bandage over the yawning, vulnerable hole that my confession's blasted in my chest, and move on.

"Not so fast." Bea yanks the doughnut bag away and slides down the length of the sofa, out of reach. "No talkie, no doughnut . . . ie."

I glare at her. "Put down the doughnuts, BeeBee."

She shakes her head. "I mean it. I'll—I'll . . ." She glances around the apartment, before the lightbulb goes on. "I'll throw them out the window."

"You wouldn't."

She bolts toward the tiny kitchen window. "Don't test me, Kit-Kat. And let me be clear: I cleaned out Nanette's maple and facon bits doughnuts. Good luck going back and buying more."

"Fine!" I yell. "I'll tell you. Now, hand over the doughnuts."

Bea arches an eyebrow. "Spill first. Doughnuts after."

A heavy sigh leaves me as I flop back on the couch, nearly drowning in the abundance of throw pillows whose sheer volume has Jules written all over it. It's easier to tell the truth when I say it to the ceiling, so that's what I do.

"Christopher always makes digs at how little I'm home, my choice to travel all over for work. He talks down to me like he sees my lifestyle as immature or . . . I don't know, inadequate. When he was younger, he ignored me, like I didn't even exist. When I got older, he started picking apart everything I did. He's either looking down his nose at me or he's not looking at me at all, and no-body's ever done anything about it."

"KitKat." Out of the corner of my eye, I watch the doughnut bag lower like a deflated balloon, until Bea's holding it limply at her side. "I didn't know. I never saw . . ." There's a beat of silence, then: "Why didn't you say anything?"

Still staring at the ceiling as Bea leaves the kitchen and joins me on the couch, I blink away the rare, unwelcome sting building be-hind my eyes. I *hate* crying. "I figured everyone saw what I saw and didn't care."

"No." Bea wraps her hand around mine, squeezing tight. "I promise you, we didn't. I'm sorry."

"I believe you. Besides, why would you? He's always been nice to you and Jules, so why would you assume the worst in him when he's only ever shown you his best? Same with Mom and Dad—he's like the son they never had. In their eyes, Christopher can do no wrong."

Bea wrinkles her nose. "I mean, they clearly weren't thrilled with how he spoke to you on Thanksgiving. Mom made him not only scrub but put away an obscene pile of dishes on Thanksgiving. Then, after you left, he took care of Dad's nightly haul of food scraps to the compost bin *and* Puck's litter."

And after those couple of measly tasks, I'm sure Mom and Dad have already forgiven and forgotten.

Struggling to read my silence, she says, "I've just made things worse, haven't I?"

"No." I shake my head. "It's okay."

"You can tell me if it's not okay. I know you're protective of me, KitKat—you always have been, even though you're my little sister. When Jules was being a social butterfly and people took their shots while my twin was gone, you came in swinging."

I smile faintly. "I do have pretty strong Big Sis Energy."

"You do." Her eyes search mine, before they dance down to where she holds my hand. "But I don't need your protection anymore."

My heart twists. Another way things have changed. Another way I'm not needed. I nod. "Okay."

Staring down at my hand, Bea takes a deep breath, then meets my eyes long enough to say, "Let me be big sister for once and take care of you. Let's stop talking about Christopher and enjoy Sister Day."

"Sister Day?"

She gives my hand a firm squeeze, then releases it. "Sister Day."

I shift on the sofa, nervous. Unless Sister Day consists solely of sitting on our asses, eating these doughnuts, whatever we do is going to cost money I don't have.

I can use the credit card, I guess. And then I'll make myself double down on gig hunting tomorrow, send out emails to photographer contacts in the city and put out feelers to see if any of them need help getting caught up with editing their photos.

"Don't worry," Bea says, misinterpreting the unease I'm sure I'm broadcasting on my face. "We'll keep it low-key. How about we hit up a couple of those vintage shops you love, grab some street food, then come home, get into jammies, and watch a foreign film. They always make you cry while you pretend not to cry and put me to sleep; I could use a nap."

I wallop her with one of the fifty-five ridiculous throw pillows on this sofa. "I do not cry. My eyes may mist up sometimes, but only because of this city's dry-ass air."

"Sure, KitKat." Bea dodges another pillow lobbed her way.

Just as she pops the last of her doughnut in her mouth, Bea's phone dings and she scoops it up. A smile I've only seen in the past few days brightens her face.

"Jamie?" I ask, leaning back on the sofa and biting into a new doughnut.

She nods, smiling as she types back.

"You don't want to spend the day with him?"

Bea frowns my way and sets down her phone. "One, I was with him the past two days nonstop. Two, he's working today, then he has plans with a friend this evening."

"Anybody worth introducing your sister to?"

Not that I'd have the first idea what to do with them, even if they were. It's not a high-speed highway for me, the road between meeting someone I find compelling and wanting them sexually. Since realizing attraction seems to work differently for me and trying to be open about that with people I thought I might be into, I've been met with impatience, dismissal, frustration, and ignorance. I got fed up. I stopped trying, stayed busy with work, exhausted myself, ignoring that quiet ache inside me that wished someone would understand how I worked and want me as I was.

Bea grimaces.

"What?" I poke her gently. "You don't like this friend of his?"

She shakes her head. "No. I like him."

"Then what is it?"

She lets out a weird half laugh, half choke. "Can I plead the Fifth?"

"Oh, come on. You're not betraying Jamie by just talking about someone besides him."

"No." She shakes her head. "It's not that. It's just . . ." Groaning, she digs around the doughnut bag, unearths a powdered sugar doughnut hole and pops it in her mouth, then says around her bite, "It's Christopher."

My jaw drops. "Jamie is *friends* with that Neanderthal?"

"Since we started dating. They get along really well."

I raise my coffee mug, my voice solemn. "To another brave soul, lost."

She snorts a laugh and smiles. "No more talking about Jamie. Or Christopher. Today is Sister Day. Only us. Got it?"

I smile back. "Yeah. That sounds perfect."

FOUR

Christopher

Fiona's is one of my favorite pubs, so when Jamie suggested we meet there after work, I was more than happy to say yes.

As I stroll in, Fee's familiar sounds and scents—the soccer game on TV and the Irish grandpas who sit at the bar swearing at its screen, cold foamy beer and crisp fried food—greet me like an old friend.

Jamie half stands from his seat at a booth along the wall and raises a long arm in greeting. I weave through the tables toward him, and we lean in to clasp hands, then offer each other a brisk, backslapping hug.

At six two, I'm used to being the tallest person in a social setting, stooping and bending when I greet people, but not with Jamie, who's six four, his height emphasized by a lean runner's build. We pull apart and drop across from each other at the booth, which is a little tight for two people our height, but we make it work, stretching our legs in opposite directions and opening our menus.

"Let's see what there is," he says, before clearing his throat. Twice. I haven't known him long, but I've learned it's something he does when uncomfortable or nervous.

I lower my menu, looking at him carefully. Jamie stares with deep concentration at his menu.

"Jamie."

"Hmm?"

"Those are the desserts."

He drops his menu like it's burning, then snatches it back up. "Perhaps I'm craving something sweet."

I arch an eyebrow. "I thought you didn't like sweets. Something about how they're hard on the endocrine system."

"Well." Another throat clear. "They are. But I'm loosening up on that a little."

"Wonder under whose influence."

Bea has the biggest sweet tooth of anyone I've ever met. Jamie's faint blush as he grins and flips the page of his menu confirms my theory.

"First time here?" I ask him.

"Hmm?" He glances up quickly. "Oh. Yes. It is."

My gaze slides down the list of familiar appetizers. "The Reuben nachos are great if you haven't—"

"Well, look who it is!" As if he's materialized from thin air, Bill Wilmot stands beside our booth, smiling widely. Salt-and-pepper hair, deep blue eyes magnified slightly by his wire-rim glasses, he squeezes my shoulder affectionately. "Fancy seeing you here!"

Jamie drops his menu, eyebrows raised. "Bill! What a surprise! Say, why don't you join us?"

My gaze dances between them. I have never met two more earnest men than Bill Wilmot and Jamie Westenberg. They're up to something, and they're doing a terrible job of hiding it.

Slowly, I close my menu, observing Bill slide into Jamie's side of the booth. Bill's not short himself, so the sight of these two men over six feet crammed together is almost comical.

"What brings you here?" I ask Bill, who immediately accepts the menu Jamie's offered him.

"Little of this, little of that." Bill sniffs, dropping his chin so he can read the menu through the right part of his glasses. "Maureen told Fee she'd send in some flowers for the wake they'll be having here tomorrow, and I was in the mood for shepherd's pie, so I brought in the flowers for her, ordered carryout, and here we are."

"Which means you're searching the menu, why?"

Bill flips the menu page. "Browsing, in case something else strikes my fancy."

I narrow my eyes. Maureen and the pub's owner, Fiona—Fee, as everyone calls her—are old friends, and Maureen is a master gardener whose greenhouse bursts with blossoms that she's always generous with. Bill's both devoted to his wife and, especially since his retirement, about as inclined as Kate to stay still, so this story about delivering his wife's flowers in the city for a wake at Fee's is entirely plausible. It might even be true. It just doesn't mean that's *all* there is to it.

Jamie clears his throat. Again.

I sigh as I set my elbows on the table and lean in. "Okay, you two. Out with it."

Bill meets Jamie's gaze, blinking owlishly. "Jamie? You feel like sharing any thoughts?"

Jamie's eyes widen to saucers. "Me? This was *your* idea!"

"Well, it was easier in my head," Bill mutters. "I prefer my battles and confrontations left squarely in literature." Drawing in a breath, he sets a hand on my elbow, then says, "Christopher. You know I love you like a son."

A knot forms in the pit of my stomach. I hate when he says that as much as I love it. I've tried to protect myself, to keep myself from getting too close to Bill and Maureen, seeing them like a second father and mother to me. Moments like this remind me that ship sailed years ago.

I was thirteen when my parents died, when my paternal grandmother came to live with me and offered about as much comfort as those needle-packed pincushions she left all over the house. So

I found comfort next door in my parents' best friends, Maureen and Bill, in their daughters, who became even more like sisters to me—

Well, at least two of them.

I push away aggravating thoughts of Kate as quickly as they arrive, focusing on Bill.

"I know," I tell him quietly.

"Good." He pats my elbow once more. "Bear that in mind with what I'm about to say." Clearing his throat, he laces his hands in front of him, elbows on the table. "What happened at Thanksgiving, as well as some further . . . insight"—his gaze slides to Jamie, then back my way—"has led to an epiphany."

"Whose epiphany?"

Bill tips his head from side to side. "Mine. Maureen's. I won't speak for others."

Jamie is quiet beside him, adjusting his watch so the face bisects his wrist bones.

"And what was that epiphany?" I ask, trying not to sound testy, but the fact is, I'm not used to being the one in the hot seat, waiting for insight. I run a company and my life with utmost control. I don't do well with unknowns and anticipation.

Staring at me intently, Bill says, "Indulge me in a Socratic inquiry, Christopher."

I rub the bridge of my nose. "You can take the professor out of the classroom—"

"But you can't take the classroom out of the professor," he says. "Too true. And the Socratic method of teaching served me well for many years, young man, so stay with me."

"I'm staying."

"Good. Now. How do you think Kate feels about how you two get along?"

I blink at him. "Feels? I think she feels that we get along terribly."

"And why do you think that is?"

"Because we get along terribly. Because since she graced this fine earth with her presence, she's provoked me and I gave it right back. Because unlike the rest of you, I haven't hidden my disagreement with her choices, my concer—my disapproval, I mean—of how she lives."

"How do you know that we see it like you do?" he asks.

I frown. "Don't you? How can you not? How can you not take issue with her living that way, taking on so much risk, even outright danger?"

"When you have children, Christopher—"

I snort skeptically.

"—you'll understand. They're your heart beating outside your chest, but there's no putting it back. You learn to live with the fear, because that's what it is to love them."

"That sounds hellish."

"It can be," Bill admits. "But what's truly hellish is seeing your child hurt. And it's not just Kate I'm talking about. What Juliet just went through, the toll that took on Beatrice, the toll *this* is taking on Bea now . . ."

I glance toward Jamie. "The toll on Bea?"

Peering down at his cuffs, he straightens them. "Well. To put it . . ." He sighs. "Oh hell, I don't know how to put it in a way that spares your feelings, so I'm just going to be honest."

"Please."

"Bea called me very upset this morning. She said Kate told her things about your relationship, explained it in a way Bea had never picked up on that made her feel terrible. That made her feel like she has to take sides. And now she's worried it's going to be how things were with Juliet and Jean-Claude all over again, having to choose between people she loves because of this, creating tension and factions in the friend group, in your family."

I sit back, wrestling with what I'm hearing. "What did Bea tell you specifically?"

Jamie hesitates, then says, "I don't feel like I can say that without betraying Kate's confidence in her." He glances at Bill.

"In fact," Bill offers, "I'd suggest that *Kate* is the perfect person to talk to about this."

I stare at him, struggling to find a way to convey how impossible that is without revealing myself.

Well, you see, Bill, I've been a moth to the flame of your youngest daughter's animosity for a long time, and I've fed it like a wildfire with the fuel of my own frustration. Because I don't look at Kate and see her how I see your other daughters. I don't look at her and think "sister." I look at her and see a tumbleweed who'll never stay in one safe place, a money-hating hellion who despises what I covet for its stability and power, a fierce, electrifying woman who could send me up in flames if I got too close.

"Whether you talk to her or not," Bill says, reading my disdain for this idea in my pinched expression, "how you two interact has to change."

Dread seeps through my system. "Change? How?"

"I need you to make peace, Christopher," Bill says, holding my eyes. "I know Katerina isn't the . . . tamest of personalities, that you and she don't have the most commonality to bring you together, but I believe you both have the capacity to be kinder to each other. You can get along well enough that holidays and homecomings don't turn into a war zone with everyone who loves you both caught in the cross fire."

"Does Kate know you feel this way?" I ask. "Is she getting the same speech?"

Bill adjusts his glasses. "No."

"Why the hell not?"

"Because"—he smiles gently—"I know my daughter. And I know that she cannot be told to reexamine something or change her perception; she must be shown and . . . perhaps . . . led, without her precisely knowing."

"You mean deceived?"

His smile fades. "Would it be a deception if you were simply gentler to her? Kinder to her? If you tried to make amends? Would it matter who started it, when all's well that ends well?"

"I can see it mattering to Kate very much."

He searches my eyes. "Then perhaps you'll find a way to tell her the truth—that you didn't know how damaging your dynamic was until others helped you recognize it."

His words land like a blow to the gut, knocking the wind out of me. It's never gone that far, has it? Our dynamic's *damaged* her? Feisty, fiery, tough-as-nails Kate? With a few honest words, the natural clash between our personalities, innocuous years spent ignoring her when she was young, then keeping my distance once she was grown up?

I've wanted distance from Kate. I've wanted to feel indifferent to her. Never to hurt her.

I can't have hurt her, can I?

"I think you're wrong," I tell him.

Bill's smile returns again, tinged with amusement. "Maybe I am. Or maybe *you're* wrong. You'll figure it out soon enough, if you do what we've asked and try to make things right."

"'Make things right.'" I sigh as I massage my temples, which have begun to thud dully.

"Talk to her," Bill says. "And then listen to her."

"How about I just keep a low profile until she's gone?" I offer, knowing I sound desperate, but too desperate to care. "She'll leave soon. She always does."

Bill shrugs. "She might leave. Or she might stay awhile. Who knows."

My stomach drops. How am I supposed to share a city with

that woman when I can barely survive her typical four-day visits? We haven't regularly coexisted in the same hemisphere since I was eighteen and she was twelve. Back then I was a teen on the verge of adulthood, Kate a kid who delighted in my annoyance. She'd jump out of tight corners to scare the shit out of me, stick fake spiders in my shoes, give me wet willies while I did homework at the Wilmots', desperate for the comfort of a homemade meal and a parent to ask the occasional question. She was a menace whom I menaced right back, six-year age difference be damned.

Kate was still that menacing little girl when I left for college and stayed away all four years, letting my grandmother live her best cranky life alone in my childhood home. I rented an apartment with the disgusting amount of money left to me by my parents after their death and hid from the Wilmots. Because two days into being at college in the city, I realized how badly I missed them. And I feared what missing them meant—that they mattered to me, that I loved them, that I could lose them, and it would crush me. I'd sworn to myself after I lost my parents that I would never love and lose again. Distance was my only coping strategy.

That strategy lasted me through college and two years postgraduation, until my grandmother died. And then there was no one left in the home my parents had filled with memories. Their photos still lined the walls. My mother's quilts draped across the beds. My dad's family recipes still sat on their shelf in the kitchen. I couldn't sell it, couldn't let it sit empty, unloved, left to fall apart and be forgotten.

So I moved home. And there was Kate, out on her parents' porch next door with some small helpless creature cupped in her hands. Tall and lanky like her father, with her mother's sea-storm eyes. Freckles on her nose and streaks of auburn in her dark hair from all the hours she clearly still spent outside.

I looked at this eighteen-year-old in front of me, who'd shot up into a woman, wild and electrifying, barely recognizing her, while a very different kind of recognition blazed through me.

I knew right then that peace was the last thing we were ever going to share.

"Christopher?" Bill presses. "What do you say?"

I blink, torn from my thoughts. "I'll . . . try."

And by "try," I mean I'll make myself scarce, even if Kate stays a bit longer than she typically does. I'll stay away and she'll cool off. It'll blow over. Then she'll be gone, and I'll have kept my distance. No more fights will have happened, and that will appease our family and friends.

The sound of Bill's name cuts through the uneasy silence at our table. Hearing Fee call him, Bill glances toward the bar, where she pats a to-go bag and offers him a smile.

"Well." Bill stands slowly. "I've said what I came to say. And now my shepherd's pie is ready to go." He raps his knuckles gently on the table. "Don't blame Jamie for this intervention, by the way. I asked him if I could crash your meet-up."

Jamie scrubs his face.

"I am sorry about the other night," I tell Bill. "And I'll try to smooth things over."

Gently, he clasps my shoulder again. "Thank you."

As Bill walks away, Jamie sits back against the bench and rubs his eyes beneath his glasses. "Well, that was stressful."

"Says the one who wasn't in the hot seat."

"God, I'm sorry. I didn't want you to feel like that."

"It's all right," I tell him. "I appreciate your honesty. I think I'm just . . . wrapping my head around it."

Two pints of Guinness are set at our table, then a shot beside my beer, which, judging by the smell, is a strong Irish whiskey.

Jamie frowns in confusion and says to the waiter, "We didn't order these."

"Compliments of Fee." They jerk their head toward the bar. "She said you both looked like you needed it. You especially," they tell me.

"Cheers to that, I guess." I raise my beer glass and knock it with Jamie's as he lifts his, too.

After tipping back our pints, we set them down on heavy exhales. "I'm not touching the whiskey." I slide the shot toward Jamie, who slides it away from himself, toward the edge of the table.

"Me neither," he says. "A shot and a beer, and I'd be laid flat. I'm too old for that nonsense."

A laugh leaves me. We're both only in our early thirties, but I feel the same way. "Hangovers in your thirties hit hard."

"They really do," he says. "I'm glad I'm not the only one who feels like this. You're, what? Thirty-three?"

My laugh fades. "Yeah."

This coming April, I'll be thirty-four. One year closer to being as old as my father was when he died. Since I've realized how close I'm getting to outliving him, I dread each birthday a little more.

"Something wrong?" Jamie asks.

I force a smile and lift my hand for the waiter. "Nothing a plate of Reuben nachos won't cure."

FIVE

Kate

"We've arrived!" Bea trills. Shouldering open the door of the Edgy Envelope, she enters the store on a dangerously lopsided twirl that almost takes out a standing display of greeting cards. "Bring Your Sister to Work Day has commenced!"

I shut the door behind me on a sigh. "You are aggressively cheerful when you're in love."

"Aren't I?" She grins.

I roll my eyes, a begrudging smile tugging at my mouth. Bea's happy in a way I haven't seen her in years, maybe ever. For her sake, I'm trying to act happy, too. But the truth is I've never been good at faking much, especially happiness, and I'm too on edge to be happy right now. This is officially the longest I've been home in half a decade, and as I step inside the Edgy Envelope, the place that seems to knit my sisters' friend group together, worries tangle into an anxious knot beneath my ribs.

How will they see me, what will they think of me, these people who've always been more Jules and Bea's than mine, if I'm not the wild-child sister who shows up once in a blue moon for a couple of fun days that are a blur of board games and beers and not enough time to be known beyond that?

"There you are!" Sula waves from behind the glass-topped

checkout desk. The owner of the Edgy Envelope, the custom stationery and paper shop for which Bea both designs and works the sales desk, Sula was Jules's friend first but clearly has become just as close with Bea, whom she squishes into a hard, affectionate hug.

I love hugs, the sensory joy of being wrapped tight and receiving pressure, but something about me must broadcast that I don't, because I've observed how readily people hug my older sisters yet not me. Maybe it's my height. Maybe it's my resting bitch face. Maybe today it's simply because I'm wearing the sling.

Sula turns my way, beaming like the sunrise outside, with her bright smile and burnt orange–dyed buzz cut. "Good to see you, Kate. I'm so glad you're here!"

"They're here!" Bea's friend Toni calls, strolling in with a smile and wave for me and another hug for Bea. "Aaand the moment you've all been waiting for," he says. With a flourish, Toni whips off a floral domed lid on the desk, revealing a glistening tower of glazed doughnuts that smell like autumn incarnate: tart apples and cinnamon, pumpkin and pungent nutmeg, warm vanilla and rich maple syrup.

I stare at the doughnuts, my mouth watering. "Wow."

Bea smiles up at me. "A welcome home treat. I told him doughnuts and fall flavors were your favorite."

"She did." Toni smiles. "And I have to say, they were a nice break from the same three cookie recipes that keep this one smiling for the customers."

Bea pokes his side. "I smile for the customers! On the rare occasion, I might come off as a little artistically aloof."

Sula gives Toni a chiding look. "Bea does great with the customers."

"Thank you!" Bea *hmph*s. "So there, Ton."

"It was a joke!"

It's bittersweet, watching them talk with so much familiarity and affectionate teasing. I've never been close to anyone like this.

Their teasing stops as Toni takes doughnut orders, setting them on delicate Edgy Envelope house-brand multicolored plates that are made of recycled material, according to their soy-ink-stamped label on the back.

"These are beautiful," I murmur around a bite of cinnamon-spiced apple cider doughnut, lifting an unused plate to the light.

Bea watches me with a smile on her face. "You've got your photographer's face on."

"Hot damn." Sula gasps, dropping her doughnut onto its plate.

"What?" Toni clutches her elbow. "Too sweet? Not fried long enough?"

"The doughnuts are perfect," I tell him.

"Agreed," Bea says, before licking maple glaze off her thumb. "What are you gasping about, Sula?"

"I," she says proudly, "have a fabulous idea. Kate, you should work here! Take photos for the website. Work some front desk hours, too. Bea's planning to reduce her hours so she can dedicate more time to her independent commissions, now that she's back at painting, so you could take some of her hours. Heck, take all of them!"

Bea and I choke on our doughnuts.

"I still need *some* hours, Sula!" Bea says.

I whack a fist into my chest and use my default excuse for whenever I'm feeling cornered and caught off guard. "Not sure how much longer I'll be here. Probably not a good idea."

"What's the rush?" Sula asks. "You're not staying home through the holidays? They're only a month away."

Only a month. I haven't lived at home for a month since before I left for college. I can't deny the thought crossed my mind over the past five years when a homesick pang struck around the holidays and I was far from my family, but every time I considered acting on it, the fear that I'd come home hoping to feel less lonely, only to find myself lonelier than ever around the people I loved most, would stop me in my tracks.

"Um. Well. That's really kind of you . . ." I blink at her like a deer in the headlights. "I'm just not sure what I'm . . . doing?"

I haven't heard from the few photographers I still know in the city, and I haven't let myself think about how many of my contacts didn't get back to me when I was still in Scotland, trying to pick up leads for work once my shoulder was healed. Was it something I did? Sure, I was late to some shoots, I missed a few deadlines, but in general, I think I built a decent reputation among the people I worked with. Whether my recent professional dead ends are a coincidence or the universe is doing me dirty, I can't deny my current desperation makes Sula's offer enticing.

"Oh, and I can pay you cash," she says. "Keep it under the table."

Little dollar signs dance in my eyes. My finances have dwindled to the last bit of cash Mom left, and I've used my credit card sparingly, but rent will be due soon for Bea, and I want to at least contribute something toward it. I don't know how long I should stay here to make my story about why I came back convincing enough not to raise suspicion when I leave, but I do know I'm not comfortable staying in the apartment any longer with no income to contribute.

"No pressure, of course. Take the time you need," Sula says, even as she smiles at me like she already knows I'm going to say yes. Then she helps herself to what smells like a chai doughnut and mercifully changes the subject. "So. Bea. How are things since reuniting with that tall, dashing beau of yours?" She wiggles her eyebrows. "Makeup boinking is the best kind of boinking, isn't it?"

"All right," Bea says, taking Sula's shoulders and gently turning her toward the back of the store. "That's enough out of you. Take your doughnut and get number crunching. This place doesn't bookkeep for itself."

Sula throws a scowl over her shoulder as she tromps toward the back hallway. "Cruelty, thy name is business management."

Toni shakes his head. "It's like a cosmic meddling void was created after Jules left, and now Sula's filling it." Turning to me, he says, "She just wants you to feel welcome and included. Whether or not you take her up on the job offer, I hope you spend as much time here with us as you want."

"Toni," Bea singsongs. "Why don't you just say what you're buttering her up for?"

Toni laughs nervously. "Who, me? Last time I buttered up something was my morning croissant."

Bea snorts a laugh. "Just ask her."

"Okay." Toni drops his doughnut and faces me, slapping his palms together in a prayer. "I might be *massively* behind on content for the store's social media."

"Ooh, Sula's gonna get you," Bea croons.

"You hush your mouth," he hisses, then turns back to me. "But if I had someone with your creative credentials, your photographic finesse—"

Bea snorts again. Toni gives her a death glare, then smiles widely at me.

"—I'd have a prayer," he continues, "of digging myself out of this mess."

"For pay," Bea says pointedly.

"Of course for pay," Toni tells her, then says to me, "Do you accept baked goods as currency?"

"Toni! You can't ask her to do your job, then pay her in doughnuts."

"Well, I'm sorry, okay? I never even *wanted* to do social media content, but no one *else* around here seems inclined," he says, widening his eyes meaningfully.

Bea's jaw drops. "I've been a little busy! Sorry I've only been making art for the place and selling it, not marketing it on social media, too—"

"I'll do it!" I say, loud enough to bring the bickering to a stop.

Toni snaps out of it first. "Oh my God. You're a lifesaver, a goddess, a—"

"Woman who requires payment in *cash*, not doughnuts," Bea tells him, poking his side.

He yelps. "Of course. No, you're right. I'll pay you—"

"As a consultant," Sula says from just a few feet behind, startling all three of us and making us spin around. "I wasn't *trying* to eavesdrop, but you're all unavoidably loud. I know things have been chaotic this fall, and we're all wearing a lot of hats right now." Gently, she squeezes Toni's elbow. She gives Bea a soft smile.

Then she turns toward me. "Still no pressure to answer today, but we'd love to have you taking photos for our social media. You'd have carte blanche. Get creative, have fun. I'd also love to update the website photos, too, but we could discuss that separately, if you want. I'm a shit baker, so my offer stands to pay in cold hard cash."

I feel a little kick of excitement, a flutter in my belly like a kaleidoscope of butterflies taking wing. It's been a long time since I did the kind of photography she's talking about—purely aesthetic, just for fun, playing with light, experimenting with perspective. For years, I've taken job after job, staying too busy to process the emotional toll of covering such intense material. The news is often focused on the worst in the world because that's what sells, and I do believe in shedding light on what's bad to wake people up and compel them to fight for change, so I've sought out those hard stories. And yet, while it's been a privilege to try to do *something*, to uplift voices and advocate through my camera, it's also worn on me. I told myself that it should, that I should feel burdened and sad and angry about the injustices and human failures that I captured, that I shouldn't feel joy after seeing firsthand how much is profoundly broken in this world.

But something about standing here, surrounded by beautiful things, and good food, and kind people, makes me think maybe wanting to feel a bit of joy for just a little while wouldn't be so terrible after all.

I glance my sister's way, watching Bea's attempt to hide her hope dissolve into a full-on smile. That's when I realize I'm smiling, too.

Finally, I turn back to Sula. "When do I start?"

———

Two days later, I'm hired and officially trained, dunking a piece of pumpkin glazed doughnut (made by Toni, of course) into a cup of cold coffee that I forgot about this morning.

"Well," I tell Toni and Bea, who sit across from me at the back of the store, all our feet up on an old crate. "This is exhausting shit."

They both nod.

"But it's energizing, too."

"You're a natural at it," Toni says. "You caught on so fast."

Bea beams my way. "She's like that with everything. When Kate's compelled by something and decides she's going to learn about it, she throws herself into it, works her butt off, and figures it out. Every time. I've always admired that."

Happiness, thick and sweet as honey, seeps from my heart through my limbs. "Thanks, BeeBee. That's nice of you."

"I say what I mean, KitKat." She toes my Doc Martens with

hers. I've always privately loved that while Jules wouldn't be caught dead in Doc Martens (in her words, they do *not* flatter her silhouette), Bea's always been my Docs twin.

Toni clucks, nodding his chin toward our boots. "Tell me you two brought shoes with less tread to change into later."

"Shit." Bea groans, dropping her boots to the floor. "I forgot."

"Forgot what?" I ask.

Toni rolls his eyes. "I swear to God you two need a personal secretary."

"Sula's birthday party," Bea reminds me, voice lowered. "Tacos and Tangos. You said you didn't think you were up for it."

Toni frowns. "Wait, why not?"

I glance back toward the office, where Sula came in to work hours ago and hasn't come out since, birthday be damned. Two days of being here, after all the kindness she's shown me, I can go to her birthday party. "I wasn't sure I'd feel good enough," I lie to Toni, pointing to my shoulder.

"Ahhhh," he says.

"But I'm doing better," I tell him and Bea, glad, for once, *not* to be telling some degree of a fib. "I'll be able to make it."

"We just need to go home and grab the right shoes," Bea says.

"That works perfectly," I tell her. "I forgot the scarf I knit Sula at home. I can grab that, too."

"Let's go, kids!" Sula yells, tromping out of her office. "Time to close up! Tacos and Tangos, here we come!"

Bea says, "Only Sula would work on her *birthday*."

"Business doesn't sleep on birthdays," Sula tells us. "Besides, I have to live up to my mantra: work hard, play hard. Everyone knows Tacos and Tangos is trashed-Sula night. I'll still be dancing on tables while you children stumble off to your beds."

Toni sighs. "She's such a Sagittarius."

"Tacos and Tangos, huh?" I peer around as we step into a classic loft-style apartment—exposed brick, tall ceilings, industrial finishes.

"Tacos and Tangos," Bea confirms, her gaze scouring the gathering of people. The place could be painfully echoey, but colorful tapestries hang along the walls, and large abstract-print rugs cover the wide-plank wood floors, soaking up sound.

"So," she says, shrugging off her jacket.

I shrug mine off with Bea's help as she lifts it from where it's draped over my shoulder with the sling. She takes it and hangs our coats beside each other. "So?"

"I'm just checking in," she says, "making sure you're okay, given—"

"Christopher!" Margo hollers from the kitchen. "Stop feeding my child sugar."

My gaze swivels to a hot pink club chair, where the jerk in question sits with a baby (toddler? who the hell knows) in his lap, holding what looks like a churro for them to gnaw on.

"It was the churro or my finger!" he calls back. "She's just sucking it more than anything, anyway. Is she teething?"

"When isn't she?" Margo says over her shoulder, walking up to us, giving both Bea and me bracing hugs, even with my sling, which goes a little way to make up for the fact that Christopher's here. "You came! I saved you tacos!"

"Sorry we're late," Bea says. "We had to circle back for shoes with low tread."

"And Sula's gift." I lift the bag containing her scarf.

Bea hands over a bottle of tequila with a bow on it.

"Thank you kindly. I'll take those." Margo gathers the gifts into her arms, then inspects our footwear. "Tell me those aren't your low-tread shoes."

We both shake our heads. "We've got flats in our bags," Bea tells her.

"Good," Margo says. "'Cause the tango in Docs, good luck with that."

"Jamie's coming," Bea tells her. "He's just working at the shelter this week, but he said he'd be here—"

"As soon as possible," Jamie says from right behind us.

Bea spins and practically jumps into his arms for a hug. I watch him kiss her on the temple and breathe her in. It's the visual version of hearing a language I don't know—melodic, mysterious. I feel like I'm seeing something intimate and private, so I look away.

"Christopher's drugging Rowan with refined sugar," Margo tells me. "But once he's done, I want you to meet her! For now, while my child's happily occupied, let's get you fed and liquored up."

As we stroll toward the open-concept kitchen, I get a closer look at Rowan. She has a gorgeous halo of Margo's tight black curls and gazes up at Christopher like everyone else seems to—with a sickening level of adoration.

I roll my eyes.

Standing in the kitchen, housing a veggie taco, I try not to look at Christopher. But my attention insistently swivels back to him. There's something odd stirring low in my stomach, seeing Christopher hold this little person so comfortably, getting cinnamon sugar all over his business suit, which probably costs more than most people's monthly rent. He still wears his suit coat, which is a dark, moody charcoal against his crisp white button-up. The tie's gone, his shirt unbuttoned a few, enough for my eyes to fasten on a wedge of golden skin, a shadow of dark hair.

Rowan shoves her churro in Christopher's face, but unfortunately he catches it just before she can smash it into his nose. A slow, sweet smile lifts his mouth as he says something to make her giggle that I can't hear.

The moment vividly reminds me of his dad, whom he's built so much like, and I think about what Christopher would be like as a father. My stomach does a funny twist again.

I want to say he'd be a terrible dad. Harsh. Impatient. Perennially dissatisfied. Except that's only how he is with me, apparently. Watching him with Rowan, I can't help but think he'd be an amazing father, smiling down at his kid like he is now, making Rowan laugh as he does a swift maneuver that involves tickling her until she drops the churro, and slipping it out of sight before tickling her again.

"Yeah," Sula says, sidling up to me with a cocktail I don't even look at. I just take a healthy swig, because Lord, do I need it. "He's good with her. And it's not even some angle he's working to bag a lady. The only single folks here are guys, and Christopher's unfortunately a confirmed straight, otherwise Phil would be *perfect* for him." She grimaces. "Wait, well, except you. You're single, too. Anyway. Hi! You came. It's been a long hour and a half since I saw you. Were you this tall last time?"

I pat Sula's shoulder. "Happy birthday, Sula. You're very drunk already, aren't you?"

"Well on my way. Tequila makes me chatty and happy." Her sigh is content as she looks around. "Even without the help of tequila, how could I not be happy? What's there not to be happy about?"

My gaze slips once again to where Christopher now stands, handing Rowan to Margo, who takes one look at his suit and pinches the bridge of her nose. He waves it off, making a show of brushing away the churro grease and cinnamon sugar as if it's nothing. When Margo walks past him with Rowan, he peers up, his gaze meeting mine.

His eyes flash with surprise, before he schools his expression. A slow tip of his head. An arched eyebrow, raised in challenge.

I tip back the rest of my drink, my gaze never leaving him. He holds my stare as I arch my eyebrow, too, and tell him in that silent, unspoken way we have:

Challenge accepted.

SIX

Christopher

Well. So much for trying to avoid Kate.

When I asked Jamie to find out from Bea if Kate planned to come to Sula's party, he said she'd told Bea no. Clearly, that plan changed.

Kate stands across the room, pointedly ignoring me since our eyes met. Fine. I can handle being ignored, even if I'm not terribly familiar with the experience, thanks to the sheer luck of my genetics. I might have done jack shit to earn my looks and presence, but I have no qualms about thoroughly, frequently enjoying the physical pleasures that transpire from possessing what draws so many women.

Jaw clenching, I stare at the most obvious exception—Kate.

"Bea only told me when I got here that it was a last-minute decision," Jamie says beside me, handing me a beer. "I'd have warned you if I knew sooner."

I take a long pull from the bottle and tear my gaze away from Kate. "It'll be fine."

"If you say so," he mutters, before taking a swig of his own.

"Okay!" Sula claps her hands to get the group's attention. She is, of course, standing on the coffee table, her cheeks flushed to a bronze almost as deep as her hair.

"She's lit, isn't she?" Jamie asks.

I nod, smiling as I remember the first Tacos and Tangos Sula birthday party I came to three years ago. It was just a few months after Jules dragged me to my first game night, but Sula and I had already formed a fast, intense bond over Risk and board-game world domination. "Every birthday," I tell him. "Tango, tacos, and a very intoxicated Sula."

Jamie grins as she does a few dance steps across the coffee table and explains that folks who know how to tango go to the left side of the room, those who need a tutorial, to the right.

"You familiar with the tango?" I ask him.

"I am. My mother insisted all of her sons take ballroom lessons. You know the tango by now, I assume?"

"I was brought into the tango fold three years ago."

He whistles appreciatively. "We have a master on our hands."

Kate's smoky laugh cracks through the air like a whip and lassos my attention. I glance her way and see she's talking to someone who I have to begrudgingly admit is good-looking, standing at just about her height, well-dressed, put together. They've got a softie-with-nerd-glasses vibe going. Kate doesn't smile for them, but they have her attention—worse, her laughter.

Hot aggravation slides beneath my skin.

I tear my gaze away and refocus on Jamie, who's watching me curiously. "I know the tango, but I'm no master at it," I tell him, trying to move past my little slip. "As you'll see very soon."

As if on cue, Margo saunters my way. "Let's go," she says. "Sula's too busy hollering at the newbies about tango's fundamentals. Whisk me away."

"As the lady wishes." I hand Jamie my beer and shrug off my jacket, setting it aside. Then I take the beer back and bolt the rest of it. Margo hoots appreciatively. Next, I make quick work of my sleeves, cuffing and pushing them up my arms to my elbows, and offer her my hand. "Shall we?"

She smiles. "We shall. West—shit, I mean Jamie. Sorry."

He dips his head. "No apology necessary."

Margo jerks her head toward Bea, who walks back into the room from the hallway, searching the floor. "Your dance partner awaits." She bites her lip. "I say this with the deepest love for Bea, no trash talk, just truth—you do know the beating your toes are about to take?"

Jamie grins, his gaze finding Bea. "I have some experience dancing with Beatrice." He sets down his beer on the table beside him and says, already strolling toward her. "She knows she can step on my toes all she wants."

Margo sighs as we watch them meet and talk, Bea smiling up at Jamie as he wraps an arm around her waist and their hands find each other's. They take one slow step, then another, then shift, quickly, Bea laughing as they bump into each other. Jamie bends to whisper something in her ear.

"They're so damn cute," Margo says.

I grunt.

She rolls her eyes. "Now, now, no grunting. Some people are happy to find a partner for the dance of life, and we're happy for them."

"We both know that's not my thing. Why would it be?" I take her waist and she leans in. "When I already have you?"

"Stop flirting." She laughs, falling into rhythm with me, our steps aligned. "I'm a happily married woman."

I grin down at her as we turn and take another slow, long step. We pass Kate as the hot nerd extends a hand, as if offering her the dance. I miss a step and nearly twist an ankle when I trip over Margo.

"Sorry!" Margo yelps. "My bad. Sula says I'm always topping from the bottom. I can't help but do it tangoing, too."

I blink, wrenching my gaze away from Kate and focusing on Margo. "You shouldn't be sorry. That was all my fault."

Margo's gaze trails to where mine just left, landing on Kate. Then she smiles up at me. "Actually, you know what, I better make sure Rowan's not eating another churro."

"Margo—"

"Thanks for the dance!" She presses a kiss to my cheek, then spins off, leaving me a few measly feet from Kate, who stands alone. With no hot nerd beside her anymore.

Our eyes meet. Kate gives me a dispassionate once-over. "Petruchio."

"Katerina."

"Lost your partner pretty quick, didn't you?" she asks.

I feel myself losing the battle with my self-control as I stare at her.

Be nice, the voice of reason inside me whispers.

Goddammit, I don't want to be *nice* to Katerina. As I look at her, every thought racing through my brain is as far from *nice* as possible.

"What happened to yours?" I ask. "Lost them before you could even dance. Did you make them cry?"

Kate shrugs idly. "He might have shed a tear or two when I declined his offer."

I cluck my tongue. "Sorely low on your daily quota, then, aren't you?"

"Oh, the night is young," she says breezily. "I still have plenty of time to catch up."

A beat of thick silence falls between us. This is when I should excuse myself, keep my promise to Bill and Jamie, and make myself scarce so the night can pass in peace.

Except I can't seem to move. I just . . . stand there. Staring at Kate, my gaze drawn once again to her right arm still in its sling. I tell myself not to look too closely, tell my chest not to knot as I see how she stands by herself at the edge of the floor, looking beat-up and proud, her chin held high, that fiery glint in her eyes.

Kate observes me inspecting her and arches an eyebrow. "Can I help you?"

"You can." I set out my hand.

She stares at it like it's roadkill.

A smile lifts my mouth. I'm absurdly delighted by that.

What are you doing? You're supposed to be walking away, not toward her, dammit!

Ignoring that sensible voice, I ask her, "Don't tell me you haven't learned the tango in all your worldly travels."

Slowly, Kate drags her gaze up from my hand and meets my eyes. "I'm . . . passably familiar with it."

"Well." I take a step closer, hand still outstretched. "Let's see it, then."

"I have one functional arm," she says silkily. "As you were so happy to remind me the other night when you ran into me—"

"*You* ran into *me*."

She rolls her eyes, but then her expression shifts as she takes me in, standing there, hand outstretched. Waiting. Our gazes hold, and our surroundings dim to a blur of moving bodies, the heavy thrum of the bandonion and guitar's melody.

Prove your family wrong, I silently beg her. *Show me I haven't fucked this up like they say I have. Show me what you always do— that fire you throw my way, that I throw right back at you.*

Kate takes a step my way and slaps her hand down on mine. "Fine."

I grip her hand and ignore the fierce rush of heat that floods my body as her palm settles, light and warm on mine, her fingers' grip hard and uncompromising. She doesn't look it, but God, she's strong.

I draw her close, until our bodies meet—chests, hips, lower.

Instantly, I recognize this moment for what it is: a devastating lapse in judgment.

But it's too late, because Kate stares up at me, her face only a few inches lower than mine. Challenge dances in her eyes as she says, "Well, Petruchio, who's leading? Me or you?"

I wrap an arm around her waist, drawing her closer. Air hitches out of her, and a rosy blush splashes across her cheeks. "I am."

Gaze locked on mine, she pulls her hand free from my grip, then wraps her arm around my neck. Heat seeps through my clothes where her hand splays across my back, where the soft weight of her breasts presses into my chest, and her hips rest, snug against mine.

I take the first step, holding her eyes as she moves with me, again with the next slow step. When our steps quicken into a turn, her head whips in the next direction, and her leg kicks up as her hips twist with a flourish.

Christ.

I stare down at her. "'I'm passably familiar with it.' Was that what you said?"

She flashes me a wide, satisfied grin, the cat who's had its cream. "Yes."

Recklessly, I drink in that grin, and my hand slips lower down her back as we whip into a quick turn, then take a long slow step together. My other hand tightens around her waist, to make up for the lack of her other hand for me to hold and keep her steady. That's the only reason my palm is wide across her back, holding her hips to mine, my other hand wrapped around her ribs, my thumb sliding over the curve of her waist.

"You're holding me rather tightly, aren't you?" she asks. Her breathing is a little unsteady. Mine is, too.

Then again, we're tangoing our asses off. But it doesn't feel only like that—her body turning and twisting with mine. It's the way we'd move if there weren't layers of clothing and decades of dissonance between us, her breath hot on my neck as I worked her hard and slow, her cheeks flushed, her nails raking down my skin.

"Petruchio."

I swallow, meeting her eyes, trying to cool myself down. "What?"

"I said you're *holding* me *tight*."

"And? Otherwise, one quick turn and you'd go flying."

"I have my left arm hooked around you. I'm not going anywhere."

I sigh, exasperated. "Could you just trust me for once and not have an argument for every—*Christ*."

Her heel slams on my toe. I glare down at Kate as she stares up at me serenely and says, "Oops."

"I suggest you hold on with that all-powerful left arm of yours," I tell her.

She frowns. "What—*ack!*"

It's not the right moment for a dip, but I do it anyway, smooth and fast, leaning forward. Kate arches back reflexively in my arms and gasps.

"Jesus, Christopher," she hisses as I draw her upright, bringing her even tighter against my body. "You could have dropped me."

My hand tucks her hips against mine, and a swallow works down my throat. "I'd never drop you, Kate." She doesn't answer me, but our eyes hold, hers hot as blue flames, as we take a slow step, then another. "You don't trust me?" I press.

On our quick turn, her knee connects with my thigh.

I groan in pain. "I'll take that as a no."

"Take that as a 'no, and I'm pissed at you.' You startled me, dipping me without warning."

"You're right," I tell her, a pang of guilt echoing in my chest. "I startled you on purpose, and that was wrong."

Kate nearly trips as we slide into a slow step, her head whipping my way. "What did you just say?"

"I said I was wrong. I know it's hard to wrap your head around," I tell her dryly, "but I can be wrong sometimes."

She bursts out a smoky laugh that draws a few heads. "What's hard to wrap my head around is that you'd admit it!"

My jaw clenches. "It's not exactly a phrase you've practiced, either, Katerina." Wrenching her to me, I pick up our pace and complicate the footwork, a thrill racing down my spine as she catches on and meets me, step for step.

"Guess what, Petruchio?" she says breathily, her hand clawing into my back to anchor her to me. "I have news for you. It's a phrase I know *very* well."

"Could have fooled me," I grunt, my grip sinking into her waist.

"Because I reserve apologies for people who deserve to hear them." She leans in, her breath hot on my ear, her mouth a whisper away from my neck. A rush of dizzying heat burns through me. "You just aren't one of them."

Her heel lands on the same toe, twice as hard as last time. And then she wrenches herself out of my arms and walks away.

SEVEN

Kate

I tell Bea I'm tired and heading back. I promise I'll take a cab. I hug Sula goodbye and tell her happy birthday again, not that, based on her drunkenness, she'll even remember. I hug Margo and let her cajole me into taking a shot with her that I needed desperately.

I walk the whole way home.

And because the brutally cold wind wasn't enough to extinguish the aggravated heat pumping through my veins, I take a brutally cold shower, too.

I'm shivering when I get into bed, wrenching the sheets over me, and yet I'm *still* burning hot. I must have a fever.

Lying on my back, staring up at the dark ceiling, I count to one hundred in three different languages I've learned in my travels, and when I'm still wide-awake, I know I'm not ready, that I won't be able to sleep for a while. There's a pulse between my thighs, a fierce, nagging ache coiling through my limbs. I feel agitated and antsy.

And so goddamn unnerved.

How dare Christopher dance like that? How dare he be so good not only at the tango but also at getting so far under my skin?

Restless, I whip off the sheets and stomp into Bea's room, flicking on her soft nightstand light. There sits Cornelius the hedgehog, doing his nocturnal hedgehog thing, snuffling around.

Sighing, I plop down beside his elaborate living space and scratch gently against the screen. "Hey."

Cornelius perks up when he sees me, big, dark eyes and wiggly little nose. He waddles closer and sniffs my finger, then, when he realizes it's not food, turns and waddles off.

I watch him snuffle around the tiny doughnut-print sleeping bag I made him and sent Bea in my last care package while I was gone. Reaching up, I ease open the lid and slowly lower my hand. "Want to hang for a minute?" I ask. "I bear no mealworm treats, but Mom says you can't have too many in one day or it's unhealthy, and we gotta do what she says."

He makes an irritated snuffle sound.

"I know. She's such a party pooper, making sure you have your best chance at a long, happy, hedgie life." Gently, I bring my hand closer. He steps onto it, and I cup my other hand around him, bringing him out of his cage.

Settling back against Bea's dresser, I savor the ticklish comfort of his paws against my palm. He peers up at me. He's obscenely cute.

Unlike someone else. Who, with his sleeves pushed up to his elbows, his shirt collar still smelling vaguely of churro from a little girl he held and tickled, melding too well with the spicy warmth of his cologne, is not remotely cute. He is high-handed and pushy and very goddamn good at tangoing and holding me so tight it felt like the world could spin off its axis, straight into the universe, and I'd still be steady.

"I don't care how Christopher dances with me," I tell Cornelius. "Or what he thinks of me. I don't care that he keeps staring at my messy bun and my ratty clothes."

I've been telling myself for a very long time that I don't care what Christopher thinks of me. Because if I do that, then all that time he ignored me growing up doesn't hurt so much, his relentless disapproval of the path I've made for myself doesn't sting so badly.

Most of the time, at least.

Cornelius gives me a skeptical blink and yawns.

"Hint taken," I tell him. "I'll let you get back to your fun."

Sitting up, I return Cornelius to his cage and watch him waddle toward his little sandbox to scratch around. "I wish I had your prickles, Cornelius. It would make it so much easier to protect myself."

My fingers slide along the screen, tracing the arch of his quills. "But my prickles are *inside*. And those seem to hurt a lot more. Me more than anyone, I think."

Cornelius turns around and peers my way, looking vaguely concerned.

"Don't worry. I'm just tipsy and getting pointlessly in my feelings." I stand, a little ungainly, feeling the shot with Margo along with the cocktail I pounded when I got to the party creeping up on me. "I'm going to go to bed and sleep it off."

After turning off the light in Bea's room and traipsing back across the hall, I fall into bed, curl up, and thankfully, not long after, sleep wraps around me, though it's anything but peaceful.

It's filled with dreams. Terribly vivid dreams.

A warm, strong body, guiding mine from a dance floor, down the hall. A hand holding me steady, until it touches me where I ache and thoroughly *un*steadies me.

A deep, decadent dip to a bed.

A new, feverish dance that lasts all night long.

EIGHT

Christopher

If the tango incident at Sula's birthday party affirmed anything, it's that maintaining my distance from Kate is the only way to survive this.

Especially if I want to keep my toes.

And yet here I am, strolling down the sidewalk from the nearest train stop to the Wilmot sisters' apartment.

Walking right toward her.

To my credit, it's been ten days. I've stayed away for a week and a half, busied myself with work, declined friend-group invitations. For ten days, I've surrendered the world that's mine. I was so sure ten days would be more than enough time for Kate to grow restless and leave town, like she always does.

I was wrong. And like hell was I going to just stay away forever, let her take from me the people who are like family because she's decided to stick around.

Even though it's just game night, I feel like I'm about to head into battle. So, like any sensible person who's possibly marching to their doom, I've brought a right-hand man.

"Christ, it's cold," Nick mutters. Icy wind hits us like a hard uppercut that I lean into, cold and sobering. Nick's shoulders climb toward his ears. "How are you not freezing your nuts off?" he asks.

I slant him a wry grin. "Have you ever seen someone built like me complaining of being cold?"

Our reflections glance back at us from a building's darkened windows—wiry, mid-height Nick, and my tall, bulky frame like my dad's. Tonight, my reflection could be his double, with my face hidden in shadow, the only part of me that favors my mother obscured. It makes me do a double take.

"Stop checking yourself out," Nick says.

I shove him away, making him laugh. "I wasn't, you ass."

"Sure you weren't."

"Where's this bullshit coming from? You mad I gave you a bigger client portfolio at work? Bummed we're slated for our best quarter yet?"

He rolls his eyes. "It's not about work. Believe it or not, some of us think about things besides ROIs and investment strategies. It's about you pulling your Casanova bullshit on my baby sister."

"I did not!"

"Maybe not on purpose," he grants, "but the end result was the same. Forgive me if I still haven't recovered from the fact that, after you left early from our happy hour meet-up last week, Gia said she would, and I quote, 'let you step on her neck.'"

I cough, studiously avoiding his eyes. "For the record, all I said to her was, 'Good to see you, too.'"

He shakes his head wearily. "Just isn't right. You can get any woman you want and you refuse to date. Then there are guys like me who'd settle down in a heartbeat, and nobody wants us. They want you and your Henry Cavill bubble butt."

I stop dead on the sidewalk, making Nick trip into me. "What the *hell* did you just say?"

"That's what Gia told me. Do you know how much I didn't want to think about my baby sister thinking about your ass? How much I didn't want to google Henry Cavill's ass—spoiler alert, curiosity won out and I did google Henry Cavill's ass—only to then have to look at *your* ass to form my own opinion on this comparison? I'm very upset to report, by the way, that my sister was right, you have Superman's butt."

I turn away and start walking. "I deeply regret bringing you with me."

"Ah, c'mon, it'll be fun. At least, it will be once you fess up about why you *really* want me to be there. You've been doing these game nights for years and never once have I had an invitation. What's different tonight?"

I slant him a menacing glare.

He lifts his hands and widens his eyes. "Oooh, now I'm scared."

"You should be. I don't just have Superman's ass, I have his biceps, and they'll happily launch you toward the nearest train station."

"You'd never." He hooks an arm around my neck, tugging me close and ruffling my hair. "Beneath that grizzly-bear growling is just a big old teddy."

"Get off," I tell him.

"C'mon." He claps his hands and rubs them together, trying to warm himself up. "Let's hear it. Let's hear why your old pal Nick Lucentio is being dragged to board-game night when he's never been dragged there before."

I sigh, planting a hand on his chest to stop him from marching into the intersection and getting flattened by a cab that runs the light. "I have to be around someone who . . . I'm not sure how to . . ." Sighing, I scrub my face. "I just need a little backup tonight, okay?"

Nick frowns my way. "Is this you being . . . sincere? Expressing . . . emotion?"

I mutter something very rude in Italian and start across the street.

"I'm just fucking with you," he says on a laugh. "You know I'm happy to come. Besides, you never know. Tonight could be the night I meet my lady fair after all."

———

"Sweet God." Nick gapes as I shut the apartment door behind us and shrug off my coat. I'm roasting already. "Who is *that*?"

I frown, trying to follow the line of his gaze. Everyone's crammed in the kitchen, animated about something I can't make sense of amid the laughter.

Jamie, taller than everyone, spots us first and steps out of the crowd, walking our way. "There you are!" he says, taking our coats and hanging them up. "You, uh"—he lowers his voice—"know that Kate's here, right?"

"I'll be on my best behavior," I reassure him. We do our typical handshake to backslapping hug, then I introduce him to Nick, who can barely drag his gaze away from whoever's caught his eye.

"Lucentio."

Nick doesn't blink. "Huh?"

"How about you stick your tongue back in your mouth and use it to tell me what's gotten into you."

"She's perfect," he whispers. "Who is she?"

Jamie and I glance in the direction of his gaze.

"Sitting on the counter?" Jamie asks. "Petite, light brown hair?"

"Eyes bluer than the sea and a smile brighter than the sun?" Nick adds.

I snort.

Ignoring me, Nick sighs. "That's her."

Jamie clears his throat uneasily. "That would be Bianca, who's just taken a job in the city and moved here. She's Bea and Kate's—"

"Cousin." I groan, shaking my head. "No, Nick. Anyone but her."

Finally, he peels his gaze away long enough to look at me, distraught. "Why?"

"Because she's . . ." My voice dies off as the crowd shifts, a rift just wide enough that I see Kate, her head thrown back in laughter, before she tips up her beer bottle and takes a long, deep drink. Her hair's piled high on her head, an auburn-streaked chestnut mess. Her cheeks are pink. Her shirt's black but a little see-through. Before my gaze drifts any lower, I make myself look away.

"She's what?" Nick asks me.

Jamie grimaces, connecting the dots.

I rub the bridge of my nose. "She's important to Kate. And Kate despises me. Soon as Kate realizes you're with me, she'll disapprove of you, and you can kiss talking to Bianca goodbye."

"I'd rather kiss Bianca," Nick says, staring at her again. "So how about we pretend we don't know each other?"

"Wow. Thanks again for the moral support."

"Hey, come on. Unlike you, I don't have women fawning over me all the time. I've never felt like this about anyone before."

Jamie frowns. "You haven't *met* her."

"True," Nick says wistfully. "And now I'm going to go fix that."

"Wait. Nick!" I reach to stop him, but he's gone. And judging by the coy, sweet look Bianca gives him as he approaches her, well on his way toward being a goner, too.

Jamie offers me a sympathetic back slap. "How about a beer?"

———

To anyone else, Sequence is an innocent old-folks game of cards and five chips in a row.

To this crowd, it's a gladiator arena.

"Sonofabitch," Toni mutters as Kate drops a one-eyed jack and flicks his chip off the board. "You're so hostile!"

"I play to win, Antoni." Kate lifts her eyebrows at me, then takes a deep drink of her cocktail.

"You know you *could* play offense," I tell her, tossing down my card and playing a chip to build us a three-in-a-row on a diagonal. "Then maybe this game would end before we're all in a retirement community."

"I know this is a novel concept to you, Christopher," she says airily, "but just because that's how *you* play doesn't mean it's the only right way."

Hamza, Toni's boyfriend, sets down a card and plays his chip right where Kate vacated Toni's, giving their team four in a row.

Kate's cousin, Bianca, groans in frustration at this turn of events. Nick stares at her like she hung the moon.

"Yeesh," Bianca mutters. "I don't remember it being this cut-throat when we played at the family reunions."

"Because it wasn't," Bea says. "At least, not at Wilmot family reunions. Mom's side of the family, however, is a whole other matter."

Kate grins wickedly. "I *love* O'Reilly family reunions."

"Someone lost a *finger* at the last one," Bea reminds her.

"Eh. They've got nine more," Kate says, plucking a cashew from a nearby dish and tossing it in her mouth. "The fireworks got a little out of hand. It happens."

Bea laughs disbelievingly, then turns back to Bianca. "You're not misremembering. Sequence is usually pretty tame. We just tend to get carried away on game night."

Jamie clears his throat. "I read an article recently about the mental health benefits of play in adulthood. Board games were specifically mentioned."

"Really?" Margo grumbles, playing a card and setting a chip in no-man's-land. "Because this feels like the time I drove through the car wash and only too late realized my windows were stuck halfway down."

Sula laughs. "You're just a sore loser."

"I'm shit at board games!" Margo protests. "I wanna do *physical* things, blow off some steam, not sit on my ass and get it whupped at board games. Let's go ax throwing—"

"No!" Jamie and I yell. Kate would kill me with her first throw and Bea would take off someone's arm.

"What about paintball?" Bea asks.

Jamie gives her a look I can't read.

"Not sure you can do that this time of year," Sula says, "given it's outdoorsy, but I honestly don't enjoy anything that involves even a facsimile of a firearm."

"True that." Hamza lifts his beer.

A chorus of *same*s echoes around the table.

"Ooh," Toni says, slapping down his cards. "I just remembered, I saw something recently about a new paintball place. It's supposed to be play focused and nonviolent."

"Nonviolent?" Hamza sounds skeptical. "But it's . . . *paintball*."

"Well, relatively nonviolent, at least," Toni concedes. He pulls out his phone, tapping open a web browser and typing quickly. After a beat, his eyes scanning the screen, he says, "How cool is this? Biodegradable paintballs that you throw freehand or you can use slingshots to launch them. Peace, Love, and Paintball. It's an indoor-outdoor space, so they run it all year long. We could go anytime."

"I'm in!" Margo hollers.

Jamie grimaces. "It sounds *extremely* messy."

Bea's eyes glow. "It sounds *amazing*."

"We should do it!" Bianca says.

"I'm in, too," Nick tells her.

Kate glares death at him.

"Hey." I knock her knee under the table. "Take it easy. Despite his proximity to me, he's a good guy."

Her lip curls, her eyes still on Nick. "I swear to God, if he messes with her, a bad haircut is going to be the least of his worries."

"Ah, nice. Judging someone's character by their appearance."

"I'm not—" Kate's cut off as a cascade of beer sloshes onto her shirt and mine, too.

"Sorry!" Bea says, picking up an empty pint glass that up until seconds ago was holding Jamie's beer. "I didn't even see it there and just knocked it right over."

Kate and I stand simultaneously, flicking beer off our hands.

"It's fine, BeeBee," Kate says.

I force a smile. "No worries."

We storm down the hall simultaneously, wedged close, thanks to its narrowness.

"I'm taking the bathroom," Kate says, throwing her good shoulder into me, charging ahead.

"You have a bedroom!"

"I have to wash off the beer. I smell like a frat house."

I stop dead in the hallway, furious. "Fine. I'll handle my wardrobe change here."

Kate freezes as I unbutton my dress shirt from work. "What are you doing?"

"You aren't the only one who doesn't enjoy being drenched in hefeweizen."

Her eyes widen as I shake off my button-up, then grip the back of my undershirt. Some small, rational corner of my brain says this is about as far as I could possibly get from keeping my distance and de-escalating tensions with Kate, but a bigger, baser part feasts on her pupils' dilating, that deep red flush creeping up her throat to her cheeks.

"Take the bathroom," she croaks.

I wrench off my shirt. "Too late."

She slaps a hand over her eyes and stumbles back into the wall. "You're naked."

"Half-naked."

A shaky exhale. "What is *wrong* with you?"

I step past her, headed toward Juliet's—now Kate's—room.

"Why are you going in my room?" she shrieks.

"I keep some casual clothes here. I know you can't relate, but your sisters actually want me to feel at home when I'm here."

I riffle through the bottom drawer in Jules's dresser and find a spare T-shirt, then tug it on.

The room is suspiciously silent. When I drag the collar of my shirt past my head, I see why.

Kate stands with her back to me.

Her *naked* back.

"Fucking hell." I scrunch my eyes shut, turn abruptly for the door, and walk right into the wall.

That hoarse, smoky laugh dances through the air and whispers over my skin. "Don't enjoy the taste of your own medicine?"

My eyes are closed, but she's burned into my retinas—the curve of her waist, the line of her vertebrae straight to two soft dimples at the base of her spine. Heat rushes through me, tightens my body, as I picture my hands on her waist, my thumbs tracing those dimples, hoisting her up by the hips and dragging her close so I can bend and spread her wide, drag my tongue—

Shit. *Shit.*

I can't stay here. Or see this. Or hear it. The *shush* of cotton slipping over her skin, the *snap* of a bra being smoothed out. On a pained, frustrated growl, I feel my way toward the door, then storm out, slamming it behind me.

"There you are!" Nick's right on me in the hallway. "So, did you straighten things out with her?"

"What?" I walk past him, but Nick chases me down.

"With Kate. The one who keeps looking like she wants to castrate me every time I smile at Bianca."

I laugh emptily. Like anything could ever be that simple with her. "Yeah, Nick. I just told her you're a nice guy and she said, 'Swell, Christopher. He has my blessing.'"

He smiles. "She did?"

"No, dipshit. She bit my head off like she always does."

He wilts. "Now what?"

I jut my chin toward Bianca, who offers Nick a sweet, coy smile. "Now you talk to her anyway. You don't need Kate's blessing."

"I need my nuts intact."

"Your nuts will live. Kate will probably warn Bianca you're like me and try to dissuade her, but you can't do anything about that. Focus on what you can do—prove her wrong."

Nick smiles at Bianca and sighs. "She's perfect."

I roll my eyes. "You've talked across a board game for thirty minutes."

"It's a soulmate connection," he says defensively. "Not that you'd know anything about that."

For some odd reason, that stings. I know it's unfair to expect Nick to understand my motives for my one-and-done policy, when I haven't told him the real reason I refuse to date or have a relationship, but it still leaves a hollow ache in my chest, to hear what he thinks of me.

"What have you done," he prods, "that Kate's so against her cousin talking to an acquaintance of yours?"

"So we're *acquaintances* now, are we?"

"You gotta fix this for me," he begs. "I'm a man possessed—'I burn, I pine, I perish'!"

I stare at him. "You *have* to stop reading so much poetry."

"It's not poetry, it's—"

"Shamelessly overromanticizing half an hour spent with a woman you can't possibly already have feelings for?"

"I know you don't understand, but, please"—he steps closer, looking desperate, making my resolve crumble—"please just try to smooth things over? Bianca's a grown woman who can make her own choices. I know that . . ." He glances over his shoulder, to where Kate, now dressed in a snug dark green T-shirt, is hiss-whispering something at Bianca, who glances our way, looking wary. "I just need a little help."

"I'm not so sure you do."

Bianca walks our way and stops beside Nick, smiling up at him. "Sorry to interrupt," she says. "Do you think . . ." She clears her throat and takes a step closer. "Do you think maybe we could talk a bit? Out on the balcony?"

Nick smiles. "I'd love nothing more."

I feel Kate's stare before our eyes meet from across the table where she stands. I'm trying so hard not to remember what she looked like with her shirt off—long back, smooth skin, wisps of auburn kissing her shoulders—to revisit that filthy fantasy that tore through my mind.

Resentment knots my gut. I don't want one more thing about Kate stitched into my memory, tugging at my thoughts when she's gone again.

Forcing my gaze away from her, I rejoin the crowd, which has abandoned Sequence for snacks and another round of Margo's cocktails in the kitchen.

Soon enough, I'm introduced to Sarah, who seems to have showed up while Kate and I were torturing each other with our wardrobe changes. A coworker of Jamie's, she's not a pediatrician like him but a general physician with whom he volunteers at local shelters in the city, providing medical care for folks in need.

She's smart and pretty, a bright-eyed fast talker with gorgeous, full curves and a confident smile. Any other night, I'd know exactly where we were headed—straight to bed, until my body was spent, my mind finally quiet, and she was blissed-out with orgasms, too exhausted for more. Then I'd get dressed while she slept and write the same note I always do—brief, sincere, and very intentionally without any contact information.

But not now.

Now, as we make small talk, I have to force myself to focus on what Sarah's said. I have to count seconds until it's been five minutes before I let myself glance around, only to see no sign of Kate in the small crowd of people. I make myself pay attention to the woman in front of me. I don't wonder where Kate's gone or second-guess if I've done the best thing in walking away from her.

I don't worry that I'm getting much too attached to knowing I can search this crowd and find the feisty, messy-haired woman who's already woven herself deep into its fabric.

NINE

Kate

From my shadowy corner of the hallway, I can see a woman beside Christopher in the kitchen, where they've been the past half hour. She smiles as he talks, looking like she's got cartoon hearts for eyes. I have no idea what she sees in him. When I look at Christopher, my brain doodles little devil horns on that annoyingly, perfectly tousled dark hair, a forked tail pinned on that high, round—

I scrunch my eyes shut, mentally kicking myself. What the hell is wrong with me, looking at his butt, noticing the way it stretches his slacks and flexes when he shifts his weight?

When I open my eyes, even while keeping them decidedly *not* on his butt, I remember the sight of his bare chest as he yanked off his shirt in the hallway, broad and solid, fine dark hairs dusting golden skin, arrowing straight down his stomach to—

"There you are." Bea leans on the wall beside me and gives me a concerned once-over. "You okay?"

"Barf," I grumble, glaring at Christopher.

She snorts a laugh. "I'm assuming this is about seeing Jamie's coworker hit on Christopher and not a case of the spins."

"Affirmative."

"If you stick around much longer, you're going to have to get used to it," she says. "You do realize pretty much everyone besides you, me, and Jules wants in his pants, right?"

"More like we're the only people who haven't *been* in his pants," I mutter into my cocktail glass. Margo's mixology genius is the only thing getting me through this night.

"Not that we're going to shame someone for who and how many people they've slept with," Bea says pointedly.

I roll my eyes. "Of course I'm not shaming him for *that*. It's the hearts he's messed up along the way."

Bea stares at me, looking curious. "Why would you assume that he's messed up anyone's heart?"

"Because that's what players do, and he is the definition of a player."

"We gotta go." Sula stops near us, fishing around the coat hooks, Margo right behind her. "Rowan's going to wake up soon, screaming for Margo's boobs."

"The joys of nursing a toddler," Margo says.

Sula helps her shrug on her coat and adds, "Who's cutting teeth."

Bea and I both reflexively cover our chests.

"Yeah, it's as fun as it sounds." Margo hugs Bea hard, then hugs me, too, careful of my arm in its sling. I'm getting so damn tired of this sling act. I want to hug with two arms. Play Sequence with both hands. Clasp Christopher's jaw, wrench his attention my way, and find some way to wipe that arrogant smirk right off his face.

"Night, kids!" Sula calls, blowing everyone a kiss.

"Oof," Bea says, watching them go. "Teeth and nursing. That sounds scary."

I watch the door shut behind Margo and Sula, then turn to see Bea gulping a glass of water. I should do the same, but I'm a little too attached to the numbing buzz of alcohol in my system right now. "The things parents deal with," I tell her. "Makes you even more sure you never want kids, right?"

Bea coughs into her water. Bringing away her glass, she wipes her chin. "Did I say that? Long ago?"

"Like the last time I saw you."

"Which was a year and a half ago."

"Touché." I sigh into my cocktail glass before I tip it back and drain it. Turning, I face Bea fully and land against the hallway wall with a clumsy *thud*. "So you want kids now? What happened to your grand plans to travel Europe with me and be a famous painter?"

She bites her lip, staring into her empty glass. "They . . . grew. I still want to travel with you again. I want to refocus on my painting career. But that doesn't mean I can't want kids, too."

Teasing her, I start to hum "Another One Bites the Dust."

Bea rolls her eyes. "I'm not saying it's happening right now or even anytime soon," she says. "I'm just saying . . ." She glances over her shoulder. As if he's felt her gaze, Jamie glances up from his conversation with Hamza and Toni in the kitchen. Their gazes lock. He smiles softly. She smiles back, then turns and faces me again. "One day."

It hits me with the force of a cosmic freight train. Everyone's lives are changing. Last time I was here, Margo looked like she'd swallowed a watermelon, and now she and Sula have a *kid*. Toni and his boyfriend, Hamza, talk about their future decades down the road, so sure they've found "the one." Bianca's already been swept away by Nick. Bea and Jamie steal glances and secret smiles and now Bea wants *babies*, and I'm . . .

Home again. Exactly where I started.

I want nothing more in this moment than to escape how restless and uneasy this makes me. Well, besides the ability to scrub the memory of bare-chested, arrogant, smirking Christopher from my brain.

As if he knows I'm sulking about him, Christopher glances over the short, gorgeous blonde's head. His eyes pin mine, and a jolt of electricity snaps through me. I drop back, disappearing into the hallway's shadows.

"KitKat?" Bea says, noticing me shrink away. "You okay?"

"Yeah. Just hot." I bring my cocktail glass holding mostly melted ice to my flushed cheeks. "I'm gonna get some fresh air and cool off."

Before my sister can respond, I skirt the edge of folks gathered around the kitchen and spot a nice Irish whiskey sitting on the bar. I slide it off the counter as subtly as possible, then slink past the crowd again, waiting as I see Bea weave around the other side and get swept into Jamie's gentle hug.

Making a break for it, I escape down the hallway toward the balcony at the back of the apartment, off the tiny studio where Bea paints. I step over rolls of canvas and wood frames for stretching them, then open the door to—

"Christ on a cracker." I shudder. Christopher's sidekick, Nick, cups Bianca's face as she wraps her arms around his neck and tugs him close, their mouths fused in an impassioned kiss.

They don't even notice me.

I'm tempted to say something, but what's the point? I already warned Bianca. I told her what Christopher's like and said I couldn't promise anything different about the company he keeps. She made her choice. She sought out Nick. I'm going to respect that choice, even if it makes me want to hurl.

Speaking of hurl, I feel a little nauseous.

I don't think it's the alcohol. It's this night, the realities pressing down on me that everyone's so fucking happy and well-adjusted. It's the agitation I can't shake over that petty showdown with Christopher and our beer-soaked clothes, seeing his body, knowing I made sure he saw mine. It's the unsettling sensation of the hairs on my neck lifting all night that's made me feel like I'm being watched, even though I haven't caught a single person looking my way, the same electric fizz that rocketed through my veins when Christopher's eyes found mine.

Stomping back through the studio, I make my way down the hallway, hidden in shadow. My gaze slips toward Christopher as he smiles at Jamie's friend and tips back his beer, his throat working in a long, deep swallow. My stomach churns. It's definitely not the alcohol.

It's this claustrophobic, disorienting sensation that the walls are closing in, the floors moving out from beneath me, that time and change have swept by me and now they're about to knock me on my ass.

I need an escape. I have a bedroom, of course, but it's at the other end of the apartment. To get there, I'd have to walk by everyone in their domesticated bliss and Christopher fucking Petruchio flirting over tapas with that cute-as-a-button doctor and her three-hundred-dollar haircut and high-quality clothes and eight times more luscious tits than I'll ever have—not that I'm comparing us. So, I'm just going to slip into this closet with my trusty whiskey, have a few sips for good measure, and curl up with the jumbo roll of recycled paper towels.

Settling in, I prop my feet on the lowest shelf, yank the cork out of the whiskey with my teeth on a satisfying *pop*, then spit it into my hand.

And then I drag the closet door shut, letting darkness swallow me up.

· TEN ·

Christopher

I'm going to wring Kate's neck. Once I find her, that is.

It's a one-thousand-square-foot apartment. It shouldn't be this hard to locate a grown-ass woman. Which means she's either in a particularly vindictive mood and left for an unknown destination at midnight without telling anyone or taking her beat-up phone, which sits on the kitchen counter, or she's hiding somewhere around here.

Either way, so help me God, when I find her.

"Any luck?" Jamie asks, returning from searching the bedrooms—again—at the other end of the apartment. His voice is quiet on account of Bea, who fell asleep on the sofa an hour ago, right around when everyone was leaving and before we realized Kate was nowhere to be seen.

He nudged her awake then and asked if she knew where Kate was, but she just frowned and said, "Here? Right?"

Wisely, Jamie let her drift back off.

Which means we're the two fools turning the apartment upside down for a woman gone rogue.

I shake my head. "No. And I've looked everywhere. She has to have left."

He sighs, scrubbing his face. But then his hands drop slowly.

He peers past me, in the direction of the hall behind me. "Have you checked the hallway closet?"

I blink at him, then glance over my shoulder at the tiny hallway closet that I've never actually seen inside. I assumed it was a shallow storage space, too small to hide a person.

Swearing under my breath, I storm down the hallway and yank open the door. "Goddammit."

There she is, cuddled up against a jumbo pack of paper towels, clutching a bottle of whiskey like it's her teddy bear. The bands squeezing my ribs pop, and I suck in a deep, steadying breath. Leaning past the door, I call to Jamie, "Found her."

His head drops back with relief. "Thank God."

I'm kicking myself for not checking here. There are a dozen closets at the Wilmots' house, perfect for slipping into for hide-and-seek, for popping out of and scaring the shit out of innocent people just walking to the bathroom.

Oh yes, I have extensive experience being at the receiving end of those juvenile jump scares. The closet is the first place I should have checked.

Twitching in her sleep, Kate mutters something as her head slumps forward, about to connect with the edge of a shelf.

I crouch and catch her just in time, exhaling with relief. "Come on, Kate. Wake up."

"No," she mumbles. Flailing away, she thumps her head back on the paper towels. "Tired."

"Which explains why you're *here* of all places. What is with you Wilmots and closets?"

"Gowaylemmesleep."

"You're not sleeping on paper towels in a closet. Get up."

"Nuh-uh," she says sleepily.

"Dammit, Kate."

A deep snore rolls out of her.

Jamie joins me outside the closet and peers down at Kate. Her mouth is slack, her head back at an uncomfortable-looking angle. "She's really out of it," he says.

"She was lucid for a second, but"—another snore rolls out of her—"she could fall and stay asleep through the Second Coming," I tell him, hating that I know it, that I have a catalog of memories of Kate growing up—gangly limbs, freckled nose, tangled hair, out cold beneath the backyard trampoline; curled up on the landing of the stairs; even once snoring in the bathtub of the third-floor bathroom, where she stashed herself for hide-and-seek and fell asleep because no one found her.

Kate twitches in her sleep again, flopping onto her back. The whiskey she was clutching rolls away from her.

I scoop it up and inspect the bottle. I know without a doubt that bottle was sitting unopened at the bar earlier this evening because I brought it. A good quarter of it's gone.

A low whistle leaves Jamie as he notices that, too.

"And apparently she's drunk as a sailor." I set the bottle aside.

"I'd like to check for signs of alcohol poisoning," he says, crouching beside her. "Sorry for the physician mode, but I'd be remiss if I didn't."

I crouch beside him, feeling a harsh, sharp pang in my chest as Jamie holds her wrist and feels her pulse, then gently lifts her eyelids, examining her. "Is she all right?" I ask.

He nods. "Fine. Just a little tipsy and tired. We should make sure she sleeps on her side in case she gets sick."

"Jamie?" Bea calls groggily from the main room. She stands from the chair she was sleeping on and rubs her eyes. "What're you doing?"

"Just, uh . . ." He clears his throat as we both stand, too. "Closing up for the night. Coming." Quickly, he turns back to me and asks quietly, "Can you manage helping Kate to bed?"

I arch an eyebrow, glancing from Kate's slight form back to him. "I think I can handle it."

Bea sleepily wanders toward him and Jamie backtracks, catching her when she slumps into him and wraps her arms around his neck as she whines about being tired. Jamie sweeps her up and shifts her high in his arms, then turns and carries Bea toward her bedroom.

Sighing, I crouch down again and say, "Wake up, Kate."

I get a snore for an answer.

"Kate, wake up."

"No," she grumbles.

I had a hunch she'd do this. She's a deep and cranky sleeper. I'd rather poke a sleeping bear than wake up Kate. Which means I just need to suck it up and pick her up, then dump her in bed.

Except I can't quite seem to make myself do it. I stare at her as she sleeps, long legs tucked up, knees to her chin, snoring like a truck driver. Like a fool, for just a moment, I watch her sleep and count the constellations of her freckles. I stare at her full lips parted, her expression smooth, utterly at peace.

I'd give anything to feel as peaceful as she looks, but this is what Kate does—hooks me by the innards and wrenches me open, like a gutted fish. This is what happens when twenty minutes pass and I don't know where she is, a world of difference from twenty months when she's on the other side of the planet, out of sight, out of mind.

Anger and resentment knot beneath my ribs.

"Kate." I grit my teeth and clutch her unhurt shoulder, squeezing rather than jostling it, so I don't shake her body and hurt the arm still tucked inside that sling I can't look at. "Wake up," I tell her.

She snores.

"Fine," I snap, my head swimming, the warning pulses behind

my eyeballs signaling a migraine coming my way. "If you won't get your own ass to bed, I'll get it there."

After the worry she just put me through, I should let her sleep all night in a cramped storage closet and earn the sore muscles she deserves, but goddammit, that is untenable to me.

So I slip my hands beneath her, my palms grazing her shoulder blades, the tendons at the back of her knees, before I lift her into my arms.

"Hmm." Her head flops against my chest on a *thud* that reverberates through my body.

"*Hmm* yourself," I mutter sourly, tucking her tighter against me, "you sanity-shredding shrew. You heart attack of a hellion. You've got me so angry, I'm being alliterative."

"Hmm," she mumbles again. A smile quirks the corner of her mouth.

It brings me to an abrupt, wrenching stop. I stand in the middle of the apartment, staring down at her—the straight, proud line of her freckled nose, those tiny wisps of auburn curled lovingly around her jaw. I stare at that dimple in her cheek that's as good as a black hole, a vortex devouring time and space, catapulting me through a kaleidoscopic blur of memory.

I look at Kate and see her when she was a baby, then a child, that same dimple in her cheek.

And then I see her just how I did that day I came home for good, a box of shit from my city apartment clutched in my arms, as she stood on the porch, no longer a pranking, conniving little girl, but a woman. No smile, no dimple in sight, her eyes holding mine.

The world melted away to nothing but the slivers of sage in the cool blue of her eyes, the smoky gray ring around each iris that darkened like the sky as a storm rolled in above us, whipping the trees, flooding the air with ozone and a crackling, electric warning.

Dragging past to present, marrying memory with this moment,

lightning flashes outside, chased by an ominous *boom* of thunder. A rare, sudden storm for this time of year.

I tell my feet to move, my body to cross the distance to her room, drop Kate on the bed, walk away, and never look back.

But instead, my gaze disobediently slips to her mouth. And I find myself wondering how well this distance-and-disdain tactic of mine has ever worked. If what's actually worked has just been that she's been gone.

And now she's home for who knows how long.

In short, I'm wondering if I just might be fucked.

"Doughnuts," she mutters, wrenching me from my thoughts.

I lose the battle against the smile that tugs at my mouth. "You and your damn doughnuts."

"Hmm." The dimple grows as she smiles in her drunken sleep, and, God, it gets worse, she throws her free arm around my neck. That's enough to wrench my body into gear, propelling me across the apartment toward her room, before I ease open the door with my foot.

As I lean down to lay her on the bed, Kate's grip tightens. Her nose, then lips brush my neck. I freeze as lightning jumps from the world outside straight into my veins.

"Smell good," she whispers as her nose slides along my neck. Heat licks up my body.

"Kate." My voice is rough and thin, my breath stuck like smoke in my throat, choking my resolve.

"Topher," she mumbles.

My heart clutches. She called me that when she was small, when her loud, busy mouth wasn't up to the task of my full name.

"Kate," I beg, clutching at her arm. "Let go."

She doesn't hear me. Stubborn, infuriating torturer, she doesn't wake up.

I kneel on her bed and lay her down until the mattress holds her weight, desperate to escape, to peel her off me and rush out into the frigid night air and let it douse the flames, cool my mind and body until I'm myself again and she's Kate, and we're back where we should be. On opposite ends of the room.

Of the world.

Whining faintly, she finally surrenders her grip around my neck, her arm slipping down my chest, her fingertips branding my skin. Her head lands on her pillow and flops to the side, her forehead pinched as if she's in pain. I hate what it does to me, seeing that furrow in her brow, the taut pull of discomfort at the corner of her mouth.

So I don't look at her mouth or her face anymore. I gently tug off one sturdy boot from her foot, then the other. I peel away her thick, fuzzy socks, and she sighs in her sleep. Her toes wiggle.

Then I lift the blanket and slide it up her body, resting it at her shoulders, forbidding myself to touch her any more than I already have.

Another sigh leaves her, then she mutters, "Topher."

I stare down at her, telling myself to leave, hating myself as I stay right beside her bed and say, "Yes, Kate."

She licks her lips, flails her arm in her sleep, and rolls onto her bad shoulder, not even wincing. I'm worried she'll hurt herself, sleeping with the sling, so I bend over her and carefully undo the Velcro holding it together. Then I reach behind her and slip it off her body.

Kate's sigh gusts across my face. "S'nice," she mumbles. And then she slides her hand across the sheets until it finds mine.

Her eyes flutter open, slow blinks, her gaze unfocused. Her smile is soft and so impossibly sweet. "S'you," she whispers.

I nod, words lost to me.

Her smile dissolves. "I forgot," she says, her eyes drifting shut.

Don't ask her, I tell myself. *Don't ask her. Don't ask her—*

"Forgot what?"

"That you hate me," she whispers.

My heart cracks and spills aching, sour regret. I despise myself so much. "Never, Kate. I swear."

"You do," she says, her mouth pulling in a frown, the tiniest sparkle at the inside corners of her eyes.

The crack in my heart becomes a clean break. Tears. They're tears.

"I never . . ." I swallow roughly. "I never wanted you to think I hated you, Kate, I . . ." My voice dies off. Another snore lifts her ribs. She's asleep.

And, like a coward, I tell her what I don't have the courage to say while she's awake.

"All I've ever wanted is for you to hate *me*. I couldn't hate you if I wanted to. I wish I could, but I can't." My thumb slides along the smooth, warm skin of her hand. "I don't know how to do this, so all I've ever tried is *not* to—not to see you or touch you or think about you, because I can't . . ."

She exhales shakily, curling in on her side, as if protecting herself, shielding herself from me. Those pleas to make peace that have been thrown my way by our friends and family are pebbles to the landslide of her tears, her hand clutching mine, her truth that's slipped between the cracks of her awareness.

She thinks *I* hate *her*.

It's the last thing I ever wanted. I have never loathed myself so much.

"I'll fix it," I tell her, gently tucking behind her ear a hair that's caught in the tears wetting her cheek. "I promise, Kate, I'll fix it."

I know she's asleep, but her silence feels damning, skeptical, a warning that nothing but a long, hard struggle lies ahead.

I meant what I said, when I told her that I don't know how to do this, how to share a world with Kate without disdain safely wedged between us, without distance maintained by living an ocean apart.

But that's not enough to stop me, not anymore.

I can't—I *cannot*—live in a world where Kate believes, even if she only reveals it in her most unguarded moments, that I hate her. I can't let tears wet her eyes and that ache of heart-deep pain pinch her expression. I can't live with myself, knowing I hurt her.

And now I have to fix it.

I know walking that tightrope of healing what I've broken without bonding us together won't be easy. I won't even try to tell myself otherwise. But I'm goddamn Christopher Petruchio. Nothing stops me. Every part of my life, when I've set my mind to something—in my work, in the kitchen, in sparring, in my bed—I haven't settled until I've come as damn close to perfection as is humanly possible.

Forcing each step back toward her doorway, out of her room, I tell myself what I'm about to undertake won't be any different. It can't be.

Because if it is, I am in some deep shit.

ELEVEN

Kate

Waking up is offensive. My head pounds. A sharp ache pounds between my thighs, too. Not for the first time since coming home, I'm hungover and horny—my personal hell.

Shuffling from my room to the kitchen, I squint miserably against the sun.

"And here I thought *I* had it rough," Bea says.

I jump a foot and spin toward the sound of her voice, tripping on the coffee table, stumbling back and landing on the armchair in a cloud of dust motes. "You scared me."

Bea clutches the side of her head, eyes shut. "Sorry. Apparently it runs in the family. You scared Jamie and Christopher last night."

I ease upright on the chair, experiencing a sudden swell of nausea. "What?"

"They couldn't find you after everyone left. They were scouring the apartment for you."

Guilt twinges through me like a plucked string. I want to ask Bea what she's talking about, but I've got a bad feeling about how she's going to answer me. Before I hear whatever drunken nonsense I pulled last night, I need coffee.

Pushing off the chair, I slip into the kitchen, fumble for a mug, drag the carafe off the warming plate, and pour a hot, sloshing cup of desperately needed caffeine.

"Should you be doing that?" Bea asks.

"Drinking coffee?" I ask, poised to savor that glorious, piping-hot first sip. "Fuck, yes."

"Using your arm," she says. "Not wearing the sling."

The coffee I've just swallowed flies down my windpipe. I smack my chest.

"You okay?" Bea asks.

I nod, lifting a hand. "Fine," I croak.

She frowns at me and my lifted arm. The one I've been faithfully tucking into a sling for the past two weeks, even though my shoulder's fully recovered from the run-in with Christopher.

I drop my arm.

"I had it seen yesterday," I lie off the cuff, loathing myself for lying again, but not knowing what else to do.

Her frown deepens. "Oh?"

I set down my coffee and kill two birds with one stone, turning toward the cabinet with the ibuprofen to fish some out and avoid my sister's eyes. "Yeah, I'm okay to take it out of the sling now."

"Huh. I figured shoulder injuries would need longer than that to heal. That seems pretty fast."

"I didn't break it right before I came home. It was a little while before I left."

That feels good, sharing some truth.

Bea makes an understanding noise. "Of course. I didn't consider that you've been healing for a while."

"Plus," I add, "you know how they're always changing what they recommend, how soon you start using it, what you can and can't do." I make a derisive noise in the back of my throat. "Doctors."

Of course, that's when I remember her boyfriend's a pediatrician. "I mean, besides—"

"Chill your cheeky briefs," she says, pushing off the couch, mug in hand. "I'm not offended."

I peer down, and lo and behold, I am indeed in my cheeky briefs. "I coulda sworn I put on pants."

Her hand lands gently on my messy bun, which she tweaks affectionately. "I think you might still be a little drunk."

"It's possible." Cautiously, I try for another sip of coffee. "I inherited Mom's knack for languages but not her tolerance for whiskey."

"Only Jules inherited Mom's tolerance for whiskey, which is freakish and unfair." Bea tops off her mug and leans against the counter beside me. "So. How much do you remember after you passed out in the closet?"

Oh boy. Here we go. "Nothing. Why? Did I reveal myself from my hiding spot in some gloating and spectacularly inebriated fashion?"

A little nervous laugh trickles out of her. She takes a gulp of coffee. Then another. "Not exactly."

Unease slithers down my spine. "What happened?"

"It's not a big deal." Bea sets her mug in the sink, the dregs swirling around the bottom.

"That's exactly what you say when something *is* a big deal."

"Christopherfoundyouandputyoutobedthat'sit."

I blink at her. "I . . . He . . . What?"

She walks backward, which is not a wise idea for Bea—she's the only one in the family more accident-prone than me. "Christopher. He found you. Put you to bed." She dusts off her hands. "No big. That's it."

Hazy, liquor-soaked memories saturate my brain and float to the surface. I remember now, my head flopping onto a shoulder, my cheek pressing into a solid chest that radiated heat, hard and warm as a sunbaked boulder.

I remember breathing in that familiar scent, spicy woodsmoke, soft as a whisper on his clothes and skin.

Oh God. His skin. I buried my face in it. I wrapped my arm around him. I *touched* him.

"Are you okay?" Bea asks.

I scrub my face. "Brilliant. Fabulous."

"You're upset."

"Christopher carried my drunk ass to bed like a damsel in distress after he found me spooning a whiskey bottle in a closet, *yes*, I'm upset!"

"To be fair, Jamie said they did try to wake you up. The damsel-in-distress bit was a last resort."

"Argh. I'm . . ." I press the heels of my hands against my shut eyes, savoring the temporary relief from the pain thudding behind them. "I'm just upset with myself"—and Christopher, because he's very easy to be upset with. "I don't like looking back at a situation and seeing what a mess I was."

"I mean, consider it this way," Bea says encouragingly. "This happened in the safety of your home, with someone who's practically family, who would never do anything untoward. Christopher just tucked you in and left, and that was that."

I hate it, the intimacy of that image—Christopher seeing my things strewn about the room, laying me in my bed. God knows what I looked like, what I said to him, my limbs and lips loosened with sleep and whiskey. How humiliating.

Trying to cover my discomfort, I throw back my coffee in hot, painful gulps. "Yes, thankfully that happened with someone who has no interest in taking advantage of me, not that I needed you to remind me."

Bea rolls her eyes. "I meant he believes in consent and consciousness."

"Yeah." I set my mug on the counter with a *thunk*. "Well, I'm gonna puke if we talk any more about Christopher carrying me around, seeing me at my worst. Let's move on."

"Fine." Bea lifts her hands wearily. "We gotta get ready for work anyway."

My legs buckle. I slump against the counter. "Oh God."

She pats my back. "It's just a morning handling sales, taking a couple photos, then you can crawl home and back into bed."

"Why?" I moan against the counter. "Why did I say yes to this?"

"Because you're broker than broke and secretly you love the Edgy Envelope, maybe even more than me."

"It's Toni and his baked goods. And Sula plying me with samples; you know I'm a sucker for samples. And working with you." I nudge her shoulder. "That doesn't totally suck."

"Life at the Edgy Envelope is pretty spectacular, especially with Toni's cookies."

Pushing off the counter, I groan and stomp past her toward the sobering hot shower calling my name. "There better be a platter of Toni's cookies the size of Texas waiting for me when we get there."

There is not, in fact, a platter of cookies the size of Texas waiting for me at the shop. But, like a hangover-cure miracle, sitting on the glass-top desk, beside sparkling delicate gold chains, colorful bricks of artisanal chocolates, and a precarious tower of hand-poured, zodiac-themed candles, is a massive pastry box tied with twine, NANETTE'S stamped on the lid.

Beside it sits a bouquet so grand and elegant it looks like a Dutch still life painting, a masterpiece of color palette, texture, and composition.

My stomach plummets when I see the name on the card and tug it from its perch, wedged inside the breathtaking flowers.

Katerina

"Look at this!" Toni says, easing open the box. The aroma of savory herbs in a rich buttery quiche, maple glaze, and pumpkin spice wafts into the air.

Bea swats away his hand. "Back off!"

"What? I just checked what was inside."

She jabs her finger toward the card bearing my name. "It's for *her*."

"How was I supposed to know that? The name's on the card in the flowers, not written on the box!"

"Shhh. My head," Bea whines. "Your voice hurts."

"Excuse me for having a voice box. And by the way, *your* voice hurts, too. You're not the only one who hit the booze a little hard last night—"

"Then stop yelling!" Bea yells.

"Sweet Jesus!" I stare at them, wide-eyed with exasperation. "Would you two just shove some pastries in your mouths and hush? You're like an old married couple with low blood sugar."

Grumbling, they open the box and poke around in it. I shove a hand in the box, too, and pull out the first thing I find, a tiny glazed doughnut hole that smells like cardamom and vanilla.

"Toni." I flick the card toward the bouquet. "Who delivered this and the pastries?"

Toni turns my way, tugging back his dark hair into a small ponytail at the nape of his neck, presumably to avoid getting it in the massive cinnamon bun he's about to chow down on. "Some delivery person on a bike showed up right as I did to open." He shrugs. "No one I knew or recognized."

I stare at the card, the deep, slanted handwriting that's shaky and jagged around the edges, and slide my thumb along the letters. I wonder if it was written by someone at the flower shop where this bouquet came from, if the person who sent it wrote it themselves.

I wonder what made their hand shake as they wrote. I hope it wasn't pain.

With some kind of gut sense there's more to the card, I flip it over and stare at the words, written in that same unsteady, craggy writing.

Better hate than never, for never too late.

"Ooh!" Toni gasps around a bite of cinnamon roll. "Poetry?"

"I don't know." I stare at the words, trying to make sense of them.

Bea frowns and peers closer. She's got a fleck of quiche on her cheek that she brushes off. "Why does that look familiar?"

"Good morning, sunshines!" Sula hollers, slamming the back door of the shop and making all three of us wince. Bea and I clutch our heads. Toni whimpers. "Long day ahead," she barks, walking her bike toward the back of the store. "Eat up those pastries, pop some painkillers, and let's get to work!"

"Speaking of the pastries," I call, "did you send these?"

"No!" Sula calls back. "But I'm glad someone did, because you three look like corpses and corpses aren't much use for restock day."

Another whimper leaks out of Toni. "I'm gonna die."

"I'm dead already," Bea whispers.

"Wait." Toni points at me. "No more sling? You can help with restock!"

I grimace exaggeratedly and rub my shoulder. "Don't think so. It's still healing."

Setting down the card, I help myself to a wide wedge of quiche that's speared by a tiny flag with lettuce printed on it, signaling it's vegetarian. Plucking out the flag, I take a hearty bite and sigh with pleasure. That creamy tang of goat cheese. Bright, crunchy asparagus. It's a favorite flavor combination.

Bea shoves the last bite of quiche in her mouth and goes for another slice.

"Hey," I say around my mouthful. "These are for me!"

"I need another piece so I can get my veggies in," she says primly, helping herself to another wedge. Hers looks like broccoli cheddar. "Jamie will be so proud."

Toni rolls his eyes. "You could subsist on lollipops for the rest of your life and that health nut wouldn't crack one bit."

Bea smiles to herself. "Yeah, I know."

My sister has a number of textural aversions when it comes to food, and vegetables have proven to be a tough frontier. I can admit I found it a little surprising that my vegetable-loathing, sugar-loving, erotic-artist, tattooed sister ended up with a nutrition-conscious, straitlaced, marathon-running, polite and proper pediatrician, but I've been pretty delighted to see all the ways Jamie seems completely taken by the things about Bea that are different from him.

In fact, maybe I'm just a tiny bit jealous.

Just a *tiny* bit. And only on the very brief, rare occasions since I've been home, when I allowed myself to think about the fact that I've never met someone who saw the hard-to-like parts of me and liked me anyway. The only people who've liked me are the people *like* me.

I used to think it was closed-mindedness, people's aversion to my inconvenient fuck-the-system views, that it was on *others* that I didn't click with those who were different from me, who disagreed with me.

But lately I've been wondering how much I had to do with that, too. If I've held at a distance people I perceive as being at odds with me not so much because I disagreed with their views, but because I was protecting myself from *their* rejection for those differences, because it felt safer to write someone off rather than risk being written off first.

It's a bleak path to go down, and I'm saved from wandering it any further when the bell jingles on the overhead door as it opens, bringing in our first customers of the day.

"Not it," Toni mumbles, grabbing his cinnamon roll and high-tailing it toward the back.

Bea sighs and drops her quiche.

"I got it," I tell her.

Her head snaps up. "What?"

"I'll handle these customers. You go ahead and help Toni get stuff sorted for restock."

One of Bea's biggest struggles with working here is how draining it is for her to interface with lots of people, especially when she's tired, let alone hungover. I'm not in a much better place myself, but the need to help and take care of my sister is overwhelming.

"You sure?" she asks. "You've only done customers two other days and—"

"I promise I'll text you if I start to drown. I won't overreach."

She nods. "Okay."

And then she slips—with the pastry box under her arm, the brat—toward the back of the shop.

I don't greet the customers with a chipper welcome, but I do offer them a polite nod, before turning back to my plate and popping the rest of my quiche in my mouth.

"'Scuse me," a small voice calls.

I turn around, covering my quiche-stuffed chipmunk cheeks with one hand, signaling with a lift of my finger that I need a moment.

A kid who stands as tall as my hip peers up at me, wide brown eyes and a cheery smile.

"Sorry about that," I tell them, after forcing myself to swallow my barely chewed food. "What's up?"

"You got journals?" they ask.

I nod. "Yep. Right over there." I point toward the second row of thin shelves taking up the right side of the store.

The kid frowns up at me. "What's on your neck?"

"What? Oh." I peer down at my camera. "That's a camera. I take pictures for my job."

"I thought you sold journals for your job."

That makes me laugh. "Guess I'm a jack-of-all-trades."

"That's my name. Jack. Not Jackie. He/him/his." He offers his hand, and I take it.

"Nice to meet you, Jack Not Jackie. I'm Kate Not Katie. She/her/hers."

Jack's smile is pure joy. "Cool."

His eyes dance to my camera, brightening with curiosity. "Can I take some pictures with your camera?"

"Sure." I lift my camera off my neck and crouch, handing it to him. "This is a really valuable camera, so can you be super careful?"

He nods. "Yeah." Frowning down at the camera, he taps a button, bringing the digital display to life. "You can see your pictures when you take them? Like a phone camera?"

"Yep, same deal. What do you want to take a picture of?"

He bites his lip and looks around, then settles on me. "You."

I laugh, surprised. "Me?"

He nods, then without preamble, lifts the camera, and with that confidence I love in kids, snaps a picture. "Now can you take a picture of me?"

"Sure. So long as whoever takes care of you is okay with it."

"We are," a voice says, making me glance up. A gorgeous couple stands together, smiling our way. Jack is the perfect blend of them.

"I'm Hugh, Jack's dad," the man says. "And this is Jack's mom, Tia."

Tia waves.

I smile up at them. "Hi, Hugh and Tia."

"Yay!" Jack yells. "C'mon, picture time!"

"Okay, Jack, where do you want to stand? Anywhere along this wall is good, so you won't be backlit."

He rushes over to the display, near the bouquet of flowers that were waiting for me when I got here. "How's this?" he asks. "By the pretty flowers."

"That's perfect."

Jack puffs up his chest proudly and smiles, hands on his hips. "This is my first picture with my new haircut."

"You got a new haircut?" I ask, squinting as I tweak the lens's focus. "It looks great."

Jack nods, rubbing a hand over his tight, close-cropped black curls. "Day after Thanksgiving. I love it."

I smile. "Good. You look picture-perfect. I'll take it on three. One, two, three."

Click.

"Can I see?" he yells, scrambling toward me and clawing at my arm in that affectionate, guileless way kids have that makes them instantly feel like a friend.

"Here you go." Tipping the screen, I show Jack his picture—the dark-wash jeans stretching down his knobby-kneed kid legs, his bright green and orange striped sweater.

Jack traces his hand along the screen, outlining his image. Over his short hair, down the line of his sweater and his jeans. "I love it."

"Good."

Jack smiles at me. "Thank you, Kate."

"You're welcome, Jack." I stand and slip the camera off my neck, setting it in its case on the desk. "Can I email this to you? Would you like that, if I sent this to Mom and Dad?"

He nods. "Thank you! I'm gonna go get my journal now." And then he runs off.

"Thanks for doing that," Tia says warmly. "I'm going to go make sure he doesn't take out a row of stationery."

Which leaves me with Hugh, who offers a friendly smile. "That was nice of you," he says. "I hope it wasn't a bother."

"Not at all. Kids are always fun to take pictures with. They don't generally have all that internalized self-loathing adults do, so they aren't harsh critics of what I show them."

"In that case," he says, "if you really don't mind sending that photo, can I give you my email?"

"Absolutely." I pull out my phone and start an email that I'll save as a draft, then send when I can upload my photos from my camera to my laptop. "Ready when you are."

"It's 'Hugh Lang'—all one word—'at Verona Capital dot com.'"

I drop my phone. It lands with an ominous *thwack*. Verona Capital is Christopher's company. "Sorry." I stoop to pick it up, not the least surprised to see a big, fresh crack across the screen. "Did you say Verona Capital?"

"I did. Best place to work in the city. Your phone going to make it?" Hugh asks.

I blink at him. "Uh. Yeah. Wait, so you . . ." I bite my lip. "Would you mind explaining exactly what you do there? It's a hedge fund, right?"

Hugh smiles. "Not your typical hedge fund, but yes. It's ethical investing. Putting my clients' money into avenues that promote social equity, environmental responsibility, and the like, while ensuring my clients see a healthy return."

"And that's . . . possible."

He laughs. "It is. But it's not easy. Or I should say it's not as easy as dumping money anywhere the market indicates will make the highest profit for you, ethics be damned. But that's why I like it—the challenge of finding initiatives and companies that not only fit our ethical requirements but promise excellent returns. It's stressful, and it's a high like no other, when you do it well. The higher-ups are adamant about work-life balance, so we don't burn out. That's why I'm here on a weekday with my family rather than at the office. I took a personal day that I really needed, and it was granted, no questions asked."

I swallow roughly. Okay. So, fine. Christopher isn't a *completely* evil capitalist. But he's still definitely a capitalist.

With an amazing chest.

Who tangos like a fucking god.

And smells so damn good.

Gah, the inside of my brain is bumper cars this morning.

"Well, that's great," I force out. "I'll be sure to send you this photo soon as I'm off work."

"Look at those flowers," Tia says, as she and Jack rejoin us, Jack bringing himself to a bouncing stop beside me. "Such a gorgeous bouquet."

I glance over my shoulder, my stomach knotting. Velvety peach ranunculus stand tall, wedged against sunbursts of yellow dahlias. Tall, willowy delphinium petals spill down their stalks in a violet-blue waterfall. Scattered throughout are splashes of blush-pink roses and lacelike baby's breath. It *is* a beautiful bouquet.

"Who's Katerina?" Jack says, pointing to the card I set against it when they entered the store.

"That's me," I admit. "My full name."

Jack frowns. "Do you like it?"

I bite my cheek, hearing in my head Christopher's deep voice, the way he says *Katerina* that makes the hairs on my neck stand on end, that sends heat searing through my veins. "It's complicated."

"Well," Tia says on a smile, "whoever sent them must be quite the admirer."

"Or they've got quite the apology to make." Hugh throws his wife a look. "Not that I have any experience needing a bouquet like that to make amends, right, baby?"

"Bleh," Jack says as his parents link their fingers together and Hugh kisses Tia's hand.

"When you have," she says, "it always worked."

"Think it'll work for you?" Jack asks.

I peer at the bouquet, a weird, woozy feeling in my limbs that has nothing to do with last night's poor decisions lingering in my system.

I don't begin to know how to answer his question.

· TWELVE ·

Christopher

I'm tired, on edge, and shaky, after riding a rough migraine through most of the night and suffering through what little sleep I did get, which was tortured by dreams I can't admit or let myself dwell on.

Because they were straight from hell.

A long, willowy body pressed against mine. None of the curves my hands typically seek, nothing soft or yielding—just sharp angles, blissful bite marks, ruthless nails scraping down my back. A hoarse, smoky voice crying my name while I sucked and licked, dragged her legs wide open and—

The ding of my laptop announcing a calendar reminder abruptly ends those thoughts. I press my palms to my eyes and breathe deeply, envisioning a slow, painful walk into a frigid lake.

I need to get laid.

The past two weeks since Kate came home and upended *everything*, I've abandoned my routine—a meal at the bar, a flirtatious conversation and then a frank one (*I'm yours all night. Only one night. No repeats.*), then a hotel room, the exhilarating challenge of a new body to learn and become an expert of, the thrill of wrenching orgasm after orgasm from her, the blissful mindlessness of my own release.

I don't care to examine why the past few weeks have gone the way they have. No matter why I haven't been getting out and getting laid—given my foul mood, my hopelessly erotic dreams—that needs to change.

I need a good hard night of fucking. A luxurious meal. One nice glass of red wine. And a beautiful woman by 10 p.m. beneath me, on top of me, beside me—hell, whatever way she wants it. I'll get back into my routine and reset. No problem. Easy.

This is what I always do.

Which is why it makes no sense that when I start to draft an email to Curtis, my assistant, to clear my schedule after five and make a reservation at one of my favorite places, I can't seem to make myself do it.

Shit. *Shit.*

This is bad.

I push back from my desk, reaching for my coat.

"Curtis!" I bark. "Going for a walk."

"You're due back in thirty," he calls as I storm by.

"Got it."

I nod politely to Luz at the front desk, then take the stairs, because fuck elevators, jogging down, pushing open the door into the cool air. The sky is cloudless, the sun a pale lemon yellow squeezing drops of light between tall buildings. I start to walk, hands in my pockets, and try to clear my head.

For a while it works, as I soak up the ambient sounds of traffic, the steady stream of people going about their lives, until I realize where I've ended up and slow to a stop.

Bello's.

I stare at the familiar sign on the Italian restaurant I haven't been to in twenty years. I can tell the place has hardly changed when someone with a food order rushes out to a delivery bike waiting for them and acoustic guitar music floats out in their wake.

The door eases shut, but slowly, giving me time to soak up its ambience. The clink of plates and glasses, the melodic lilt of spoken

Italian, sharpens memories that have faded at the edges, fuzzy and softened by time. Plates of pasta swirled with Parmesan and cracked black pepper, tall glasses of deep red wine. Mom's bright laugh and Dad's warm smile. Old music, flickering candlelight, my belly full of too much frittelle.

The memory expands, like a widening lens. Bill's deep chuckle. Maureen's rosy-cheeked grin. Bea doodling on a napkin, Jules with her nose in a book.

And a little pigtailed menace with freckles on her nose and wiggly legs, kicking my shins, sharp, stormy eyes boring into me.

I blink, wrenching myself from the memory, though it's hardly a relief. My present is just as haunted by Kate as my past.

I think of the work I have ahead of me to fix things between us, enough so that I don't feel sick every time I replay what she said.

You hate me.

I wonder if there will ever be a world where we could walk in here as something gentler, something forgiven, split a bottle of wine, pick at each other's plates, our forks knocking in a battle for the perfect bite.

That'll be a cold day in hell, the voice of reason mutters in my head.

Finding my phone in my pocket, I pull up Curtis's email from this morning, confirming the flowers and pastries were delivered, and type a response, asking him to clear my schedule after five but not to make any reservations.

Where I'm going after work, I won't need reservations.

More like head-to-toe body armor.

· THIRTEEN ·

Kate

I'm sure I look ridiculous, clutching a bouquet the size of my torso as early December wind tries to rip it out of my arms, but I don't care. Like hell was I leaving those flowers at the store.

While I couldn't give a shit less what brand my clothes are, while I'll never want diamonds or cashmere or any sort of personal luxuries—anything that costs the kind of money that makes me ill when I think of the poverty and inequality that ravages so much of the world—I have a weakness for flowers. I *should* care that once each stem is cut, a flower's life dwindles exponentially, that such an extravagant, costly arrangement could have been assembled from my mother's greenhouse for a few dollars, its blossoms grown dirt cheap from seeds nurtured by the simplest of things—sunlight and soil, water and waiting.

But I love flowers too much. So I clutch my precious bouquet and breathe it in. The card wedged inside it, with my name penned in dark ink, pokes against my chest, reminding me, since having determined via text it was not my parents, of my many unanswered questions:

Who sent it? And why?

Who knows my full name?

Who knows I eat vegetarian and love pumpkin doughnuts?

Who knows where I work right now?

Reminded of work, my mind makes one of its nimble leaps and reroutes, drawn to memories of the day, how happy they made me. After Jack and his parents left, a fresh batch of customers came in. I took care of them, helped them pick out a card for Grandma, stationery for a friend, a small art print for their grown child who just moved into their first place. During restock, I laughed with Bea, teased with Toni, traded a knowing look with Sula as my sister and Toni bickered like old biddies.

I hadn't planned to stay all day, but time passed so easily. Hours flew as I snapped photos of the store in between customers, capturing its loveliness as the sun made its journey from butter-yellow morning light to honey gold at high noon, then to rich russet as it dipped below the horizon.

Before I knew it, we were closing the door, flipping the sign from **OPEN** to **CLOSED**. And when I clicked through my camera's screen display, Toni, Bea, and Sula gathered around me, their *ooh*s and *aah*s a soothing chorus to my ears, I felt it—a rare, precious ember, small and glowing, right in the center of my chest.

Belonging.

Warmed by that little nugget of happiness, I clutch my flowers, impervious to the determined wind, contentedly alone, about to start my walk home. It took a bit of maneuvering to get myself here—standing outside the pub next door to the Edgy Envelope, having just waved goodbye to Toni, who hopped on the back of Hamza's Vespa while Sula whizzed by on her bike, her bell chirping a merry *ding* goodbye—but I managed it.

Jamie stopped by a half hour ago with pho in hand for Bea and me, a cab waiting to take us home. I declined, lying by saying I was going to get a bite at the pub next door and would catch my own cab home. Because Jamie and Bea need it—time alone at the apartment, time to be happy in a way that I don't understand because I've never known it but that I'm happy for them to have, nonetheless.

I told the same lie to Toni and Sula, a little disconcerted by how readily I've deceived people since I came home, knowing it's something I'll have to sit with at some point and face. The reasons I tell my little white lies, the choices I make to stay separate, the roots I refuse to let sink deep.

But not tonight. Tonight, my belly full of the quiche and doughnuts I snacked on all day, my face buried in the luscious perfume of flowers, I'm letting myself bask in a sliver of joy.

That is, until I see someone leaning against the streetlamp a block away, hands in his pockets.

He tips his head back, scrapes a hand through his hair, exposing the line of his throat, a thick Adam's apple kissed by the sunset's glow.

I stare as a bolt of awareness races down my spine. There's something so familiar about him. The way he scrubs at his scalp, then lets his hand fall. The way he lifts his wrist, examines his watch, and slides his thumb across its surface.

That's what I recognize first. His hands.

Hands that pushed me on a swing when I was a scrawny girl who wanted to fly so high I could kick the clouds. Hands that dragged Puck, the family cat, out from under his front porch's crawl space where he'd hidden for shelter from a sudden, violent storm. Hands that scooped me out of a closet last night.

Christopher.

His eyes meet mine. "Katerina."

Reflexively, I hug the flowers tighter to my chest. The card pokes my skin and my stomach drops as I remember the name written on it.

Katerina.

No. It couldn't be him. He'd never.

Would he?

I shift the bouquet in my arms and lift my chin, forcing myself to meet his eyes. Two glowing embers in the dying light, fringed with thick black lashes. Dark half-moon shadows beneath them. He looks exhausted.

Not that I care, of course.

"Christopher," I finally manage to say. "What're you doing here?"

He pushes off the streetlamp post and strolls my way, so intensely . . . *there*. Solid and sure, unmoved by the wind tugging his wool coat, whipping back his hair. Sunset gilds his profile and, when he faces me fully, lights up his amber eyes as it spills, burnished bronze down his body.

My breath is doing funny things, turning short and tight in my chest. I feel the danger, the draw of leaning too close to a roaring fire after a long, frigid day.

He's so near now, I catch a wisp of his spicy smoke scent on the wind, see his chest rise and fall.

Snapping me from my reverie, he says dryly, "Apparently you're 'staying at the pub for dinner.'"

I arch an eyebrow. "Are you *following* me?"

He arches an eyebrow back. "I asked relevant parties where I could find you after work. That was the answer I was given."

"You didn't ask *me*."

"I don't have your number, Kate. You never gave it to me."

My stomach knots. "You never asked."

His eyes hold mine as he says quietly, "Fair point."

Suddenly, I am desperate to go.

I don't want to look at him glowing in the sunset like he was made for light to love every angle of his face, every contour and powerful line of his body. And I *really* don't want to think about why he's here, the ways I might have humiliated myself in front of him last night when I was drunk as a skunk and half-awake. I want to move on. I want to walk past him and just keep walking.

"Well," I say, falsely bright, "I'll just be on my way."

I start past him, when his hand darts out and clasps my elbow, bringing me to a stop.

I try to wrench my arm away, but his grip tightens, strong, yet still gentle, like when we crashed into each other that first night I was home.

"What do you want, Christopher?" I say between clenched teeth. I'm a raw live wire surging dangerously, my skin hot, agitated, too tight for my body.

His hand slides down my arm until it clutches my bare wrist. Despite the chilly weather, his palm is warm and dry, his fingertips rough as they graze my skin. His thumb drifts along my pulse where it flies as fast as I want to move down this sidewalk.

He takes a step closer, his hip brushing mine. Then he brings a hand to my flowers, to the wide-open rose slipping from the bouquet, its petals bruised by the wind. Gently, he slides the stem back, secure once more.

He meets my eyes again. "I need to talk to you."

"So talk."

"Let me walk you home. We can talk there."

"Walk yourself home and go to bed. You look tired as shit."

"Why, thank you, Katerina, I am. And I will. But you first. You shouldn't be out alone, especially when it's nearly dark."

"This again." I sigh, shifting the bouquet in my arms.

After a beat, he says, "I'll compromise. Let's walk and talk."

I swallow nervously. "Is this about last night?"

"In part, yes."

My cheeks heat. "I don't want to talk about last night."

"Doesn't mean we shouldn't. Just let me walk you home. I'll keep it brief, then leave you alone, I promise."

I tug my hand away and take a step back. "I'll pass."

"Goddammit, you're stubborn."

"Goddammit, you're bossy!"

Christopher holds my eyes and steps closer. His face softens. A sparkle settles in his eyes. "Katydid." That ridiculous childhood nickname. My stomach does *not* do a somersault. "Let me walk you home."

I roll my eyes. "Is this you trying to charm me? Make me swoon? Whatever it is, stop. It's not working."

"And yet you're clutching the flowers I sent like they're your favorite camera."

I peer down at the flowers, my stomach souring. "You sent these?" I ask, trying to keep my voice calm.

His mouth lifts at the corner. "Yes."

"An unconscionably expensive, gorgeous gift? Trying to buy your way out of something?" I give him a wide-eyed, exasperated look. "Of course you did. It's got you written all over it."

"So you *do* think they're gorgeous?"

"They're obscene. I can't stand them."

His smile widens, those warm amber eyes heating as they dance over my face. "I don't think so, Katerina. You love flowers. You always have."

A sharp, searing pain slides down my sternum. It's been so long since I let myself expect kindness from Christopher. I'm scared to trust it, bewildered by his sudden change in behavior. "Why are you doing this? Why are you sending me flowers and a card with some cryptic line on the back and enough pastries to feed the whole damn store?"

His eyes widen. He blinks at me like he's stunned I'm not just gobbling up this suave and debonair act. "I thought . . . the flowers would make your day a little better. And the pastries, I figured you'd share, that everyone working at the store had been drinking a good bit last night and could use some hangover food."

My heart's sprinting in my chest. Why would he be nice? Why

this sudden change? I want to reach out with both hands and take his olive branch, just as much as I want to protect myself and snap it clean in two. "So you were just being...*nice*?"

He throws out his arms in a gesture of helplessness. "Yes, though apparently little good that's doing me!"

Ah, there's the truth. Little good it's doing *him*. My heart sinks. "This nice-guy act is about *you*, then. I see. Given that"—I shove the flowers at him—"leave me out of it."

Two steps past him, and I can't do it. I backtrack and yank the flowers out of his arms. "Never mind, I'm taking these."

"Kate," he calls as I start to power walk down the sidewalk. "Wait!"

"No!" I yell over my shoulder. I'm walking as fast as I can, but even my long legs are no match for his. "Go away, Christopher."

"I can't let you walk home alone, Kate," he says, slapping the crosswalk button for pedestrians. He waits, but I cross the street, a car whizzing between us.

"I don't want to talk to you," I yell.

Except, God, I really do. I have so many questions, even though I'm scared of the answers. I'm scared I'll *like* his answers. And if I like those answers, I'm scared most of how easily I could lower my guard and let him in.

"I won't talk, then," he calls back. "I'll walk you home, and then I'll go, I promise."

I'm about to tell Christopher where he can shove his promise when I notice a guy walking toward me down a perpendicular sidewalk. My shoulders tense. I've been on my own long enough to trust my instincts about these things. Immediately, I turn and close the distance between me and Christopher, falling into step beside him. The man pauses when he notices Christopher now beside me, then he starts toward the street, like he's going to cross.

My heart pounds. I'm waiting for some snide remark from

Christopher about his point being made, but none comes. Instead, he sets a hand low on my back and takes one smooth step around me so he's walking on the outside of the sidewalk, his body close to mine, shielding me from the man.

I scowl, despising myself for the rush of relief cascading through me. I don't need protection. Or care. But some small part of me that's been alone for so long, that's worn out from having to always look over my shoulder, assume the worst, be on the defense, stretches out and sighs like a cat in its favorite sunny corner.

I don't want to like how he's behaving. But I do.

After three long blocks of spinning my gears, I peer up at him, my curiosity about this odd one-eighty too intense to keep me from examining him.

He frowns into the distance, hands in his pockets. Then he glances my way and catches me staring at him.

"You really do look like shit," I tell him honestly.

He sighs tiredly. "I feel like shit."

I can't manage to ignore the band of concern squeezing my ribs. "What's wrong? Make yourself less than a million dollars today? Were you for once in your life turned down by someone with a square head on their shoulders?"

His mouth lifts faintly at the corner as he stares back ahead. "I wish it were that simple. You, on the other hand," he says, throwing me another one of those charm-the-pants-off-a-nun looks, "do not look like someone who chugged a quarter bottle of whiskey and slept half the night in a closet."

"Stop it."

His eyes widen again, that Casanova smile slipping. "Stop what?"

"Saying nice things you don't mean. Flirting. I look underslept and hungover, my hair's a bird's nest, I smell like the whiskey I'm still titrating out of my system, and we both know it."

"I know what you're doing, and it doesn't work like that. You can't gross me out, Kate. I've seen it all with you. You've literally shit on me before. And puked, for that matter."

I glare at him. "I was an *infant*."

"With a vendetta against dashing elementary school boys."

"More like with a prophetic gift for recognizing little shits when I meet them," I mutter.

He slaps a hand over his heart. "I'm wounded."

"Like you care what I think."

Peering my way, Christopher sighs heavily, the teasing humor suddenly drained between us. He stops walking, and I stop, too. "Kate . . ."

"You promised no talking."

He ignores me. "Do you remember last night?"

Now it's my turn to ignore him. I start walking again, the fastest I have yet. I'm only one block from the apartment now. I need a hot shower and ten hours of sleep and miles between me and this weird new side of Christopher and whatever scheme he has going on, asking these questions, bringing up something best left behind.

"Kate, stop running off."

"As you said on Thanksgiving," I tell him over my shoulder, "it's what I do best."

"I'm sorry, all right?"

I come to such a sudden stop, he slams into me, clutching my body and steadying me. I stare up at him. "Did you . . . just . . . *apologize?*"

His jaw ticks. He's breathing roughly, staring down at me. "Yes. I apologized and I apologize now. For what I said at Thanksgiving. For losing my shit on you in front of the family . . . For a lot of things."

I search his eyes. I'm so disoriented, I'd swear the world's turned upside down. "Is this all because of last night? What happened? Did I say something?"

"Not *all*, no. But . . . yes, somewhat." He hesitates, then says, quieter, "It messed me up, Kate."

"So, what? You had a sudden crisis of conscience? Based on some drunken nonsense I muttered in my sleep, you determined, after twenty-seven years of acting like I'm either as invisible as the breeze or gum stuck on your shoe, that you were going to buy me flowers, send some doughnuts, and boom, problem solved?"

He pinches the bridge of his nose and sighs. "Yes. No. I didn't—"

"Listen to me." I step closer, holding his eyes. "Whatever I said last night, whatever made you decide to have a personality transplant and treat me any different than you ever have, ignore it. It was nonsense."

He stares down at me, intense, wary, something turning his expression fierce and unreadable. "I don't think it was, Kate."

My heart plummets to my feet. Oh God, what did I say? I know my track record, that when I'm drunk, I unfortunately tend to say things I've buried deep inside.

Some of it is pure, whimsical silliness.

Some of it is my deepest, most vulnerable feelings.

Judging by how Christopher's looking at me, it was the latter.

"You had no right," I tell him, barely holding back my fury, "to take advantage of me like that."

"I didn't," he says, shaking his head. "I wasn't trying to. You wouldn't shut up. Trust me, all I wanted was to drop you on that bed and get the hell away."

"Of course!" I yell. "All you've ever wanted is to shit on me or get rid of me as fast as you can, and the one time you didn't is when you had a chance to take advantage of my uninhibited state. How shocking!"

"It wasn't like that," he says sharply, stepping closer. "You think I wanted to hold you, to watch you smile in your sleep and say weird, funny shit, to feel your arm wrap around my neck like it was supposed to be there? I didn't. I *never* asked for that."

"No one asked you to be Mr. Fucking Chivalrous, Christopher!"

"That's the problem, Kate," he mutters between clenched teeth, so close his thighs brush mine, my flowers the only thing keeping us apart. "I can't help it, not with you. And then you had to open your goddamn mouth—"

"Ignore it," I tell him. "Just ignore what I said—"

"You said I *hated* you," he grinds out. "I never...I never meant..."

I stare up at him, trying and failing to hide the sadness that bleeds into my voice. "You *do* hate me."

"You infuriating woman, I have *never* hated you."

"Maybe you've never said it," I tell him, "but you've acted like you hated me."

"If I have, so have you."

I shove his arm, but he doesn't budge. "You started it."

"Because I had to."

I open my mouth to challenge that, but my words die away the moment his hand curves along my jaw.

"Because you," he whispers, his head lowering, "have tortured me. For as long as I can remember. And I have dealt with it terribly, I admit that. I pushed you away and put our differences between us, and you gave it right back to me, but I never, *ever* . . ."

His mouth hovers so close to mine, I breathe him in. I feel him breathe me in, too. His thumb slides along my jaw. His nose grazes mine.

"I never hated you, Kate. And I can't stand for you to think otherwise."

"You can't just . . . say that," I whisper, my eyes slipping shut. His thumb drifts down my throat, tender, featherlight, scattering sparks beneath my skin.

"I know."

"It doesn't change anything," I tell him, my body listing traitorously toward him.

"Not yet," he says quietly. "But I'm trying."

"How? We can't stand each other."

I hear the smile in his voice. "You so sure about that?"

My eyes drift open, meeting his. "What?"

His gaze drops to my lips. "My mouth is very, very close to yours, Kate."

I swallow. "I'm aware."

"And you want it there. Otherwise, I'd have a knee in my nuts right now."

A breathy, exasperated laugh leaves me. "You're such an arrogant—"

"Infuriating," he adds.

"Frustrating," I growl, wrapping my hand tight around his coat, pulling him close.

"Menace," he whispers, dragging me by the waist until I'm pinned against him. He dips his head as I peer up at him and our noses brush. Our lips are a breath apart. We both draw in a long, rough tug of air.

"God, Kate," he whispers.

A current surges between us, white-hot, crackling, as his mouth lowers toward mine. The world careens off its axis, tipping me toward him, up on my toes.

My mouth brushes his, and a shock jolts us both. But neither of us pulls away.

Christopher lets out a low, aching sound of satisfaction as he cups my face, guiding our kiss. At first it's soft, a whisper of warmth and promise, then it's hungry, velvet-hot, slow, searching tastes, his mouth learning mine.

Deep inside me, a spark ignites to a flame, flooding my body with heat. It makes me lean in, desperate for more. Christopher senses this somehow, or maybe he wants it as badly as I do, because as I throw my arm around his neck, his grip spans my waist, then tightens, dragging me against him.

One hand splays up my back, arching me into him, until it settles at the nape of my neck and rubs gently. Our mouths fall open on twin moans, and his tongue softly strokes mine, coaxing. I gasp and lean in, consumed with helpless, restless need.

Christopher's hand slides higher up my neck, scraping into my hair. He tips my head for a better angle and groans roughly as our kiss deepens, wet and warm, slow, steady strokes of his tongue.

I'm panting, aching, because this kiss is an ember and my body is a blaze, burning awake, begging for longer kisses and stronger touch to ground this frantic energy bringing me to life. I need him. I need this. I need *more*.

But when I try to pull us closer together, my shoulder twinges sharply. A quiet cry of pain jumps out of me.

Christopher tears himself back, breathing hard, his gaze searching me frantically. "I hurt you."

"No. No, I'm fine," I tell him, my hand sliding up his chest. "It's not you. My shoulder is just a little sore."

He ducks his head as if he's gathering himself. He breathes out a slow, concerted breath. "I shouldn't have . . . I didn't mean to . . ,"

Those words echo in the air and sour it. My pride stings like a slapped cheek.

Christopher shakes his head, staring down at the ground, scrubbing his forehead. "I'm sorry, Kate. I just—"

"Wanted to talk?" I ask, stepping back and wiping my lips with the back of my hand, trying to erase the memory of him from my mouth. I hate how weak I just was, wanting that. Even more, I hate that he's humiliated me *again*.

I can't believe we just *kissed*.

Christopher and I kissed.

Where's the sign of the end times? The meteors raining down from the sky? The pestilence and rivers of blood and the Four Horsemen?

Christopher swears under his breath. His eyes meet mine, dark with regret. "That wasn't supposed to happen."

"Of course not," I say tightly. "You could kiss anyone, why kiss me?"

"Now you're twisting my words," he says. "Don't do that."

"You're right. How unfair of me! Our history dictates that, without hesitation, I should give you the benefit of the doubt!"

He yanks at his hair. "I'm sorry, all right?"

"Yes, you've made that very clear! How sorry you are! How much you regret kissing me!"

His eyes narrow and he erases the small amount of space I put between us. "What are you angry about, Kate? The kiss, or what I said about it?"

"I don't know," I snap. "I don't even know who the hell *you* are. You send me flowers, you send me food, you're waiting outside my work, insisting on walking me home, then you're hauling me against you like this is some—some fucking romance book of Juliet's, and none of it makes sense!"

"I'm trying to talk to you so it *will* make sense, but you won't let me!"

"Because it doesn't make sense! Because you don't treat someone the way you've treated me my whole life, then magically want to 'talk about it.'"

"And those twenty-seven years are all on me? You provoked me, taunted me, hounded me—"

"I was a fucking kid, Christopher! I was a child who just wanted to be a part of what you and my sisters, and hell, even my parents, had. I just wanted to belong!"

"You've made very interesting choices for being someone who wants to belong," he says, breathing harshly, "considering you left and never looked back."

"Because I wanted to live! I wanted to see the world. And I have some fucking pride. Because I wasn't going to hold myself back, only to want things from others that weren't wanted of me, too."

"You aggravating, maddening, clueless woman—"

"Please, insult me more."

He clasps my jaw, his thumb sliding across my lip, reminding me of our kiss, and God, I'm weak, because I want it again. I want teeth and tongue and his body moving with mine, hard, urgent, chasing something this has awakened inside me, something I despise him for.

His forehead hits mine, his mouth a breath away from meeting my own. He says, his voice dark and quiet as midnight, "As if anyone could not want you."

Then he drops his hand, draws open my building's foyer door, and hauls me inside, before slamming the door closed between us.

I'm rooted to the floor as Christopher spins in a fury and storms out into the night.

While I stand, stock-still.

Stunned by his words. Burning from his touch.

FOURTEEN

Christopher

"You are in a foul mood today."

I glare at Nick. "Did I say you could talk to me?"

"Oof." He looks to Hugh and makes a *get a look at this guy* gesture.

Hugh, one of my best employees and all-around stand-up guy, just smiles my way as he tells Nick, "Take it easy on the boss. He's got a lot on his plate."

"Yeah," Nick quips. "The world's largest, butteriest pile of toast."

I sigh, biting into another piece of toast, which is indeed stacked on top of a number of other extremely buttery slices of toast, but after a migraine, I crave salt and simple carbs. That, combined with a cold, sweet fruit smoothie, generally sits well and eases the lingering nausea I feel.

"How's Jack doing with moving schools?" I ask. I'm desperate for a subject change. I don't want to think about how many migraines I've had lately, how high my stress is, how epically last night backfired, how lost I am, now that I've abandoned the old manual with Kate.

And I really don't want to think about the fact that I kissed her, that I can still taste her, a trace of maple glaze on the soft pillow of her lip; still feel the warmth of her skin beneath my hand.

God, I *kissed* her.

I can't stop thinking about it.

I *have* to stop thinking about it.

Hugh finishes chewing his bite as he sets down his sandwich and wipes his mouth with a napkin. "Jack's doing so much better. It was the right call."

"Good."

"Here." Hugh pulls out his phone and opens up his photo album, spinning it so I can see. "Look how good he looks."

I smile. Jack's hair is close-cropped now, making his expressive brown eyes look even bigger and wider. His hands are on his hips, his jeans dark and perfectly tailored, his green and orange striped sweater almost as bright as his smile.

"He looks perfect. And happy."

Hugh nods, angling the phone for Nick to see.

"God, he's cute," Nick says. "I can't wait for kids. I want at least five. No. Seven. Definitely an odd number."

Hugh laughs. "You say that now. Wait until you have one and you don't sleep for a year."

I can't help but glance at the photo again as Hugh spins it his way. It's a stunning image. The angle the photographer used, the way light glances off Jack's cheekbones and catches his eyes. How softly out of focus the background is, but not so much as to render the elegant bouquet of flowers behind him unrecognizable—

Wait.

"Sorry," I mutter, picking up Hugh's phone and zooming in.

"Everything okay?" he asks.

I zoom in a little more. Holy shit. "Was this taken at the Edgy Envelope?"

Hugh smiles. "Yeah. We got Jack a journal there. His therapist recommended it after our last session, and her office is just down the street, so I figured we'd stop by. Tia loves that place, too. I got her a perfume there last Christmas that was not cheap, but let me tell you, that investment paid dividends, you know what I'm saying?"

Nick offers him a fist pound, cracking up. "I'm gonna check it out, then. Get something for Bianca," he says, before biting into his sandwich.

I give him a sharp look. "You will not."

"Why not?" he asks around his mouthful.

"Because Kate's working there and will not take kindly to you showing your face." I tap the screen on Hugh's phone. "That's who took this photo, isn't it, Kate?"

"Yeah, wait, how do you know her? She was so good with Jack. Tia was like, 'Can we see if she babysits?'"

"Unless you want Jack burning bras and rubbing shoulders with an anti-capitalist, I would not recommend Kate as a babysitter."

He laughs. "Ah, there are worse things than a kid spending time with an adult fired up about the world's injustices. I mean, I want that, truth be told. We all do. It's why we work here. It's why you took your family's company in an entirely new direction."

I stare at the photo, knowing he's right, how in many ways—in spite of how I've tried to tell myself otherwise—Kate and I share similar goals for the world, albeit through very different methods.

And now I'm back to remembering those kisses.

Jesus, I'm screwed. The mess I'm trying to clean up just became messier.

I have a decade of experience wooing women. But I have never had to work to repair a relationship with one. Especially one I don't *want* a relationship with, for so many very sensible reasons. How do you make things right with someone without making things good between you? How do you set a break without grafting yourselves together in the healing?

Apparently you kiss them, then dream about them, then beat

off in the shower to thoughts of them, and obsessively replay kissing them in your head.

I'm losing it.

And it's all her damn fault.

"Do you think she'd be free to watch Jack?" Hugh asks, shattering my thoughts.

"Probably not. She's a traveling photojournalist," I tell him. "She won't be here for long. She never is. She disappears for months, even years sometimes."

"Wait, a photojournalist? I have a *brilliant* idea." Nick drops his sandwich and claps his hands together. "You should hire her to do the new company headshots."

I blink at him, gently setting down Hugh's phone. "Why the *hell* would I do that?"

Nick leans in, smiling. "You've been grumbling that they need to be updated. And you're not wrong, Hugh's creepy uncle goatee was rough—"

"Hey." Hugh throws a chip at Nick's head. "You leave me and my goatee alone. It was artistic."

"It was not your best look, my friend." Nick turns back to me. "Listen, I know you and Kate don't get along, but—"

"Wait. You don't?" Hugh frowns. "She seemed so friendly. What's the problem?"

"A complicated multitude of ills," I mutter.

"And who knows better what cures a multitude of ills than us?" Nick says. "Money."

"With pretty much anyone else," I tell him, "but not Kate."

"So what *does* she value?" Hugh asks.

I try very hard to push away the memory of last night, her confession that she's felt excluded, shut out, pushed away. It makes my chest ache.

"She just . . ." My throat feels thick. "She just wants to feel like she belongs."

And I made her feel like she didn't. Guilt sours my stomach. I push my food away.

"Hmm." Hugh frowns thoughtfully. "Well, never thought I'd say it, but for once, I think Nick's onto something, then."

"Thanks," Nick says, before he realizes the implications. "Hey."

Hugh laughs. "I'm just messing with you, man. It's a good idea and not your first."

"Hiring her to do our photos?" I ask Hugh, turning it over. "Why is that a good idea?"

"You said she needs to feel like she belongs. So give her something to belong to. You want to smooth things over with her and let her feel like a part of your world—"

"But keep things distant," I clarify.

He shrugs. "What better way than establishing a professional dynamic?"

I blink at Hugh. "Damn, that's good."

"Hey." Nick smacks my arm. "It was *my* idea."

"Pat yourself on the back, then, Lucentio. And wish me luck." I stand, my chair scraping back. "Because I've got a business proposition to make."

FIFTEEN

Kate

This is an IDGAF playlist and new clothes from the vintage shop kind of day. The silk top I'm wearing was probably originally a couple hundred bucks, with its smooth, invisible seams, the eccentric dark blue print against a steely gray background. I got it for six dollars when Bea and I went shopping on Sister Day. The sleek-soft fabric, the happy memory of our day together, wraps around me, soothing my raw nerves, which haven't left me since last night.

I wander the Edgy Envelope with my camera around my neck, trying to keep my mind busy, snapping shots while a group of customers congregate around the Prurient Paper Collection, which is Bea's work—hidden erotic designs in gorgeous abstract artwork.

"Excuse me!" one of them calls.

I lower the camera, swallowing a groan. After that shit show with Christopher last night, I'm not in a peopley mood. I'm not even technically here today to provide customer service. I'm just taking photos for the store's website. But Bea's off and Toni left a little bit ago to pick up lunch for us, so I'm the only employee on the floor right now.

I could call for Sula in back, but after how generous she's been, offering me work, paying me under the table, I can handle a small group of customers even when I'm not in the best mood.

"Hi." I let my camera drop around my neck. "Need something?"

The customer smiles slyly as I walk her way. "I've heard these have, like . . . sexy pictures in them, but I can't figure any of them out."

"Some of them are abstract," I tell her. "Others are more overt. Like all art, it's a matter of your perception. It's open-ended."

She sighs, glancing toward her friends. "Does it have to be so philosophical? I just want to send Lex a card with sixty-nine."

"More like with feet," another one quips.

"Shut up!" she says, swatting her friend with the card, as they all shriek in laughter.

I smell the booze on their breath, and this starts to make sense. They had a liquid lunch, or at least lunch with lots of cocktails. They're all a little drunk and uninhibited.

"This one could be pegging, couldn't it?" another one of them asks me, shoving the card my way.

Heat creeps up my neck as I stare at it. As much as I absolutely do not judge anyone for openly and freely talking about sex, I've never been able to relate to conversations like this. I know I'm a sexual person, but I don't feel like I'm sexual how most people I know are.

I was raised without shame about sex or sexuality—my mother sat us down and talked frankly about how it worked, the healthiness of masturbation and birth control, our right to feel safe, and the necessity of continual, mutual consent. I'm enlightened about the fundamentals of sex, but I'm still deeply uncomfortable talking about them with strangers.

The bell to the overhead door jingles, mercifully interrupting us.

"Holy *hell*," one of the women whispers, staring over my shoulder. The rest of the group follows her gaze and responds in various forms of appreciation.

It's either Toni, who'll take my place, or a customer I'll turn my attention to. Whomever the tipsy ladies are checking out, they're currently my favorite person for saving me from this torture.

Turning, I feel an actual smile on my face.

It swiftly dies.

Christopher steps inside, golden midday sun shining behind him, sparkling off the tips of his hair. He's in that same long coat he wore last night over a whole damn bespoke suit. Dark blue so perfectly tailored, it looks poured down his body. Crisp white shirt. Bloodred tie. From the neck down, he looks straight off of Wall Street. From the neck up, he looks like a pirate. Sable hair a little too long and messily wavy for his fancy corporate job, his lashes absurdly thick and dark, that roguish gleam in his warm whiskey eyes.

I stare at his mouth and remember it moving with mine last night, hot and wet and hungry. I don't want to, but I can't stop. Until I remind myself what he said.

I shouldn't have. I didn't mean to.

"Katerina."

I scowl at him, folding my arms across my chest. "What do you want?"

A slow smile that I think is meant to charm me tugs at the corner of his mouth. "That's a very pretty top."

He walks closer, examining the fabric.

"Stop deflecting with false compliments," I tell him. "And stop ogling me."

"The compliment was genuine, and I'm not ogling you, Katydid. I'm appreciating the print. Also trying to figure it out. I thought it was paisley, but . . ." His smile deepens. "Are those *piranhas?*"

"They are. Watch out. They're not the only thing on me that bites."

His gaze drifts to my mouth. "That's not the threat you think it is, Kate."

That was definitely sexual. And unlike the awkwardness of those strange women talking about pegging and feet, Christopher holding my eyes as he says that makes my whole body flush. Heat rushes up my throat and floods my cheeks.

He watches its progression and smiles his widest smile yet. All bright teeth and wide, sensual mouth.

Doing my best to ignore that I'm blushing head to toe, I ask him, "What do you want, Christopher?"

His expression sobers. It's so reminiscent of last night, which I still can't begin to let myself think about—what we said *or* that kiss. If I think about it, I might believe him, and if I believe him—that he's sorry, that our dynamic (which I can admit I've played a healthy role in) got away from us, that he doesn't hate me—I don't know what will happen, what I'll feel.

How badly I could get hurt if I ended up being wrong.

"Can we talk?" he asks quietly.

I arch an eyebrow. "Need I remind you what happened last time you led with that request? I'll give you a hint. It was last night and it involved—"

"All right," he says, that smooth facade cracking as he steps closer. "Just . . . hear me out. Right here, okay?"

"Fine."

"I have a proposition for you," he says. And then he immediately realizes how that came out. His eyes widen. A rare rush of pink warms his cheeks. "I—wait. Just—"

"Mm-hmm." I shift my weight onto one hip, stony-faced.

He clears his throat. "I'm going to try that again."

"By all means."

"I have a *business* proposition. Strictly professional."

"Does it involve me working for you?"

He smiles. "Not really. Just under my roof. My company's."

"I'm good, thanks."

His smile falls. "Kate."

"Christopher."

"It's business. Good business."

"I know," I tell him. "I'm more than a good photographer. I'm great. It would be *great* business for you. But you could not pay me enough to spend all day rubbing shoulders with you and your money-grubbers—"

"Who grub money for good things," he says patiently. "Which you already know. You met Hugh. He's a class act, isn't he?"

Of course those two made the connection. My stomach knots. I was hoping I could pretend like I hadn't met a sweet person who worked with Christopher, but alas.

"Everyone there is like him," Christopher says. "Good people who care about good things. And they need updated professional photos. Everyone's headshot is five years old. Hugh has a creepy-next-door-neighbor goatee and Nick has such a douchey hairstyle, I'm worried it's hurting his client opportunities."

My mouth twitches. That gleam in his eye deepens. I think, despite my best efforts to resist, I'm being a little charmed. "Nick's hairstyle really is terrible."

"Hey, take it easy on us Italian boys," he says, taking on a thick accent I remember his dad using playfully when we were kids. "We got a lotta hair and no idea what to do with it."

"Excuse me," one of the women in the group says, raising her eyebrows at me. "Can we have some help already?"

I tear my gaze away from Christopher, then glance her way, gritting my teeth as I remind myself that being in a position of service is not demeaning, even if this group's treating me like it is.

"Yes?" I ask.

One of the women opens her mouth, but before she can answer me, Sula strolls in from the back. "Hi, folks! How can I help you?"

She practically shoves me sideways into Christopher. "Take five, Kate," she says warmly. "You haven't had a break today."

"Oh, that's—"

"Perfect," Christopher says, wrapping his hand around mine, dragging me toward the back of the store.

We're halfway down the hallway when I tug my hand from his, before I can let myself enjoy the warmth and solidity of his grip. "Stop hauling me around like a bag of bagels."

He spins, his coat swishing. "Kate, last night—"

"Please," I whisper, trying and, I think, failing to hide how raw I feel from last night. I haven't recovered from the whiplash when that tiny spark of hope soared through me as we kissed, then did a nosedive as he told me he regretted it, that he hadn't meant something that meant a lot to me.

I can't take that two days in a row.

"You've made yourself clear, Christopher. If you say you regret it or you're sorry or you didn't mean it one more time, I can promise you if you think you've seen a feral Kat, that's nothing to what's coming, so *drop* it."

He stares at me, jaw tight. Then a rough, slow swallow works down his throat. "All right."

My shoulders loosen with relief.

"So . . . will you do it?" he asks. "The company's headshots?"

I stare up at him, still so . . . lost. Who is this man I'm seeing? Where are the biting words? The fast steps away, constantly putting distance between us? I search his eyes. "Why?"

A beat of silence, then he says, his voice quieter, "I told you, I want to fix things between us. At least . . . make them better."

"Better?" I ask incredulously.

He rakes a hand through his hair. "I know we'll never get along *easily*. But I want to find a way to at least get along. While you're home. When we're with friends and family. That's what yesterday was about—the flowers, the food. And hiring you to do these photos. I thought they could be a reset, allow us to move on."

Move on.

Two little words. Why do they sound so terrible? Why do they make me feel like I've been kicked when I'm already curled up on the ground?

Christopher's eyes search mine, as if he senses how badly I'm spiraling. "Talk to me, Kate. What are you thinking?"

I don't feel very rational right now. And I don't know why. Because what Christopher is saying is the very thing I've told myself I wanted. For him not to be an asshole to me or pretend like I don't exist. For him to smile that warm, charming smile that he smiles at everyone else. For him to fold me in like I'm just part of the group and not give me every special kind of hell for simply existing in the same space as him.

So why does it feel like my stomach is a giant knot? Why does the mere idea of Christopher treating me like everyone else make the coffee I gulped ten minutes ago crawl up my throat?

And what am I supposed to do with what he did yesterday? The flowers are explained but not the cryptic note, the unexpected kiss, or the even more unexpected words he said before he left.

As if anyone could not want you.

Like I wasn't turned around and off-kilter enough from yesterday, he has to come in here and knock me sideways even harder.

But maybe he's not trying to knock me sideways. Maybe this is the emotional equivalent of those first steps on land when you still have your sea legs. I'm not used to standing still beside Christopher, quiet and peace wrapped around us as we search each other's eyes. I'm used to sky-high swells and raging storms. Of course this would feel weird. And different.

And, frighteningly, pretty ... wonderful.

If I can trust it. *If* he means what he says. *If* he really docs want us to, as he says, "get along." Praying I hide it well—the thrill of curiosity, the tiniest, most tentative hope, humming through my body, I offer him my hand. "Deal."

Christopher stares at me warily, his gaze dancing over my face. "Deal? That simple?"

The threat of a smile tugs at my mouth. I'm not the only one who doesn't know what to make of this new dynamic, then. "I do have a few stipulations. We do it when it suits me, scheduled around my commitments here, but yes. Those are my terms. If you accept, then it's a deal."

Gently, he takes my hand. His thumb sweeps across my skin as he holds my eyes. "Then it's a deal." A bright, satisfied smile warms his face. "Pleasure doing business with you, Wilmot."

I wage a battle inside myself to hold my calm expression, not to sigh at the warmth of his hand wrapped around mine. It's a small concession to strike a deal. It would be too grand a surrender to reveal this little bit of business we're doing actually feels like pure pleasure.

"Likewise, Petruchio."

SIXTEEN

Christopher

"So." Jamie clears his throat before sipping his green tea. "How are . . . things?"

"'Things' are fantastic." Looking both ways, we stroll into the crosswalk, shoulders up against the biting December wind. "Kate walloped me with the flowers I sent the other day and nearly got herself run over by rushing into traffic just to get away from me."

And you kissed her, that stern voice in my head reminds me. *You can't stop thinking about that kiss. You've had decadently filthy dreams replaying that kiss, taking things much, much further.*

I don't tell Jamie that.

"Then, when I pivoted and tried another tactic—extending an olive branch, asking if I could hire her to take new professional headshots at the firm—she just . . . agreed."

He frowns in thought, sipping his tea again. "And that's bad? Her agreeing?"

"It's suspicious." I take a long swig of my coffee, turning over my memory of the moment, that unreadable glint in her eyes as she peered up at me. "It was too easy."

"Or maybe it's just that simple."

"Nothing's ever simple with Kate," I mutter.

Jamie frowns my way, examining me. "She accepted your offer

to take photos for the firm, which you're suspicious of, but that's because *she* acted differently than she normally would, and that's what you want from her, too, for things to be different—"

"To be *better*," I remind him.

"Well, it takes time for things to get better. Different can be a good first step on that path." He gets one look at my incredulous expression and sighs. "All I'm saying is, Bea told me—and from what I've witnessed the past few days when I'm around her, I agree—Kate's seemed *happy*. That's a good sign, I think."

My heart kicks against my ribs. "She's seemed happy?"

Jamie nods, a grin lifting his mouth. "She has. And that means Bea's been happy, too."

Which means Jamie's happy, a fact that's obvious by the satisfied smile he wore when we met up, the kind of smile a man wears when his needs are being enthusiastically and frequently met. I'm well acquainted with that relieved, clearheaded look.

Not that I've seen it in my reflection the past three weeks.

God, if I could just get past this . . . block I have against my usual routine, if I could stop replaying every moment my mouth was on Kate's, my hands gripping her, tugging her close—

I shake my head and draw in a deep breath, pushing away the memories. I'm taking a page out of Kate's avoidant book.

I'm grateful that she's ignoring those kisses, pretending they didn't happen; that she acted as annoyed as always to see me when I walked into the store yesterday, with those little carnivorous fish on her shirt and a feisty glint in her eyes, and asked me to stop bringing up the incident in which I mauled her mouth outside her apartment and told her anyone would want her.

I'm glad about that. I *am*.

"Christopher?"

I blink, pulled from my thoughts, and force myself to meet Jamie's eyes. "Sorry. My mind wandered."

His mouth quirks at the corner. "Hmm."

"Don't you and your 'hmm-ing' have a job to go to?"

His smile deepens. "They do. I was saying, if you're feeling unsure about how things are progressing with Kate, why don't we put together a friend-group activity? Something fun and bonding."

I grimace. "I don't know. So far group settings have been a disaster with me and Kate."

"Give it one more try," he says. "I'll handle it, all right? You've got enough on your plate. Fun activities aren't my wheelhouse, but I'm good at outsourcing. I'll have help."

"Oh, Lord no. You're going to fold in the whole friend group, and you have no idea the meddling mayhem those fools can cause."

Jamie tips his head. "Why, Christopher, it's almost like you're aware there's some precedent in this group for meddlesome chaos."

I point a finger at him. "That . . . was different. You and Bea were different."

"How? I mean, I'm not displeased with the results, but the means, my friend, they were dicey."

"You two had a spark. As an expert on flirtatious chemistry, I am qualified to make these judgments, and the spark was there. You just got off to a terrible start. You needed a little nudge to give each other a chance."

"'A little nudge to give each other a chance,' you say?" Taking a step backward in the direction he'll head for his practice, Jamie grins. "Hmm. Sounds like it just might be time to take a page out of your own book."

I scowl at him. "I liked you, Jamie. We had a true bromance, a good thing going. And now you gotta throw my own behavior in my face."

He laughs. "Don't worry, we'll take it easy on you. Just a fun, bonding group outing, something that might move you and Kate a little farther along the path to peace."

"Have you met that woman? Peace is about as familiar a concept to her as a savings account."

"Give me some credit." Jamie takes another step back into the flow of morning commuter foot traffic. "I'll make sure it's in your interest to play nice, for *both* of you to. You'll be right there with her, on the same side."

I narrow my eyes. Kate and me? Side by side?

Sounds like a disaster waiting to happen.

SEVENTEEN

Kate

Christopher's office is different than I expected. No massive, chilly, corporate skyscraper with a bird's-eye view, pedestrians turned to insignificant specks on the ground.

From three floors up, people are still people, yet somehow more vulnerable from this perspective—a sea of ducked-down heads and hunched shoulders against the cold, shrunk to miniature size, delicate and numerous. I wonder if this is intentional. If Christopher meant for his employees to see and be reminded that there are people out there, on the other side of every choice we make.

I turn away from the tall, nearly floor-to-ceiling windows overlooking the city block, taking in the view from his desk.

Office doors here are open, so energetic voices carry down the halls that lead to Christopher's office. Luscious green-leaf plants and plush, dense carpet soften the hard edges of the space's midcentury furniture and severe, geometric layout.

Spinning in Christopher's desk chair, I curl my hands around its worn leather armrests until the world is a blur that looks as mixed-up as I feel sitting here, waiting for him.

The walls of his office are a warm, cozy color dancing between white and taupe—the color of a sleepy Sunday, a rainy afternoon nap. His desk seems old but well maintained and tidy, polished walnut that reflects the sunlight pouring in. No papers on the desk, only a calendar to the left with a word of the day, which I didn't see coming, and to the right, a beautiful black-and-white photo of his family that makes my chest ache.

Either they used the world's best family photographer or it's a candid shot, because it's so damn hard to get people to relax and be themselves when they're posing for you. I've perfected the art of telling people I got the shot, then snapping it as soon as they relax, but that doesn't always work. Sometimes you have to stay and be patient, find that moment they loosen up and joy comes back and their personality shines through. It took me years to hone that skill.

Gio's in profile, clear proof of where Christopher got his tousled waves and sharp jaw, deep laugh lines at the corners of his eyes and a wide smile as he looks down at his wife and son. Nora's curly dark hair is a halo around her head, her amber eyes, just like Christopher's, sparkling and warm. She sits with her arms wrapped around Christopher, her chin on his head as both of them smile up at Gio.

I sweep my thumb along the edge of the frame, sadness twisting my heart. I can't remember Gio's and Nora's faces without a photograph's help anymore, which I suppose shouldn't surprise me—I was seven when they died. I wonder if Christopher can still close his eyes and see them. I wonder why he never talks about them, why, once they were gone, he never did.

Selfishly, I feel a pang of gratitude for my parents, for the fact that I could hop on a train and hug my mom right now if I wanted, feel her softness and warmth and smell lavender in her hair, let my dad squeeze me tight and breathe in his peppermint scent and hear him call me Katie-bird.

My gaze slips to the right, to the next and only other photo on his desk besides his family's. Another family photo, taken years later. *My* family.

Curious, I scoop it up, then lean back in Christopher's chair. I set my thick-heeled boots on his desk, cross my feet at the ankles, and sway from side to side as I examine the photo.

It's an oldie, taken at Christmas. All of us stand in front of the tree at my parents', wearing some variation of warm sweaters, comfy pants, and slippers. Dad smiles, his eyes shut because they always are in pictures, his arm wrapped around Christopher, who's in his high school–hunk glory, already as tall as Dad and grinning arrogantly, his dark wavy hair in its almost-to-his-shoulders phase that he thought made him look super cool.

I snort and roll my eyes.

Next to him is Mom, her chin-length hair rich brown threaded with auburn like mine, her eyes crinkled cheerfully at the corners. Bea and Jules stand beside her, looking around thirteen and almost identical still, like they did until they hit high school. You can see the first signs of Juliet's beautiful curves, and a pen-drawn tattoo adorns Bea's right hand like a premonition. Then there's me, holding Puck, the family cat, who's looking much spryer in this picture, with his fluffy, long white fur, his pale green eyes twinkling with mischief. I'm about eleven in this photo. Scrawny, squint-eyed, freckled.

And wearing my fucking orthodontic headgear.

"That asshole."

I set the photo back on the desk with a *thunk* and glare at it. Of course, of all the photos he has, it's one where I have more metal in and on my head than there is in an aluminum factory.

Annoyed, I decide that if Christopher's going to keep a photo of me looking my all-time worst, it's time to find some dirt on *him*. I yank open the middle top drawer, surprised it's not locked. I'm met with an anticlimactic sight: blank notebook paper, blue, black, and red pens, a tiny pile of paper clips.

Next, the first drawer on the right. I open it and poke around.

Two prescription bottles that I don't look at or read—yes, I'm doing a little snooping, but give me *some* credit—mints, mint gum, and a thin stack of thank-you cards that have the Edgy Envelope logo stamped on the back.

"Boring," I mutter, shoving it shut.

Opening the second drawer, I riffle around. A slender leather-bound notebook that looks promising. A condom that upon further inspection accordions out to *ten* condoms.

"Ew." I drop the condoms and scoop up the notebook, which my gut tells me is some kind of diary or journal.

A decision is before me, a proverbial fork in the road. Do I read it? Do I not?

I'm annoyed at Christopher. I'm wary of whatever he's been up to the past few days . . . But the thought of violating his privacy makes my stomach sour.

"Dammit," I grumble, exasperated with myself.

I miss my reckless wild side. But this is growing up, I think. That and my ADHD meds, which I've managed to take pretty regularly lately, helping me with my impulse control, like metaphorical brake taps that slow my brain from acting on its natural inclination to press the pedal to the metal.

Still, this is even more than recognizing my maturity, the impact of my meds. This is caring. And I don't like it. I just can't seem to override it, either.

Sighing, I drop the notebook back in the drawer, then freeze when I notice something that's slipped partway out of it.

A faded bit of paper-white cotton with a poorly stitched deep blue border.

My stomach drops.

That looks eerily like my first, frustrated attempt at embroidery. Like a handkerchief I abandoned a decade ago.

Slowly, I slide out the fabric. My stomach plummets down, down, down.

In the corner, just like I knew it would be, is a terrible rendering of forget-me-nots. Uneven stitches of periwinkle and midnight blue form lopsided petals, silvery white and yellow gold knotted in lumpy pistils. Lime green leaves hover too far from the flowers, floating aimlessly.

A lump forms in my throat.

I made this on the tenth anniversary—what an awful word to use for such a sad occasion—of Christopher's parents' death. But I never gave it to him. I hated it. How inadequate it felt, how poorly done. I pricked my finger so many times and lost my patience, and after I'd deemed the handkerchief a failure, I shoved it God-knows-where, threw out the embroidery hoop, and settled on knitting when my hands needed to be busy and I wanted to make something for someone I cared about.

How did he get this?

Why does he have it?

As I sit back in his office chair with the handkerchief, my thumb dancing across the bumpy threads, a new voice carries out in the hallway.

Christopher's.

I drop my feet from his desk, shove the handkerchief hastily back inside the drawer, and bang it shut. I might have been ready to see him for these corporate headshots five minutes ago, but five minutes ago, I was not holding a humiliating reminder that (1) I used to not only foolishly care about Christopher but also try to make him care about *me*, and worse, (2) he has that proof carefully tucked away in his desk drawer.

Frantically, I scan the room for an escape until my eye snags on another door besides the one I used when I found his office. Voices come from the other side of it, reassuring me it leads toward a viable escape.

That's when I do what anyone would when their snooping's got the better of them—

I run.

EIGHTEEN

Christopher

My desk chair is empty yet swaying when I walk into my office. Frowning, I glance around the room and stroll toward my desk. I slide my messenger bag off my shoulder and set it on the chair opposite from where I sit, then round the desk, examining its surface.

I don't leave out loose papers. My desk has very few things on it, and none of it's been disturbed—except the framed photographs. Both of them are slightly skewed.

My jaw clenches in irritation. I reposition both frames until they're how I left them, my thumb lingering on Kate in her headgear orthodontics, holding Puck, who's so plump he's as big as her entire upper body.

A double knock makes me look up and drop my hand.

Curtis, my assistant, smiles. "Good morning!"

I arch an eyebrow. "Is it?"

"It is now," he says brightly, walking in with a steaming espresso, a mini chocolate-dipped biscotti nestled on the saucer.

"You're a saint." I dunk the biscotti in the espresso and bite off half of it.

"It's self-preservation," he tells me, adjusting his thick, black-frame glasses. "When you're happy, I'm happy."

"I'm happy," I say defensively around my bite.

He snorts. "Sure you are. You've been a real peach the past three weeks. A pure delight."

I drain half of my espresso and curse under my breath. It's scalding. "It's the end of Q4. I'm always 'a peach' this time of year."

"True," Curtis says, interlacing his hands in front of him. "However, you forget how much you rely on me to maintain your calendar and that I am thus aware of how ... *unoccupied* your evenings have been the past few weeks ..." He purses his lips meaningfully and raises his eyebrows.

I glare at him. "Did you have a point to make?"

He lifts his hands in surrender. "Nope. No point. Just plenty of thoughts that I'll keep to myself."

"Excellent." I take a small sip of espresso this time, careful not to burn myself again, before draining it. "While we're on the subject of calendars, what happened to this morning's schedule? Everything was as it should be before I got on the train, then by the time I was walking to the office and checked again, you'd cleared the all-hands meeting and blocked us off until two."

"When else was I supposed to update the calendar to make time for the professional photos you rescheduled to today, seeing as I found out about it from the photographer herself this morning?"

My espresso cup clatters out of my hands onto the saucer. "I ... what? When?"

He steps forward and gingerly takes both from me. "You didn't reschedule and move it up to today?"

Planting my palms on the desk, I tell him darkly, "No."

"Ah." He takes a cautionary step back. "Well, then it seems there's been a slight misunderstanding. I'll take care of it. Get the all-hands meeting back on everyone's calendar, cancel the catered lunch, well, or maybe keep the catered lunch—"

"*The catered lunch?*"

He laughs nervously. "She said you'd guaranteed her a vegetarian catered lunch, and I just assumed you'd forgotten to mention it, like the reschedule."

My expression must be thunderous, because Curtis gives me a chiding *don't be dramatic* look. "Keep your heart rate down. I said I'll handle it."

"I'm sure you will. It's Katerina who's got my blood boiling."

Curtis looks confused. "Who?"

"Kate," I explain impatiently. This little rescheduling stunt has her written all over it. "Kate Wilmot, the photographer. She's the one who told you it was rescheduled, wasn't she?"

"Oh, yes! Well, she didn't say 'rescheduled,' actually. She just showed up this morning, saying she was here for the corporate headshots," he explains, as I lower toward my chair. "She acted like she was supposed to be here, so I assumed you two had discussed it."

Just as he says that, a familiar-looking woman darts past my door in a streak of messy upswept hair and fire-engine red.

I miss the chair entirely and fall straight on my ass.

"Oh goodness!" Curtis yells. "Are you all right?"

"Fine," I bark. Rolling onto my knees, I spring upright and storm past him out of the office and down the hall, a poked bull charging its red flag.

Scouring the reception room, I search for Kate.

I'm not seeing things. It was her, in a red so vibrant I should be able to spot her instantly. But as I circle the office, wending my way down the halls, through our conference and break rooms, she's nowhere to be seen.

And then my gaze settles on the one place she could be hiding where I couldn't find her—the restrooms, right near the front desk.

"Everything okay?" Luz, our receptionist, asks.

I glance away from the row of single-stall, non-gendered bathrooms that line the wall, knowing Kate's in one of them, and there's fuck all I can do about that.

"Yes, Luz. Everything's fine." I sidle up to the desk and offer my most ingratiating smile. "Can you just do me one small favor?"

They smile back. "Of course."

"Did you happen to see a woman dressed in head-to-toe red dart into one of the bathrooms just a moment ago? Our photographer for the day, Kate Wilmot."

They nod. "Yes, I did."

"When she walks out, kindly let me know?" I hesitate, then add, "Immediately."

———

Of course, my office phone lights up when I'm on a spur-of-the-moment call with a client—one of our biggest investors, who needs reassurance about this latest green energy company that's part of her portfolio. This is what I get for being transparent and open with my clients about their investments.

Much as I *want* to tell Lydia Bel Sur she'll just have to hold on a sec while I take a call because I have my receptionist doing reconnaissance on the woman wreaking havoc in my office, I can't.

Which means it's not until I hang up with Lydia fifteen minutes later that I'm able to storm out of my office and immediately identify Kate's whereabouts. A semicircle composed of at least a third of my team encircles Kate, who leans against the conference table in head-to-toe red, looking like a warning sign.

Rohan barks a laugh. "Christopher in a tricorn hat and breeches. This is priceless."

I roll my eyes, knowing exactly what photo Kate's sharing from the Independence Day party when my dad demanded everyone come in costume.

"You should see him in lederhosen," Kate tells him, scrolling through her phone. "I have to dig around back at my parents' house for that photo, but let's see. Ah! Here's a goodie. He's . . . nine in this one, I think?" Kate zooms in on the photo that fills her phone screen, which she angles for everyone to see.

"Oh my God," Jia says, pointing at the screen. "Is that a *bowl* cut?"

"It is," I say casually, making everyone jump and turn except Kate, who slowly glances up and locks eyes with me. I close the distance between us, my employees parting to make a path.

Kate pushes off the conference table and stands to her full height, just a spare inch south of me, which means she's got heels on. I don't risk a once-over to find out the details.

"Christopher," she says.

I tip my head and force a wide, easy smile. "Katerina."

Tearing my gaze away, I look down at the photo. "I see why you chose to share this one. It predates your extended orthodontia season."

Her eyes narrow. "My 'extended orthodontia season' seems front and center in your mind, Christopher. I wonder why."

I grin. "Saw that photo, did you?"

Now the empty swaying chair makes sense. She was snooping around my office.

Kate sniffs, pocketing her phone.

"Oh! There she is!" Curtis appears out of breath, his glasses slightly askew, forcing a smile as he power walks into the conference room and says to me, "Like I said, definitely handling it—"

"No need." I wave him off. "We'll stick with the updated schedule."

He glances frantically between us. "Uh . . . You sure?"

Kate frowns. "Is something wrong?"

"Okay, folks." I clear my throat, smiling politely at the team. "Fun as this has been for you to get a little trip down memory lane, let's get back to it. Curtis will let each of you know when Kate's ready to take your headshot."

The group disperses with polite *nice to meet you*s for Kate, some of which linger a little too long until they notice me watching them like a hawk.

Kate turns on me, arms folded. "What was that about?"

I wait until the last person shuffles out and Curtis shuts the door behind them, before I turn on her, so close our chests nearly brush. "I'd ask you the same question, Kate. What are you playing at, showing up here today and pulling a prank like this? If it were just me, that would be one thing, but Curtis has been bending over backward to accommodate this little stunt of yours."

"Christopher, it's just some vegetarian sandwiches and soups. All your assistant had to do was place the order I'd lined up with the café and spend a little of all that money you bathe in every night. What's the big deal?"

"First of all, I don't bathe in money. But nice to know you're thinking about me bathing. At night."

She rolls her eyes. "Am I that transparent? Yes, Christopher. It's all I think about."

"Second of all," I tell her, ignoring her dripping sarcasm, "I'm not talking about the catered lunch—well, not *predominantly* the catered lunch. I'm talking about you showing up, acting like today is photo day, sending Curtis into a tailspin."

Her eyes widen. She blinks at me. "I . . ." Glancing away, down at her camera bag, she fiddles with its straps. I watch her shoulders set, her jaw harden. I've never been so aware of watching Kate slip on her armor.

And I've never been so aware of how hard I'm used to being on her. I assumed she showed up on the wrong day intentionally and tore into her for it, but what if she didn't? What if she got her dates mixed up?

It's been over a decade since I've spent enough time around

Kate to observe her executive function when it comes to time management, but I remember when she was younger it was hard for her.

I feel a sucker punch of guilt. Kate hides her struggles that come with ADHD so well, I forget she has them. I shouldn't. I, more than most people, know that hiding your struggles doesn't make them disappear—it just makes them less visible to others. I know how lonely it gets when no one knows why I canceled plans or left early, when I'm a last-minute no-show at game night or I cut a meeting abruptly short because my brain's decided it's a great time to incapacitate me with a migraine.

"You didn't mean to show up on the wrong day, did you?" I ask her.

She throws a sharp glance my way, her eyes flashing. "I . . ." Her jaw works, like she's searching for words.

Stepping closer, I slip my hand around her elbow. "Katydid—"

"Stop calling me that, Topher Gopher."

I grin faintly, remembering that nickname from a long time ago, when I hadn't quite grown into my front teeth. "I'm sorry I assumed you pulled a prank. How about I make it up to you with that fancy catered lunch you had Curtis order?"

"Just have him cancel it," she mutters.

"Nah. We can afford a catered lunch here and there."

She still won't look at me, but the furrow in her brow softens as she gently steps out of my grip, fiddling more with her camera bag. "Good. I woke up craving those roasted eggplant and red pepper pesto sandwiches."

After a beat of silence, watching her, I tell her, "You rely heavily on your calendar to organize your commitments and keep you on time, I bet."

Kate throws me another sharp glance, all pricked pride and

fire. "Yes. Which is generally the reason one has a calendar. It just bites me in the ass when I rely on something I've entered inaccurately, but that's my brain for you. I'm sorry about today, okay?"

"Kate, it's all right."

She stares up at me, searching my eyes, quiet for a long, drawn-out minute.

"What is it?" I'm starting to get uneasy with the intensity of her examination.

She sighs bleakly. "I'm finding it hard to despise you right now, and I resent that."

I smile, wide and genuine. "Well, I *am* supremely likable."

Rolling her eyes, she drags her camera bag higher on her shoulder. "The moment's passed. You killed it real quick."

A soft laugh leaves me, earning her attention. Kate meets my eyes, a faint uptick at the corner of her mouth—the closest I've come to earning her smile.

She steps away from the conference table, backtracking steadily. I can't stop my gaze from finally raking down her body.

Jesus. H. Christ.

Her jumpsuit has wide legs, soft, fluttery sleeves, a fabric belt cinched tight at her waist. Shoulders, hips, and legs for miles.

Heat rushes through me as the memory of last night's dream floods my mind's eye—long legs straddling my waist, lean, strong arms outstretched, hands planted on my chest, hips riding me hard and fast—

I clench my teeth and beg my brain to recall with vivid detail the photo on my desk featuring middle school Kate in her orthodontic headgear, hoping it's enough to douse the fire coursing through me.

It doesn't work.

If Kate notices I'm suffering, she doesn't let on, and given how much she seems to delight in my suffering, I don't think she's noticed. She points her thumb over her shoulder, then says, "I'm going to use that small southwest-facing meeting room for the photos, if that's all right. It'll be the best light."

I stare at her, managing only a silent nod.

Finally, she seems to notice that I'm looking at her differently.

She arches an eyebrow. "Just wait for it. Business in the front. Revolution in the back."

And with that cryptic statement hanging in the air, she spins and wrenches open the door.

My eyes snag on the back of her jumpsuit, spotting the classic Rosie the Riveter icon printed across the top, except in this version, Rosie holds a sledgehammer in her raised arm; below her reads, the letters cracked and compressed like shattered rock, SMASH THE PATRIARCHY.

When the door slips shut, I let out the laugh I've been holding in.

NINETEEN

Kate

"Saving the best for last?" Christopher eases the door to the meeting room closed behind him.

"You caught me," I deadpan.

As the door shuts, the hairs on my neck stand on end. I glance over my shoulder and catch his gaze on me, then darting away. Christopher clears his throat and rakes a hand through his hair.

"I see you've noticed Rosie," I tell him, assuming that's where his eyes were.

He gives me a wry smile that makes my insides fizz like a just-popped bottle of champagne. "If you were hoping to scandalize me or anyone here with your fuck-the-patriarchy sentiments, Katerina, I'm sorry to disappoint you."

"Meaning what?"

He eases onto the stool I gesture toward, the one I've had everyone sit on to take their photo. "Meaning lots of things. Women's rights are human rights," he says. "Diversity and inclusion isn't something you phone in for brownie points but work your ass off to actually achieve. We don't just invest in companies committed to that ethos, we embody it ourselves. Verona Capital offers its employees fully paid insurance covering and affirming their right to all procedures and medications their bodies need, extended paid sick leave and work-from-home accommodations, menstrual leave, extended parental leave, subsidized daycare and pre-K, zero tolerance for harassment, an ADA-certified accessible workplace, dedicated lactation rooms, gender-neutral bathrooms . . . You get the idea, I think."

Lifting my camera, I plant my forearms against my nipples, which are rock hard. Goddamn, that shit turns me on.

"Well," I manage, scowling as I flick through my camera screen's display, not even seeing the photos I've taken, "it's the least you could do. It's what everyone should do."

"Completely agree."

I clench my teeth. Great. Not only is he making me horny with his progressivism—he's *agreeing* with me.

"You seem flushed, Kate."

I shrug, then clear my throat. "Just a little warm."

His grin is slow and satisfied. He knows exactly how he's affected me, and it's so damn irritating. "I can open a window," he offers.

"I'm fine."

I'm clutching my camera so hard it's going to crack. I let it drop around my neck, telling myself to cool down. So what if he can tell what he said turned me on? Turning on people is as unremarkable to Christopher as the sun lighting up the sky.

Which is just one of the many ways we are so deeply different. Sex is effortless and central in his life, his expertise and enjoyment of it a given. Sex is anything but effortless for me, my attempts to enjoy it fraught with misunderstanding and disappointment.

Christopher leans in, elbows on his knees, and clasps his hands together, bringing him closer to me, a shock jolting me back to the present. Our eyes meet.

A flush sweeps through me as his gaze holds mine. Maybe it's because it's so rare for me, but the intensity of this sexual pull I feel toward him nearly knocks the air out of me. I stare back at him, struggling to make sense of the weighty warmth settling in my breasts, deep in my belly, and between my thighs.

I haven't liked Christopher in a long time. But that doesn't mean I haven't known him. It doesn't mean I haven't noticed him. Yes, he's familiar, his scent, his voice, his presence—something I've known my whole life—but shouldn't it take more? A lifetime of existing in my sphere, a few days being nice to me, and my body's throwing itself at him. It's unacceptable. And frankly, it's unsettling.

"Penny for your thoughts," he finally says.

Squaring my shoulders, I try to rein my body in. "Revolutionary as this idea might be for you, Petruchio, some things cannot be bought."

He tips his head, grinning. He's such a flirt. "No? How are they . . . acquired, then?"

I stare at him, despising and also despicably enjoying how warm I am, the sweet-sharp ache ebbing through me. "They must be earned."

"Earned," he says softly, an appreciative grin warming his face. "Hmm."

Leaning so close I can feel the heat of his body, he peers up at me, brow furrowed, jaw tight. His throat works with a swallow. Mine does, too. Every inch of me is *aware* of him, goose bumps dancing across my skin. I feel my fierce blush creeping up my throat.

What is this? Does he feel what I feel? He's so experienced in a woman's pleasure that he has to recognize the signs—the way I've subtly pinned my thighs together to relieve the ache between them, how I've rolled back my shoulders, hoping I can shake off the hot, heavy waves of desire coursing through my body.

Does he stare at me like this, watching what he does to me, because it interests *him*? Does he want me?

As if anyone could not want you.

I haven't let myself dwell on what he said the other night. Because I'm scared I might latch on to those words. Count on them. Hope in them.

That sobering thought finally makes me step back. I scoop up my camera and put it between us, focusing on Christopher through the lens, adjusting and angling myself to capture the best light.

I grunt in frustration as I bring him into focus.

His cheeks are swept with a hint of pink, like he's hot, too, but otherwise, his expression is smooth, unreadable. "That bad, huh?"

The camera drops around my neck. "Some people look fresh as a daisy seven hours into their workday. You are not one of them."

He laughs tightly, raking a hand through his hair again. "Thank you, Katerina."

Closing the distance between us, I stop just outside the narrow V of his legs. They're so long, his feet are planted on the ground rather than the bottom rung of the stool he's sitting on.

His jaw tightens. His guard's up. "Can I help you?" he asks.

"I'll help myself, thanks." I kick his feet wide and step in between them, making Christopher mutter a curse as he sets his hands on my hips to steady himself.

"Jesus, Kate."

"I'd like to fix your disheveled appearance for this photo so you look like a business owner worthy of people's millions instead of somebody's stunt double after a rough day on set. May I?" I ask, gesturing to his hair.

He blinks up at me. "I . . ."

I shift my weight to one hip. Which is when I process that Christopher's hands are still on my hips, his grip tight.

And I like it.

And I shouldn't.

"You what?" I ask, forcing myself to breathe steadily, to keep my voice even.

A rough swallow works down his throat. I stare at his Adam's apple as it bobs, his jaw as it clenches. "I'm still hung up on the past ten seconds."

I ignore that because I have to, because if what he said the other night knocked me sideways, what's happening now, the way he's touching me, is about to send me spinning clean off the earth's surface. "Is that a yes?" I ask.

His eyes hold mine. His fingers flex on my hips, holding tight. "Yes."

I slide my hands into his hair, thick and cool, silky locks that slip through my fingers as I tidy the disheveled waves. As I comb my fingers through his hair again, his eyes fall shut. A low, satisfied sound rumbles in the back of his throat.

My fingers trace down the ends of his hair, over neck muscles that are so tight, they make me wince in sympathy. "Lord, Christopher, you ever heard of a stress ball? A day off? Your muscles are like steel cables."

He grunts pleasurably as my fingers rub down his neck, and his head *thunks* forward onto my chest. It feels simultaneously like the most natural and shocking thing we've ever done. His hands tighten their grip on my hips, and he breathes roughly when I sink my fingers into the base of his neck, then across his shoulders. "Fuuuuck," he groans.

"All this money you bathe in, and you can't spring for the occasional massage?"

"That's the bad part," he mumbles against my chest. "I do get massages. I'm worse than this without them."

I *tsk*, working my fingers beneath the collar of his dress shirt, kneading those tight ropes of muscles banding his neck to his shoulders. Air rushes out of Christopher, and he turns his head sideways, resting it against my chest, his grip its tightest yet on my waist.

"Kate," he says roughly.

I answer, redirecting my touch to the safer territory of his hair. "What."

"E-enough." His voice breaks on the word.

"I'm not done," I tell him, smoothing back the pieces curling around his ears and jaw.

"I am," he grunts. Easing away, he sits straight again and sighs heavily, eyes scrunched shut.

"Did I hurt you?"

He tips his head back and blinks up at the ceiling. Another heavy sigh leaves him. "In a manner of speaking."

He's clearly not in actual pain, so I go back to sorting out the last few straggling pieces that need to be smoothed back. "What *is* with your hair these days? It's so long."

He shuts his eyes again and lets out another long-suffering sigh. "I've had to cancel my last few haircuts, then it just got to the point that I said, 'Fuck it, I'm wearing it this way.'"

"Why'd you have to cancel so many haircuts?" I ask, leaning back, examining how I've arranged his hair, deciding one last comb through with my fingers will do the trick—

His hands come up to mine and clasp them, stopping me. Gently, his thumbs circle the sensitive skin of my wrists. I'm not sure if he draws me nearer or if I take a step, but somehow I'm now closer between his legs, staring down at him.

Christopher swallows roughly, his eyes searching mine. "Migraines. The last three appointments I had migraines, so I had to cancel."

I blink at him, stunned by this admission. The last time Christopher admitted to or, hell, even *spoke* about his migraines was before his parents died.

Gently, I tug my hands from his grip. Like an unspoken chore-ography, my hands land on his shoulders as his wrap around my hips again. We both jump a little, then settle like a circuit com-plete, energy humming between us.

"For that to have happened on three different appointments, the chances of that," I say quietly, my fingertips curling toward the base of his neck, toying with the soft dark licks of hair that hit his collar. "You must get them a lot."

His hands' grip flexes on my hips. "I manage fine, Kate."

It's a nonanswer that's answer enough. He's not even trying to dismiss their frequency, meaning it must be really rough. He's a pain in my ass, but the thought of him hurting so badly makes me feel sick to my stomach.

"I'm sorry," I whisper.

He makes an impatient noise in the back of his throat. "Don't apologize for something you aren't responsible for. If anyone should be saying sorry right now, it's me."

"Why should you say sorry?"

His palms slip across my lower back, so gentle, as his thumbs graze my waist. "I gave you hell earlier," he says quietly, "when you showed up today. I didn't even consider you'd gotten your schedule mixed up instead of messing with me. I forgot—"

"That I have ADHD?" I snort. "Once I stick around more than a few days, it's impossible to miss, isn't it?"

His hands glide higher up my back and draw me closer. "Why *have* you stuck around, Kate?"

I bite my lip, my fingers curling into his hair at the nape of his neck, softly scraping up into the silky strands. "It's complicated," I mutter.

"Tell me," he says quietly but fiercely, his hands drifting over my back in a lulling, sensual circle.

"Why should I tell you my secrets?" I ask.

He's quiet for so long, staring up at me, searching my gaze. Finally, he says, his voice rough and hoarse, "Because you know that while I've been an ass to you plenty, Kate, I'm safe. You can trust me."

Our eyes hold as those words sink in. The fearful part of me wants to deny that I somehow know deep down I can trust him, to stop myself from opening my heart to him even a crack. But the brave part of me wants to kick my heart's doors wide open and run headlong into the notion of a trustworthy Christopher Petruchio and all that's possible because of it.

"As a gesture of good faith," he adds, "to prove my point, here's what I'm prepared to do. When you first came home, and I told you I'd collect payment at a later date, for my silence about what you were up to the night we ran into each other . . ."

My grip on his shoulders intensifies as I remember how deeply he pissed me off that day, towering over me in the foyer on Thanksgiving and threatening to tell on me. "What about it?"

"Well," he says quietly, his touch wandering higher, his thumbs sweeping so close to the underside of my breasts. "I'll surrender that."

I arch my eyebrows, incapable of hiding my surprise. "Are you serious?"

"Very serious."

"You'd do that, just because you want to know why I'm here?"

He hesitates. His knees brush my legs as they tighten around me, holding me close. "I want to know, yes. But . . . mostly I want you to trust me, because your trust matters to me."

My heart's pounding. I bite my lip so I won't smile in pleasure at the warmth his words suffuse through me. Tipping my head, I peer down at him and notice his tie's loose and crooked. Gently, I straighten the knot, then tighten it a little. "I came home because I wanted to fix things," I tell his necktie, still fiddling with it, simply to avoid his eyes. "Because if Jules got away, she could have a place to heal, and if Jules was away, Bea and Jamie could be together without worrying about how it might affect her. If I left Scotland and came here, all of that was possible."

His hands go still on me. "You came home . . . for them."

I smile wryly and meet his gaze. "Yes, Christopher. Hard to believe I could pull my head out of my ass long enough to show up for my family?"

"I wasn't thinking that." He bites his lip, his grip firm on my waist. "I just wondered . . . is there another reason you came, one that was just for *you*?"

It's so tempting to tell him everything, when he holds me this way, when he looks at me like this—*Because I was tired and sore and broke and lonely. Because this life I've been living that used to fix all my problems started feeling like the source of them. Because it felt so good to feel needed, and even better, knowing I could help.*

But I've given him more than I ever thought I would, in what I've already confessed. That's enough vulnerability for one day.

"I have my reasons for me, too," I hedge. Sliding my hands off his shoulders, down his arms, I take my first step back until he reluctantly lets go, his hands landing heavily on his thighs. "But those . . ."

"You're not ready to tell me," he says.

"Girl's gotta have some secrets." I lift the camera and force myself to focus on its mechanics, my eyes on Christopher not as someone who's touched me tenderly and offered an olive branch of trust, but as my subject, contained safely in its frame.

He stares straight at me, jaw clenched, his eyes two glowing embers that burn through the barrier I've tried to put between us. "I can wait," he says. "Until you are. Ready, that is."

I lower the camera for a moment and search his eyes. "And

what if I told you that you might be waiting a long time, Petruchio?"

His eyes hold mine. "I'd tell you, I'm a patient man, Katerina."

I clutch my camera like a shield and bring it between us, capturing frame after frame, reminding myself why I came here today in my feminist red power suit, armed with my best camera, my fiercest boots, ready to take charge—not get myself emotionally twisted up and melt into a puddle of lusty goo.

But as I snap photo after photo, as I look into those warm amber eyes locked on me, sure and steady, all I can think about are those photos on his desk, the handkerchief in his drawer, his gentle touch, his eyes searching mine, his voice, low and steady, revealing kindness, promising patience.

I can wait.

I have more than enough photos of him, but I keep my camera up, firmly between us, hiding the fact that Christopher's managed something I stopped hoping he would a long time ago: to put a smile on my face.

TWENTY

Christopher

"Turn that frown upside down." Nick smiles from where he leans a shoulder against the threshold of my office.

I stop swaying in my chair, pinning him with a flat, weary look. "And why should I do that?"

"Because you are clearly making some progress with the ballbuster—"

"*Don't* call her that."

Nick lifts his hands. "Okay. My bad."

I scrub my face. "Sorry I snapped. I'm tired."

"So go home. Get some sleep."

I laugh emptily. Spoken like someone who can simply lay down their head and sleep, whose head pounding with pain doesn't wrench them awake half the time, whose nightmares don't keep them up the other half. "Yeah."

Slowly, I ease out of my chair and reach for my coat. "Walking to the train? I'll join you."

"Oh. Uh . . ." He wiggles a finger in his ear, Nick's nervous tell.

"Uh, what?" I ask, slipping on my coat.

"I actually have a dinner date with Bianca. I just wanted to stop by and say . . . thank you. Whatever you're doing with Kate, I think it's working. She took my picture today and didn't judo chop me, just told me if I broke her cousin's heart, she didn't know where I lived, but she had her ways of finding out. I've been holding my breath since Bianca and I scheduled this, especially since Kate saw me earlier, nervous Bianca would cancel on me, yet here we are."

I glance away, focused on packing up my cross-body bag, securing the clip, willing myself to ignore the dull ache spreading through my chest. "That's great. I hope it goes well."

Nick's quiet. So quiet, for so long, that I glance up. I catch him examining me carefully. "Thanks," he finally says, then after a beat: "You doing okay?"

Before I can answer him, my phone, faceup in the middle of my desk, dings with a text message from a number I don't recognize. I read it, and my heart jumps against my ribs.

> Hi. This is Kate.

"Christopher?" Nick says.

I slap a hand over my phone, oddly protective of this first. Kate and I have never had each other's numbers. Never texted. Doing my best to ignore my heart drumming inside my chest, I flash him an easy smile. "I'm good. Thanks. Enjoy your date with Bianca. I hope it goes well. Have a good night."

Nick narrows his eyes at my phone. When it dings again, and I nearly jump out of my skin, a knowing grin lifts his mouth. "You have yourself a good night, too."

As soon as he eases off the doorway and disappears into the hall, I lift my hand and read the new message lighting up my screen.

> **KATE:** Pretty sure I left my phone at your office.
> Mind looking for it? I can come by tomorrow and

look for it myself, but I figured I'd ask you to look now. I assume you're still at the office, counting coins and inventorying your empire.

A dry laugh jumps out of me.

CHRISTOPHER: I already finished inventorying my empire today, but I'm still at the office. I was about to leave. Let me find your phone and I'll bring it to your place, if that's where you are. Any idea where you might have left it?

My phone dings with her response.

KATE: I'm at the apartment, yes. Maybe the room where I took photos? I honestly don't remember. Enjoy the scavenger hunt.

CHRISTOPHER: I expect some kind of compensation for this favor.

KATE: Of course you do, you soulless capitalist.

Another laugh jumps out as I type back, See you soon to collect my due.

———

After knocking a few times with no response, I let myself into the Wilmot sisters' apartment with my key. The door swings open, and I shut it behind me gently. "Kate?"

Glancing around, I take note of the place—the main room dark and empty, only the pendant lights on over the kitchen island, where I see her laptop sits open to Messenger. That explains how she was able to text me without her phone. Beside her laptop are those familiar bulky headphones and a bag of dill pickle chips, their crumbs strewn across the counter.

As I set Kate's phone on the island, my ears snag on the sound coming from her headphones. The volume must be incredibly loud because even as they sit a foot away, I can tell it's a person's voice, clipped and urgent. I glance up at her laptop and briefly see what's on the screen. I can tell it's news, and it's not good—a rough hand-held video of emergency vehicles, a crowd in chaos, people's clothes and skin stained ominously red.

I look away from it quickly not just to respect Kate's privacy but also because I hate the sight of blood.

The bathroom door opens, and I turn, facing the hallway. Kate steps out, then, when she notices me, comes to a halt.

She stands, hair in its messy knot, red-rimmed eyes locked on me, chest heaving unevenly like she's trying very hard not to cry.

My heart twists as a terrifying need rattles my bones like they're prison bars—begging me to wrap her in my arms, to take from her body to mine whatever is hurting her.

A tear spills down her cheek, a winding rivulet that slips past those freckles to her trembling lip. She wipes it away and tries to exhale slowly, but it comes out a broken half breath, half sob.

My feet move, closing the distance between us. My bag drops from my shoulder. My coat slides off my arms, past my hands, freeing them to grab her by those sharp elbows and drag her against me. Her head lands with a *thud* over my heart, and her arms wrap around me like a vise. Another deep, stilted sob wrenches out of her.

I clutch her tight, one hand cradling her head, the other low on her back, holding her hard against me. "Kate," I murmur. "Shhh. It's all right."

"No, it's not." She shakes her head. "So many people . . . I'm just so"—she exhales a shaky sob—"so tired. So many good people, trying to live good lives, and it's so fucking easy for bad people to ruin *all* of it. I hate it. I hate it so much," she growls, another sob wrenching out of her.

"Shhh." I rock her in my arms, swaying her, knowing there's nothing I can say, knowing she's right—how irrevocably people's carelessness and selfishness and hatred can destroy lives, the terroristic violence humans have normalized and accepted, how defeating it is, how hard it is to have anything hopeful to say.

"Katydid," I whisper, my mouth against her temple as I comb her hair back from her tearstained cheeks. "Take a nice slow breath."

"D-don't tell me what to do," she says unsteadily. But then she sucks in a slow, shaky breath.

"Good. Now another."

She takes in another breath, this one a little slower, a little more even.

I hold Kate as she takes more breaths, as her head gets heavier on my chest, calm settling into her body.

It could be minutes or hours that we stand there. I have no concept of time. Frankly it doesn't matter. What matters is this: holding her, comforting her, knowing, even in some small way, that being here, wrapping myself around her, helps.

"Thank you," she whispers, her head still resting over my heart.

I nod, clenching my jaw tight so the truth won't spill out: that I hate that she's hurting, but I'm so glad she's letting me comfort her; that I could hold her like this forever, wrap myself around her, shield her from everything that would hurt her, if she'd let me.

I don't confess that. Not when I've spent so long battling those feelings that admitting them would be to surrender to them. Not when she's upset like this, when such a proclamation would ring hollow coming from someone who's spent so long trying to make her think I feel the very opposite of that.

Kate lets out a long, heavy sigh that tells me the tears are done for now, that she's calmer.

I should leave now. I brought her phone, gave her comfort when she was upset. I should get the hell out of here before I lose the last grip on my dignity, before it's impossible to hide what I've hidden for so long:

How much I want her.

How *long* I've wanted her.

How much I've hated that want, gnawing at me like a sickness.

It's always been Kate. And in my fury that my feelings for her were entirely beyond my control, I've pushed her away and hurt her. In repressing my worry for her, my fierce desire for her, the only woman I want and the woman whose wild lifestyle puts my heart most at risk of losing a loved one *again*, my feelings have pressurized into a festering knot of misery.

I'm so tired of being miserable.

I'm so tired of resisting what I feel.

Which is why I should go. Because I'm about to not just give up the act but give in to it, and I've done more than enough to reveal myself today—when she touched me at the office, and I clung to her like a dog panting at the pleasure of being petted.

But God, I want her. I want her so deeply, so badly, it's an ache in my marrow. I don't know if I can fight that ache anymore when she's here, in my arms, and finally, she *wants* to be.

My arms tight around her, I tell her quietly, carefully, "I can go, if you want to be alone." She tenses in my arms, and I hold her close, praying she feels how badly I want to be here with her, how badly I hope she wants me here, too. "Or . . . I could stay for a while."

It's a lifetime in a moment as I wait for her answer.

Then her arms tighten around me, and she whispers, "Stay. Please."

TWENTY-ONE

Kate

My eyes scrunch shut as those words hang in the air. *Stay. Please.*

I feel so exposed. So scared. All day long, I've been warring with myself. My brain screams this is the man who's made me miserable for so long, I can barely remember when he didn't. My body firmly disagrees, each calm beat of my heart saying that what I'm seeing of Christopher isn't a ruse but a revelation, that he's always cared, always been safe, but for some bewildering reason, didn't want me to see him that way.

Maybe it's only been a few seconds since I asked, but it feels like it's been hours, when Christopher dips his head, his cheek resting against my hair. Gently, his hand drifts up my back in slow, soothing strokes. "Of course I'll stay."

Relief rushes over me like water across parched earth, until I'm overflowing with it. There's a lump in my throat again. My eyes prick with fresh tears.

As he holds me, I soak up the comfort of resting in his arms, the trace of spicy woodsmoke mingled with something warm and familiar, the simple scent of his skin. It feels strange and wonderful and right. It feels like home.

Christopher's stomach growls, and the sound reverberates up to my ear, pressed against his torso. "Someone's hungry. Have you had dinner?" I ask.

"I haven't. Have you?" he asks quietly.

I burrow deeper against his chest, not wanting this to end, not knowing what comes next. "Sort of."

He circles his hand over my back again. "In case you're wondering," he adds, "dill pickle chips do not qualify as dinner. Not even when combined with a doughnut."

I smile in spite of myself. "Tragically, we don't have any doughnuts right now. If dill pickle chips don't count, no, I haven't had dinner. And we're low on groceries. As in, we have none. But I order a mean take-out meal."

A soft laugh gusts out of him. His fingers glide through my hair at the nape of my neck, massaging. The pleasure of my sensory needs being met finally settles the waves of disbelief that have been cresting inside me, how not *us* this is—his patience and calm, my quiet stillness, my arms squeezing him tight, his hands rubbing steady circles over my back, his fingers combing softly through my hair.

"I could make some pasta," he says, "if you're hungry for that."

"Pasta sounds good. I don't know if we have any, though. I was supposed to go to the store and grab groceries, but when I came home, I got sidetracked with cuddling Cornelius the hedgehog, then he shit on me, and I had to change my clothes, which is when I realized I had a lot of dirty laundry, but I hadn't put away my clean laundry, either, which meant I couldn't tell what was clean from what was dirty, and then I got really overwhelmed by the mess and debated throwing out all my clothes and joining a nudist colony, except I'm not at all into the concept of communal nakedness, so that was out." I suck in a breath, then exhale unsteadily. "And then I sat down with a bag of chips to eat my feelings and fell down the horrible news rabbit hole. So, yeah. Not sure about the pasta."

Christopher makes a small, dismissive noise in the back of his throat. "What use would I have for store-bought pasta? I said, 'make pasta' and I meant 'make pasta.'"

I pull away, peering up at him. A dense five-o'clock shadow darkens his jaw and makes him look a little different, which feels fitting. I know it's Christopher I'm looking at, Christopher who's holding me. But this isn't the man I've known for so long, not exactly.

I have the stomach-dropping feeling of the first time I ziplined, knowing rationally I could rely on the harness, the line, a straightforward path, and a clear final destination, but so keenly aware of how foreign the idea was, flying through the forest, wild and unpredictable, not knowing what would come my way.

It took courage to step off that ledge, and it takes courage now. Finding it, I meet Christopher's warm amber eyes, counting their tiny goldleaf flecks. He looks at me like maybe I've given him that first-zip-line feeling, too.

"You'll make pasta from scratch, for me?" I ask.

His mouth tips up at the corner, something I've never seen before, small and soft, none of that grinning Casanova charm, nothing like his familiar antagonistic smirk. Just Christopher fussing with my hair, tucking a lock behind my ear that feels like a strand pulled, slowly unraveling me.

"Well," he says, "you bet your ass I'm making pasta for me, too. But yes."

I poke his hip, where he's freakishly ticklish. He catches my hand and laces our fingers together. His thumb gently circles my palm.

It's the tiniest thing, his thumb circling my palm, his fingers tangled with mine, but it feels like it contains a whole world inside it. He and I stand, silent, touching. The intensity of his eyes holding mine, the steady sweep of his thumb against my skin, it's like he's seeing everything I'm too exhausted to fight or hide anymore.

I spend so much time keeping myself busy, distracting myself from slowing down long enough to feel everything I carry inside me, until I collapse into a rare episode of chest-aching cries and lying in the fetal position. I know that my empathy, the depth with which I experience emotions, makes me impassioned, makes me care and fight and speak out, that my capacity to feel is a strength, but it doesn't always *feel* like a strength.

My capacity to feel is . . . overwhelming. But here, in his arms, I wonder if maybe it's so overwhelming because I never tried to unburden myself, to give it to someone else for a while.

The way I am, even in just this small way right now, with Christopher.

For so long I have prided myself on not needing others, loving people from a safe distance, through brief visits and playful care packages and entertaining emails. But beneath that pride, that fierce determination to be independent, is the desperate need for someone to grab me by the elbow and haul me into their arms and let me fall apart until I can put myself back together.

Just like Christopher has.

"Katydid," he says softly, pulling me from my thoughts, back to his arms, to his palm steadily circling my back. "Let me make you pasta. All I need is flour and eggs. And those Kitchen-Aid pasta-maker attachments I gifted Jules a couple Christmases back."

"I don't know if we even have that," I tell him. "The flour or eggs, I mean."

Slowly, he steps back, but his hand stays with mine, lacing our fingers together. "Let's find out. We'll run to the store if not."

I let him tug me toward the kitchen and try not to feel deprived when he untangles our hands, using his to shut my laptop, power off my headphones, then slide them down the island, out of sight.

He wraps up the bag of chips, sweeps away the crumbs, and wipes the island clean.

"Sit," he says, tipping his head toward the chairs on the other side of the now-tidied island.

I don't want an island between us. I want to be close to this new Christopher, so I can examine him and indulge my needy fascination. Instead, I hop up on the counter beside him, legs swinging. "Seated."

He gives me a wry smile, then turns toward the kitchen cabinets, more at home and familiar with their contents than I am, even after weeks living here. I watch him find flour, then open the fridge and locate a carton of eggs.

And then I watch him do something I've never watched someone do so closely. His fingers deftly unbutton his cuffs and make quick work of rolling the fabric of his shirtsleeves up his arms, until it's nestled right above his elbows, like they were when we tangoed. He turns on the water over the sink and starts a soapy lather in his palms.

I stare at his hands and forearms, these practical parts of his body that I've seen countless times. They don't make *me* feel very practical right now.

They make me feel warm and unsteady as I look at them—long fingers and the rough joints of his knuckles, the muscles in his arms visible beneath a dusting of dark hair.

My breath feels tight. I think about touching those hands, sliding my fingertips across his skin, feeling fine, soft hair and hard, thick muscle. I think about taking those hands and pulling them toward my body so they can ease the ache between my thighs, which I squeeze together.

"Want to make it with me?" Christopher asks, eyes on his task as he sets out a wide nonstick mat and measures out flour onto it.

I set a hand against my hot cheek, trying to cool myself down. "I'm not sure."

"I think you should."

"Why?" I watch as he settles the flour into a circle, then hollows out a crater in the center of it.

"It's cathartic." He cracks an egg seamlessly, dropping it into the flour crater. "C'mon. Roll up those sleeves and wash your hands, Katydid. You'll see."

When I don't answer him right away, he doesn't seem to mind, doesn't pressure or heckle me. He just cracks a few more eggs, then sinks his hands into the eggy lake in its flour valley and crushes half the yolks on the first kneading squeeze.

I never got the "food porn" concept, but if this is it, I do now.

Some kind of pained noise must leak out of me, because Christopher peers up, a furrow etched in his brow. "What is it?"

"I . . ." Riveted by the pasta-making porn, I search for words I don't have.

He glances down, following my line of sight, then swears quietly under his breath. "My watch." He lifts an egg-and-flour-covered hand in my direction. "Would you take it off?"

I stare down at his messy hand, his wrist where his pulse pounds steadily. Gingerly, I take his wrist and draw it closer, so I have a better angle to undo the buckle. Christopher observes me as I take off his watch, unusually quiet. I'm careful as I turn it over, examining the face, knowing, as I search the catalog of my sharp visual memory, that it's familiar. "It was your dad's."

He stares down at it resting in my palm. "Yes."

"I think that would make him happy. I think . . . he would be very proud of you."

Christopher's head snaps up. His eyes meet mine, and the impact hits me like a tuning fork, reverberating through my body in a bone-tingling hum. "Proud of what?" he finally says dryly. "My soulless capitalist success?"

I hear it in his tone, half humor, half plea—*Be gentle with me. Don't toy with me, not when it comes to this.*

Regret carves its way through me, sore and sharp. For the first time, I understand something I didn't before—I'm not the only one who's been hurt in our messy past. Along the way, I hurt him, too.

Holding his eyes, I tell him, "Perhaps calling you a 'soulless capitalist' was a slight exaggeration. Perhaps . . . I've realized I assumed the worst of you and your company. And perhaps recent events, particularly my time at your office today were . . . illuminating."

A small, satisfied grin tips his mouth, makes his eyes glow like dawn breaking through a sea of autumn leaves. "Illuminating?"

I tear my gaze away and force it back down on the watch, examining its face. "When you take people's picture, they do best when they're relaxed. I've learned to make conversation with people to put them at ease, and when I talked to your team today, when they shared their relationship to their work and their values, what the firm does to support them and what it believes in . . ." I shrug. "What they said, what you told me yourself, made me see things differently. I have a lot of respect for it. I think your dad and your mom would, too. They'd both be immensely proud."

Christopher stares at me so intensely, I feel it like sunlight heating my face on a bitter-cold day. I can't keep myself from peering up again, meeting his eyes, any more than I can stop my heart from thudding against my ribs.

"Thank you, Kate," he says quietly. "I'm not always sure about that."

"Why not?"

He shrugs, eyes down on the flour as he traces his finger through it. "I've done a lot of things differently from my parents, different from how I imagine they'd have liked me to. I overhauled and restructured my family's company. I haven't been to mass in a decade. I'm thirty-three, unmarried, no kids."

Carefully, I set down his dad's watch, far from the flour and eggs. "Just because you've made choices different from them doesn't mean they wouldn't admire you and be proud of you. If I've learned anything by living in places whose culture and language aren't mine, it's that differences don't have to hold people at a distance if we're willing to try to understand each other. Our similarities are much vaster than what sets us apart—we just have to want to see them."

A thoughtful frown tugs at his mouth as he sinks his hands into the eggs and flour again, then says, "I can't imagine doing that."

"Imagine doing what?"

He shrugs, working the eggs into the flour. "Going all those places you've been to. Not knowing the language well or the social expectations, how to get where you want or who you can ask. It sounds like chaos."

I hop off the counter, stepping beside him at the sink to wash my hands. Maybe I'll try this pasta-making thing after all.

"It *is* chaos," I tell him, working a soapy lather through my fingers. "But my brain loves that chaos. When there's too much 'same' in my life, it's like I'm suffocating, like novelty is air and I'm gasping for it. When I end up somewhere I've never been before, hearing unfamiliar words and sounds, seeing new sights; when roads are other directions, and food's texture is unexpected, and music I've never heard before plays so loud it rattles my chest, I feel like I can breathe again, like my skin fits right over my body, like that perfect feeling when you float on water, and you're weightless, and you hear your breath in your ears, your heart pumping life through your body, and the world feels like nothing and everything and just as it should be, all at once."

Christopher stops kneading. A furious flush heats my cheeks. I just rambled. Again.

Rambling is a lifelong habit, and one people haven't often been kind about, the refrain *Kate talks too much* following me wherever I went as I grew up. I learned to shut up around people who resented my rambling not because they were right but because I didn't want to waste myself on people who couldn't appreciate me as I was.

Conversely, with my people—my family, the rare fast friendships I've built—I've always felt safe to ramble, trusting those who love me to love my brain and how much it makes my thoughts spill into one another and out of my mouth, sometimes strange, sometimes funny, always honest and real and *me*.

But Christopher is in some unnerving no-man's-land. He isn't a stranger. He isn't family, no matter how much *my* family says otherwise. He isn't a friend, either.

And even though, as I scroll quickly through the lengthy catalog of his offenses over my lifetime and come up short of any memories of Christopher shaming me for how much I talk sometimes, I'm nervous, not knowing how he'll respond.

I shut off the water and hide the heat staining my cheeks by turning my back to him, drying my hands.

"Kate."

Slowly, I turn, forcing myself to face him. He steps back, leaving space between him and the counter, and tips his head. "C'mon."

I step in front of him against the counter and feel him settle right behind me.

His voice is quiet and warm, so deliciously close. "I want you to know that I think what you do, how you live, is beautiful and brave. I know I haven't shown it. But I respect it. Deeply."

I blink, stunned. "You do?"

Silence hangs in the air before he says, carefully, "I do. But it was hard to focus on that admiration when I was scared, Kate. And I was scared a lot. I worried about you, and I didn't want to."

My pulse pounds in my ears. *What's he saying? . . . What does it mean?*

"I didn't disapprove of what you did because I thought it was inadequate or wrong," he goes on. "I thought it was incredible. But I hated that to do your work, you took risks and put yourself in danger. So I focused on what I hated because it made it easier for me to put distance between us, to tell myself I didn't care what happened to you. But I did care. I buried it while you were gone, then made us both miserable when you were home and I couldn't escape it."

I'm speechless as I glance back over my shoulder and find his eyes. God, his eyes. They're a fire's flames, rich whiskey warming me from the tips of my toes to the crown of my head.

"You cared?" I ask hoarsely.

Staring down at me, he searches my eyes. "Yes, Kate. I cared. I *care*. I've been shit at showing it, but I have always cared about you." He swallows roughly. "And admired you."

My heart skips. "Well . . . if it makes you feel any better, I've cared, too." Oh God, now my heart feels like an elevator plummeting to its doom. Admitting this shit is hard. "And . . . admired you. For a capitalist, at least."

Christopher's smile turns so bright, its wattage could power a city block. I turn back toward the counter, smiling, too.

"For a capitalist, huh?" The pleasure in his voice, an edge of almost laughter, makes goose bumps dance across my skin.

I shrug, biting back my smile as it grows.

"Is that a smile I just earned?" Christopher dips his head, nuzzling my shoulder with his chin. It makes a very juvenile noise squeak out of me.

"Christopher." I nudge him halfheartedly in the stomach with my elbow.

"Katerina," he says, so close his mouth nearly brushes my neck. A shiver dances down my spine.

"Stop tickling me," I tell him, forcing my posture to straighten, my voice to steady.

"Fine." He sighs, tapping the counter. "Now, come on. Everything that's been upsetting you today, work it out on the pasta dough."

I hesitate for a moment, then step closer. Slowly, I push up my sleeves higher, before sinking my hands into the eggs. I squeeze as hard as I can, squealing in pleasure at the slimy, runny whites, the satisfying, tactile resistance of the remaining yolks slipping out of my grip.

"Feel good?" he asks.

"Uh, it's just a sensory *delight*." I lift my hands and show him the way I'm savoring the sticky texture of the flour and egg between my fingers. "This is incredible."

He steps closer behind me and sinks his hands into the flour and eggs again, too.

It feels so good, his body behind mine, his hands and my hands, messy together.

Our hands touch, our bodies brush. I feel his breath, warm and soft on my neck, his eyes on me, watching me as I lose myself in our task, and soon we have a ball of dough. Christopher shows me how to knead it, his hands on mine, folding the dough over itself, pressing it into the counter.

"Still doing okay?" he asks.

"Yes," I whisper, knowing my voice is uneven but helpless to do a damn thing about it. "Very okay."

Maybe he hears how affected I am. Maybe he's affected, too. Because he falters with the dough, fumbling it for a moment before smoothly folding it over. Somehow, he suddenly feels closer, but I know he hasn't moved. I think maybe I have. I think maybe I've leaned back into him like I'd sink into a hot, long-awaited bath.

For just a moment, I shut my eyes, luxuriating in the nearness of his body and its heat, the thrill as he nuzzles my hair and breathes in, slow and deep. When he breathes out, his mouth brushes the shell of my ear. "I've never done this before," he says, so quietly I barely hear him.

"Made pasta?"

He laughs softly, like a sigh. "You're such a pain in my ass," he says. "I mean I've never done this . . . with someone else."

I bite my lip, inordinately pleased. I sort of figured Christopher's done just about everything there is to be done with someone else. "And?"

"And I like it." I feel his swallow down his throat, his hands covering mine as we shape the dough together.

"I like it, too," I tell him quietly.

"We can do it again," he says. "Whenever you want."

I stare down at our little masterpiece made up of a few humble ingredients, feeling like this night is a masterpiece itself, born out of a few humble ingredients of our own. Kindness, honesty, the work of seeing what we share, not what sets us apart.

A smile, bright and deep from the heart of me, lights up my face. "I'd like that."

Christopher's quiet, but I feel it like the wind on a sun-bright autumn day, soft and warm and real . . .

He smiles, too.

———————

One giant plate of cacio e pepe and one very large glass of red wine later, I stand at the door, watching Christopher shrug on his coat and set his work bag over his shoulder.

Nervous energy flutters in my stomach. I pin my cheeks hard between my teeth so I won't say again the same thing that started this all:

Stay. Please.

Christopher sets a hand on the dead bolt, unlocking it, then the door handle's lock, too. I feel time slipping like sand between my fingers, the moment almost lost to me.

My hand shoots out and wraps around his wrist, stopping him. "Thank you," I blurt, feeling that damn flush crawl up my throat to my cheeks.

Christopher lets go of the door, turning his hand until our palms slide together. "Thank you for letting me teach you something with only one threat to my delicate bits."

I bite back a smile. "You got very condescending about the pasta roller."

"You were very close to breaking it."

I roll my eyes. "I was not."

A smile tips his mouth. "Next time, I'll show you how to make marinara. You can take out your frustrations with the world on tomatoes."

Next time.

That tiny sentence hangs in the air. Christopher senses it, and so do I.

I don't refute that "next time." Because the truth is I want "next time." I want to tell Christopher more about where I've been and what I've seen. I want him to tell me more stories about his co-workers and share more about the nerdy, philosophical beauty of his ethical investment approach. I want to sit beside him at the kitchen island and bump elbows, demolish a big bowl of pasta, and get a little tipsy on wine.

I want *more*. More touches like the way he touched me when he walked me home that night, the way he held me in the office today.

More hugs like every hug tonight. More kisses like the one he pressed to my lips outside my apartment that made my knees weak and lit a fire inside me aching for whatever mysterious alchemy that keeps it burning bright.

But I don't know how to ask for that. If I should.

If he wants what I do.

As if he senses my internal battle, Christopher tugs me close, until I land with a comforting *thump* against his chest.

It feels as wonderful as his hug when he first walked in.

And infinitely better.

His hand slips from mine and drifts around my waist, tucking me close. His other hand curls around my jaw, smoothing back my hair.

And then he presses a kiss to my forehead, long and tender.

My arms wrap tighter around Christopher and travel up his back. Air rushes out of him, and his head dips, his mouth grazing my temple, my cheekbone, the corner of my mouth, so close to where I want him.

I want him to kiss me so badly, a tiny desperate sound of need leaves my throat.

One hand tightens at my waist, pulling me harder against him. The other sinks into my hair, kneading it. I press my lips to his jaw and breathe him in.

"Kate." His voice is tinged with warning.

"Hmm?"

He swallows roughly. I kiss his Adam's apple, too. "I'm trying to be a gentleman."

I groan in frustration. "Stop."

"Please," he says quietly, his thumb drifting across my lip. "Let me. For once. You've had a big glass of wine and a long day."

"And?"

"And I'm not taking advantage of that."

I scowl as he starts to pull away. "I *am* capable of making my own decisions, even when navigating a few emotions and eight ounces of wine."

"I know that. And next time, if you want the same thing from me, I promise you"—he bends and presses a swift, deep kiss to some dangerously sensitive place on my neck, his voice hot and dark against the shell of my ear—"I will not be able to say yes fast enough."

My mouth parts as he whips open the door and disappears past it, fast, purposeful strides taking him away from me.

And yet, hours later, lying in bed miles from where I picture him lying in his bed, too, I feel so close to him.

Closer than I ever have.

TWENTY-TWO

Christopher

The lights in Nanette's flicker to life, and I think I scare the shit out of the employee who spots me right outside the window, dripping in sweat, breathing heavily, my hair messily half-tied back to keep it out of my face.

I couldn't sleep. So I read in bed, then I used my makeshift garage gym and lifted weights until my muscles couldn't take any more. The moment the sun started to glow on the horizon, I got on a train into the city and ran Kate's neighborhood until it was time for Nanette's to open. I'm sleep-deprived, my body shaking from too many reps, too many miles, but my mind is crystal clear, one single thing its focus—

Kate.

My head says that this is madness. My heart says that this was inevitable, that the moment I let myself get close enough, the moment Kate touched me like she did yesterday, the moment she gave me just a sliver of her fiercely guarded heart, which I've spent so long trying not to want, trying not to get too close to, there'd be no stopping myself.

I'm not thinking about everything that used to hold me back. I'm not thinking about everything I'm still afraid of. I'm only thinking about *her*.

Which is why I'm standing outside Nanette's at the ass crack of dawn in the morning, then opening the door the moment it's un-locked, the first customer to walk in. Promptly, I order a box filled with the doughnuts I know she loves, every autumn recipe rebel-ling against the Christmas flavors that shouldered their way in the day after Thanksgiving. No chocolate and peppermint or ginger-bread and eggnog for Kate. She loves pumpkin pie and spiced ap-ples, cinnamon and maple syrup, everything that reminds her of the grandeur of turning leaves, the cozy joy of starlit bonfires and sipping mugs of cider, the quiet beauty of waking up to a misty autumn morning.

And so, even though we're well on our way toward Christmas, I buy a box of autumn doughnuts and a pumpkin pie for good measure, then walk out and make my way toward her apartment, an unseasonably mild December wind whipping my workout clothes against my body, sunrise's golden rays spilling across the pearly blue sky.

With quiet feet, I take the stairs up to the Wilmot sisters' apartment and let myself in. The main room and kitchen are tidy and dark, how we left them after making pasta, eating, then clean-ing up.

Bea's door is still open, which is no surprise, since Kate said last night that her sister planned to stay at Jamie's.

And Kate's door is still shut.

I stare at it with a kind of longing that feels like a hook in my heart, reeling me toward it.

Instead of obeying that tug, I step into the kitchen, set the doughnuts and pie on the counter, then prep the coffee I know Kate wanted but forgot to set up. I grind beans, muffling the grinder's noise by running it inside my hoodie, then I pour in fil-tered water. I set the coffee maker to brew at eight, which seems safe, since she said she works at the Edgy Envelope today, and I know they open at nine.

Then I locate one of Bea's colorful pens on the coffee table and write in electric blue letters on the doughnut box—

These are for breakfast. Have some milk with them, while you're at it.

—C

I set down the pen, then walk to the door, forcing myself past it, to pull it shut and lock it, triple-checking it's secure.

Down the stairs, out the door, I stop outside her building, greeted by dawn's progress. Like a fire finally caught, its flames fan across the sky, burning away the shadows.

I stare at the sunrise and feel its transformation inside me, too—a spark of hope, once only the faintest flame surrounded by darkness, now glowing, growing.

Brightening to an unrelenting blaze.

———

I'm buried in paperwork at the office hours later when my phone dings with a new-message alert. There is no dignity in how quickly I drop what I'm doing and scramble for my phone.

> **KATE:** Donuts & pumpkin pie are for whatever meal I say they are, Petruchio.

I smile, unlocking the screen so I can answer her.

> **CHRISTOPHER:** You had leftover pasta for breakfast instead, didn't you?

> **KATE:** Hell yes, I did. So damn good, even cold.

CHRISTOPHER: Cold? Christ, Kate. Why?

KATE: I was running late. I dumped some in a container & ate it on my walk.

CHRISTOPHER: Every Italian ever is rolling in their grave, mourning that you ate and walked.

KATE: I am aware it's a cultural faux pas, but I'm sorry, there are Italians with ADHD, & I guarantee you they walk & eat. They probably just hide their food in their pockets like chipmunks, shoving it in their mouth when no one's watching.

I snort.

CHRISTOPHER: I didn't know chipmunks had pockets.

KATE: Shut up. You know what I mean. ANYWAY. Thank you for the treats from Nanette's. I packed some for lunch, so even though I had pasta for breakfast, your generosity did not go to waste.

CHRISTOPHER: Tell me you at least had some milk, too.

KATE: Listen, Dad, if I did have milk w/ my donuts & pie, it would be because I enjoy milk w/ donuts & pie, not because you told me to. However, if I didn't have milk, it might be because I can't stand cow milk & I'm trying not to drink almond milk since an almond requires an atrocious amount of water to grow, so if I drink a cup of almond milk, I'm sucking up a bunch of water from some poor California grandma's yard & now I'll feel personally responsible if it succumbs to wildfires.

KATE: Also, I might have forgotten my lunchbox full of donuts and pie at the apartment. But never fear, I'm eating them now. I left work at 2 & now I'm home alone, sprawled on the couch in my underwear, happily covered in Nanette's pastry crumbs.

I groan as I picture that. Kate's long legs stretched out on the sofa, swinging and bouncing like they always do. Probably a mismatched pair of fuzzy socks on her feet, cheeky panties that hug her sweet little ass. An oversized sweatshirt draping down her body yet unable to hide the fact that she's not wearing a bra, not when her nipples do what they did last night and poke right into the fabric, begging for my mouth to suck and tease them, until she's panting, squirming—

My phone dings, wrenching me out of my lusty thoughts. I clear my throat and read her text.

KATE: Well, I just verbal vomited. Kindly delete this text thread & pretend it never happened.

CHRISTOPHER: Even if I did, text messages might last only a minute, Katydid, but screenshots last forever.

KATE: Listen, Topher Gopher. I can't find my meds right now, so I'm a little more labially liberated today. Don't tease me about it. It's ableist.

A laugh jumps out of me so loud, I hear Curtis startle outside my office and drop something.

CHRISTOPHER: "Labially liberated"?? Where do you come up with this shit?

KATE: Come up with what? Labial means lips. Ask the New York Times Crossword. "Labially liberated" is my fancy way of saying I'm loose lipped.

CHRISTOPHER: My mind goes somewhere else when you talk about liberated labia, that's all.

KATE: CHRISTOPHER PETRUCHIO YOU PHILANDERING PHILANDERER THIS CONVERSATION IS TERMINATING IMMEDIATELY.

Choking down a laugh, then taking a deep, steadying breath, I type my response.

CHRISTOPHER: I'm sorry. That was inappropriate of me.

KATE: You're lucky I liked the donuts & pumpkin pie & the pasta you made. Consider yourself forgiven.

CHRISTOPHER: Thank you. I promise next time I see you, I'll be on my best behavior.

KATE: I can't promise the same, because I'm me & life's too short to be well-behaved. If I can find my meds, I'll at least be better at avoiding alliterative slips of the innuendo variety.

My phone dings with a new message preview, and I tap on it to read it fully.

JAMIE: We're on for this Saturday, 4 pm, at Peace, Love, and Paintball with the usual motley crew. Bea

invited Bianca and Nick too, but Bianca opted not
to come because she said she doesn't trust Kate
with projectiles around Nick yet, which I'm inclined
to agree is wise.

I switch back to my message thread with Kate.

> **CHRISTOPHER:** Looks like our well-behaved reunion
> will be sooner rather than later, Katydid.

> **KATE:** Just got Bea's text. Paintball! Better watch
> your back, Petruchio.

> **CHRISTOPHER:** No need. We'll be on the same team.
> Jamie made sure of it.

> **KATE:** Both of us on the same team sounds like a
> recipe for disaster.

> **CHRISTOPHER:** We made a pretty good team last
> night, making pasta, and that recipe was anything
> but a disaster.

> **KATE:** Yeah, but paintball isn't going to be nearly as
> delicious.

> **CHRISTOPHER:** I disagree, at least, if you plan on
> being extra labially liberated.

> **KATE:** I'M DELETING YOUR NUMBER. I BID
> YOU GOOD DAY SIR.

When Curtis comes in with next meeting's notes, I'm still wiping away tears from laughing.

· TWENTY-THREE ·

Kate

I don't have butterflies in my stomach. I don't glance up every time someone enters the room, hoping it's him.

Because I am *not* crushing on Christopher Petruchio.

I'm just possibly slightly affected by his kindness and care and friendly text messages the past few days. And my dreams the past few nights, which have possibly involved obscene moments in the kitchen that started off how we did and ended very differently. Me pressed back on a counter, hands I know so well, strong and beautiful, skating up my thighs, easing the ache between them. Hard, slow kisses turning my limbs loose, liquid gold.

"Everyone suited up?" Hank, the Peace, Love, and Paintball employee in charge of orientating our group, asks from the middle of the gear room as everyone trickles in from changing.

I crouch to retie my bootlaces, which don't require retying, to hide the fact that my face has turned bright red as my thoughts wandered down Lusty Lane, and to avoid Bea's eyes because my sister's looking at me curiously, like maybe she has a guess as to what's running through my head.

"This is an aggressively unflattering green on me." Toni plucks at the hunter-green fabric of his coveralls.

"It is not," Bea tells him. "You look cute as a cabbage."

"Cabbage?" Toni sighs bleakly.

"That's how you tell someone they're cute in French," Jamie explains. "Call them cabbage—chou."

Toni bats his lashes. "Jamie. Stop it."

Hamza laughs and hooks an arm around Toni's neck, pulling him in for a kiss to his temple. "I already told you that you look cute."

"You're obligated to say that." Toni pouts. "Plus, cute is nice, but I want to look *sexy*."

"I got news for you," I tell Toni, peering down at my own green coveralls as I stand. "None of us looks sexy in these getups."

Which is of course when Christopher strides out of the changing room, looking sexy as hell in his green coverall paintball suit. I shouldn't be surprised—the color complements the golden undertone in his skin, his amber eyes and dark locks. It's obscene what happens to my body as I watch him rake back his hair and set a pair of goggles on his head.

Toni throws an accusatory hand Christopher's way and says to me, "You're really going to try to tell me you still stand by that statement?"

"Ready when you are," Christopher says to Hank as he finishes doing the last few top buttons of his coveralls.

He stands beside me but doesn't look at me. Doesn't even acknowledge me.

It feels like a slap.

A sinking dread settles in my stomach. Maybe I got it all wrong. Maybe two nights ago didn't mean to him what it meant to me. He's trying to fix things, he said. Maybe that's all the other night was, Christopher trying to "fix things," doing it how he knows best—sweet-talking and flirting, hugging and making homemade pasta, promising a satisfying time in bed when I was clearheaded enough to know I really wanted it. That whole routine has to be as natural for him as breathing.

If that's the case, if I've misread this so badly, I feel like a fool.

"Okay, folks!" Hank claps his hands as Margo and Sula join us in their green suits, goggles on their heads. "Welcome again to Peace, Love, and Paintball, the ultimate progressive paintball experience. The rules go like this: you and another team will—"

"Wait." Jamie lifts a hand. "Sorry to interrupt. You said *another* team? We were hoping for a friendly time out there for our group only. When we called and inquired about that, we were reassured it was possible."

"It is," Hank says, sounding apologetic. "But only if no one else shows up. This group came in while you were all getting changed. We're up against a lot of competition with the more traditional, rifle-style model of paintball, so we're not really in a position to turn down business."

Jamie sighs and peers over at Bea.

"That's understandable," Bea says encouragingly. "I'm sure it'll be fine."

"If by fine, you mean 'about to get your asses reamed,'" an obnoxiously loud voice calls from behind us, "then it sure will be."

We turn around to see ten dudes in head-to-toe black, clutching paintball guns. I roll my eyes.

"Uh." Hank clears his throat. "Folks, this is a gun-free establishment. You'll need to leave those in your vehicles."

"C'mon, man," the guy who yelled and is the obvious ringleader says, "paintball without guns is for pussies."

His whole posse chuckles.

Everyone else is behind me, so Christopher is the only one I see opening his mouth to say something, but I speak before he can. "How about you boys take your sexist bullshit along with your inferiority complexes and give them a flex somewhere else?"

Bea, standing on my other side, slips her hand inside mine and squeezes. I don't squeeze back. I'd crush her fingers if I did, I'm so angry.

"I'm sorry, what was that, baby doll?" the guy says. He's bigger than the rest of them, red-cheeked, eyes narrowed, chest puffed up as he stares me down.

I snort. He's such a misogynist cliché.

"Something funny?" he sneers.

"Your pathetically uninspired insults would be funny for how predictable they are, except for the fact that they reveal your disgusting bigotry," I tell him.

He smiles, but it doesn't reach his eyes. "Aw, we got ourselves a little snowflake who likes big words, boys." They laugh again. "Did I hurt your feelings, princess?"

"The only feelings I have when it comes to you, Chad, is pity for every poor soul who's had to suffer your presence."

The asshole takes a sudden step toward me. I take a step toward him. Which is when Christopher wraps an arm around my waist and drags me back. "That's enough," he growls at the jerk, then he spins us both so I'm settled in front of him, facing Hank, with Christopher between me and Chad the Asshole behind us.

Hank takes that opening and says once again to the butthead brigade, "As I explained, you'll need to return those paintball guns to your vehicles if you want to play. Otherwise, we do ask that you leave."

I glance around Christopher long enough to see Chad or Brad or whoever the hell he is curl his lip and stare me down as he tells Hank, "Nah, we're staying." He smiles, a creepy, predatory glint in his eyes. "We'll stash these and be right back."

As soon as they wander out, I finally manage to yank myself out of Christopher's grip. "Don't manhandle me, Petruchio."

Christopher opens his mouth like he's about to answer me, but infuriating tears prick my eyes, and I can't let him or any one of those dick bags see it. Spinning away, I stand with my back to him and glare at the ground, blinking until my eyes clear and the threat of tears is gone. Hank answers Jamie's questions about the history of Peace, Love, and Paintball while we wait for the team of jerks to come back. I'm too angry to hear anything that's said.

When the bros in black are back, paintball-gun-free, Hank starts to go over the rules, droning on about minimum proximity permissible to strike someone, parts of the body that are off-limits, and other instructions so bone-dry, I'd have a hard time paying attention to his words on the best of days, let alone when I'm fuming.

A sudden nudge of an elbow makes me glance up.

Christopher's finally looking at me. I hold his eyes, clinging to my anger and hurt.

"I dragged you away," Christopher says under his breath, "because he's not worth it, Kate."

"Gee, I wonder why men keep acting like vile creatures," I hiss-whisper. "Oh wait, I don't wonder—I *know* it's because other men enable them. You should've been telling him to shut the hell up and exactly why what he said was offensive; instead, you're corralling *me*."

Christopher lowers his head, his breath warm against my ear as he says quietly, "I tried, but you got to him first. When I could get a word in edgewise, I told him it was enough. There is a giant paintball field out there where we can make him suffer for his assholery, and I promise you we will. I pulled you away from him because I'm trying to make sure you actually make it out there to put him in his place."

I blink up at Christopher, a little stunned, right as Hank says, "Any questions?"

Christopher drags down his goggles, then drags down mine, too. "C'mon, Katydid. Time to kick some ass."

I really thought that without the whole firearm aspect of paintball, this would be less stressful.

I was wrong.

Perhaps that's because Chad and his goons are acting like this is guerrilla warfare. It's half-ridiculous, half-terrifying, how intense it's become, with nothing but slingshots to accelerate our paintballs, stray obstacles scattered across the field to deflect them when they fly our way, and this fierce sense of urgency to not get pelted with surprisingly hard balls filled with paint.

So far Sula and Hamza are out, watching grimly from the sidelines, their bodies covered in splotches of yellow and pink paint.

Toni screams as a paintball whizzes by and tackles Margo to the ground, saving her from being hit.

Margo laughs, but it's an *oh shit* nervous giggle. "Toni! You okay, bud?"

"This is *terrible*!" he yells, glaring at a few of the bros in black, who duck when Christopher tugs back the band of his slingshot and rips a paintball their way. It nicks one of them on the shoulder, and he wavers for a second, like he might try to pretend it didn't happen and stay in the game.

"You got clipped, fucker!" Christopher yells. "Find a scrap of pride and walk the hell off."

Jamie sighs. "This was supposed to be *fun*."

"It's not very fun," Bea admits, crouched beside him.

"We gotta spread out," Toni says, glancing around, looking rightfully paranoid about being ambushed.

Jamie grimaces. "He's right."

"If I didn't want to beat these caveman turds so bad, I'd say let's call it quits," Bea grumbles, "but I really want to beat them."

"You?" Jamie says, grinning as he tucks a stray hair behind her ear. "Competitive?"

Bea flashes him her full, bright smile. "Just a smidge."

"Wait." Toni eases upright, glancing around. "Have any of you seen signs of the catapult?"

We all blink at him.

"The *catapult*?" Christopher asks.

Toni nods. "I overheard Hank ask one of the other employees if he'd moved the catapult from the last session—"

"And you're *just* now mentioning that!" Margo yells.

Another paintball whizzes by us. We all duck. Toni swears loudly in Polish, which is apparently when you know he's truly worked up. Still cursing, he loads his slingshot and snaps a paintball toward one of the guys, who narrowly avoids it, falling out of view. "As you can see," Toni says, breathing heavily, "I've been a little busy trying not to turn into a human Jackson Pollock painting to share that anecdote."

"Regardless of how late it's being mentioned," Jamie says diplomatically, "if we find that catapult, we have a legitimate advantage on our hands." He blows out a breath, surveying the range, a disaster zone of paint splatters marring tree bark and boulders, knee-high grass and looming haystacks.

"I suspect it'll be midsized," he says thoughtfully. "Something a single person or maybe a duo could operate. We get that catapult, lure them into the right spot for an attack, then we can take out a number of them at once. We just might beat them."

"What if they have it already?" Margo asks.

"They don't," Jamie says. "We'd know it. We'd be getting beaned in clusters. I imagine you load the bucket with as many paintballs as possible, then launch it. They're coming one or two paintballs at a time."

"All right." Christopher nods. "Given that, what do you think we should do?"

Jamie clears his throat. "Well . . . I mean, who am I to say?"

Bea peers up at him and grins. "Jamie. Now is not the time to be bashful about all those history of ancient battles and medieval weaponry books you nerded out on in middle school."

Jamie blushes. "I might have nerded out on a book or two."

"Let's hear it." Margo wipes sweat off her forehead, arms braced on her knees. "Whatever helps us beat these assholes."

As Jamie talks, I fight a shiver, trying my best to focus on his voice rather than how hard my teeth want to chatter. The plastic dome surrounding us still has its sides open, allowing the wind to tear across the field. With the sun sinking toward the horizon, the temperature's begun to drop, and sweat's settled on my skin, damp and chilly. I'm freezing my ass off.

A shiver finally wins the battle and shakes me. I manage to keep my teeth from clicking, though.

Christopher doesn't look at me, eyes on Jamie, but he moves closer, so my whole side is wedged against his. It feels like cuddling up to a radiator. I lean in even more and soak up every ounce of heat he'll give me.

After Jamie's brief tactical plan explanation comes to an end, we split off, first Jamie and Bea deeper into the small gathering of trees to look for the catapult. We've deduced from our collective surveillance of the field, that's the one area none of us has covered and is thus likely hiding it.

Toni and Margo split off next, army crawling toward the large boulder that we can see from here is now empty, ever since Jamie and Margo nailed two of the goons hiding there.

Now it's only Christopher and me, sneaking toward the high ground, where four out of the remaining six creeps are stationed.

The plan is Margo and Toni will wait for Jamie's whistle signal that they've found the catapult and are in good position for an attack, or a different whistle if they haven't found it but they're in close enough range to use slingshots. Then Margo and Toni will draw the douchebags' attention from their place of protection behind the boulder, Jamie and Bea will catch them from the front, with the woods offering them coverage, and then Christopher and I will ambush them from behind.

The nerve-wracking part is we have no idea where the other two guys are.

"Nothing like a little wildly stressful paintball combat with a bunch of wannabe GI Joes to round out your week, huh?"

I'm nervous-blabbing, and I know it. Since his brief explanation before we walked out onto the field, Christopher hasn't spoken to me, hasn't acknowledged me but for that offering of warmth while we strategized. For my pride's sake, I wish I could stop talking to him.

Unsurprisingly, he doesn't answer me, just creeps ahead, surveying the area as we sneak toward the high ground.

I don't want to blab and beg for his attention. I know I *shouldn't* be blabbing if we don't want to give ourselves away. But it needles me that I'm once again in that old familiar territory of being ignored.

Would it be so hard to just say something to me already?

From behind, I flick his ear. Christopher glares over his shoulder at me and sets a finger to his mouth. I stick out my tongue.

His gaze flicks to my mouth and darkens.

And that's when all hell breaks loose.

Jamie's first whistle, an owl hoot, sounds in the distance. I silently fist pump, because that means they found the catapult. Next, Toni and Sula start the diversion, making the bros in black glance their way. The first deluge of paintballs from the catapult rains through the air from the woods and catches them off guard, nailing three out of the four guys before they even know what hit them.

Christopher's ahead of me as I reach for a paintball, nailing the last man standing square between the shoulder blades. All four of them whip around and give us death glares.

"Aw, guys. Did we hurt your feelings?" I say, throwing their ringleader's words back in their faces. "You look so glum. It's just a game. Cheer up."

Their jaws twitch in anger. Christopher stands beside me, silent, glaring at them stonily. I let myself appreciate the view as they have some kind of unspoken stare-down.

The green coveralls are tight on Christopher, strained against his thick biceps, chest, and thighs. I haven't let myself even glance at the backdoor view—I'd rather not trip and face-plant in the middle of paintball war because I'm too distracted with ogling his ass, and I would definitely ogle it. Ever since I noticed it at game night, it takes Wonder Woman–level strength not to let my gaze wander there.

"Run along," he tells the guys finally, jerking his head toward the sidelines.

Grumbling under their breath, they stomp past us.

I'd bet my best camera that if big, glaring Christopher weren't there, they'd have some real choice words for me. In spite of my pride, my fury that I have to deal with men like this at all, I'm grateful Christopher's here so I don't have to find out.

I grin as I watch them join the other guys from their team who already stand off the field, legs wide, arms folded, looking pissed. Even though it's a small victory, it's a victory, nonetheless.

And that victory is short-lived.

I hear them in quick succession, Toni's and Margo's yelps.

Christopher and I scramble up to the high ground the douche canoes had and peer over the ledge. "Shit," Christopher mutters.

Toni and Margo are splattered in paint, walking gingerly away from their boulder toward the sideline.

By some kind of silent agreement, the two of us stay in our spot for the moment, Christopher focused on the direction we came from for our ambush, me scanning the outlook for signs of the two remaining assholes.

Our brief surveillance screeches to a halt when we hear Bea's scream. I move without thinking, pure reaction, leaping over the ledge of our hiding spot and landing with a bone-rattling *thud* before I sprint toward the woods.

I hear another set of footsteps close at my back and glance over my shoulder, relieved to see what I already knew—Christopher's right behind me.

"What the *fuck*?" I hear Bea yell.

"Beatrice." Jamie's voice is calm, infused with patience.

Right before I run into the clearing, Christopher grabs me by the waist and pulls me flat against him behind a tree. I'm about to tell him off for stopping me, when his hand slaps over my mouth. The last two guys from the team stand ahead, right where I was about to run, two feet away from Jamie and Bea, who are stationed on either side of the catapult.

I drag Christopher's hand off my mouth, but he only wrenches me tighter against him, his chest rising and falling quickly, his breath hot against my ear.

A shiver runs through me again. And this time it's got nothing to do with being cold.

I feel every inch of him that's touching me. The hard muscles of his thighs pressed against the backs of my legs, his groin wedged into my butt, the obvious thickness that's . . . oh God, I can't think about what I feel or this instinct to press back and rub myself on him. His heavy arms pin me close, his chest a broad, firm landing place that I let my head fall back on as I drag in a breath, needing oxygen, needing *something* to make my body behave itself.

My sister's voice is a good distraction, redirecting my attention as she steps into my line of sight, hands on her hips, glaring up at the bros in black. "You fucking assholes."

"Easy, sweetie," the ringleader says. "It's just a little fun."

"A little fun?" she shrieks. "Listen, dickhead, I don't pretend to be a big rule follower, but when it comes to safety, rules matter. You slingshotted a fucking paintball point-blank into his face."

"Beatrice," Jamie says again, still so patient and calm.

"What, Jamie?" she yells.

Slowly, he pulls her into his arms and presses her head to his chest. "I'm fine. My goggles took the brunt of it, and my face is fine."

"*I'm* not fine," she mutters, her voice suspiciously thick. She sniffles.

"You are," he says gently, swaying her from side to side. "You're okay. Just take a deep breath."

"I'm *not* okay with this," she grumbles. "You hid me behind you and they nailed you in the face, much closer than the rules allow." She pulls away long enough to yell at them, "The face is off-limits, you cheating, shriveled-up nut sacks!"

The big guy rolls his eyes. "Y'all are hit. You gonna walk off the field or what?"

Both Jamie and Bea ignore him as Bea settles her head on his chest again and takes a slow deep breath, displaying a hell of a lot more class than I would. After a moment, the two of them pull apart and without a word to the jerks, turn their backs on them, walking right in our direction.

"Stay quiet," Christopher whispers.

I couldn't even speak if I wanted to. I'm still tongue-tied by the sensation buzzing through my veins, pulsing everywhere we touch, my back to his front, his hand splayed low across my belly and high across my shoulder, pinning me against him.

I'd swear my swallow echoes in the woods, but either it's quieter than I think, and Jamie and Bea don't notice us, or they do and they're the best actors ever.

Right when they're passing our tree, Jamie seems to stumble, falling to his knees.

"Jamie!" Bea bends over him. "You okay?"

"Fine," he says, standing up. "Just caught my toe on a root."

That's when I see what he's just laid at our feet during his "fall"—his satchel filled with a treasure trove of paintballs.

Relief fills me like a balloon, buoying me up. I have one paintball left in my satchel, and I don't know if Christopher has any. We were going to restock after the ambush, but obviously that didn't happen.

Now restocking is the last thing we have to worry about.

My gears start to turn. We're so close to beating these tool bags who played dirty, who had us outnumbered and acted like cutthroat, petty jerks. Best yet, the ringleader is still on the field. And I'm going to take him down.

Slowly, I peer over my shoulder, craning my neck so I can whisper in Christopher's ear as quietly as possible. Christopher dips his head at the same time, as if he had the same thought.

We freeze.

It's that night outside my apartment all over again, his mouth so close to mine, right before we kissed like I've never kissed.

Christopher's hand slides up my neck, his thumb gliding over my jaw. His eyes dart to my mouth as he lets out a long, shaky exhale that presses his chest to my back.

Wrapping my hand around his wrist, I feel his pulse pound, a thrill coursing through me as I touch evidence of what I've hoped: he wants me just as much as I want him.

But now's not the time for that, for weak knees and hazy longing and aching to kiss. No distractions, nothing that jeopardizes kicking these jerks' butts.

Forcing myself to exhale slowly, steadily, I meet his eyes and whisper, "I'll run across the clearing. Draw their attention. I call taking down Mr. Misogynist. I'll aim for him first. You take out his henchman while they're focused on me."

Christopher's gaze snaps up from my mouth. He shakes his head quickly and whispers, "No. You'll stay right here. *I'll* go."

A twig snaps. We both go quiet and glance toward its sound. The jerks from the other team are poking around the catapult, which they can't seem to figure out how to maneuver. I wonder if Jamie somehow found a way to compromise it. I hope so. Because now's my moment.

I try to turn in Christopher's arms, and he loosens his grip so I'm able to. His touch softens, his hands settle on my shoulders, as I spin and face him.

Reaching up on tiptoe, I press a kiss just below his ear, then whisper, "Go for the jugular."

Christopher pulls back, eyes narrowed. "Katerina, what—*shit*!"

I lurch out of his reach and spin, bending to scoop up two paintballs. Adjusting them in my grip like the good old softball days, I rush out into the clearing, sprinting across it and letting out a shrill whoop that makes the bros in black startle and fumble in their bags for their paintballs.

The first ball snaps from my hand and smacks Chad the ringleader right in the—irony of glorious ironies—balls. On a pained groan, he drops to his knees and falls sideways.

The last man on their team stares at me with pure rage, winding up and whipping a ball at me. I dodge it as I sprint farther across the clearing, so he'll turn as he tracks me and not be able to see Christopher coming up on him.

"Sucker!" I yell, hopping a rock in my path. My ankle wobbles, and I stumble forward, but I wrench myself upright back into a sprint.

He's tracking me, winding up again as I run, before he snaps a ball that I try to dodge but which nails me on my chest, right over my heart. I groan and throw my head back in frustration. When a ball strikes me again, my groan morphs to a shocked gasp, though I shouldn't be surprised. The rules say you stop when your opponent's hit, but of course he's thrown another ball, aiming for my face.

The jerk reaches into his satchel and grips a new ball as he growls, prowling toward me, winding up, "You fucking cu—"

A paintball splats right into his windpipe, making him go wide-eyed and gape like a fish as he stumbles back, the ball falling from his hand.

Slowly, I turn my head.

Christopher stands at the edge of the trees, and our gazes lock. The world dims around me, a peripheral blur of the bros in black stalking off, until all I see is Christopher. Jaw tight, chest heaving, standing with me in a little forest of bare paint-splattered branches and dwindling leaves, the last slice of ripe persimmon sun dissolving on the horizon.

As I stare at him, the surge that's built inside me, flipping breaker after breaker, shutting down reason after reason for why I should pull back from this longing that's unfurled inside me and protect myself like I always have, for why I shouldn't crush my mouth to that high-handed, infuriating, sweet-talking, shamelessly flirtatious, hot-as-hell-in-skintight-green-coveralls pain in my ass, blows my re-solve into a shower of white-hot sparks that rocket through my limbs, urging me to move.

I take one step toward him.

And then another.

And then I run.

TWENTY-FOUR

Christopher

I watch Kate run toward me, her feet pounding into the dirt as fast as my heart pounds in my chest. For so long, I've denied myself this—the pleasure of watching her, the thrill of admiring her, the ache of longing for her.

But not anymore.

Surrendered, free from the last of my resistance, I drink her in as she barrels toward me, beautiful and wild, splattered in paint, ribbons of chestnut hair flying out of their messy knot in the whipping wind.

I take a step toward her. Then another. Long, fast, then faster strides eating up the earth, and fuck, my heart, it feels like for the first time it's stretched its arms, drawn in starved-for air, and roared out joy.

We're three paces away from each other.

Two.

One.

She leaps onto me, scaling me like a tree, and our mouths crash, knocking teeth, rough exhales as I clasp her face in one hand and slide the other around her thigh, over her ass, wrenching her close.

"Christopher," she gasps, threading her hands through my hair, arching against me.

It's frantic and fevered, not so much a kiss as a consuming, mouths hot and hungry.

"Kate," I groan, unleashing myself on her, no finesse, nothing I've practiced and perfected guiding my mouth or my hands. As I tip my head and take our kiss deeper, her legs tighten around my waist. Her heels dig into my ass, and her fingers claw through my hair. I'm so hard, every brush of her body against mine is sweet, terrible torture. I need her so badly, nails raking down my back, teeth grazing my skin, hoarse, sharp cries as I lose myself in her.

Air rushes out of me as Kate rocks her hips with mine. I crush her closer, moving her tighter over me.

"Yeah." She nods, grabbing a fistful of my coveralls and pulling me in for another bruising kiss. "More."

My hand leaves her face, drifts down her chest, molding over her breast, palming it. I find her tight, hard nipple and rub it as she pants into my mouth. When I try to tug at the buttons of her coveralls, rip them open, my grip slips on paint, reminding me what she did—how recklessly she ran into danger.

I don't care that it was just paintball, a few splatters of biodegradable material striking her skin. Those fuckers had it in for her and she knew it. She put herself right in their line of fire anyway. My anger rushes back, as red as the paint smearing my hand—rage and frustration and fear braided in my blood. I walk us back to the nearest tree and pin her against it. "Don't run off on me like that, straight into harm, Katerina. Don't ever do that again."

"That wasn't harm," she pants, working herself against me, head thrown back against the tree, eyes shut.

"It was," I growl, nipping her neck, dragging my tongue up her throat, tasting her, breathing her in as I punish her with my hips, rutting against her, then pulling back, holding myself away, my hands hard at her waist, denying her what she wants. "Kate, when you're in danger, listen to me. Let me protect you."

She plants her feet against the tree, leans into the trunk, and shoves, making me stumble back, hurtling us backward until I land against another tree. Tightening her thighs around my waist again, she straightens her spine, until she's half a head above me, her hands cupping my face.

I stare up at her, helpless, hopeless, lost in those stormy eyes peering down at me, flashing like lightning as she drifts her fingertips down my cheekbones, dancing them along my jaw. "I was fine," she murmurs. "I'm fine right now."

"Dammit," I growl, craning up, kissing her, squeezing the sweet curve of her ass, dragging my hands up her back. "Tell me what it'll take. I'll beg, Kate. Anything. Just don't scare me like that, stop running headlong into danger."

"I'm safe," she whispers. "You don't need to worry." Setting her teeth on my bottom lip, she gently bites. "I got hit by two biodegradable paintballs. That's it."

I swear against her mouth, lightheaded with need as I drag her closer, crushing my mouth to hers. "It's still unacceptable."

She laughs as we break our kiss. "You're ridiculous."

"You're impossible," I groan, cupping her neck, slipping my fingers into her sweat-soaked hair, tangling with those wild locks knotted high on her head. "God, I can't stop. I can't stop and—"

And I've tried, I almost tell her. *I've tried for so long.*

She searches my eyes, perplexed, serious. Her thumb sweeps along my temple to my cheekbone, gentle and reflective. "What is it?" Leaning close, lowering her mouth to a breath away from mine, she whispers, "Tell me."

My hands travel gently up her back, tucking her closer. I draw in a breath, my heart pounding, searching for the bravery to unburden myself. "I—"

"We WON!" Bea's voice pierces the air.

More voices whoop and yell. Feet pound toward us.

Kate searches my gaze, her eyes dancing between mine. Sticks break under feet. Voices grow closer.

"Hold that thought," she whispers. Then she plants one last, long kiss to my lips and leaps like a cat from my arms, scoops up a paintball, and launches it toward her sister as Bea steps into view.

"Paintball fight!"

TWENTY-FIVE

Kate

It's the longest train ride of my life.

Christopher sits beside me, staring straight ahead, his thigh pressing into mine, hard, insistent. Those kisses on the paintball field play on a loop in my brain, and a flush creeps up my throat, flooding my cheeks.

Our eyes meet in the reflection of the train's glass across from us. His eyes pin mine, sharp, hungry. My eyes say the same thing—*Want, want, want.*

Peripherally I'm aware of the group's conversation, Toni and Sula dramatically replaying the highlights, Bea cackling with joy about defeating the bros in black.

All I can focus on is the sound of my breath sawing from my lungs. The heat pouring off Christopher. Every point of contact between my body and his.

My thighs squeeze together.

Christopher's reflection smirks knowingly.

Never one to turn down the chance to retaliate, I lift my arms over my head, acting like I'm stretching out my shoulder, putting on full display the diamond bits that are my nipples poking into my sweater.

His smirk dies away. I watch his grip curl around the edge of his seat, until his knuckles are white. There's still a splatter of green paint on his hand, flecks of yellow and blue clinging to his wrists, his neck, his hair, that make me flash back to just an hour ago at Peace, Love, and Paintball.

I see him as he looked then, turning right as I crept up on him and splattered a yellow paintball over his head, the grin on his face as he crushed one in his hand, then wiped it down the side of my face, making me scream with delight.

The train slows to a stop and we all ease out of our seats gingerly, walking slowly, sore as shit. Everything hurts.

The group leads the way, while Christopher and I fall behind them. I feel his hand settle low on my back, warm, comforting, torturously good.

He slants a glance my way, his eyes meeting mine, before they dance down to my mouth. The pressure on my back increases.

He wants me. And I want him.

I want his hands and mouth, I want more of those kisses that made my skin spark and dance like a live wire, arcing, lit up with relief as I grounded myself—my mouth to his mouth, my hands on him, his hands on me, welcoming the energy thrumming through us.

Up on the sidewalk, everyone pairs off and hugs goodbye, shivering against the cold. I participate in the ritual, barely paying attention, hardly knowing what I say.

And then it's just the four of us on the sidewalk, Bea curled into Jamie for warmth, Christopher shoulder to shoulder beside me, giving me his heat.

A car whooshes by, pounding bass, a raw ache rattling the air like an echo of what's inside me.

"Well, my lady." Jamie wraps an arm tighter around Bea's shoulders, smiling down at her. "May I escort you home?"

"My dear sir, how about *I* escort *you* home?" Bea says as she grins up at him.

"I won't say no to that. There's a cab," Jamie says, waving it down. "You two coming?"

I shake my head. "I want to walk."

Christopher says, "I'll walk her home."

Jamie and Christopher seem to exchange some kind of look I can't read as Bea rushes my way, hugging me hard, whispering in my ear, "You okay?"

"Yes. I promise. Love you."

She wraps her arms tighter around me and says, "Love you, too. I'm one call or text away. Because, uh . . . just in case it wasn't obvious, I will not be coming back after I take Jamie home. Well, not until tomorrow morning."

I snort a laugh, then pull away. "It was obvious, yes."

She grins. "Okay. Night, KitKat."

"Night, BeeBee."

After Jamie tucks Bea into the taxi, he follows her, pulling the door shut. I look up at Christopher and find him staring down at me. He steps closer and zips my coat all the way.

"Do you mind walking?" I ask.

"Of course not," he says, eyes on his task as he tugs up my coat's collar to cover my chilly neck, a smile lifting the corner of his mouth. "I had a sneaking suspicion that despite going hard for two hours at paintball, after that train ride, you'd need to move."

"I had to sit still the whole time." I wiggle my legs at the knees, working out the restless energy that's built up in my system. "I feel like a shook up bottle of bubbles."

"Hmm. What should we do about that?" Christopher squints into the distance, eyes on the empty sidewalks. Then, out of the blue, he says, "Race ya."

And he takes off.

I'm stunned for a split second, before I explode after him. "No fair!" I yell. "You got a head start."

He glances over his shoulder and flashes me a grin. "I'll make it up to you later."

"No, you won't," I holler, pushing my legs, which used to take me ahead of all the other kids on the playground, which got me middle-distance track medals, the thrill of air burning in my lungs, my muscles working until they were spent and finally able to rest. "Because I'm gonna beat you."

He laughs. Actually laughs. "Sure you are, Katydid."

A green light for opposing traffic makes him screech to a halt and makes me stop beside him. I stare up at Christopher, my chest rising and falling heavily, a smile lighting up my face.

"You are so getting burned," I tell him, bouncing on the balls of my feet. "You weren't around for my track-and-field days, Petruchio, so you don't know you're up against a second place in states for the eight-hundred-meter and *first* place for the sixteen-hundred-meter races."

He stares down at me, dark eyes filled with something knowing and warm. "I was there."

"What?"

He looks up at the light, watching it, waiting for it to turn red. "Just because you didn't know I was there, doesn't mean I wasn't."

I'm still gaping when he runs through the crosswalk.

"Christopher!" I yell, pumping my arms tight against my body, evening out my stride, then fucking leaning into it.

He glances over his shoulder. His eyes widen as he sees me gaining on him. "Shit!"

"Yeah, you better be scared!"

He laughs like it's disbelief, turning the corner onto my apartment's block, making a fatal mistake, swinging wide and losing precious ground. Which is when I lean tight into the corner and pour everything into the last stretch of our race, streaking past him and taking the lead five feet before we make it to my building's door in a stumbling mess of ragged breaths and hands slapping against the glass.

I laugh deliriously, my back against the door, Christopher's hands planted on either side of my head.

The fun and laughter of our race dwindle in the silence. The wind stings my cheeks and beats against my thick coat. I watch it plaster Christopher's jacket against his body, wrenching his hair off his face.

I can't take my eyes off him.

And he can't seem to take his eyes off me.

Staring at him, it's like I've lost a layer of my skin, so raw, so keenly aware there's nothing I can hide, nowhere to escape how much I want him.

I slide my hands up his chest, breathing unsteadily, feeling his chest work like bellows as I search for words I don't know how to say. For all my bravery and badassery, traveling the world, learning new languages and customs, rules and regulations, finding places, getting lost, learning from mistakes, scraping by, I can't find my voice or the words I need.

Christopher dips his head, his nose brushing mine. "Tell me what you want, Kate." His hand cradles my jaw. His thumb traces my lip. "Tell me."

Maybe it's the fact that I see it so clearly in his eyes, that I feel it in the faint tremor of his hand, in the rough, uneven gusts of air leaving his lungs. Maybe I'm finally finding my courage not just to fight but to *feel*. Maybe I'm finally safe to let myself desire and need and say it. Whatever it is, it swirls and builds, a violent, beautiful storm coursing through me, filling my lungs, making me brave.

"I want you." I breathe the words, staring up at him, my hand over his pounding heart. "And you want me, too."

"God, yes," he groans as I reach for him, as he crashes down on me. Our kiss is hard and bruising, rough and perfect. I open my mouth and wind my arms tighter around his neck, while his hands drift down my back, over my ass, then grip my legs, hoisting them around his waist until he's lifting me up. He slips his hand into my coat pocket, pulling out the key, then clumsily slides it into the lock and yanks open the inner door.

"Hurry," I beg, tightening my legs around his waist, moving myself shamelessly against him.

"Hurrying." His mouth grazes my earlobe, my jaw, my throat, as he takes us up the stairs two at a time.

A whimper leaves me as he walks me up to the apartment door and pins me there, breathing harshly, fumbling with the key again and cursing under his breath.

A sound escapes me, half whine, half belly laugh.

Christopher laughs, too, then steals a hard kiss, silencing us both.

Finally the door to the apartment flies open and we stumble inside. He shoves the door shut, flips the bolt, then nearly dumps me onto two feet, yanking down the zipper of my coat.

I wrench it off with his help, then tackle his coat, too. His hands slip under my sweater, around my waist as he tugs me against him, then walks me backward toward the sofa.

Bending his head, he brushes his lips against mine, tender, soft, his tongue dancing with mine. I sink my hands into his shirt and feel the fabric crumple. "More."

He groans against my mouth, his hands gliding higher up my sweater, cupping my breasts. When the backs of my knees hit the sofa's arm, I yank him with me, making him grunt as we fall, him on top.

"Easy," he mutters. "I could hurt you."

I laugh. "Petruchio, if you think you're the biggest thing to land on me, you are sorely mistaken."

I'm about to brag about the incident involving the biggest

thing to land on me in all my work travels (that would be an adolescent alligator), and who came out on top (that would be me), but
given his freak-out earlier about a couple of paintballs coming my
way, I decide to keep that little anecdote to myself so he'll keep doing this thing with my nipples that's making me pant like I've just
run wind sprints.

"These tits," he grunts. "Torturing me with that little show you
put on in the train."

I'm wild, mindless, and I slide my hands beneath his shirt, feeling hot skin, the solidity of his body, that line of hair trailing down
from his navel. "Kiss them."

Christopher's mouth is hungry, a blissful dance of wet and
warm and teasing as he kisses his way down my throat with nips of
his teeth, silken flicks of his tongue. His hands cup my breasts,
palming them appreciatively.

"I said *kiss* them," I whine.

His thumbs flick my nipples, then he pinches them gently.

"Shit!" My head falls back as I arch into him.

"Still have something to complain about?" he murmurs.

I slip my hands beneath the back of his jeans, then his underwear, until I'm touching his big, glorious ass, yanking us closer together so I feel him, thick and hard inside his jeans, wedged right
against me.

"Shit," he moans against my neck.

"Still think you were right about keeping your distance?"

I'm pressed back on the sofa, even more of his weight on me
making me gasp. "No." He dips his head, planting a slow kiss over
my heart that makes goose bumps erupt across my skin. "Not
anymore."

My fingers rake through his hair as he kisses across my collarbones to my shoulders, lingering on the one that I broke. He gives
me his body weight, gliding his hands slowly up my arms, pinning

them over my head. He's so heavy and it feels so good, the sensation of pressure that my nervous system craves.

His mouth moves lower, down my chest, nuzzling my shirt aside so he can tease my skin with silken hot sweeps of his tongue. One hand cups my breast and tortures my nipple with slow, aching tugs. The other hand drags my thigh wider and slides up, his thumb swirling in teasing, torturous circles. "I want to kiss you here, too, Kate."

I nod, half-thrilled, half-terrified, trying not to dwell on how little I've experienced, how little I know. "I want that," I whisper. "I want you to kiss me everywhere."

His hand drifts higher up my thigh until he's cupping me between my legs, grinding his palm against my jeans, making the seam rub over my clit.

I moan, loud and shameless. It feels so damn good.

With his other hand, Christopher lifts my breast, then drags my nipple through my shirt between his teeth.

Another loud, uninhibited noise leaves me. I'm feeling too much that's too good to be self-conscious. Wrapping my legs around Christopher's waist, I work myself against him as he licks my nipple and tugs it rhythmically through the cotton in hot, wet strokes.

He's breathing so hard as he pulls away and starts to crawl lower.

Then he stands, frantically unlacing my boots, throwing them over his shoulder, bending over me, stealing a deep kiss as he braces himself on one hand and uses the other to flick open the button of my jeans, then drag down the zipper.

He stands, grips the cuffs of my jeans, and yanks them straight off my legs, wrenching me down the sofa with them. My legs hang off the arm of the sofa and he drops to his knees, hauling me closer by the hips and kissing up my thighs. I am keenly aware of the fact that I'm in mismatched fuzzy socks, the most basic-ass pair of dingy, once-white underwear, and the landscape down under is pure wilderness.

Before I have time to let my head run away with worries about my inexperience, my insecurity about if he'll like what he sees, he says quietly, "Whatever you want or don't want, Kate, tell me. I'll stop if you say stop. I'll do whatever you need. Just tell me."

"Okay." I nod, trying desperately to overcome my nerves, to focus on how good it's felt, to take reassurance in what he's said. "Maybe let's just . . . start like this?"

Nodding wordlessly, he kisses up my thighs, his tongue swirling against my skin, making me writhe and lock my legs tight around his shoulders. And then he's there, his mouth warm over my underwear, the pressure of his tongue against the cotton firm and perfect. I gasp and throw my head back, sinking my hands into his hair. "Like that. Just . . . more."

He makes a low, satisfied sound as he sucks me gently over the cotton of my underwear. My body feels so tight, everything between my thighs aching and hot and desperate for relief.

I'm so aroused from moving against him as he kissed and teased my nipples, so achingly close, but release is out of reach. I feel empty, agitated, knowing at some fundamental level that I want more.

"I need you," I whisper. "Inside me."

He groans against me, then gently pushes my underwear to the side, just enough to slip in a finger, then crook it forward.

"Oh God," I yell hoarsely. "There. Just like that. Faster."

That's when the sound of footsteps coming up the stairs makes us both stop, lifting our heads, staring at the door. There's the low timbre of Jamie's voice. Bea's cackling laugh.

"Shit," I hiss.

Christopher stands up so suddenly, he looks like he got electrocuted. "Fuck."

"My jeans!" A bubble of nervous laughter jumps out of me.

"Right." He spins around, scraping both hands through his hair. "Where the hell are they?"

The key's sliding into the lock. I stare at it. So does Christopher.

Shockingly fast, he bends and hoists me over his shoulder firefighter-style, then runs down the hallway, sliding into the bathroom with me and slamming the door shut just as I hear the front door open, then close.

The lights are on over the sink—I must have forgotten to turn them off before we left for paintball—so I can see as he crouches and eases me off his shoulder. I'm imbalanced, jelly-legged, and I thump back against the door.

Christopher stares up at me as he slumps from his crouch onto his knees. His forehead lands heavily against my hip. "Jesus Christ," he mutters. "That was close."

Jamie's and Bea's voices linger briefly in the main room, then die away, headed in the opposite direction in the apartment toward the bedrooms.

Peering up at me, he asks quietly, "Why are they here?"

I listen for a second and catch the high-pitched voice Bea uses for her pet hedgehog. My eyes slide shut with regret. "Cornelius needed his dinner. She probably tried to call and text to remind me to feed him, but I missed it."

Come to think of it, I actually have no idea where my phone is. Hopefully buried in my coat pocket.

"Dammit, Kate," he groans.

"Well, I'm sorry I was a little busy with you getting me off!" I hiss-whisper. "You want me preoccupied with modern technology while you're going down on me?"

A groan rumbles out of him. He slides his hands around my waist, down lower, and wraps them around my ass. "I want you to make those sounds you were making again." He lifts my shirt and presses a kiss to my stomach. "I want your heels digging into my shoulders."

"I wasn't making sounds," I protest weakly. His mouth is on my hip bone, lower, over my underwear again. He kisses me there, slow and wet, and my legs buckle. Thankfully he catches me, pinning me by the hips against the door.

"You were. And I loved them." He kisses me again, then nuzzles me, breathing deep. "Fuck, I don't want to stop."

"I don't want you to, either." My fingers slide into his hair.

He peers up at me, his hands rubbing my ass, kneading it. "Kate, can you be very quiet?"

I exhale shakily, moving my hips against his thumb as it starts to tease me over my underwear. My nipples feel hard and tight as they brush my shirt, the ache between my thighs so close to sweet satisfaction. "Probably not."

"Try for me, honey," he mutters, before kissing me between my thighs again, sucking and licking. Between his tongue and my own arousal, my underwear is soaked, plastered to my skin. "I need this so bad."

What he's doing feels good, but what I want is more. I want the hard, thick ridge of his erection grinding against me. I want his groans and pleas in my ear, those sounds that reassure me he's as undone as I am.

I tug his shirt at the shoulder and yank him toward me until he stands.

"What is it?" he asks. "Too much? I can stop—"

"No." I shake my head, wrapping my leg around his hip, showing him what I need. "Like this."

He presses a slow kiss to my jaw, then my neck. I sigh as I feel him on the first perfect grind of his hips that makes him, stiff and heavy inside his jeans, rub over my clit. His mouth meets mine and

I tighten my thigh's grip around his waist so I can move faster, gripping his shoulder for leverage, panting against his mouth.

After only a few strokes, my breathing has turned hoarse and jagged. His has, too.

Christopher's grip on me intensifies, moving me against him. "Hold on," he mutters.

"Don't tell me what to do—*ah!*"

Two fingers push aside my underwear, curling up inside me, stroking just where I need. A warm, sweet ache spreads through my veins.

"So good," I whisper. "Oh shit, you're good at this."

"For you," he whispers against my neck. "Just for you."

Reaching down, I find him so hard inside his jeans, stretching the fabric, it has to hurt. Tentatively, I stroke along his length. Christopher curses into my neck.

"Is that okay?" I ask.

"So much more than okay," he pants.

I tug at his belt, then the top button. "Can I touch you?"

"I'll die if you don't." He shifts his hips, just enough so I can slip my hand inside his jeans, curling my fingers over his erection straining his briefs. He's so thick, so hot even through the fabric. I whimper as I stroke him, thrilled that I've made his body like this.

"So good, honey." He kisses me slow and deep, his tongue stroking mine. "Keep going. Yeah, that's it. Fuck, that's perfect."

My head lands against the door with a *thunk* as his fingers change their rhythm, rubbing faster. I'm so close, trying so hard not to scream with pleasure on each thrust of his hand, as it brings me right to the edge.

"You gotta come for me, Kate," he grits out. "Come on, honey. Give it up."

"So close," I whisper, working myself on his fingers, making a fist with the fabric of his shirt as I crush my mouth to his.

That's when we hear voices coming closer again.

We freeze, our breathing so ragged and loud, I don't know how they don't hear us.

But then the front door eases open again, then shuts; the lock engages with a click.

And then we crash down on each other. The door thumps as Christopher thrusts into my hand, as my hips roll with him, banging into it.

"God, Kate." He throws his head back when I bite his neck and chase it with my tongue. He starts to work his thumb over my clit in fast, expert circles, his fingers still pumping inside me.

I gasp as heat pools, a white-hot flash flood that tears through my limbs, washes between my thighs, through my breasts, making my toes curl. "Gonna come," I beg. "I'm gonna—"

"Yeah," he grunts. "That's it, honey. Ride my hand. Come all over it."

I slam my head against the door as pleasure pounds through me in seismic waves. A low, pained groan tears out of Christopher as he punches his hips into mine, as warmth and wetness seep between us and he comes against my waist.

Panting, messy, we kiss. Slowly, he lets my legs go and steadies me as I find my footing. I stare up at him, touching him, cresting my hands over his shoulders, down his arms, while he holds me tight to him, his hands savoring my ass, kneading it as he kisses me, reverent and deep.

And then the real world begins to seep into my awareness. The soft *plink-plink* of water dripping from the faucet. The muffled sounds of traffic outside, a siren wailing.

Christopher stares at me, his expression unreadable, chest heaving. He cups my face and presses one last soft kiss against my lips, breathing in. Exhaustion sweeps through me. Between paintball and the most intense orgasm of my life, my eyes feel heavy, my limbs heavier.

I want to drag him down the hall and make him fall on me like we did on the couch, for his big, heavy body to weigh me down. I want to sleep for a week. My legs wobble.

"Easy," he says quietly. He paws around for the light switch and turns it down, until it's low and dim.

Then he sweeps me up in his arms, making me squawk. "What are you doing?" I ask.

"Putting you to bed."

Then leaving, is the unspoken remainder of that sentence.

I can tell by the way his expression turns serious and focused, its playful, passionate fire dimmed; the way that he walks me to my bed and lays me on it, then drags the blankets up.

"Stay," I whisper, brave in the darkness, in the raw need that I feel. No one's ever touched me like this, made me feel free and weightless and known, a fire billowing in the air that feeds it, hot, wild, alive. I don't want to be left alone in that. "Please."

He's quiet for a long moment, his hand on my hip, his thumb sweeping tenderly against the skin beneath my shirt.

Then slowly, he stands.

My heart plummets. He's leaving.

Except, he isn't. He stops at my bedroom door and pushes it shut, bathing the room in darkness.

I hear drawers open and close. Fabric slide off his body. I hate the darkness for what it hides, knowing he's changing out of the clothes he came all over.

A shirt hits my face. "Put that on," he says quietly.

"You're so bossy," I grumble. But I still drag off my shirt that's wet at the hip and throw it somewhere in a corner of the room before I pull on the new shirt. It's as soft as I love my shirts to be, but surprisingly loose. I get a whiff of his scent and smile to myself. He gave me one of his shirts.

Christopher crawls onto the bed, pointedly on top of all the sheets, like he's going to "try to be a gentleman" again, as if he didn't just dry hump and finger me into orgasmic oblivion against a bathroom door. Then again, even with my wardrobe change, I'm still a mess of grass stains and paint and sweat, so maybe he's just protecting himself from that.

Then *again*, he's covered in all that stuff, too.

So why the distance?

Gently, he tugs the sheet up to my chin, then drifts his fingers across my forehead, down my temple, across the bridge of my nose. "Time to settle that busy brain of yours, Katydid. Go to sleep."

"Don't tell me what to do," I mutter, feeling my eyelids give in to the temptation to slip shut. "Besides. I'm not"—a yawn rudely interrupts me—"tired."

"Of course you're not. You're not exhausted," he says, his fingers slipping through my hair along my scalp until they bump into my messy bun. "Your eyes aren't sleepy. Your limbs aren't heavy."

Another yawn. "Nuh-uh."

I hear the smile in his voice as his knuckles tenderly graze my cheek. "And you definitely won't have sweet dreams."

I wish I could say his reverse psychology doesn't work. But my eyes drift shut. My limbs are heavy.

And I dream the sweetest, filthiest dreams.

TWENTY-SIX

Christopher

I wake up groggy, my body heavy and loose with the unfamiliar pleasure of feeling rested. Blinking, I stare up at the ceiling and smile as I remember Kate cuddling with me in her sleep, her head on my shoulder, her arm across my stomach, her leg over mine.

Watching her sleep, listening to each steady breath, holding her, feeling her hold me, I could have stayed there forever.

My smile falls.

Because now I remember where I am.

I'm not with Kate in her bed. I'm in my bed, which I stumbled into after I slipped out from her arms and dry swallowed my abortive med as a migraine scraped across my brain and sunk in its teeth.

It comes back to me in patchy flashes of memory. Battling waves of nausea on the train ride back as my pain level skyrocketed. Collapsing onto my bed. Covering my head with my ice cap and a pillow as agony pulsed through my brain, until mercifully the med kicked in, and I slept.

But Kate doesn't know any of that. All she knows is I touched her and kissed her and put her to bed, then left. I tried to write her a note before I left, but my hand was shaking so badly from the pain, I couldn't write. By the time I got on the train, I couldn't stand to look at my phone's bright screen and text her. I told myself I'd message her as soon as I woke up. I'd only sleep a few hours, like I always do, before nature's call or more pain woke me up.

And of fucking course, the one time I counted on only a few hours of sleep, I slept straight through the day.

Goddammit. The thought of her waking up to an empty bed makes my chest ache.

Reaching for my nightstand, I feel around clumsily for my phone, then spin it toward me. I turn up the screen brightness so I can see it, now that the light won't hurt my eyes.

I want so badly for the time to reassure me that this darkness is a sign of early morning, that the rare surge of rested energy coursing through me is a fluke, but I know it's not. It's the deep velvet darkness of an autumn evening, and I couldn't possibly feel this good after only a few hours of sleep.

"Fuck," I groan as my phone screen reveals the time: *5:45 PM.*

And then I see the email notification, its sender and subject. My heart starts to pound.

I tap on the notification and open the email, eyes scanning the text, dread knotting my stomach:

Dear Mr. Petruchio,

Please see the attached link to your team's headshots. This link is private and accessible only to employees of Verona Capital. Both color as well as black and white high resolution files are available for download, per our agreement. If you or your employees notice anything *minor* that you'd like edited in any photo, please note that Photoshop enables me to erase zits and stray hairs, but it does not make me

God or a plastic surgeon—there are limits to what can
be done.

Regards,
Kate Wilmot

Oh God. This is bad. Not only did she *Mr. Petruchio* me, she
used *Regards*, the corporate email equivalent of a big old "up yours."
She's angry.

She's hurt, a quiet, wise voice inside me says.

I can't honestly imagine what Kate thinks, waking up to me
gone after what we did last night. She's probably drawn the worst
possible conclusion, and to be fair, I've never done anything to
make her think I'm more than an unapologetic one-and-done se-
ducer. To her, I got what I wanted, and then I left.

"Shit." I kick away the blankets and stand from my bed, scrubbing my face. I have to find Kate and explain myself. I have to
make this right.

"Shower," I tell myself, getting a whiff of how ripe I am. "Shower
first, then . . ."

Meow.

I glance toward my doorway, where the Wilmots' cat, Puck,
slinks across the threshold, deceptively smooth for such an old,
cantankerous animal.

"Puck. You can't keep doing this, man, escaping and sneaking
over here. It stresses them out when they can't find you."

Meow, he says, stretching lazily, then sauntering toward the
foot of my bed and jumping up.

"I know you like my treats better, but that's no excuse for
sneaking out. We have our scheduled visits when I bring you home
and you get to enjoy them. I always bring some to Sunday dinner,
too . . ." My eyes widen. Relief whooshes through me.

Sunday dinner. Today is Sunday. And Sunday dinner starts fifteen minutes from now. Kate will be there. Jamie said she's come to every Sunday dinner that I've missed, trying to keep my space while she was here. I start frantically stripping off my clothes, tripping over them on my way to the shower.

This is one Sunday dinner I'm not going to miss.

TWENTY-SEVEN

Kate

Hopping down the main stairs of my parents' house, I pass the coffin-sized storage bins labeled CHRISTMAS in the hallway and spin into the kitchen, where Dad stands stirring something that smells so mouthwateringly good, it makes my stomach growl.

Which reminds me that I haven't eaten all day. I spent it lost in editing photos and sending Christopher a terse professional email, trying not to think about how empty my bed felt when I woke up, even though I told myself not to hope he would be there in the morning, even though I told myself not to expect another generous pastry or gorgeous flower delivery, another one of his little scribbly notes, anything indicating that what we did meant to him anything close to what it meant to me.

Foolish, foolish Kate.

"Katie-bird," Dad says, opening an arm to me.

I slip inside the crook of his arm. "Hey, Daddy. What's for dinner?"

"Creamy potato with facon bits. No animals were harmed in the making of this soup."

I smile and give him a squeeze around the middle that makes him groan. "Sounds perfect, thank you. Where's Mom?"

Dad adjusts his glasses, which have steamed up over the soup. "On the lookout for Puck. He's made a jailbreak again."

"That little master of feline mischief," I say proudly. "I raised him right."

Dad chuckles. "He certainly keeps us on our toes." As he glances my way, my dad's expression changes. "You weren't wearing that when you got here, were you?"

"Oh." I step back and peer down at myself. "No. I was in a questionably stained Tweety Bird sweatshirt and leggings with holes in unmentionable places. 'Not exactly Sunday dinner attire,' Mom said. I raided my closet upstairs and changed for her sake."

More like you wanted Christopher to see you looking like a million bucks, if he finally came to family dinner, that taunting voice says in the back of my mind. *You wanted him to see you looking good and feeling A-OK, just in case he's worried you took a few companionable days and thoughtful gestures, and one glorious orgasm at his hand, then ran with it and now you have expectations that might have been dashed when he was gone in the morning, like he's always been with everyone else he's done that with.*

Oh God. *Everyone else.*

That phrase is the emotional equivalent of a ripped cuticle—small, concentrated, sharply painful. A vicious double wave of jealousy and humiliation crashes through me.

"Where'd your mind go, Katie-bird?" Dad asks mildly.

I blink, wrenched from my thoughts. My dad's smiling at me, patient, kind. Like always.

I absolutely cannot tell him where my mind went.

Still, I need some outlet for what I feel, so I wrap my arms around his waist and squeeze again, burying my face in his sweater, breathing in his scent—old books and peppermint pillow mints.

On a deep breath, I blink away tears. I've felt so weepy all day.

A soft kiss lands on the crown of my head. "I love you, Katie-bird. You can always talk to me, all right? I'll just listen, if you want. No advice. No judgment."

"I love you, too. And I know," I mumble against his sweater. "I've missed you so much. You and Mom. Bea and Jules. Everyone."

"We've missed you, too," he says. "But as Grandma used to say, the ones we love are always with us. Wherever you've been, I've had you"—he taps a hand over his heart—"right here." Smiling down at me as I give his ribs a break and release him, he says, "Every year that passes, you remind me of Grandma even more."

I smile. "She was a badass. She also had *no* filter."

He laughs. "She certainly spoke her mind." His gaze dances over me. "When you wear that color, that deep blue, it changes your eyes, and you look"—he grins—"very much like her."

"This was hers. Vintage cashmere."

"I thought it looked familiar," he says, returning his attention to the soup. "So why did you have to raid the closet to freshen up for dinner?"

I get out a salad bowl and tongs, setting them on the counter. "Ah, well, I'm a little behind on laundry, so I didn't have anything nice enough to wear that was clean. I keep forgetting to go to the laundromat. I can't handle the apartment's basement laundry. Not since this thriller I read, the main character went down to the basement to switch over her clothes and—"

"Nope. Don't tell me." Dad shakes his head, tapping the spoon on the edge of the soup pot, then turning off the burner. "I don't touch that genre for a reason. My worst-case scenario, doomsday-inclined imagination comes up with plenty of terrible possibilities without the help of thrillers."

The doorbell rings, making both Dad and me jump.

"See?" he says, taking off his fogged-up glasses. "No help needed."

"Probably just a delivery person leaving a package," I tell him.

"Or Christopher," he says.

My heart skids to a stop. "But Christopher doesn't ring the—"

Now there's a knock at the door. I frown, confused. Christopher doesn't knock, either. He walks right in like he owns the place. He always has.

Who else could it be, though? Not Bea and Jamie. They're missing Sunday dinner for Jamie's office holiday party.

"Why don't you go see?" Dad says. "Oh, and by the way, if it's those two young fellows with their Bibles again, I'm not home."

"I—"

"Look who I found." Mom strolls in from the mudroom, Puck in her arms. His little bell jingles as she sets him down and he scampers toward me. "He's lucky he's cute, that's for sure."

"Where was he?" Dad asks.

"In the greenhouse, trying to eat my roses again. Who's at the door?"

As if on cue, there's another knock.

My eyes dart toward the front door, panic seizing my insides.

"Katerina," Mom says, walking briskly past me toward the soup pot. "Why don't you get that?"

"Me?" I ask pathetically.

Meow. Puck twines around my legs, then scampers off into the hallway, his little bell jingling.

Sighing, I follow Puck, because if my cat's brave enough to face Christopher Petruchio, then I am, too.

"Okay," I tell myself, as I try to regulate my breathing. "You are fine. Your pride is a little wounded that Christopher wasn't around when you woke up and didn't pull another stealthy pastry delivery or reach out all day. But that's all right. You're an adult. You can just move on."

Meow, Puck says. I scoop him up and cuddle him close, comforted by his rumbling purr.

"Okay, maybe not move on," I admit to Puck. "I can have a

conversation with him about it, though. I. Can. Communicate! I can put on my badass big-girl pants and talk to him. And until then, hopefully make his eyes bug out of his head with this very flattering sapphire-blue, plunging-V-neck sweater."

Meow, Puck agrees.

"Well, now it's sapphire blue *and* covered in your white fur."

Puck plops his head on my shoulder and purrs happily. I glide my hand down his fur in rhythmic, soothing strokes and take a deep breath. "I've got this. I can do this."

Meow, Puck says, and with that encouragement bolstering me, I yank open the door.

Christopher stands on the porch with a small bouquet in his hand, a canvas bag in the other.

He's in an emerald-green long-sleeve thermal that hugs his thick arms, expensive-looking dark-wash jeans, and saddle-brown lace-up boots. His hair is wet and a little messy, like he just got out of the shower, the waves curling around his jawline. I take a steadying breath and catch his scent, woodsy candle smoke and spice.

Not that it's affecting me.

Not that I'm remembering when I sank my teeth into his neck like an animal last night and tasted that scent on his skin.

He clears his throat, then says, "Can I come in?"

I clutch the door, because the world feels like it's tipping. "You always let yourself in. Why are you asking this time?"

His eyes hold mine. His throat works in a swallow. "Because they're your family first, and if you didn't want to see me, after last night, well, this morning—though I promise I can explain myself— if you didn't want me here, I didn't want to force myself." He's quiet for a moment, before he says, "I want you to let me in, Kate, but only if *you* want to."

I'm as frightened as I've ever been, standing on more than one threshold—not just this physical space but one in my heart. I want to trust him so badly. And I'm so scared he's going to break my heart before he even knows how long he's had it.

I have hated Christopher Petruchio for so long not only—not even primarily—for his distance, his aloof superiority, but because it hurt so badly to be rejected and pushed away by someone I cared about.

But I'm Kate Wilmot. I'm a globe-trotting badass who doesn't shirk risk or avoid a challenge simply because it might end badly. I'm brave in so many other parts of my life. I'm going to be brave now, too.

Slowly, I ease open the door and step back. "Come in, then."

Christopher crosses the threshold. Our eyes hold as he steps closer and his fingertips brush mine, the lightest touch that makes a shiver race up my arm. "Thank you," he murmurs.

"Christopher!" Mom calls from the back of the house. "What on earth were you knocking for? Come in!"

Christopher shuts the door behind us and follows me into the kitchen while I keep clutching Puck like he's a life raft.

Carefully, Christopher sets the bouquet, then his bag on the counter, unloading a bottle of chilled white wine and a beautiful loaf of rustic bread whose crust glows golden, intricate leaves carved into its surface. Then he pulls out a small container whose sound immediately sends Puck leaping from my arms.

I watch Christopher crouch and set a handful of treats on the ground for Puck, who gobbles them up like he's been on a starvation diet.

Empty-handed, I focus on brushing Puck fur off of me, eyes averted so I can't watch Christopher pet Puck as he purrs loudly, so I won't feel that awful mushy warmth flood my heart.

When Christopher stands, brushing off his hands, he glances

up at me, then does a double take. I think, with Puck gone from my arms, he's finally clocked the neckline of my sweater.

Avoiding his eyes, I step up to the refrigerator and open it, grabbing components for the salad I was going to contribute to dinner.

"What the hell are you wearing?" he asks.

I crack open the container of greens and add some to the salad bowl. "This would be a sweater, Christopher."

"A sweater," he mutters to himself, setting the bread on the cutting board and reaching for a knife from the knife block.

Mom strolls in through the swinging dining room door and sweeps up the flowers Christopher brought. "Well, that explains Puck's foray into the greenhouse."

"Sorry about that," Christopher mumbles. "He must have snuck in with me, and I didn't notice."

She pats his back gently. "It's fine."

As Mom sets them gently into a crystal vase, I realize that the flowers he picked—roses, dahlias, delphinium—are my favorites. Christopher picked my favorite flowers and made a bouquet.

Did he do it for me?

Glancing my way, Mom smiles. "Now, this is much better than Tweety Bird. That sweater on you is so lovely."

"Thank you," I tell her. "At least *someone* here likes my outfit."

She frowns, glancing toward Christopher. "What's wrong with what she's wearing?"

"Nothing," he grumbles, sawing viciously into the bread.

Mom shrugs, walking past me. "Either of you want some wine with dinner?"

"God, yes," Christopher says.

"Just a splash," I tell her as she sweeps up the bottle of white Christopher set on the counter and tears off the seal around the cork. "I shouldn't have too much now, since I'm going out after dinner."

The knife clatters to the cutting board. Christopher's stare bores into me from across the island.

"Out?" Mom asks distractedly, struggling with the wine opener.

"Mm-hmm."

Christopher rounds the island and says to her, "Let me."

She steps aside and leans against the counter, wide smile, eyes sparkling. "Out where?"

"Fee's maybe? A club? Who knows." I return to the salad, sprinkling some chopped almonds across the top. Then I scoop up a handful of pomegranate seeds, adding those, too. "Wherever I go, I imagine it'll end up being a wild night."

The cork flies out on a loud *pop*. Christopher stares at me, jaw tight, fire in his eyes. "Of course. I forgot."

Mom glances at him. "Forgot what?"

"That I'll be going with her," he says, unwinding the cork from the corkscrew.

My stomach knots. I have no idea what he's talking about. Granted, I'm making up shit, whatever I can think of to provoke him, to get under his skin the way he's gotten under mine. Maybe he's just bullshitting right back to mess with me.

"Going with her?" Mom asks. "Why?"

"I asked Kate if I could keep her company tonight, make sure she can have fun and stay safe." He glances over my mom's shoulder, holding my gaze. "She said yes."

Thank God my mom has her back to me. My eyes practically bug out of my head.

"Really? How sweet of you, Christopher," Mom says to him. I wipe the shock off my face just as she glances over her shoulder at me, her eyes bright and happy. "Isn't that sweet of him, Kate? What a gentleman."

"Very sweet and gentlemanly." Never to be outdone by Christopher, I force a bright smile at my mother as Christopher drags an empty glass his way, pours himself a hefty glug of wine, then throws it back like a shot. "He's on a roll, lately. Christopher was *such* a gentleman last night that he saw me home after our paintball group outing and made sure my *every* need was met before he left."

Christopher chokes on his wine.

Mom slaps him on the back. "Serves you right for shotgunning a gorgeous Sancerre like it's moonshine. I'm going to take this with me and attempt to extricate Bill from the book I saw him pick up as soon as I left the room. Wish me luck."

Sweeping up the bread Christopher half massacred and the wine bottle in the crook of her arm, she disappears through the swinging dining room door.

He watches the door fall shut, then rounds on me. "Give me a chance to explain first, before you go on some vengeful bender tonight."

I hold his eyes, nerves coursing through me. "Fine. Explain, then."

"I—" His eyes rake down me slowly, then slip shut. He hangs his head and pinches the bridge of his nose, blowing out a slow, heavy breath. "*Christ*, Katerina."

"What?" I ask, hearing how defensive I sound, but frankly, it feels justified.

"I can't think straight, let alone talk right now, looking at you."

"Why not?"

He groans, dropping his hand. "You know what you're wearing. You know how beautiful you look. And you know it's killing me."

Warmth crests up my throat and spills into my face. I set a hand against my cheek, trying to cool it. "Maybe I wanted to wear something . . . a little eye-catching. I was feeling vindictive. I woke up this morning, and you were gone, and I was . . . upset. I wanted to make you pay for leaving me like you've left every other woman you—"

"Don't," he says, storming toward me. I step back as he advances on me, until my back hits the counter. I can't help but remember not even a month ago being in this very same position—caged inside his arms, his hands planted on either side of the counter, staring me down.

You were always *needed.*

That's what he said. I hate that passive sentence structure. I want to know *who* needed me. I want it to be him. I want to know why he's looking at me the way I'm looking at him, like he's searching for solid ground to stand on, like he's just as lost in this as I am.

"There is nothing," he says quietly, his hand settling at my waist, "routine or typical about what happened last night. I didn't leave because you were 'just some other woman.'"

I pull back, stunned. "Christopher—"

"Please." He swallows roughly, stepping closer, his hand massaging my waist, drawing me toward him. "Give me the chance to explain. Don't go, Kate. Don't leave."

Those words do something to me, turn the part of me that's always been hard and implacable, soft and pliant. I feel warm and willing and a little frightened.

Our eyes hold as I do what I haven't felt brave enough to do before—reach out when I'm afraid; try, even when I'm nursing wounded pride. I lace our hands together and squeeze his, a reassurance.

"I'm listening," I whisper.

His eyes flicker; some of the tension eases in his shoulders. "This isn't an excuse. And I can only promise you I wouldn't have left otherwise, but it's up to you to believe me." His jaw clenches as he stares down at the ground, sighing heavily. "I started a migraine.

A bad one. I panicked. I didn't want to get sick in front of you. I don't . . . I don't do that around other people. I'm used to handling it myself. So I took my preventative med and rushed home, and then I slept the whole fucking day somehow and woke up in a panic because I knew how it would hurt you, for me to be gone, for you not to hear from me all day. I . . ." He swallows roughly, tearing his gaze up, finding mine. "I never want to hurt you, Kate."

The kitchen is quiet, my parents' voices distant, somewhere deep in the house. Steam curls off the soup on the range. The lights are soft, glowing. I feel like time's dissolved, like the world's been paused as I stare at him, my heart flitting like a hummingbird against the cage of my ribs.

Gently, I slide my hands up his chest and feel air rush out of him. I search his eyes, crossing that bridge inside myself from familiar fear to newfound trust. To hope. "I believe you."

His eyes dart back and forth, searching mine. "You do?"

I nod, my hand circling his pounding heart. "I do. I'm sorry you were hurting so badly. I wish—"

"I'm fine." Words evaporate on my tongue as Christopher drags his thumb over my bottom lip, his fingertips whispering along my throat, then down, across my collarbone. "After this," he says quietly. "Let me take you home. Please."

I bite my lip, a thrill coursing through me. "You want me to come to your house?"

"Your apartment, I meant. In the city." He leans in as if he's going to kiss me but seems to stop himself. His eyes dart down to my breasts, and he groans.

"What is it?"

"That damn sweater. Don't you have anything else to wear? I can see straight to your belly button."

"I don't mind if you see straight to my belly button."

"*I* mind," he says darkly.

"Are you two coming?" Mom calls from the dining room.

I smile and shrug. "I'm happy in my sweater, so you're stuck with it. Now, come on. I'm starving."

"I'm starving, too," he grumbles as I gather the salad bowl and tongs, then head for the dining room. "And it sure as hell isn't for potato soup."

TWENTY-EIGHT

Christopher

Dinner lasts a lifetime. And it doesn't last nearly long enough. Because I'm just as desperate for Kate as I'm terrified of what I'm about to do—try something I've never done before, something I've actively avoided my entire adult life: brutal honesty, naked intimacy.

Emphasis on naked.

It's taking superhero strength not to think about every erotic thing I want to do with her after this, when I'm sitting between her parents at their dinner table.

A rush of something primal and possessive burns through me as I watch her laugh at a wisecrack her dad tosses into the conversation. Her cheeks are pink from the warmth of the room, her dimples deep, her hair an upswept swirl of chestnut and auburn that I ache to undo and watch spill down her back.

My hands curl into fists beneath the table.

Goddamn that sweater wrapped around her the way I want to be, kissing her collarbones, gliding over the slight swells of her breasts, hugging her waist. I see exactly where my hands belong, stroking her nipples, sweeping down her ribs to her hips.

My teeth grind as my cock helplessly hardens, thick and angry in my jeans. I'm in agony.

"Christopher?" Maureen's voice earns my attention.

"Hmm?"

She tips her head. "You seem distracted. Everything all right?"

Kate picks up her water glass and lifts her eyebrows.

I stare at Kate, struggling not to broadcast in my expression how fiercely I want her, how good it feels to have told her the truth in the kitchen, to know she believes me. I still can't really believe that she's letting me sweep her away after this, that soon I'll have the satisfaction of taking my sweet time with her instead of our frantic chaos last night, incredible though it was. I stare at her and can't make myself stop picturing how slowly I'll strip away her clothes and kiss her everywhere except where she wants. How I'll work her up until she's begging for my mouth, my cock, my hands, to give her relief.

"Christopher?" Maureen says again.

I blink, a rare rush of heat hitting my cheeks. I can't believe where my mind went, when her parents are sitting right here.

"Sorry." I shake my head a little and have a sip of my wine. I don't taste it at all. "I'm fine, yes."

Kate lifts a spoonful of chocolate mousse to her mouth and slowly slides it past her lips, hollowing her mouth when she does. Her mouth parts and her tongue flicks the tip of the spoon.

I put a fist in front of my mouth and breathe deeply. I'm going to die.

Kate tips her head, then leans in, which presses her breasts together. By some superhero strength, I manage not to look at them. "I'm ready to go if you are," she says.

The final thread of my restraint snaps. I stand abruptly, sending my chair scraping back, then pick up my plate and bowl to hide how physically in hell I am. "Yes. I'm ready. Thank you for dinner," I tell Maureen and Bill.

"Of course, dear," Maureen says, smiling up at me.

"Don't worry about the dishes," Bill tells us as Kate and I gather up our plates and silverware. "Go on and have your fun."

"We can throw them in the dishwasher," Kate says. "It'll take ten seconds."

I'm already ahead of her, storming into the kitchen, rinsing my plate, bowl, and silverware under the water, then setting them in the dishwasher.

"Okay. Love you!" I hear Kate tell her parents.

The door swings open from the dining room and Kate walks in. I watch her set down her dishes, then stop abruptly and turn, disappearing from the kitchen, before reappearing. She shrugs on her coat and her beat-up cross-body bag, while I shove her dishes into the dishwasher. Somehow nothing breaks, even though I'm not remotely watching what I'm doing.

I stare at Kate, who looks so *her* right now, with that messy bun and her ratty jacket and beat-up bag. Something inside me snaps. I kick the dishwasher closed, close in on her, then walk her back to the counter, my hands on her hips, my mouth a whisper from hers. "I want to kiss you, Kate. Very badly."

She blinks up at me, her eyes growing hazy as her hands drift up my arms to my shoulders. For a moment, I'd swear I have her, that her mouth's about to meet mine, but then she ducks out from under my arms and spins away. "Not yet."

"Not yet?" I turn, breathing roughly.

Slowly, she backs toward the door, like a cornered animal, a flush on her cheeks, a feisty glint in her eyes. "Not yet," she says again.

"Katerina, what's—"

My voice dies off as she turns the handle, then wrenches open the door.

TWENTY-NINE

Kate

I've barely made it to the bottom step of the back stairs when Christopher's arm wraps around my waist and spins me his way. I gasp, shocked by how fast he is, how quickly he whips me around and pins me against him.

And then he bends, scoops me up, and throws me over his shoulder.

I squawk as he starts to march us across the yard.

"Christopher!"

"Katerina," he says pleasantly.

"What are you doing?" I squeak.

"Giving you exactly what you deserve for trying to run off." He lifts a hand and swats my butt.

I squeak again. "Did you just *spank* me?"

"And if I did?"

"Stop it!"

He grins. I hear it in his voice. "Why? Because you don't like it? Or because you don't think you should?"

I turn bright red. Reaching down, I swat his ass back. "Put me down, you caveman."

Immediately he stops and crouches, letting me slide down his body.

I'm a little wobbly, and I grip his arm, steadying myself as he slips a hand around my waist to steady me, too. Words evaporate on my tongue as I stare up at him, his face cast in sharp moonlight and shadowy darkness, as the wind rattles bare branches and whips between our houses.

"Why did you tell me not to kiss you yet?" he asks quietly.

I stand there, silent longer than I'd like, struggling for the courage to explain myself, to confess that I'm scared of how much last night meant to me and I'm scared it isn't the same for him—that for him this is a low-stakes bet, and for me, it's the wager of my life.

"I'll tell you," I promise. "Soon. Just . . . not yet."

His jaw tenses. "You keep saying that—not yet."

I smile softly. "And I mean it."

He sighs, hanging his head. "Let me get my jacket."

He darts away up the stairs to his back porch, punching in the lock code, then disappearing inside. I wander slowly toward his house, inspecting it. Oddly, it looks a little outdated and weather-beaten. The windows are the same ones I grew up seeing, at least thirty years old. The paint on the sill is peeling here and there. The house's exterior looks tidy but worn down.

Christopher's got more money than God. So why hasn't he used it to keep up the place?

"Let's go." He's beside me before I realize it, breaking me from my reverie.

Setting his hand low on my back, he guides me between our houses toward the street we'll walk down to catch the train. Heat spills from his hand through my jacket. I feel his fingers curl in on my body, his palm sliding to my waist, then drawing me closer. Looking up at him, I'm breathless for a moment. His dark hair's everywhere in the wind, the lamplight dancing down his thick brows and lashes, that strong nose and sensual mouth, the sharp line of his jaw. He's so beautiful, it makes me ache.

Maybe I do feel ready for some kissing after all.

"So." I clear my throat, biting my lip. "The kissing thing."

He peers down at me. "The kissing thing."

"I thought maybe I needed . . . a break, until we talked some things over, but . . ." My gaze drifts up to his, again. "I think maybe I was wrong."

He lifts an eyebrow. "Maybe?"

"I'm undecided, so I say we settle this the old-fashioned way. If you win, you can kiss me, whenever you want. If *I* win, you won't kiss me until I say."

"Wait, win what—"

Gently pulling away from his arm wrapped around me, I call over my shoulder, pointing to the train stop, "Race ya."

It's the fastest I've ever seen him run.

———

For how fast we raced to the train stop, we're just as slow walking to my apartment. Christopher hasn't touched me since he beat me to the train stop.

Which, I will admit, I'm confused about.

Everything about the way he was looking at me at my parents' during dinner, when he threw me over his shoulder in the yard, made me think the second he won he'd haul me into his arms and kiss me senseless.

But here we are, Christopher with his hands in his pockets, walking beside me, glancing my way every once in a while, watching me in that intent way of his.

Stopping outside my apartment, I turn to face him, fighting and losing the battle against a shiver. His brow furrows as he frowns, his hands rubbing up and down my arms. "You need a real winter jacket, Kate. Come on. Let's get you inside."

I let him turn me toward the building, my hands shaking with cold and nerves as I unlock the main door, which Christopher shuts securely behind us. I jog up the stairs to my apartment door and then start to unlock that one, too, then think twice, stopping myself.

Turning back, I clutch the doorknob and peer up at him.

Christopher tips his head, confused. "What's going on?"

"Why haven't you kissed me?" I ask him. "Even though you won the race."

Holding my eyes, he steps closer, his hands traveling my arms again, drifting around my back, pulling me toward him. "I don't want to take something you don't want to give."

I smile. "That's a good answer."

He arches an eyebrow. "I know it is. Which is exactly why your little race and wager was a ruse. Either way, I was at your mercy, Kate. I still am."

"My mercy?"

Christopher lifts his hand, his knuckles softly grazing my cheek, down my throat. "You know how much I want you. I told you the only reason I left your bed last night was because of that goddamn migraine. Otherwise, Katerina, we'd still be there. I'd be learning every corner of your body, every single thing that makes you shake and beg and sigh." His nose drifts into my hair and he breathes in, his mouth brushing the shell of my ear. "I'd have had you so many ways, so many times, you'd have lost track of them already."

A trembling breath leaves me. "And . . . that's what you want, still?"

He groans into my hair and presses a kiss there. "It's all I want. *You're* all I want." His mouth drifts to my ear and nuzzles there, tracing my earlobe, sucking softly. I gasp and lean into him. "I've wanted you for a long time, Kate."

My heart leaps—he's wanted me the way I've wanted him.

But then it plummets—because it's so hard to reconcile that

while he says how deeply he desired me, he spent night after night sharing an intimacy with others that I've never even experienced. I don't judge him for it, but I don't understand it. I know why I want Christopher—why crossing that bridge of physical appreciation to a deeper desire has been so much swifter than it has been for others. He's never been a stranger to me. Even when he made me angry, I knew him, the sound of his voice, the scent of his skin. I knew he loved my family and would do anything for them. I *knew* him, and in some way I think I knew how much he knew me, how much he saw me even though he didn't understand me, even though—as he admitted that night he came and made pasta—my choices scared him.

There's so much about each other that in simply sharing nearly our whole lives, we know—that's familiar and understood. And yet there's so much left to learn.

I'm scared of where and how to begin. But as someone who's bungee jumped, skydived, who's taken those terrifying, free-fall leaps, I know sometimes the fear doesn't leave—bravery just joins it.

And I know this is one of those moments.

I swallow nervously, my hands coming up to his chest. "Do you remember, back when I was taking photos at work, when you said you could be patient, if I needed time to open up to you about certain things?"

He nods.

"So . . . my body needs that, too."

He rears back, his eyes meeting mine. "Needs . . . time?"

"Yeah," I say softly. "I know last night happened, but . . . that's not typical."

"No," he agrees, his voice deep and rough. "No, it's not."

"Before we did that again, I'd . . ." I draw in a long breath, then blow it out, steadying myself. "I'd need time until I'm ready. Can you wait?"

"Of course," he says quickly, his hands coming gently to my shoulders, soothing them. "Of course I can wait."

"And you'd be with no one else while you waited?"

He looks deeply offended. "Kate, of course I wouldn't. I told you, I just want you. I don't want anyone else."

Can it be that easy? "What if I'm not talking days of abstinence, Christopher? What if I'm talking weeks?"

I watch it sink in. "Weeks," he finally says. He exhales slowly. "I can do weeks."

"You can?"

He scrubs his face and sighs bleakly. "Considering I *have* been the past three weeks," he says, the first nip of irritation threading through his voice. "Yes."

"You have?"

"Yes. For the same reason I'm saying I'll wait now. I wanted you and no one else, and I still do. Could you act a little less surprised?"

"I'm sorry," I whisper.

Christopher sighs, pulling me close for a gentle hug. "I'm the one who should be sorry. I shouldn't have snapped like that. It's just . . . I want you to believe me."

"I do believe you. I believe you mean it. I just don't know if it means to you what it means to me."

He sets his chin on my head and says quietly, "I don't know what you're saying, Kate."

My nerves get the best of me for a moment, but I make myself take a deep breath, then say, "For me, physical intimacy needs to be . . . emotionally grounded. I don't do casual sex. And unless I'm mistaken, that's all you've ever done."

Christopher pulls back, his jaw hard as he searches my eyes. "That's true, yes. But casual isn't what I want with you." He swallows roughly, then lifts my hand and turns it so my palm faces him. He bends and presses a kiss there, his tongue brushing my skin so lightly, I almost don't believe it happened. A shiver waves through me, and this time it's got nothing to do with being cold.

"I'll show you that. I'll wait," he says. "As long as you need me to."

"Even if I need a month?" I venture, expecting him to laugh or choke, but he just brings my hand to his cheek, holding it there.

"A month," he agrees. "*If*—"

I roll my eyes. "Of course there's a condition."

"I'd be a shit businessman if I hadn't perfected the art of a strong negotiation, Kate." He grins, rubbing my hand against his cheek. His stubble tickles, and it makes me fight a smile as he stares down at me. "I'll be abstinent for a month, *if* you promise that, even if you leave between now and then, when our time's up . . ." He brushes my knuckles against his lips, staring at me. "You'll come back."

The way Christopher looks at me makes me realize, maybe I'm not the only one with fears. For the first time I consider how it might have felt to want me the way I've wanted him, never knowing where I was going or when I'd be back.

My heart kicks against my ribs. "Of course I'd come back. I promise."

A sigh leaves him, slow and relieved. "Then you have yourself a bargain, Katerina."

He reaches past me and turns the key in the lock, gently pushing open my door. I smile up at him, a rush of happiness running through me. He'll wait for me.

Christopher smiles, too, though it's tinged with a groan. Bending, he presses a kiss to my forehead, hard and warm, breathing in. "Stop looking at me like that."

A flush of heat crawls up my chest to my throat, spilling into my cheeks. "Like what?"

"You know what." He presses a gentle kiss to the corner of my mouth, teasing and sweet all at once. "Keep your phone on you, Katerina. I'll be counting on it."

"What does that—"

I'm nudged across the threshold, the door shut behind me, before I can ask what he meant. Not even a minute goes by as I slowly tug off my jacket and hang it up, before my phone buzzes in my messenger bag.

Digging around, I finally find it.

A calendar invite for tomorrow night, 6 to 8 p.m., lights up my screen:

Event: Dinner with Christopher
Location: Kate's apartment

My phone buzzes again, this time with an email notification. I bite my lip, fighting a smile when I see who it's from, before I tap to read it:

Dear Ms. Wilmot,

Thank you for your prompt delivery of the team's headshots. I can't say they're everything I'd hoped for— they far exceed it. A direct transfer to your account paying the balance you were owed for services rendered has been completed.

And now, please consider this a formal termination of our professional relationship.

(I don't date people I work with.)

Yours,
Christopher Petruchio

THIRTY

Christopher

"You're sure?" Kate asks. "You trust me not to mess it up?"

She's got a streak of flour on her cheek. A long tendril of hair has slipped out of the knot piled high on her head. Stepping up behind her, I lift that rogue strand away from her face and tuck it back into the hair tie. It takes the kind of self-denial I've never asked of myself before the past two weeks, touching her without coming on to her, wanting her so badly, my skin practically vibrates when I'm near her, yet never acting on it.

I brush the flour from her cheek and somehow manage not to kiss it. "I'm sure."

Kate bites the inside of her cheek as she examines the sheet of pasta dough ready to be draped across the ravioli filling and pasta sheet beneath it, idly twirling the mini cutter wheel in her hand. "I don't know."

"Hey now," I tell her. "You wrestled an alligator into submission. No getting timid in the home stretch of making ravioli."

One of those pretty blushes turns her cheeks pink. "It was an adolescent alligator."

"Adolescent or not, you still wrestled an *alligator.*" Stirring the sauce simmering on the stove, I glance her way. "Don't shortchange yourself."

She peers up at me, a smile setting dimples in her cheeks, and like a fool, my heart skips a beat that I did that. I made her smile.

But then her smile dims. "I just don't want to mess it up."

I pause mid-stir, then set down the spoon. "What are you talking about?"

Kate turns toward the ravioli. Slowly, I close the space between us and clasp her elbow, turning her back toward me. "Katydid. Talk to me."

She shrugs, flicking the spokes of the pasta cutter wheel. "I get anxious about expectations. So anxious, I sort of . . . freeze."

Stepping closer, I rub my hand along her arm. "What expectations?"

"All of this." She points around the apartment. "For the food to be good, for everyone to want to be here and have fun. Jules is the hostess expert, not me. I forget things when it's time to set up and plan for company, then I get overwhelmed and cranky when there's a lot of people."

"Which is why we're working *together*. You and I are making ravioli and sauce. Jamie and Bea are handling the salad and veggie dishes. Bianca and Nick are picking up fresh bread. Toni and Hamza are bringing dessert, and Sula and Margo are going to bring way too much wine. It'll be great, because it's all of us getting together for some food and games, and whenever it gets to be too much, you can slip away and take the time you need while Bea and I hold down the fort. In the grand scheme of things, if you cut the ravioli a little crooked, it's not going to change a thing."

"Yeah." She nods, starting to pull away. "You're right."

"Hold on. I need this recorded for posterity. You said I'm *right*."

Kate rolls her eyes but doesn't laugh; my joke hasn't lightened her up like I'd hoped. She's still uneasy.

"Show me one more time," she says, gesturing with the cutter wheel toward the pasta sheet.

"Kate—"

"Please." She sinks her fingers into my shirt and tugs me toward her. "I wasn't paying attention earlier. I missed how you start."

I stare down at her, bringing my hand to her cheek, cupping it gently. "What's this really about?"

She bites her lip. "I don't know. I feel . . . antsy and nervous. I haven't done this ever, spent this much time home, this much time with other people I care about, and I think it's dredging up old insecurities, that I'm going to do something that makes me wear out my welcome. One moment, I'm telling myself everything has to be perfect so it won't happen, the next I'm dying to give in to the itch in my legs to rip open that door and run before it inevitably does."

My heart aches in my chest. "Kate, honey. Whoever made you feel like you wore out your welcome simply because of who you were, they're assholes and you're better off without them."

She blinks up at me, her eyes wet, like she's on the verge of tears. "It isn't one person or one moment, though, it's . . . having a brain like mine in a world that isn't very welcoming or understanding of it. The things that I like about myself when I'm on my own, living and doing my work my own way, they're not things that are seen as strengths or skills or advantages. They're tolerated at best, criticized at worst. And sure, my family's always been supportive and accepting, but they're the minority. So I've just learned to push people away and do my own thing. But that's not very easy when I stick around and start to care about people and they can hurt me or disappoint me when they start to see the real me, all my quirks and executive-functioning lapses. When I care about that, I feel so helpless."

I stare down at her, my thumb drifting along her jaw in a slow back-and-forth motion. "I know a little about that."

She frowns, confused. "You do?"

"I didn't run halfway across the world to hide from what's scared me about relationships, Kate, but I've been hiding just like you. The way I've lived, the boundaries I've drawn, they're how I've protected myself from that feeling of helplessness, too."

Brow furrowed, she searches my face. "You say it like . . . like that's in the past."

"I want it to be," I tell her, my hand sinking into her hair at the nape of her neck, massaging gently. "I'm trying. I want to be braver. Because I've seen what protecting myself cost me, and I never want it to cost me that again."

Kate drops the pasta cutter on the counter and sinks her hands into my shirt, drawing me close, until our bodies touch.

I hiss in a breath between clenched teeth. "What are you doing, Kate?"

"Trying to be brave, too," she whispers, pressing on tiptoe. Her mouth brushes mine, and air rushes out of me.

"Kate, honey—"

"Kiss me," she pleads.

"I promised I'd wait—"

"As long as I needed, I know. And you're wonderful—you've been wonderful—but I don't need to wait anymore. At least not for these kisses." She leans in, pressing me back into the counter, her hands scraping through my hair.

Heat spills through me, my skin burning everywhere her body presses into mine. "You're sure?" I whisper against her mouth.

She nods.

"God, I missed your taste." I wrap my hands around her back and drag her against me, taking over the kiss, coaxing her mouth open. Our tongues dance, slow, hot glides as my hands wrap around her hips, moving her with me, rocking, rubbing.

A soft, needy sound leaves Kate that makes my cock thicken,

the air in my lungs catch. "Christopher," she whispers. "I need more . . . I need you to touch me—"

"I know," I tell her, hands slipping beneath her sweater, across the satin warmth of her skin. I palm her breast and nearly come from just touching her, feeling its slight weight filling my hand, her nipple tightening as I tease it with my thumb. "If it's too much, just tell me to stop—"

She shakes her head. "Don't you dare stop." She reaches for the hem of my shirt and drags it up, out of my jeans.

"Kate, you don't have to—"

"I *want* to," she pants, tugging at my jeans, pulling my hips toward hers.

"Honey, slow down. Just let me do this." I bend enough to lift the hem of her long skirt, dragging it up her leg. I slow down as I get higher, my fingertips teasing lightly along her inner thigh.

"W-what are you doing?" she says hoarsely.

Finally, I slip my hand between her thighs, cupping her over her underwear. Her legs give out, but I hold her easily, an arm wrapped around her waist. Kissing her, I mutter against her lips. "I'm giving you what you need. Let me touch you like this? Please?"

My finger toys along the hem of her underwear, dipping beneath it. She knows what I'm asking. "I need an answer, Katerina."

"Yes," she whispers, arching into me.

A groan of relief leaves me as I slip my fingers beneath her underwear and feel her, so beautiful—soft curls, warm, smooth skin that's goddamn drenched.

"Christ, you're wet."

She sighs, tight and breathy. "You make it sound so dirty."

"It's not dirty." I kiss her deeply, loving her mouth with mine. "It's beautiful, what your body does, how it responds to me. Now hold on to the counter."

"Why—" Her voice breaks off as I drop to my knees, rucking her skirt up and away. I press a kiss to her hip, the inside of her thigh. A shaky exhale leaves her. "Christopher, what's happening?"

"I'm kissing you," I tell her, toying with the edge of her underwear again. "Let me see you, here, Kate."

A deep red blush crawls up her cheeks. "I'm all . . . natural down there."

I groan. "You're perfect."

I kiss the juncture of her hip and her thigh, breathing her in, squeezing her ass in my hands as I kiss her. My fingers toy with the hem of her panties.

"You can see me," she says quietly. "Take them off."

I tug at her underwear, and either they're threadbare or I'm hornier than I thought, because they rip right in half.

Kate gasps. "You just ripped my underwear."

"I'll buy you more," I mutter absently, too distracted with my fingers parting those soft auburn curls, discovering pink, silky skin. I stroke her gently, lap her with my tongue. She jolts and cries out, her hands sinking into my hair. God, she tastes so good.

"Christopher," she says shakily, "people are going to be h-here soon, and—" Her head drops back as I lean her against the counter and slip a finger inside her, then another.

"And what?"

"And—" Somehow, her blush deepens. "They could walk in on us."

"Hmm," I murmur against her, sucking softly, flicking my tongue, tasting her sweet, warm skin. "I think you like that, Kate."

She sucks in a breath. "The things you say."

I smile against her, lost in how much I love the ways she can be so fierce and fiery one moment, then shy and scandalized the next; how much I love the feel of her body, clenched around mine.

I devote myself to her, desperately trying to ignore the truth that reverberates through me with each thud of my heart, the knowledge racing through my mind—I love more than her beautiful contradictions, her supple body, melting for me. I love—

"Please," she whispers, tugging at my collar, toward her.

Standing, I drag her inside my arm and bring my hand back to where she's wet and tight, her hips moving against me.

Our mouths meet and she sighs as she tastes herself against me, as I groan into our kiss.

"Christopher," she whispers, her hand rubbing over my heart. "Oh God, please. I need to—"

"Shh, honey. Easy." I kiss her, slow and deep, coaxing her to relax. "Don't chase it. I'll give it to you."

Pinning her against the counter, I slip my fingers out gently, just enough to bring her body's wetness up and rub her clit.

She cries out, burying her face in my neck as I stroke her softly, working her up to orgasm. Her cries get faster, hoarse and pleading, and I feel my body tighten, begging for its own release as she chases hers. Denying myself like this is as foreign as trying to speak another language and just as difficult, but it's gratifying, pouring all my attention solely into what she needs, worshipping Kate the way she deserves.

Feeling how close she is, I slip my fingers inside her once more on a deep, curved stroke. Kate yanks me toward her by the collar, until my mouth finds hers, and I'm lost to her sounds, her cries as she comes against my hand.

Panting, she drops her head against my chest. "I can . . ." She sighs, dazed and satisfied, her hand slipping down my chest, toward my tented jeans. "I can return the favor."

My hand finds hers and stops its progress. I bring it up to my chest again, clutched against my heart. "I don't want a damn thing from you."

She scowls. "Gee, thanks."

I laugh roughly. "I didn't say that right. Sentences are difficult right now, given I barely have any blood in my brain."

"Which is why I—"

"There's no rush." I kiss her slowly, softly. "What I just did, that is more than enough for me right now."

She arches an eyebrow. "That is not what the state of your pants indicates."

I smile against our kiss, teasing my fingers lower again, ready and hungry to give her more. "Ignore that."

"Impossible," she whispers.

"Hmm. I can think of a way to distract you." Watching her smile in spite of herself, I tell her, "Now, hush, and let me make you come one more time before company's here."

THIRTY-ONE

Kate

Some things have changed over the past week—I've gotten very confident with making out and dry humping on all sorts of household surfaces. And some things have not changed. Like my capacity to stay on top of my laundry.

"Kate!" Christopher calls, followed by the sound of the apartment door shutting.

"One second!" I call back, scouring my room for a single piece of clothing that's clean and isn't riddled with holes or questionable stains on it. It's pretty difficult, seeing as my laundry is a mixed-up disaster and my room looks like a bomb went off in it.

I hear his footsteps coming down the hallway and, out of sheer desperation, yank a long-sleeve shirt from his Christopher drawer, throwing it over my head, cuffing the sleeves to a slouchy three-quarter length. Rich cerulean blue and superfine cotton, it's soft and comfy, long enough to pass for a tunic.

"I can work with this," I tell my reflection, tugging on black leggings and quickly stomping into my Doc Martens. Then I rush out of my room, shutting the door behind me right in time.

Christopher stops just short of the door and frowns. "Everything okay?"

I nod, my grip firm on the doorknob. "Mm-hmm. Let's go." I

take his hand and start down the hall, but he doesn't budge, sending me boomeranging back into him.

"Oof." I bump into his chest. "C'mon, we have to go."

He stares down at me. "You're wearing my shirt."

I grimace. "I was hoping you wouldn't notice that."

His eyes darken as he steps closer. "That was a very foolish thing to hope, Katerina."

"I'm behind on laundry," I tell him apologetically. "The machines in the basement creep me out, and I was so busy all week, I kept forgetting to go to the laundromat, but I'll do laundry soon, I promise. I'll wash it right away and give it back to you—"

He bends and kisses me, deep and slow. I lean into it on a sigh as he nudges my mouth open and his tongue grazes mine.

"Keep it," he says between kisses. "You wearing it is not the problem."

I blink up at him, a little dazed by those kisses. "Then what *is* the problem?"

A husky laugh leaves him as he wraps me in his arms. "The problem is that I'm thinking about you in *just* that shirt, lifting it while my hands wander up your thighs straight to where I want, then tearing it off of you and teasing you with my mouth and hands until you're begging me to make you come."

My eyes widen. "Me wearing your shirt inspired all of *that*?"

He sighs, then he kisses me softly, closemouthed and sweet. "It doesn't take much these days to inspire deeply erotic thoughts about you."

I bite my lip. Leaning closer, I wrap my arms around his neck.

"What kind of erotic thoughts?" I ask, pressing up on my toes, taking his lip between my teeth and tugging softly.

On a growl, he pulls himself away, putting distance between our bodies except for his forehead, which he presses to mine. "Even I have limits, and telling you what I've been fantasizing about before we have to leave for Sunday dinner is it. Now, go on, get your jacket and bag so we can leave. We'll be late if we don't head out now, and we both know how Maureen feels about that."

I grab his hand as he turns toward my room. "What are you doing?"

He arches an eyebrow and glances over his shoulder. "I was going to grab your laundry for you."

I almost laugh. He thinks he could just walk in and pick up a hamper of dirty clothes. "Why were you going to get my laundry?"

"To bring it to your parents'," he says, as if this is obvious and entirely logical. "You could get it done tonight while you're there, couldn't you?"

"Christopher. You're not getting my laundry."

"Suit yourself. Just pack it all in a bag, and I'll carry it for you."

"I don't want to make us late—"

He starts toward my room again.

"Fine!" I yell, darting past him and slipping through a crack in the door. "I'll be ready in five minutes!"

———

Christopher sits beside me at my parents' dining table. He's kept his hands to himself, but below the table, his knee rubs against my thigh, making me bite my lip as I stare into the remnants of the crème brûlée we had for dessert.

"Kate," Dad says. "You said you had a project you started this week, wasn't that right? Have any photos to share?"

Bea narrows her eyes across the table from me. "I already asked. She's been so secretive about them."

"I don't like to show them until they're edited," I explain.

"You've been editing all day," Christopher says. "Come on, Katydid."

Mom's expression perks up as she registers his use of that

childhood endearment. I freeze, realizing his slip, but Christopher doesn't seem to notice, or maybe he does but he simply doesn't care. He just sips his coffee and watches me as I dart out of my seat and dig around my bag for my phone, then come back to the table, opening up the folder where I store my projects' photos.

He leans in as I plop down in my chair, bathing me in the familiar, enticing scent and warmth of his skin. "That's beautiful," he says, pointing toward the photo that I've pulled up. "This is from the nonprofit—"

"For girls and gender-nonconforming kids." I nod. Then I offer my phone to my dad first, telling everyone at the table, "I went in at the beginning of the week and took photos for this nonprofit that focuses on emotional support and self-expression. These were taken while they ran their storytelling workshop."

"Beautiful, Katie-bird," Dad says proudly, beaming up at me, then handing the phone to Bea. "You have such a gift."

"KitKat!" Bea says, scrolling through the album and leaning toward Jamie so he can see them, too. "These are stunning."

"Thank you. I'm happy with those. Now I just have about fifty more to edit and get in similar shape tonight."

"Do you have to do them tonight?" Christopher turns more fully my way, a concerned frown on his face as he stretches his arm across the back of my chair. "Why don't you take a break and tackle the rest tomorrow?"

"Well, in theory, that would be lovely, except I told them I'd get the photos finalized before Christmas, and with all the hours I'll be working this week at the Edgy Envelope, I should try to get more done tonight."

Christopher sighs as he rubs his knuckles against the back of my shoulder, where no one at the table can see. "That's too fast of a turnaround you agreed to."

"They wanted to have it ready when they kick off funding

initiatives in the New Year. I didn't want to make them wait when I could do it now, even if it was a bit of a crunch. Besides, I don't have any other projects to tackle at the moment—"

"Besides working nearly full-time at the Edgy Envelope during its busiest time of the year," he says. "That's a lot, Kate."

Dad's eyebrows lift at the intensity of his tone. Christopher's focused on me, so he misses my dad's surprised expression. Mom hides a smile in her coffee cup that I don't understand, but doesn't say anything. Bea and Jamie don't seem to notice, their heads still bent over my photos as they talk.

Jamie, who hands my phone to Mom, peers up and asks, "What are the photos going to be used for?"

"In their new presentation they've built for prospective investors," I tell him.

Mom smiles as she scrolls through the photos. "They're gorgeous, Kate. I'm so proud of you."

My throat feels thick. "Thanks, Mom."

"Now, is this work relatively close to or different from what you did when you were abroad?" Jamie asks, wrapping an arm around Bea as she leans into his shoulder and covers a yawn.

I shrug, scraping my spoon along the burnt-sugar rim of what's left of my crème brûlée. "Logistically it's simpler here, but something like this . . . it's what I've always aspired to in my photojournalistic work—activism through storytelling, giving my subjects the chance to be heard, their voices amplified through the power of images that make people stop and listen."

Bea smiles up tiredly at Jamie. "My baby sister's a badass."

"That she is," Jamie says fondly to her.

Christopher's silent. But when I peer his way, he's watching me so intently, I feel it like a dry shock of static electricity.

"Christopher actually made the introduction for me with this nonprofit," I tell everyone, even though my eyes can't seem to leave him. "I have a handful of projects waiting for me in the New Year because he won't stop blabbing about me to his social network."

A grin tips his mouth, his eyes holding mine. "What good is a social network if you don't use it? Besides, I didn't make them hire you. I just sent them your website and told them you'd done the firm's new headshots. Your work spoke for itself."

"Do you think you'll take on those projects after the New Year?" Dad asks, leaning in, elbows on the table. "Or do you think you'll go abroad for your usual work again?"

Christopher's suddenly very interested in his empty dinner plate, eyes down, expression tight and unreadable.

I remember what he told me that night he came to the apartment and made pasta, and everything started to change.

I worried about you. I hated that to do your work you took risks and put yourself in danger.

Beneath the table, I reach out until my hand finds his clenched into a fist.

"Much as I loved what I was doing," I tell Dad, "it's burned me out. I'm ready for a change. I'll still travel, sometimes, I hope. But I plan to spend a lot more time at home."

Bea smiles at me from across the table. "So long as you don't leave before December 25, for the sake of all those who'd have to deal with Maureen Wilmot losing her ever-loving shit if you were gone for Christmas."

"Language," Mom says, before turning toward me, poorly hiding her hopes as she looks at me. "Christmas is just so soon, and you hadn't left; I assumed you were staying."

"I'm staying," I tell her while, still hidden under the table, I stretch my palm across Christopher's knuckles and feel his grip start to relax, until our fingers tangle. Christopher's gaze snaps up and our eyes meet. "And I'm not planning on leaving anytime soon."

"Mom!" I call from the mudroom, where the washer and dryer are set up.

"Yes, Kate!" she calls back.

"Something's wrong with the washer."

Popping her head in, Mom wrinkles her brow in confusion. "Oh, dear. You don't say."

Dad pops up behind her, frowning. "It is? I just used it this morning—"

"Bill," Mom says sweetly, turning and smiling up at him. "Would you be a dear and make sure the front door shut properly when Jamie and Bea left? Puck will pull it open if it's not securely shut, and I'm not in the mood for another midnight frolic in the cold, looking for that tyrannical furball."

Dad blinks down at Mom. "Maureen, the door's—"

Mom yanks Dad down by the collar and kisses him so suddenly, he grunts in surprise. But then whatever hesitation he felt dissolves as his hands wrap around her waist, drawing her close.

"Ew. You two." I shudder, shooing them with my hands. "Go do that somewhere else."

Mom pulls away from their kiss and flashes me a smile that's so like Jules's, it's startling. "I'd say the same for you and the laundry. Try Christopher's."

"Christopher's? Mom, I can't just—"

"Excuse me, Kate," Mom says, eyes back on Dad as he leans in for another kiss. "Your father and I will be back in just a minute."

"A minute?" Dad says, huskily. "That's all I get?"

Mom laughs as she walks him back from the doorway until they're out of sight.

I sigh, turning back to the washer. Puck slinks into the mudroom and meows, twining around my legs. I start to pull out my sopping-wet clothes from the washer and load them into the zip-up hamper that I brought them in. "I know, Puck. It's gross. Parents aren't supposed to act horny like that."

Meow, he says.

"Well, fair point," I tell him, reaching inside the washer for the wet clothes plastered to its sides. "I can appreciate that their horniness precipitated my existence, but as far as I'm concerned, that was twenty-eight years ago, and that should have been the end of it."

A throat clear makes me jump and slam my head against the washer. Swearing under my breath, I stand and feel my heart flutter ridiculously in my chest.

Christopher stands, leaning against the threshold, hands in his pockets, watching me.

"It's not polite to eavesdrop," I tell him sourly, rubbing the back of my head.

He pushes off the threshold and closes the distance between us, gently brushing my hand aside, feeling the back of my head, satisfied when he doesn't find any serious damage.

"Washer's busted, Maureen said."

I sigh, glancing over my shoulder at the traitorous washing machine. "Apparently."

Christopher's quiet, inspecting my sopping clothes sitting piled in the hamper. He seems to be deliberating something, his brow furrowed. Then he steps past me and picks up my laundry bag, using the shoulder strap to hike it onto his back. "I'll do it for you."

I give him a look. "You are *not* doing my laundry. However, if you wanted to invite me to your house for the rest of the evening so I could do my own laundry, that would be a different matter."

Christopher's jaw clenches. He stares down at me, clutching the hamper. "Kate—"

Taking a page out of my mother's book, I press up on my toes and silence his mouth with a kiss. He's breathless when I pull away.

"Let's settle this like we do all serious matters, Petruchio." I reach behind me for the doorknob, then turn it. "Race ya."

Christopher swears viciously as I sprint down the stairs and across the yard. I glance over my shoulder just once, shocked to see how fast he's moving for carrying a sopping wet, heavy bag of laundry on his shoulder.

I leap up the stairs to his back porch two at a time and come to a halt at his door. Above the handle, there's a code-based lock, a half-moon of numbers.

"Kate!" Christopher yells, making it to the bottom of the steps, scrambling up them.

I don't know why I do it, if I'm daring fate, if I'm wishing it into existence, but I enter my birthday.

The door unlocks.

I gape and glance over my shoulder.

"Dammit," he rasps, pushing me inside, slamming the door behind him.

I laugh, equally shocked and thrilled. "Why is my birthday your lock code?"

He drops my laundry off his shoulder with a wet *thud* and rakes a hand through his hair. He doesn't answer me.

"Christopher," I press, my heart pounding with a dawning, earth-tipping hope that's my most closely guarded, deepest-buried dream. "Why is my birthday your lock code?"

He stares at me, something so fierce and raw in his expression, my breath catches in my lungs.

My throat feels thick as I take a step toward him. "Tell me," I whisper.

"Tell you what?" he snaps.

Closing the distance between us, he grabs me by the waist and hoists me onto the counter, which hasn't changed in twenty years, in a kitchen frozen in time. Curious as I am about why his home seems unchanged since I was last here as a little girl, I don't focus on my surroundings. I focus on Christopher, who's breathing hard, staring me down.

"What should I tell you, Kate, hmm?" His voice is dark and sharp as he sinks his hands into my hips and pulls me close. "That your birthday is my lock code, that I keep your horribly sewn handkerchief in my journal at work, that I've archived every single photograph you've ever published, that I lure your cat to my house for cuddles, that I walk into bakeries in the fall just to see the foods you love, that I sit in your mother's greenhouse and breathe in the scent of your favorite flowers, because anything you've touched, anything colored by the memory of you, are relics and I'm a supplicant?

"Should I tell you that since you came home and stayed, I've been losing my goddamn mind, because I couldn't believe the lie I'd told myself for so long, and that's why I wrote the note in those flowers? Should I tell you that was my confession—that my sad attempt to feel close to you was upheld by the delusion that it was better to have your hate than your apathy? That when I realized how badly I'd fucked up, I hoped it wasn't too late to have you look at me with anything besides loathing burning in your eyes?

"Should I tell you that I have *missed* you and *ached* for you for so long, Katerina Elizabeth Wilmot, that you define those words, and I have done everything I could to break inside me what drew me to you, but I'm not strong enough?"

He steps between my thighs, his hands diving into my hair as he presses the gentlest kiss to my mouth and breathes slowly, shakily. "I can't do it anymore. Denying myself you has been like battling the tide. If I fight it any longer, I'll drown. I'm yours," he says, reverent, quiet, like a prayer whispered in a church. "For as long as you'll have me."

Hot, fast tears slip down my cheeks. "Christopher," I whisper, my voice broken and hoarse.

"I'm so sorry," he mutters, kissing my cheeks, the tears wetting them. "I'm sorry for every tear I caused, every time I pushed you away rather than pulled you into my arms. I just wanted to protect you."

"From *what*?" I plead, fisting his shirt, dragging him nearer between my thighs, hooking my ankles around the backs of his legs. He's not going anywhere.

"Me," he admits. "I'm fucked up, Kate." He thumbs away a fresh trail of tears. "Look around you. My house is an homage to people who've been dead for decades. I haven't changed anything that hasn't broken beyond repair. I can barely tolerate it being touched by anyone else, repairmen, painters, landscapers. I've never left this city because when I think about how fucking huge and cruel the world is, it makes me spiral into a panic attack so bad, the first time it happened, I thought I was dying. What was I supposed to do? Say, *Hey, Kate, the world's at your feet, but would you mind shrinking it to this sliver of its possibilities for a fuckup like me?*"

"Stop it," I tell him sharply. "You aren't a fuckup. You lost something I cannot fathom losing, Christopher. You live with the knowledge of life's fragility that many of us have and choose the privilege of blithely ignoring." I look around the kitchen, smiling through my tears, memories of this place, full of joyful sounds and smells, returning to me. Gio cooking over the stove as he sang in Italian, loud and off-key. Nora singing along with him, somehow harmonizing to the meandering melody, dancing happily around the table as she set it in the next room.

"You've held on to what you have left of the people you loved most and *treasured* it," I whisper. I draw him closer, cupping his face, holding his eyes. "And with me, you did what you thought was right—" My voice catches, the sadness of what we've missed, of what we could have had, mingling with the relief that so many years of misery now make sense, cast in the light of this twisted sacrifice he believed we had to make, for him to live the way he needed, for me to live the way I needed, too. "Even though you were so completely wrong, you were just doing what you believed you should."

"I was wrong?" he asks quietly, his hands settling on my thighs, sliding up and down them, as if it soothes him, as if it helps him remember I'm still here.

"So wrong," I tell him through new tears. "Christopher, you grossly underestimated me, what we could have had, if I had known years ago the man I've spent the past month learning . . ." I shake my head, my thumb sweeping across his cheek. "You would have had me from the moment I knew I could be yours."

Air rushes out of him, pained.

"That day you came home," I whisper, "when you moved back in, boxes in your arms, and I saw you from the porch, I . . ." Swallowing nervously, I take his hand and set it over my heart. "A storm was coming as I saw you, and this . . . electricity crackled right through my skin. I told myself it was something in the air, the promise of what the sky had up its sleeve. But then there you were, serious and strong. You felt so different from when I'd last seen you, and yet so . . . familiar. After a whole childhood of being the little kid you ignored, it felt different, like we were both . . . equals, like maybe things could be different. I realized I *wanted* it to be different," I tell him, cupping my hand around his neck, drawing his head down to press a slow, soft kiss to his lips.

"I wanted to curl up to what was familiar," I whisper against his mouth. "The sound of your voice. Your belly laugh. The way a shirt stretched across your shoulders and that curl at the tips of your hair." His touch kneads my breast, wraps around my thigh, to my hip, tucking me closer to him, until our bodies meet, our chests heaving for air. "And I wanted to learn everything that was new, every part of you I didn't yet know."

Wordless, he pulls me closer, cradling my head, kissing me deep and slow. And for just a moment, that's all the world is—the two of us, arms wrapped around each other, in a kitchen filled with memories—sad, beautiful, bittersweet—fading into the corners, making space for what's to come.

I wrap my arms around his neck and kiss his jaw, his throat. "I need you."

His hands settle low on my waist and rock me against him. "I need you, too."

Christopher wraps my legs around his waist and walks us slowly through the kitchen, toward the foyer, where stairs lead up to the second floor.

I nuzzle his nose, then pull away just long enough to glance around, drinking in the truth of what Christopher said.

Nothing's changed.

The family room's just as I remember it, and through the pocket doors, the music room, too, where his mom taught piano, the dining room with the same table, same chairs I sat at as a tiny girl.

My heart twists. Now I know why he wouldn't want just anyone to see this place. Because the polished, devil-may-care man with his fancy *this*, latest *that*, lives in a home whose heart was built by his parents thirty-five years ago, a home rich with their lingering presence and memory. The man the world sees doesn't live here. The man holding me in his arms, who's opened his heart, lives here, straddling memory and moving forward, living with what he's lost, cherishing what he could keep.

I feel his eyes on me as he slows to a stop in the foyer.

"It's as lovely as I remember," I tell him.

He stares at me steadily as I meet his eyes. "I know I should change it."

"No, you shouldn't. Well, only if you want to." I set my hand on his heart, soothing it. "I love it, just as it is."

"You do?"

I nod, wrapping my arms around his neck again and pulling myself closer. "I love old things. The memories they carry of the people who touched them, who loved and lived with them. But I could see why you'd be wary of welcoming just anyone into this. If they didn't know you . . . like I do."

Drawing me close in his arms, he hugs me hard, his head resting on the crown of mine. We stand like that in the hallway, arms around each other, quiet, still. Against my hair, soft and hoarse, he says, "Thank you for saying that, Kate."

A lump settles in my throat. I squeeze him tight in my arms. "Thank you for giving me the chance to."

His sigh is heavy and content as I nuzzle his chest, listening to his heart's steady *lub-dub, lub-dub*. Christopher bends his head until our mouths meet. We're quiet as we kiss, as he walks us up the stairs and I cling to him.

"So," I tell him. As we turn into his bedroom, it hits me like a freight train. Nerves wrack my system. He's so experienced. And I'm so not. How many women has he had in this bed? How many wild, erotic things has he done that I can't even imagine?

"So," he says, kissing me, sweet and slow.

"This is where you . . ."

He gives me a funny look, flicking on the light switch. "Where I sleep?"

"You haven't"—I jerk my head toward the bed—"you know, done it here with—"

Christopher stops abruptly halfway to the bed. "Katerina, *no*." Resuming his stride, he walks us to the edge of the mattress and sits, holding me so I settle on bent knees, straddling his lap. "Listen to me."

"I'm listening."

He sighs, running his hands along my back. "They're not here. The other women I've been with. You're the first and only woman I'll have in my bed, and what I did before . . ." He clenches his jaw, then sighs heavily. "It was pleasurable for what it was, I won't deny that. It was always mutual and consensual. It passed the time, it gave me relief—albeit faint and temporary—from wanting you and telling myself I couldn't have you, but, Kate, this, here with you, in my bed, it's new for me."

Maybe it's his admission that in some sense, he's as inexperienced in this as I am, but it makes me brave enough to meet his eyes and tell him the truth.

"That helps to hear." I toy with his hair at the nape of his neck, searching for the words I want. "Because . . . it's new for me, too. Because I don't have . . . I haven't done . . . this . . . before."

His brow furrows. "Haven't done what?"

I stare at him, wishing it didn't feel so vulnerable, that it didn't feel so weighty, so exposed.

And yet, maybe I can love that weight, that exposure I feel as I think about seeing him, letting him see me. *All* of me.

Sensing my struggle, he tips his head, cupping my face, gentling my cheek with his thumb. "What is it, honey?"

"I haven't touched someone the way we touch," I tell him. "Haven't kissed them the way we kiss. Before you, I'd never done anything like what we did after paintball, like what we've been doing the past few weeks."

His eyes widen. "Kate. Are you telling me—"

"I'm inexperienced," I blurt. "Demisexuality and one-night stands don't exactly vibe, and traveling constantly for work doesn't lend itself to long-term, emotionally grounded physical intimacy. Before I knew how I worked, I tried some stuff, but I always stopped things pretty early on. It never felt right . . . until you."

He's staring at me, mouth agape, then his mouth snaps shut, his jaw jumps. I think maybe, just possibly, Christopher's a little upset. "Kate. After paintball . . . I threw you over my shoulder and humped you like an animal against a bathroom wall."

"Technically, it was a bathroom *door*."

"I tore off your underwear in the kitchen," he groans, digging the heels of his hands into his eye sockets.

"They were falling apart anyway."

"Katerina," he warns. His hands drop from his face and his eyes meet mine, dark and troubled. "I wish I'd known."

"I wasn't trying to keep it from you. I can't explain how incredible it felt, how good it felt, after so long, being so frustrated and misunderstood by too many people, to be with you and for it to feel *right*." I swallow past the lump in my throat. "That night after paintball just . . . happened. Same with the kitchen. Every moment since then, it's felt so right. And while I wish I could have found a way to tell you everything before this moment, you and I are messy people, Christopher. We don't do things the easy way, and we don't take the direct path. I'm here now, and I'm telling you. Please don't hold that against me."

He swallows thickly, his hand curling around my jaw. "I would never, Kate. I just . . . I could have hurt you, upset you—"

"But you didn't," I remind him, nuzzling my cheek into his palm. "You asked, and I answered, and you listened. It was perfect.

And now I'm nervous that it won't be perfect again, because we have *this* between us."

"Honey." He stares down at me with such absolute tenderness, such naked longing. "Nothing's coming between us anymore. It's just you and me." His lips brush my cheek, gentle as a whisper. "That's all that matters."

I peer up at him, naked though I'm clothed, free-falling even though I'm held tight. "Promise?"

He lifts his pinkie. I lift mine and hook it around his. And just like our childhood ritual, he kisses his thumb, I kiss mine. When our thumbs meet, soft, slow, like a tender, trusting kiss, his mouth meets mine, too, as he whispers, "Promise."

When we pull away, his eyes search mine. A sweet smile lifts his mouth.

"What is it?" I ask.

The smile deepens. "That night, after paintball, was that the first orgasm someone else gave you? The first—"

"Ugh!" I slug his shoulder, making him laugh as he leans in and kisses me harder. "The 'specialness' of 'firsts,' the notion of virginity, are patriarchal constructs, Christopher Petruchio. You are taking nothing *first* from me, you are not claiming me. I am not your property."

"You're right," he says, hoisting me higher in his arms and turning us onto the bed so I'm pinned beneath him.

"As you throw me around like a bag of bagels."

"Thankfully, I've never thrown bagels around on my bed or harbored fantasies about bagels like I'm harboring for you."

A smile sneaks out of me in spite of myself. "Please. Don't make a big deal out of it."

His expression turns serious as he brushes away the fine hairs from my face. "My satisfaction at your history, it isn't what you think, Kate."

"Oh?" I arch an eyebrow.

"No," he says, pressing a hot, wet kiss to my throat. "I'm just deeply aware there are many selfish at worst, mediocre at best, lovers out there, and you, Katerina Wilmot, deserve nothing but the best. Which is why I'm so satisfied. Because I am a lot of questionable things, but a selfish, mediocre lover is not one of them."

Being reminded again of his vast experience feels like whiplash. I shrink back in his arms. "Maybe this is a terrible idea."

He freezes over me. "Why?"

"*I* don't know what I'm doing."

"Every time you've touched me says otherwise," he murmurs, easing his hand along my shirt, rucking it up toward my belly.

"Really?" I ask, biting my lip when his hand splays across my bare skin, his fingers slipping beneath the waistband of my leggings.

"God, yes. You don't need dozens of partners to know how to be a good lover, Kate," he says roughly. "You just need to listen and learn, to trust and talk and try. You've done all of that. You've been an incredible lover to me."

I blush hot and fast. "You're not just saying that?"

"No." He teases his hand up my ribs, his knuckles grazing the edge of my breast. "I'm not."

Christopher searches my eyes as I look at him, my body tense with worry, my mind spinning in countless negative fantasies of how I might mess this up with him.

Slowly, he eases up on his elbow, then peers past me toward what I recognize is his bathroom, dark subway tiles winking against the faint glow of a nightlight. I catch the edge of a big soaker tub, the silhouette of unlit votive candles scattered across its edge.

"Do you like baths?" he asks.

I glance his way, my heart racing. A bath sounds heavenly. I got so hyperfixated on my editing that I didn't have time to shower when I realized I was running wildly late for my parents' house and Sunday dinner. Soaking in sudsy water, scrubbing my hair, relaxing until my limbs are loose and heavy, sounds perfect. "I love baths."

"Then I'll draw you a bath. Get you a glass of wine if you want, let you relax."

"A bath and a glass of wine sounds nice," I tell him.

He presses a soft kiss to my temple. "Good."

My eyes slip shut as I drop my head into the crook of his neck. "I'm sorry," I whisper. "That I'm so nervous. That I'm making us slow this down."

He pulls back and cups my face, holding my eyes. "I never want you to say that to me again, Kate. We take whatever time we need. There's no slow or fast. There's what's right for us."

"You don't . . . mind that? You won't need—"

"I need you. However I can have you." I must look skeptical, because he says, "I told you, I've gone the past six weeks without it, and I'll go as long as you need me to." He stares at me intently, stroking my cheek with his knuckles. "I got tested last week, so you know. My results were negative for STIs."

"I haven't had any partners since my last checkup," I tell him. "I was negative, too."

"Birth control?" he asks. "We can use condoms."

"I got the shot this week," I tell him, blushing when he smiles, satisfied that I was clearly planning ahead, like him. "I'm set for three months. I have a reminder in my calendar for when I need to get my next one."

"We can still use condoms," he says quietly. "Whatever you want—"

I shake my head. "I don't need them."

Silence holds between us as he stares down at me, his hands caressing my skin, calming my nerves, then he eases back from the bed and lifts me up with him, until we're both standing, our arms around each other.

"Now what?" I whisper, excitement crackling through me.

He presses a kiss to my temple, breathing me in. "Now I fill the tub with water, pour you a glass of wine, and do whatever you want me to."

A mighty flush warms my cheeks. "Oh."

His smile is soft and affectionate as he sways me in his arms. "The bath will take a little to fill. And the wine's downstairs. But we can start that last part now, though."

"Telling you . . . what I want? What about what you want? What you need?"

Christopher stares down at me, his eyes searching mine. He dips his head and presses a kiss to my temple, my cheekbone, my cupid's bow. "I have everything I want—you in my arms, and what I need . . . well, I just need to make you feel good. Tell me how you want it, what you want, anything."

"Kiss me." I don't recognize how breathy my voice is. How unsteady I am. "Now. Please."

His eyes spark. Then his mouth meets mine, sweet, velvet-hot strokes of his tongue, so delicate, cherishing, they make my eyes scrunch shut against a prick of tears.

Gently, he glides his hands down my waist, to my backside, and rubs it affectionately. My mouth falls open, a desperate, needy sound croaking out.

He smiles against my lips. "I love your horny sounds."

"Shut up," I whisper.

He laughs as I drag him with me and fall back onto the bed. When he bends down and kisses me, I sigh into it, pure euphoria.

So little has ever been easy between us. Yet here's this comfort, the way he already knows I like to be held and kissed, deep and slow, his tongue stroking mine, coaxing desire like a flame inside me, brighter, brighter—

Gently, he pulls away. I make a highly juvenile noise of discontent.

Smiling, Christopher kisses me once more, soft and sweet. "Now, how about we draw that bath?"

THIRTY-TWO

Christopher

My hand shakes as I pour two glasses of red wine, only a splash for me because I'm anxious not to tempt fate with more than the one glass that I had at dinner. Too much alcohol triggers that aching at the base of my neck, the familiar scraping pain in my eye sockets. The memory of having to leave after paintball still fresh, I don't want a migraine ruining another night with Kate.

I silently beg my brain, which has shown zero signs of ever caring what my plans are or how badly I don't want them to be ruined, to have mercy on me tonight.

And then I set down the bottle of wine, telling my hands to be steady. But still, they shake. Because I've never done this—never been with someone who means too much to me, whom I want so badly to make feel good and safe.

It's Kate, I remind myself, stopping in the foyer in front of a picture of our families side by side in the dog days of summer, sweaty and smiling, sparklers in our hands. There she is, small and smiling, knobby-kneed and freckled, squinting at the camera. I stare at her and smile myself.

It's Kate. Kate who snorts when she laughs and gags when she smells barbecue. Kate who loves helpless creatures as deeply as she hates injustice. Kate who teases and touches me like no one else ever has, who gets under my skin and fires me up, who kisses me like it's the last time she'll get to and trembles when I touch her like she never wants it to end.

As I take the stairs to the second floor and my bedroom, I repeat it like a mantra: *It's Kate. It's Kate. It's Kate.*

Wineglasses in hand, I stop and lean at the threshold of my room to soak up the view. Kate sits on the edge of my bed, staring into the dancing flames of the gas fireplace I turned on. She looks pensive, breathtaking, bathed in firelight that paints her skin gold, turns her russet hair burnished bronze.

She looks perfect. She looks at home.

Glancing my way, she smiles, and my heart sighs at its rightness.

"Liar," she says.

I push off the doorway, frowning. "What are you talking about?"

"Some things *have* changed around here." She pats the mattress. "You got rid of the race-car bed."

I smile, relieved, and hand Kate her glass of wine. "I tried to upsize, but they don't make them any bigger."

She takes the wine without any questions about how small my pour is, then stands and tips her glass my way. I tip mine to hers. Our glasses kiss and *clang* quietly, still humming when we bring them to our lips and drink.

Kate sighs happily. "That's a good wine. It's also an expensive wine, isn't it?"

"It is."

She peers into the wine's depths, swirling it in her glass. "Maybe I do like money a little, if it buys this."

A laugh jumps out of me, and I curl an arm around her, bringing her close, pressing a kiss to her forehead. "Money can't buy happiness. But it can buy you really good food and wine, and that's damn close."

"Cheers to that," she says, sipping her wine again, then setting her head against my shoulder. Peering toward the bathroom, she goes very still. "Wait. I was supposed to watch the tub as it filled, wasn't I?"

"Shit." I nearly drop my wineglass as I set it down, then run into the bathroom.

"Sorry!" she yells from behind me.

"It's all right," I call over my shoulder, reaching for the handles to turn off the spigot. "It barely overflowed. Not too much water on the floor. Just be careful—"

"I started daydreaming," she says, rushing into the bathroom, clearly not having heard me, "and completely lost track of—*ack*!"

Slipping on the water that's spilled onto the tiles, Kate slides across the floor, then slams into me. I wrap an arm around her and try to steady us, pinwheeling my free arm until I catch a towel that's hanging nearby, but it just rips the towel rack out of the wall.

I clutch Kate inside my arms as we fall, me onto my back, Kate on top of me. We land with a loud, wet *splat*.

The room is stunningly quiet.

After a prolonged stretch of silence, Kate whispers, "I am *so* sorry."

"It's okay," I wheeze.

She picks up her head from where I'd tucked it against my shoulder to protect her, eyes wide as she looks at me. "Why do you sound like that?"

"Air," I croak as I point to my chest, then lift a finger. "Just need a minute."

She bites her lip. Her face is getting progressively redder.

"Swear to God, Katerina," I wheeze. "If you laugh right now—"

A cackle bursts out of her so loud it echoes off the tiles. "I'm sorry!" she shrieks, tears starting in the corners of her eyes. "I can't help it when this happens." She doubles over so hard on another cackling laugh, air wheezes out of *her*.

My shoulders start to shake as I fight a laugh, not knowing how my lungs can handle it when I've had the wind knocked out of me. Despite my worries, a hoarse, deep laugh leaves me as my head flops back onto the wet floor.

"Christopher!" She's still laughing as she buries her face in my chest. "I'm so sorry. I'm the worst."

"Hush." I drag her back down into my arms, pulling her across my body and clasping her jaw in my hand, stealing a deep, hot kiss. Gently, I tug her lip between my teeth and earn a delicious, tiny head-to-toe shudder. "You are the *best*."

Her laughter dies away. She looks at me, unblinking, and brings a hand to my face, sweeping back the hair that's fallen onto my forehead. "I think you are, too."

Leaning in, she brushes her lips over mine, sweet and fleeting. "Let me clean this up," she says. "Then I'll call you in, okay?"

"I can help—"

"Christopher." She kisses my jaw, my throat, her hand sliding down my chest. My hips lift, waiting for her to finally touch me where I ache so badly for her, but she stops just short of where I want. "Please let me clean up my mess."

Grumbling a little about it, I sit up with her carefully, then let her push me out of the bathroom, before she shuts the door in my face.

Suddenly the door opens a crack, one beautiful blue-gray-green eye blinking at me. "Oh, and by the way. Just to be clear, when I call you in. Please be"—pink dances up the sliver of her cheek that I can see—"clothed. I think I can only take one of us naked at a time, to start things off."

I lean into the crack of the door and steal a kiss. "Clothed it is."

———————

Now it's my turn to sit on the edge of the bed, staring into the fire.

"Ready!" she calls.

I straighten like I've been shocked. Clearing my throat, I stand from the bed. "Coming," I call back.

"Heh," she says. "So soon?"

"Watch it, Wilmot," I tell her, even though I'm smiling, reaching for the door and once again realizing my hand isn't steady.

"Ooh, I've been Wilmot-ed. And I thought calling me *Katerina* was as stern as you could sound."

Opening the door, I tell her, "Katerina, you haven't even seen stern . . ." My voice dies off.

A mountain of bubbles surrounds her, obscuring most of her body, but not all of it. The tips of her bare toes. Two knobby knees. The freckled tops of her shoulders. All that hair, piled high on her head, delicate wet tendrils plastered to her neck.

Her face, flushed and lovely, tight with nerves.

"Take a look," she blurts, lifting one long arm out of the water, pointing toward the polished, now-dry tiles, the neat stack of folded damp towels in the far corner where the broken towel rack rests. "I can sure make a mess, but at least I can clean it up, too. What do you think?"

Staring at her, I drag the door shut behind me. "Unimaginably lovely."

She frowns. "That's a strange way to describe a tidied-up bathroom."

I ease onto the edge of the tub and set her wine beside her. "I'm not talking about the bathroom."

Her cheeks stain deep, rose pink. "This tub," she says, staring down at the bubbles, "is incredible. Get your digs in now. I will forgive anything so long as I'm soaking in this thing, even out-landishly sweet compliments like that."

I smile, guiding a hair off her cheek that's stuck there. "Are you telling me that all I should have done when I tried to fix things with you was throw you over my shoulder and toss you in my tub?"

She laughs. "Yep! Little did I know, all *I* had to do was get drunk and spill my guts for you to be nice to me."

My heart clenches. "Just 'nice'?"

"Well . . ." She makes a thoughtful face. "Maybe a little more than nice. Maybe caring. And unexpectedly gentle. And thought-ful. And excellent at providing upright orgasms, which I have yet to master for myself."

She's rambling. Which means she's nervous. I rest a hand over hers, tracing with my fingertips the droplets of water beading her skin. That's when I feel her trembling like I have been, too.

"Kate, honey—"

"I'm okay," she says, flipping her palm, squeezing my hand hard. "I promise."

She slides forward in the water, wrapping her arms around her knees, baring a long expanse of smooth, pale back that I've seen only once before, the night at her apartment that she gave me right back what I'd given her. It does not feel remotely the same. "Would you wash my back?" she asks. "My shoulder's still a little too stiff to reach it."

I set my hand between her shoulder blades, tracing my finger-tips down her vertebrae. "Yes," I tell her, savoring the trail of goose bumps that blooms on her skin in the wake of my touch.

I reach for a washcloth and dip it in the water, then glide it over her back. She sets her chin on her knees and sighs. "That feels nice."

"Good." I scrub over her shoulders, tracing carefully over the one she broke. "Kate, should it still be stiff like that? Do you need physical therapy?"

She turns her head slightly, giving me her profile, the sight of her teeth, sinking into her lip. "I might."

Bending, I kiss her shoulder. "You have to take better care of yourself, Katerina. Or I'm going to get very high-handed and do it for you."

A smile tugs at her mouth. "I'm sort of bad at self-care, but I'm trying to be better, and you seem to enjoy bossing me around. Maybe we can meet in the middle."

I smile against her skin and kiss it again before sitting up. "Deal."

She reaches for my hand resting on her shoulder with the wash-cloth and guides my touch down her arm, into the mysterious sea of bubbles. I follow her lead, scrubbing her arm as she leans against the tub on a sigh and rests her temple against my hip. "I didn't real-ize how much I neglected myself until I came home. I just got so hyperfocused on work, things like clothes without holes in them and regular meals felt like annoying interferences.

"I loved that work, and I'm proud of what I did. I will always want to use my camera to wake people up to the world's wrongs, wrench them out of their complacency by showing them what's so much harder to ignore and do nothing about when you *see* it. But I can also recognize that work took a hell of a lot out of me. I'm ready to move on and take better care of myself."

A knot's in my throat as I bring the washcloth back up her arm and guide it slowly across her chest, above the bubbles concealing her breasts. "And let others take care of you, too?"

"Not just anyone." She hesitates, then glances up at me. "I think I'll start with a few people I trust. Who matter to me the most."

I swallow roughly, searching her eyes.

"Like you," she says quietly, grabbing my wrist, pulling me in. Her kiss is cool and faint. It feels like forgiveness. It feels like love breathed over me, seeping through my skin, to my bones, to the heart pounding in my chest.

"If I got to do one thing for the rest of my life," I tell her, "it would be taking care of you, Kate."

She stares at me, wide-eyed, a fierce flush flooding her cheeks.

I can't believe I just said that, just revealed so much. I reach past her, dragging the washcloth down her arm.

"You'd choose that over inventorying your empire?" she says, a smile suffusing her voice.

I narrow my eyes as I stare at her. "You know I would. None of that would matter if you weren't . . ." I wash her neck, which she offers me, tipping her head away. Bending, I press a kiss there, breathing her in. "It wouldn't mean anything to me if you weren't with me to share it."

"That's a good answer," she sighs.

"I know," I whisper against her neck.

She laughs, loud and smoky, then she's there, turning, her wet hand on my cheek, her mouth finding mine, hungry and hot, tongues stroking, breaths echoing in the space. I lean in, sinking a hand into her hair, wanting her, drinking her in.

Her hair starts to fall loose as I tug it, tipping her head, coaxing her mouth to open for mine, deepening our kiss.

"Kate," I mutter roughly between kisses. "Can I take out the bird's nest?"

She gasps, then pulls away and splashes me. "Asshole!"

I laugh, splashing her back. "Relax, Katydid. I love your bird's nest."

"Some way to show it," she grumbles, turning her back on me.

I lean in and press another kiss to her neck, nuzzling her hair, breathing her in. "I might be a little obsessed with it, actually."

She turns my way, her nose brushing mine. "You're obsessed with my bird's nest?"

"God, yes. I want to see it down."

She searches my eyes. Then she lifts her hands toward her hair. My hands shoot out and wrap around them, stopping her.

"You want to do it?" she asks.

I nod.

She smiles. "Go ahead, then. You can take it down."

Her hands fall away. I reach for the tie, unwrapping it cautiously, going slower than I know she would, but wanting to be careful not to hurt her. And then the tie is in my hands, free of her hair. I set it on the edge of the tub, then I unwind her hair in slow circles, until it spills down her back, a chestnut waterfall that steals my breath.

It sinks into the bathwater, so long it lands near her hips. I stare at it, gliding my hands down the silky strands as they turn wetter.

"You're so quiet," she says.

I spread my hands across her shoulders, down her arms, to the waves of hair floating in the water. "I might have . . ." I swallow roughly. "I might have wanted to do this for a while."

She smiles, carving dimples in her cheeks. "To touch my hair?"

I nod.

She leans back, dipping her head in the water, so her hair is submerged, dancing like dark, bare trees swaying against the dawn.

"You can wash it if you want," she says, gathering bubbles toward her chest. "In fact, some more bubbles might be great right about now."

I pour in more bubble bath and turn on the water, then identify the bottles of shampoo and conditioner lining the tub's edge.

Quiet settles between us as I scrub her hair, as Kate bounces her knees and wiggles her toes at the edge of the tub, humming to herself.

As I rinse the conditioner out of her hair, she peers up at me and asks, "What is it about hair that you like?"

"*Your* hair."

"Okay, what is it about *my* hair? Why did you want to take it down yourself?"

"It's always up," I tell her, pouring water down her hair to rinse it again. "It felt like, when it came down, if I had the privilege of being the one to do it, it would be . . . intimate."

A charmed smile warms her face. "So you *do* read those historical romances Jules foists on all of us."

"I might have read a few," I admit, holding her eyes, begging my body to stay put together as she leans close and scrapes her fingers through my hair, then presses a gentle kiss to my temple, my cheek.

"Kiss me, Kate."

She smiles against my cheek. "I am."

"On my mouth," I say roughly as she kisses my nose, my jaw, coming closer and closer.

"Kiss me," I beg.

She does, her sweet mouth finding mine, soft sips and bites that make me chase her for more, that make her smile against my lips as I growl in frustration.

"You like when I tease you," she whispers.

I nod, my hands drifting down her hair and her back. "Almost as much as I like when you give me what I want."

She laughs. "And what do you want?"

More, I almost say. More than fleeting touch and taste, because mere fragments and edges of her body can't sustain me anymore. I want to see her, all of her, spread out on my bed, bathed in firelight as I learn every corner of her. But I don't want her to feel pressured. I want her to feel safe. I want to show her I can wait.

"Maybe I should tell you what I want first?" she says softly.

I nod.

Her eyes hold mine. Her hands settle on my shoulders. A soft smile lifts her mouth. "I want you to take me to your bed."

Oh God. My body's taut as a string, one touch away from snapping. "You're sure?"

She nods quickly, a blush creeping up her cheeks. "I'm sure. I'm ready."

I reach for an oversized towel as I stand and hold it up, averting my gaze.

She steps out of the tub and raises her arms as she leans into the towel's edge. Then, on a laugh, she spins, rolling herself up in it like a burrito.

Kate stands in front of me, water beading her freckled skin, her hair wet and long, draping down her waist. I watch her do this sensible task, reach for a new towel, wrap it around her hair, and wring it dry as she smiles up at me.

I love you, I think, watching her. *I want this every day for the rest of my life.*

Kate breaks me from my trance, setting a hand on my chest, guiding me out of the bathroom, until the backs of my knees connect with my bed and I drop to the mattress.

Standing in the bracket of my legs, bathed in firelight, she reaches for the towel's tucked-in edge and undoes it, letting it flutter to the ground.

My heart stops. Thank God, for only just a moment, before I'm revived, my heart beating like new, harder, urgent, as I stare at her. Glowing skin dusted with constellations of freckles on her shoulders and arms, her knees and calves. Soft, slight breasts with their rosy tips, the slight taper of her waist, the flare of her hips, the long stretch of her legs, wiggling at the knees.

"Say something," she whispers.

I shake my head, setting my hands on her hips, drawing her close. I press a kiss to her heart and set my head there. "No words do your loveliness justice."

Her hand settles in my hair, stroking gently. "That's a sweet thing to say."

"It's a *true* thing to say," I tell her.

"Do you think . . . you could be naked, too?" she asks a little unsteadily.

I pull away and stare up at her. "Now?"

She smiles, all bright teeth and deep dimples and firelit freckles. "Yes. Now."

I reach for the back of my shirt collar instinctively, but as my hands did with hers, poised over her hair, her touch stops me. "Can I?" she asks.

Heat rushes through me as I stare up at her. "Yes."

Stepping closer, Kate reaches for my shirt at the hem and lifts it up my chest, over my head. Her hands drift around my shoulders, down my arms. "You're so . . . solid."

I laugh quietly, then stand as she reaches for my buckle and undoes it, then unbuttons my jeans. "Solid?" I ask.

She nods. "You feel like . . . one time, I was in Australia, and these winds came out of nowhere, so violent, I swore they were going to rip me off the earth and launch me right into space. I panicked, wrapped myself around a tree that was just as thick as my arms could reach, so steady and solid, and I clung to it until the wind died. That's . . . you." She smiles up at me, her touch gently sifting through my hair. "My tree in the storm."

My hands go to her hips, as I swallow against a lump in my throat.

"Now, stop making me sentimental." She tugs at my jeans, and I help her, shoving them down, stepping out of them, kicking them away.

Her hands settle at my boxer briefs, drifting along the waistband. I let out a slow, steadying breath.

She peers up, looking worried. "Is this okay?"

"Very." I cup a hand around her neck, massaging it, soothing her. Then she tugs my briefs down, kneeling as she goes. She stands, eyes averted before they snap up and find mine. A wine-red blush spills up her throat and floods her cheeks.

"Now what?" she whispers.

I smile, gliding my hands along her arms, savoring how beautiful she is—soft and warm and *here.* "Now we lie down."

Kate leaps onto the bed and lands like a starfish, making me laugh. I crawl onto the bed after her, arms caged over her as she smiles up at me, beautiful and a little nervous. "You can look at me," I tell her. "Touch me. Wherever you want."

Her eyes dance down my body, then widen as she looks at me, where I'm so hard, my cock is curved up against my belly.

I start to ease onto my side, but she stops me, holding me over her. Then she sets her hands on my chest, her touch smoothing across my muscles, tracing my nipples. "Christopher," she whispers.

"Yes, Kate." My voice is tight, my hands making fists with the blanket on either side of her. I have never felt so raw, so hungry, so desperate to touch and be touched.

She drifts her knuckles down my stomach, watching in fascination as the muscles jump beneath her touch. "You are very, very lovely," she whispers.

"So are you," I tell her, forcing myself to stay still, to let her learn me like I promised myself I would.

My breath comes rough and ragged as her fingertips trace the line of my hip, the muscles knitting my groin. Tentatively, she strokes a palm up my thigh, then higher, testing the weight of my cock along her palm, curling her fingers around it.

"Whenever we've been together," she says, "you've known how to touch me."

"You've told me how, too," I tell her. "You've shown me."

She nods, a furrow in her brow as she touches me so gently, experimenting with how I feel, how the skin moves over my length as she strokes it. "Can you show me how to touch you?" she asks quietly.

I reach past her for the nightstand and pull out lube. Then I open her palm and pour some in. She squeals quietly. "This feels delightful," she says.

I snort a laugh. "It feels even more delightful when it's being used on you." Lying back, I take her hand, wrap it lower, at the base of my cock, then stroke up, rotating her wrist, working the lube around me inside her hand, then dragging it back down. Heat bursts through me. My toes curl into the blankets.

She watches me move her hand in fascination, then falters when I let go. "Why?" She peers up, anxious. "Why'd you stop?"

"You know what to do," I tell her tightly, struggling to breathe normally as she eases closer, one leg draped over mine, and strokes me again.

My eyes want to shut. My heart wants to beat right out of my chest. Being touched like this has never felt so incredible.

"Is this okay?" she asks.

I nod quickly, cupping her neck, bringing her closer. "I like being kissed while you touch me, too."

She kisses me eagerly, open-mouthed, her touch uneven and unsure, but gaining confidence when I start making the kinds of sounds I can't help, deep, rough gasps that make me crush her against me, make my hips pump my cock into her hand, faster and faster. She takes my cue and moves faster, intensifies her grip. "Yeah, that's it," I tell her. "That's perfect, honey. So good. Just like that."

She smiles against the crook of my neck and presses a wet, long kiss there.

My body's tight as I groan and beg for her to keep going, my breathing sharp and short as she pumps me faster and teases my neck, my chest, with more soft, wet kisses.

"I like to kiss you, too," I tell her, "when we're doing this."

"You are kissing me."

I smile. "More than your lips."

On a breathy laugh, she falls back on the bed and lets me ease over her, my hand lifting her breast, palming it, teasing her nipple. I kiss below her ear, the hollow of her throat, the place where I feel her heart flying beneath her ribs.

When I suck her nipple into my mouth, she sinks her nails into my back and gasps, her grip on my cock tightening, her pace accelerating.

"God, Kate," I pant, sucking at her other nipple, rocking my hips into her hands. "I'm gonna come if you don't slow down."

"Then come," she says, pushing me back enough to kiss her way down my neck. When she sinks her teeth into my pec, right above my nipple, and bites, chasing it with her tongue, I shout and come all over her hand, thick and fast.

"Keep going," I manage, guiding her hand to move. "That's it. Gentler. Like I did with you. Until I tell you I can't anymore. Until being touched is too much." I slow her hand to a stop, easing it away, and drop my head to her neck, breathing roughly. "God," I groan.

"Wow," she whispers. "That was fast."

I bark a laugh and flop back onto my bed, reaching for the

towel on the floor that she abandoned from her bath. Kate takes it from me, wiping her hand clean, then carefully wiping me clean, too, before she tosses it aside. She sits upright, staring down at me, her touch softly trailing my thighs, my hips.

"Come here," I tell her, easing up on my elbow, hand outstretched.

Kate stares at me still, firelight flickering in her eyes. Then she crawls over me and pushes me right back onto the bed.

THIRTY-THREE

Kate

I thought the first time I found a person I wanted to share this with—nakedness, touch, desire—it would feel like a bridge crossed, a height ascended, a power discovered that I hadn't known before.

But as I crawl across the bed over Christopher, seeing firelight kiss his body and turn his eyes to ochre flames, as my skin touches his and we both let out harsh, winded breaths, it feels nothing like that. Not like I've crossed a bridge, but like I finally feel safe to stay with a truth that was always inside me. Not as if a height's been ascended, but as if I'm free-falling, rushing wind and the promise of a safe landing below, sweet and smooth, welcoming me into its depths. Not like I've discovered some new power, but like power itself has dissolved, leaving me and this man beneath me as naked as we were born yet infinitely more vulnerable—our innocence lost, our eyes open, knowing the loss and pain life can bring, embracing each other in spite of it.

"Kate," he says, his voice low and quiet, his hand warm and rough, scraping back my hair, cupping my jaw. "Come here, honey. Let me touch you."

I stare down at him, the beautiful breadth of his body, broad, heavy arms splayed wide across the bed, one leg lazily bent, the other hanging, thick and strong, off its edge. I have never wanted someone so much. I have never felt more overwhelmed.

Christopher seems to sense this, because he takes my elbow and gently tugs me with him across the bed, until we collapse together onto cool, downy pillows. He slips his arm beneath my neck and curls me against his body, his other hand low across my back, rubbing soothing circles. I tip up my head to see him, to try to orient myself amid this emotional vertigo. His lips brush the bridge of my nose, then one side, then the other.

"What are you doing?" I whisper.

"What I've wanted to do for a long time," he whispers back. "Kissing your freckles."

My cheeks heat. "You like my freckles?"

"Like I 'like' your bird's nest—I *love* them."

"Oh." My hand settles on his waist, then begins exploring his body—dense muscles, smooth, warm skin, these fascinating divots joining his hips to his backside that feel like they were designed for my hands to be there. "These divots are nice," I tell him.

Christopher smiles against my cheek, then kisses me there, too. "Thank you."

"I don't feel like divots should make me feel . . . squirmy, but they do."

His smile deepens. "Want to know a part of you that makes me feel 'squirmy'?"

I nod quickly, as his hand slides lower down my back, his fingertips tracing the dimples at either side of my spine, right above my backside.

"These," he says softly, his mouth trailing my jaw, below my ear, where his voice is dark and hushed. "When you gave me a taste of my own medicine at the apartment, took off your shirt, and made sure I saw your topless back—"

"Not my most rational moment."

He grins against my skin and groans. "A back and two butt dimples have never been so erotic. You have no idea how much

I've stroked off to that memory—your back and waist and those dimples—all the ways I've had you in my mind, pleased you, made you scream my name."

My body moves reflexively against him. I feel wet between my thighs, a sweet, fierce ache building from touching him, from the words he's saying.

"I like knowing that," I tell him. "I like it when you tell me."

He brushes a knuckle against my hardened nipple, kissing me gently. "I can tell."

"I want you to touch me." I take his hand and set it between my thighs. "Please."

Christopher stares down at me as he tenderly parts my legs and strokes between them. "I want to touch you, too."

I gasp and bite my lip against a noise that's stuck in my throat, loud and uninhibited. He's so gentle, so attentive, watching me.

"Tell me, Kate," he says quietly.

"Faster," I whisper. "Harder."

I reach down and guide his hand, showing him what I've learned about myself, what I recognize has built my arousal in the past and yet don't recognize at all. Because it's different, when you show someone else your nakedness, your need; when they cherish and protect it by listening like he does, groaning in quiet pleasure as my hand falls away because he's doing what I showed him, and I can't do anything but lie there and grip his arm, his hair, his chest, as he kisses me and makes me fall apart.

As he kisses me, touches me, pleasure spirals through me like a vortex, swirling from the edges of my limbs to the heart of me, and culminates in a sharp, fast release that makes me whimper against his kiss.

"Christ," he groans as he brings me with him, easing onto his back. He kisses me slowly, brushes his knuckles along my cheek, and I wedge my leg over his, feeling my body both sensitized and already needy for more.

Our eyes meet. His are tight, his expression almost pained.

"What is it?" I ask.

Christopher sighs against my mouth, shifting restlessly as my leg works itself higher over his, as my hand lands on his stomach and drifts down, over that trail of hair that leads to his erection, thick and hard, arced tight against his stomach. "I nearly came from touching you right now," he says. "And I *just* came."

"That's good?"

He smiles down at me. "It's a little disconcerting. First I came in your hand after two minutes. Now this. I have to demonstrate my sexual prowess at *some* point."

I can tell he's being lighthearted by the way his eyes warm as they look at me, the way his hand affectionately rubs circles on my back. I like that we can joke while we do this, that it's not all long stares and intense emotions. Our laughter is like a life float, when I'm nearly drowning in all the feelings flooding me.

"Your sexual prowess, what you've learned from being with . . . others," I tell him, fighting a vicious stab of jealousy. "I don't say this as judgment—I don't think I could ever want or do that. I don't understand it."

His thumb circles my palm. "I know. Which is why I feel very lucky, very . . . honored, that you want it with me."

A weird little lump settles in my throat. "After all you've experienced—"

"Kate," he pleads.

"—will you want only me? Day in and day out, will I be enough?"

His eyes search mine, so intent. Then he leans in, kissing me softly, his nose nuzzling mine. "You think once I had you, I'd ever want another soul? When I had your eyes and your touch and your smart mouth and your vicious races that remind me how damn old I'm getting, that I'd ever look at another and want anyone but you?"

I bite my lip, feeling it wobbling. "Oh."

"Oh," he mutters. A muscle jumps in his jaw. His eyes darken as he draws me closer. "Katerina Elizabeth, I told you I'm yours for as long as you'd have me, and I meant it. Tell me you believe me. Tell me you trust me."

Heat spills through me, longing and need, as he dances his fingers over mine, staring into my eyes. I drift the sole of my foot along his calf, feeling hard, dense muscle and soft, springy hair.

Suddenly I have an image in my head of Christopher asleep, rumpled in his sheets, sunshine sweeping down the landscape of his smooth skin and broad, hard muscles, caressing the curly licks of his hair. I think about photographing him when he rolls over in bed and wakes up grinning, teasing me about my bird's nest and wrapping a long coil of my hair around his finger. I picture us in the kitchen, quiet and sunlight and dust motes dancing in the air, sitting at the island, me in one of his big soft shirts, capturing with the camera the moment his dark eyes meet mine over a cup of coffee.

I want to chart the years of his life with my eyes, my hands, my camera, when those faint lines at the corners of his eyes etch themselves deeper from so much laughter that we'll share. I want to drag him places without a plan and only a Polaroid around my neck to fill the walls of this place with garlands of memories captured in tiny squares of joy. I want him for now. For always. And he wants me, too.

For as long as you'd have me, he said.

I plan to do my damnedest to be sure that is indeed a *very* long time.

"I believe you," I tell him, my voice sure and steady. "I trust you."

He sighs in satisfaction, dragging me over his body until I straddle his lap. He kisses my mouth, hot and slow, his hands tracing my body, settling at my backside and squeezing affection-ately. I shift over him, easing the ache between my legs as I rub against his length.

Air rushes out of Christopher as he stares up at me.

"Is this okay?" I ask.

He laughs roughly. "'Okay' is a deeply inadequate word for how I feel about this." His hands drift along my waist. "In fact, I would not mind at all if you . . ." He clears his throat. Is *he* blush-ing? "If you moved about two feet up the bed."

I blink at him, then do the math. My mouth falls open. "But that's your head."

"My face," he says, smiling. "Yes. Do you know what you'd do there?"

It's not hard to intuit. But it still makes me blush fiercely. "Yes . . . and no."

Christopher's hands are gentle on my hips, his smile soft. "Do you want to try?"

Insecurity pounds through me. So I answer him honestly. "I don't know."

"That's okay, honey." His hands travel down my hips, then lower, massaging gently. "We can stay just like this."

I shut my eyes, feeling his hands making this glorious circuit from my hips to my ass to my thighs, then back up, and I think about how it might feel for him to do that, while his mouth and tongue teased and tasted me, coaxed my body to orgasm. To be so close to him while he did it. To touch his hair and feel his sounds against me, to feel so lost to him and at the same time, to have so much control.

And suddenly I am incredibly aroused.

"I think maybe . . ." I clear my throat. "I want to try."

His eyes hold mine. "There's no pressure, Kate. Only if you want . . ."

I'm already crawling up his body, stopping long enough for him to pull me close and share a long, deep kiss. "I want," I whisper.

He exhales roughly. Then Christopher reaches around and eagerly knocks away the pillows except for one that he fluffs below his head and drops onto with a contented sigh.

I smile. "You're acting like a kid at Christmas."

"This is way better than Christmas," he says, grinning. "Now, get up here and sit on my face."

I slap a hand over my eyes and shriek a laugh. "You can't just *say* that!"

"I believe I just did." His hand lands with a sweet swat on my butt that makes my thighs clench on either side of his ribs. "Get up here."

Sighing but grinning like a goofball, I ease up a little higher, then stop. "Wait. What are the logistics of this?"

"Grab the headboard," he says.

I do that.

"Now, kneel on either side of my head."

I do that, too. And I blush fiercely. "Oh, God. I'm doing this."

"*We're* doing this." He presses a slow, tender kiss to my thigh that makes me feel a little more relaxed about having my vulva three inches from his face. Lifting his shoulders, he says, "Try tucking your calves beneath me."

With a little shimmy, I'm closer now, and the weight of his shoulders settles on my calves. The pressure and heaviness make me sigh contentedly.

"What's that sigh mean?" he asks.

I smile down at him. "It means it's good."

He grins up at me, something so young and sweet about it, I reach down and slip my fingers through his hair. His hands spread across my hips as he holds my eyes, then gently eases me toward him, just enough pull to show me what he wants but not so hard that I couldn't push away and show him I'm not ready.

My breath is rushing out of my lungs, not out of fear or anxiety, but out of a sheer thrill as I let him guide me down, as I feel his mouth, confident and sure, warm and wet, the first sweep of his tongue, its gentle circling of my clit, the way he learned after paintball, that night in the kitchen. He remembered so perfectly. I gasp as he does it again, a little harder. My grip in his hair tightens. "Like that," I whisper.

He groans quietly, and its hum against my skin makes me jolt, then laugh in pleasure. My knuckles are white as I clutch the headboard, trying to brace myself over him.

He pulls away with a wet *smack* that sounds so intimate, those noises I think bodies might only make when they're doing this. "Kate." His voice is a rough rock's edge, a bonfire's smoky heat. "I said *sit* on my face, and I meant it."

I gulp, my fingers sifting through his beautiful dark hair. "But what if I smother you with my vulva?"

He grins so wide, it carves two deep dimples down his cheeks. "You won't smother me with your vulva."

"How do you know?"

"You won't, honey. I could bench-press you without breaking a sweat, Kate. If I can't breathe, I'll move you, easy."

"But it's going to stress me out, and if I'm stressed, I can't orgasm."

He peers up at me, a little furrow in his brow. "How about a signal?" he offers.

"Good idea," I tell him, my voice wobbling a little as he sneaks a kiss where my thigh meets my pelvis, then he nuzzles my clit. "H-how about a double tap?"

"Not on your ass," he mutters, licking me again, kissing my clit in rhythmic, soft motion. "I'll be slapping that."

"Says who?" I yelp.

"Says you," he groans, "judging by how much wetter my mouth just got when I said that."

"Well." I clear my throat. "I suppose I like a little spank here and there."

He grins against my thigh. "How about a double tap on your leg?"

"Good plan."

"It's settled," he says roughly, his hips shifting on the bed. "Now kindly sit on my face, and come all over it."

I bite my lip, smiling at how much I like his words, their surety, like a hand holding mine not because he doesn't think I can stand on my own but because it's better when it's *us*, on this path together. I relax my thighs, still holding on to the headboard with one hand, and let my weight fall more fully on him. A gasp tears out of me. It's so intense this way, so wonderful.

Christopher groans so deeply, I feel it reverberate in his throat as he sinks his hands into my ass and moves me tighter against him.

My mouth falls open as *his* mouth makes me fall apart. Slow, velvet strokes of his tongue. Teasing flicks and hot, wet kisses that make my thighs shake, make my hips start to move on their own. But each time I start to get close to release, something manages to jar me out of it, whether it's him shifting beneath me, triggering my worry that I'm smothering him, or a shift in my hips so I won't get a foot cramp that makes that building heat inside me subside.

Easily, Christopher lifts my hips away and presses a kiss to my thigh, breathing roughly as he stares up at me. "What do you need?"

"I . . ." I slip my fingers through his hair. "I can't focus. My brain keeps dancing away and it feels so good but I can't stay with it. I'm sorry—"

In one smooth motion, I'm on my back on the bed, Christopher's body over mine, pinning me to the mattress. "Stop apologizing for what you need," he says sternly, softening his admonishment with a kiss. I taste myself on him and feel myself arch into his body. "Katerina, tell me you understand."

My eyes slip shut with pleasure. "I understand."

He reaches for a pillow and kisses me again. "Now, lift your hips."

I lift my hips as he sets a pillow beneath my butt. "Tell me you won't apologize anymore."

"I won't apologize anymore."

"Good girl."

I gasp as he gives me his body's weight, the pillow beneath me bringing our bodies so close. Relief sweeps through me as that familiar comfort of pressure settles my limbs, quiets the static in my brain.

"There," he says against my temple. "That's better, isn't it?"

I nod. "So much better."

"Kate, honey." He nuzzles me until I open my eyes. "Have you never . . ." He touches me gently, his hands moving in soothing strokes down my arms and waist. "Have you ever had someone inside you this way?"

I shake my head.

"We'll go slow." He kisses my eyelids, the tip of my nose, my chin. His hand cups my breast and fondles it gently.

"That makes it better?" I ask, already squirming underneath him. "I've been so close, so long, Christopher. I want to come."

"It makes it much better," he says quietly. "I promise it'll be worth the wait."

Gently, he adjusts my hips until his erection is right up against where I ache so deeply for more. Then he starts to move over me, hot and heavy, still kissing, his hands in my hair, brushing every sensitive corner of my body, teasing my nipples and breasts.

I've always "known" time is a construct, an abstraction, but now I understand it—how minutes can become meaningless, hours wholly immaterial. All that exists is him and me and this, the knowledge that we're safe, that he wants me, that I want him, too.

"Feels so good," I whisper brokenly, as pleasure starts to consume me like fire curling paper, scorching and swift. I scrape my fingers through his hair and stare up at him, his eyes fixed on me. I'm free, weightless, arching my back as I move under him and cry his name, begging him not to stop.

Release is a mercy, a glorious relief, plunging my molten body into a pool of cool pleasure from a height I didn't know I could climb, let alone fall from.

I'm panting, tangled hair and limbs, as he kisses me fiercely, harsh breaths, his heart pounding so hard in his chest I feel it against mine.

I sigh as our tongues twine, slow and silken, as he mutters quietly, "So beautiful. You were so beautiful. You *are*. God, Kate."

I cup his jaw and kiss him. "So are you," I whisper. I reach for him, thick, velvet soft yet so hard and hot, guiding him to me. "Please don't make me wait anymore."

He groans, dropping his forehead to my shoulder, kissing me there.

Then he eases away, reaching for the nightstand again. He pours a drizzle of lube on his fingers, then brings it between my legs and works them gently inside, making me gasp.

"Put your leg around my hip," he says as I settle my head against one of his bent arms holding him over me, as his hand cups my head, his fingers sink into my hair.

I throw my leg over his hip, a whimper leaving me as it makes every sensitized inch of me brush against his length.

"Breathe for me," he whispers as he leans in for a kiss, his fingers doing sweet, wonderful things inside me, curving forward, finding that spot that made my legs give out when I leaned against the bathroom door after paintball. Thankfully, this time I'm lying down.

I drop my forehead to his jaw and cling to his arm. He shivers when I do, and I'm reminded how much he's given me, how much I want to give him, too—the touch he loves, the pleasure he deserves.

"Should I do this?" I ask, drifting my hands down his arm, to the round, full muscles of his backside, lower down his thighs.

He groans and nods. "Yes. Everywhere. Just touch me."

I rest against the pillow of his arm as his fingers play with my hair, as his other fingers coax my body to open, to ache for him to fill it. And I touch him, too, his chest, his nipples, the dark, lovely trail of hair down his stomach, the thick muscles of his thighs, the tight, soft weights of his balls, rubbing them, savoring their feel as he moans against my mouth and brings his fingers finally from my body, wet and warm, and rubs my clit.

Then he's there, slowly easing in, just a little, before he stops, watching my wide eyes, the breath heaving from my lungs. I have no idea how the physics of this is supposed to work. But I trust him.

He bends and kisses me again, but this time feels different, the tenderness of his lips brushing mine, the sweet, sensual stroke of his tongue. I'm so dazed and distracted by these kisses, the discomfort of him easing deeper inside me remains peripheral, dull and dim.

"You okay?" he asks.

I nod. "So good. Don't stop. Please don't stop."

He kisses me, and his hand curves around my backside, drawing me down on him, filling me. "There. That's it, honey. You're there."

I gasp, tears pricking my eyes as I feel the weight of his body, fully inside me, not out of pain but out of sheer, heartrending joy.

Before he can worry about those tears, I wrap an arm around him and pull him tight to me, my mouth finding his hungrily. I need to be as close to him as I can be, I need his body to be a part of mine and mine a part of his.

Slowly, he starts to move, each stroke inside me uncoiling spool after spool of molten pleasure.

"Kate," he gasps, drawing me close, kissing me deeply, our mouths open and panting, our tongues like our bodies, working in a rhythmic, hazy, hot glide.

His hand slips between us and his thumb rubs me gently, quickly pulling wetness from what our bodies are making. "Christopher," I tell him. "I've come twice, you don't have to worry—"

I'm kissed into silence. He shakes his head. "Need you with me."

His eyes hold mine as those words echo through me. *Need you with me.*

"I'm with you," I tell him, giving him his own promise, laid at his feet, "for as long as you'll have me."

He breathes roughly, then crushes me to him and rubs me harder, kissing me frantically, teeth and tongue and gasps of air. Settling more of his weight on me, he starts to move faster, deeper. His eyes find mine.

I feel it then, this place inside me that I didn't know, that I hadn't discovered, but he has. And, entirely out of my control, a sharp, desperate cry wrenches from my throat, then another. I can't speak, can't say how beyond anything I imagined this is, but he knows. I see it in how he looks at me, in how his mouth falls open, too, and harsh, rough sounds leave him, too, sounds I've never heard, that say unbearable pleasure and need and losing himself to the mercy of his body with mine.

My eyes flutter shut, but he pulls me closer, his hand tight in my hair. "Stay with me, Kate, please."

I open my eyes as I feel him thicken inside me, hear him call my name and hold us together as I fall apart, as my release pours through me like liquid light, a pyrotechnic shower of sparks, glittering white-hot as they course through my body in time with him as he moves, as he shouts my name and fills my body in hot, wet punches of his hips.

The wake of the moment is the silence that hangs after a fireworks grand finale, ringing ears, chests echoing from the beauty that lit up the dark and shook the world.

Ragged breaths, gentle hands, we touch each other, see each other, and kiss once, long and slow. And then it's the intimacy after intimacy—naked walks to the bathroom, lying on the bed afterward, watching his big bare body move, warming water in the sink, wetting a washcloth, gently cleaning me between my legs as he kisses me.

After that, he's back under the sheets, pulling me close, weaving his legs with mine. The world is dark and still but for the faint firelight glow, its silent dancing flames. I wrap my arm around his waist and sigh deeply, staring into the fire.

His fingers stroke softly through my hair. He presses a kiss to my temple. "Penny for your thoughts," he says.

I peer up at him. "For once, my mind is blissfully blank. No sight of my brain's typical chaotic twenty-five open browsers."

His fingertip drifts down the slope of my nose. Down, over my cupid's bow, around my lips. "Blissfully blank or practically overheating, I think your brain is pretty wonderful, Kate."

"You do?"

I hear his swallow. His fingertip sweeps up my cheekbone, landing gently on my temple, which he circles. "I do. I used to be afraid of—well, I probably am, still, but I'm working on it—how bold it made you, how brave and uncompromising. How you've always known what you believed and spoken your mind and *done* something about it. Now I just see what chickenshits most of us are, compared to you. How I wish the world was filled with Kates."

"Even with their chronic inability to stay on top of their laundry? Their propensity to lose their phone weekly? Their restless legs and regular struggle to stay in one position or place for longer than five minutes? You'd really want a world filled with Kates?"

"Especially with all of that," he says quietly, kissing the tip of my nose. "There'd be Christophers in the wings, to keep things running smoothly."

My heart does a wild leap in my chest. "Christophers do laundry?"

"Christophers *love* doing laundry."

"And finding phones?"

He shrugs. "They bathe nightly in money and have time on their hands, after inventorying their empire. It's no big deal to buy a replacement or go on scavenger hunts to find them."

A bittersweet lump thickens my throat. "And are Christophers patient when Kates get wiggly and desperate for adventures?"

He's quiet for a long moment. "Christophers want Kates to wiggle their wiggles and have their adventures . . . even if they take them far away. So long as they try their very best not to fall off cliffs or get in vans with questionable strangers. Whatever makes Kates happy. It's all worth it, for a world filled with Kates."

My heart swoops and dips, then settles like a bird that's danced the day through the air, finally landing on its branch, settled its feathers for rest, at long last, content. I snuggle into Christopher, sighing happily as he tucks me tighter against him. "A world filled with Kates," I whisper. "There'd be a doughnut shortage of catastrophic proportions."

"That's the beauty of capitalism, Katydid. Demand drives supply. The proliferation of Kates would lead to unprecedented doughnut-industry growth."

A sleepy laugh jumps out of me. Christopher's fingertip grazes my forehead, then swirls around my other temple. My eyelids feel heavy. "Probably for the best there's only one me."

He's quiet, his touch circling my temple slowing. "There could only ever be one you." His mouth presses gently to my forehead as he breathes in.

I'm so relieved, so exhausted, so happy, as I drift off in the bliss of a heavy blanket, a soft kiss to my forehead, two strong arms, the warm, safe place of his chest holding that heart whose beat I treasure.

Whose closeness I hold fast to all night.

THIRTY-FOUR

Christopher

The kitchen is quiet but for the faint chirp of a few stubborn birds who stick it out here this time of year, hovering on the windowsill. I smile at them and sip my coffee, savoring how different it is to have slept well, wrapped around Kate. Even with the handful of times her long wiggly legs kicked my shins, those sharp knees and elbows poked me, her wild hair spread over my mouth, tickling my face, it was the best sleep I've had in a long time.

The peace I've never felt before, holding her, was knowing she was safe, she was with me. I know the day will come, God, do I hope only briefly, that I'll have to give that up. Let her get on a plane and go on an adventure and trust her to come back to me in one piece. That's something I'll have to seek help for, and I'll take all the help I can get, whatever it takes to make it possible.

I pick up my phone, figuring now's as good a time as any to look up therapists, and feel my smile shift up a gear as I see the picture I already set as my wallpaper. It's one I took of her when I woke up and left her in my bed, snoring, stretched like a starfish across the mattress, illuminated by the faintest dawn light seeping through the curtains.

While the pumpkin pancakes sizzle in the pan, I set down my coffee, text Curtis to let him know I'm taking a personal day, then google therapists in the area. The sizzle's a little louder than I want, so I turn down the heat.

And then I hear footsteps thundering down the stairs.

I freeze when I see Kate turn the corner into the kitchen, a mountain of sheets in her arms, her eyes red-rimmed.

A thousand explanations run through my head and none of them are good.

She deeply regrets sleeping with me.

To the point that she stripped the bed to destroy the evidence.

She thinks I'm some pervert because I begged her last night to smother me with her vulva.

Three times.

"Hey," I say quietly. Walking toward her carefully, the way I do with Puck when he's caught in the rain, wet and pissed, and is about to bolt under the porch.

She doesn't hiss. Worse, she peers past me, gets one look at the pumpkin pancakes, and bursts into tears.

"Oh, Jesus." I close the distance between us and tug her into my arms, bedsheets squished between us. "Kate, honey, why are you out of bed? And crying? What's wrong?"

A sob jumps out of her. "Y-you're perfect."

"I'm not and you know it. In fact, you're the one who generally reminds me otherwise. What's got you talking like this?"

She wipes her nose with the back of her hand. "You gave me eight orgasms last night—"

"Ten, actually."

"—and you big spooned me all night even though I know I'm a nightmare to share a bed with. I kick in my sleep. Then I woke up to a note to stay in bed because you were making me p-pumpkin pancakes"—her lip wobbles, and God, when she cries, I feel like someone's cutting out my heart—"and what did I do? I smothered you with my vulva twice—no, *thrice*—last night and woke up with my blood all over your sheets."

"Ahhh." I pull back enough to wipe her tears beneath her eyes, before I tuck her snugly back in my arms. "So that's what's got you all weepy."

"I'm not *weepy*," she weeps. "I'm *overwhelmed*. Because you . . . you did my laundry. You made the most incredible love to me all night and made me breakfast this morning and did my laundry and I bled all over your sheets—"

"Kate." I tug the sheets out of her arms and toss them over my shoulder. "First, fuck the sheets."

"They're Egyptian cotton," she whispers hoarsely, as I rub her back and she wraps her arms around me, smooshing her cheek against my chest. "One thousand thread count. I checked the tag."

"And I have more up in the closet. They're replaceable."

"According to a cursory internet search on my phone, their market value is three hundred dollars. I just bled over three-hundred-dollar sheets," she mutters tearily.

I laugh into her hair, earning her narrow-eyed glare. "I'm sorry, Katydid. I'm not laughing at you."

"Uh-huh."

"I just haven't seen this side of you in a long time. You're generally either ice-cold or fiery pissed, and this sweet, emotional side of you is very precious to me."

"I'm not *precious*," she grumbles.

"You are the most precious. Now, listen to me. I *loved* giving you those orgasms, not to mention receiving every orgasm you gave me. And while your cuddling may be a bit . . . active, I slept better holding you than I have in a very long time."

"You did?"

"I did," I tell her softly, kissing her. "So stop worrying about what's not perfect and focus on what is, Katerina. This. Right here."

She sinks into me, kissing me back, her hands tangling in my hair. But then she pulls away suddenly and sniffs the air. "Hey. Is something burning?"

I glance over my shoulder and see the pumpkin pancakes smoking in the pan. "Shit!"

"Okay." Walking down the sidewalk toward her apartment, I hand Kate a pumpkin muffin covered in cream cheese frosting, freshly unearthed from the Nanette's pastry box. "Pumpkin-based breakfast, take two."

Kate accepts the muffin, then bites into it, smiling, her gaze dancing over me.

"What?" I ask, smiling back at her, adjusting her laundry bag on my shoulder.

"You're just really sweet," she says, shrugging. "I feel spoiled."

I bite into my butter croissant and say around my bite, "I have bad news for you, Kate. I'm just getting started, spoiling you."

She rolls her eyes as she bites into her muffin again, but a pretty blush sweeps up her cheeks, and she can't hide her smile.

I stare at her, feeling my heart pound, hard and feverish. God, I love her. I *love* her.

And I do want to spoil her. I want to surprise her with plane tickets to wherever her heart desires and leave behind work, devoting myself only to those smiles and blushes and learning all the scattered, lovely things her brain notices and absorbs.

I want to wake up every day to her smoky laugh and hard kisses. I want her fierce intensity and lung-burning sprint races for the most unexpected things. I want to sleep curled around her and talk while she bathes and cook with her in the kitchen. I want to stare into those stormy eyes and feel the thrill of knowing there's so much I already know about her and so much more that I don't, this dizzying cocktail of memory and mystery.

I watch her smile up at me, her hand finding mine and lacing our fingers together. And I feel the world tip beneath me.

I want to give Kate everything she deserves. I want to promise her and ask for everything, too. I hope we'll figure out how that's possible for two people who live so differently, that somehow our lives can meet halfway.

Kate squeezes my hand and smiles up at me, reminding me what's changed—what all this is about.

I don't have answers yet, but I don't have to find them on my own. Kate and I will do that *together*, hand in hand. One step at a time.

· THIRTY-FIVE ·

Kate

"I'll take that." Stopped outside my apartment door, I reach for the massive bag of now clean laundry from Christopher's shoulder. He doesn't seem inclined to give it up.

"I'm fine carrying it," he says.

I blink at him, weighing my options. My room—Juliet's room, where I'm staying—looks like a tornado hit it. Even with most of my dirty laundry scraped into a bag, it's still a wreck of, among many other random odds and ends, half-drunk water cups and snack bar wrappers because snack bars are about all I managed to eat this week. The last time he saw my room was that paintball night, and its status was borderline hide-from-anyone-whose-good-opinion-I-value, but by the time he'd tucked me in, it was dark and he left before sunrise, so I got away with it.

Today, in the light of late morning, which pours into that bedroom, it'll be like tugging down a microscope on my mess and shoving it in his face.

No, thank you.

Christopher's home is worn around the edges and sweetly dated—all of which I adore—but for all the things others might think could use improving, its tidiness and cleanliness are not among them. Christopher is a neatnik. He likes doing things like wiping down his fancy coffee machine after each use and deploying a lightweight shiny vacuum to pick up crumbs in the kitchen's corners after cooking. He voluntarily did my laundry, for Christ's sake. He folded everything. Even my underwear.

My high-waisted, once-white but now dingy-dishwater, grandma underwear. That's embarrassing enough.

But Christopher is so stubborn, and I'm realizing that with my good old hiss-and-flex-the-claws days behind me, what this situation calls for is something we're just starting to figure out: compromise.

Resting against the door to the apartment, I attempt a casual lean and paste on what I hope is an ingratiating smile. "I propose a deal."

Christopher arches his eyebrows, resettling the massive duffel's strap on his shoulder like it's full of paper products instead of my entire laundered wardrobe. "I'm listening."

"You may carry my bag inside the apartment."

His eyebrows lift higher. "And . . . ?"

"And that's it. You may carry it in, and then you may carry it no further, most definitely not inside my room."

His eyes narrow. He purses his lips, thinking this over. "Your terms are close to but not quite what I'm looking for. I propose a negotiation."

"Nope."

He sighs, shaking his head. "Rookie mistake," he mutters.

I'm annoyed by that and turn toward the door, about to unlock it when Christopher stops me with a hand gently circling my wrist. "Hey." His voice is quiet, the brief contentious fire between us doused.

"What is it?" I ask.

He glances toward the door, then back to me. "Is Bea home? If she is, I just want to know what to say when we walk in together."

I frown. "Would we have to say anything? Couldn't we just walk in and that's that?"

"Possibly. Or it might be obvious what we've been up to."

I search his eyes, looking for some clue as to how he feels about that. And then I remind myself that I have a mouth, so I ask him, "And would that be all right, if it was?"

He smiles, slow and satisfied. "Very all right with me."

I'm nearly dizzy with relief.

"What about you?" he asks, searching my eyes, too.

I nod. "Very all right."

His smile grows. "Good."

"We can tell the friends, too," I blurt.

Christopher smiles his widest yet, eyes sparkling, warm and proud. "I'd like that."

"Good." I turn toward the door, focused on the lock, then stop, turning back. "Bea's actually at work now, so we have the place to ourselves for a bit."

He arches an eyebrow. "Is that why you were hustling me out the door, so you could sneak in here and avoid the walk of shame with me?"

"I was hustling you out the door because I wasn't sure if *you'd* want them to know. I wanted to give you an out and not have them be here when we were."

He glares at me, folding his arms across his chest. "Kate, I'd shout from the tallest skyscraper in this city what you mean to me, if you'd let me."

Oh God, my blush. "Well, now I know. But I didn't then. That was why I was nagging you about needing to go and to stop beautifying in front of the mirror—"

"I was *shaving*."

"I liked the scruff," I blurt. "A lot."

He tips his head, his gaze warm. "You did?"

I nod. "I liked how it made you look different and also . . . the same. I can't explain it."

Except that's how this *feels. Like it's you. Like it's nothing like you. Like it's better than I could have ever imagined.*

"And I like how it feels," I admit, my cheeks heating.

One of those slow, wicked grins lifts his mouth. He leans against the wall beside the door and crosses his feet at the ankles, oozing sensual self-satisfaction. "And where exactly do you like how it feels?"

I slug his arm. "Stop it. You know exactly where."

"Mm-hmm, but I like hearing it."

"Good grief." I turn my back on him, fumbling with the key as I try to unlock the door before I do something silly like tackle him in the hallway and kiss him to death.

"Kate," he says, stepping behind me, dropping his chin on my shoulder. He nuzzles into my hair.

"Yes, Christopher."

"When we tell everyone. I want to tell them . . . that you're mine and I'm yours. That we're together exclusively."

My heart pinwheels in my chest, joy spinning it fast and faster.

"Do you . . ." He clears his throat softly, then breathes me in, his nose buried in my hair. "Do you want that, too?"

I smile so wide my cheeks hurt, then glance over my shoulder, making our noses brush. "Yes. So much."

His smile is dazzling as he leans in and kisses me.

When I pull away and refocus on the door, about to cross this threshold, bringing my first-ever lover and partner inside, it hits me. The reality of all this, its immense, overwhelming, terrifying wonderfulness, brings me to a standstill.

"Kate?" Christopher rubs my back gently. "What's up?"

I shake my head. "I'm okay."

"Hey." He wraps his arm around my waist. "Don't do that. Say what you feel. This is what we do now, Kate. We talk."

"Is that what we do?" I tease, struggling with the key. "Talk?"

I feel his grin against my neck as he kisses me there, his hands wandering higher up my waist, toward my breasts. "Well, that and other things."

"'Other things' is right, like me cussing at this goddamn door whose lock is my villain origin story."

Christopher sighs, abandoning his seduction, and wraps his hand around mine, helping me jiggle the key once, then flip it to unlock. Pushing open the door, he holds it for me.

"Thank you," I tell him.

As I toss the keys onto the kitchen counter, Christopher shuts the door behind me, then strolls down the hall straight toward my room.

"Hey!" I scramble after him. "We had a deal, Petruchio!"

"Oh, I remember," he calls over his shoulder. He stops at the door to my bedroom and makes a point of dropping the bag right outside it. "I offered to negotiate and you declined. I warned you it was a mistake." Turning the handle, he opens the door and walks over the bag, right into my room.

"Christopher!" I run after him, hopping over the laundry bag sitting precisely outside my door, as promised. "What the hell!"

"It's a messy room, Kate." He shrugs, standing in the middle of the bedroom, looking like a prince in a pauper's hovel, surrounded by my chaos. "So what?"

I glare at him, my cheeks heating. "It's *my* messy room."

He stares at me. "So let me see it. You think I care? You think it's going to scare me away?"

My eyes prick with tears. "I don't know."

"So, what are we doing, then? Hiding from each other, still? You're just going to let me fuck you—"

"Don't call it that," I snap. "It's more than that."

"Exactly," he says, stepping smoothly over an empty granola box. "Which means I get to see and want you not just when you're naked in my arms and cute as hell wearing my clothes, but when you're feeling emotional about life and work, when your room's a mess and when you're drowning in dirty laundry."

"Easy for you to say!" I gesture up and down him. "You've got it all together."

He lifts his eyebrows, then pauses, tipping his head. "You think I have it all together?"

I snort, but I'm not amused.

Gently, he takes me by the elbow and tugs me into his arms. "I don't have it all together, Kate."

"You have a kajillion dollars. A straightforward career. A beautiful home. A knack for doing laundry. And a brain that doesn't make life delightful but also deeply frustrating sometimes."

"Is that right?" He peers down at me. "Kate, you more than most know how unfair and unmerited generational wealth is. My dad was a shrewd businessman who died young and left me a good company—that's hardly something *I* did. As for my house, again, inherited, and it's not beautiful by many people's standards, just yours, which, frankly, is all I care about." He bites his cheek. "And as for my brain . . . it is deeply, *deeply* frustrating. Often."

I stare up at him, noticing for the first time since we hustled out of his house the smudges under his eyes, the pinch of pain at the corners of his mouth. "And have you told me how your brain is actually, truthfully feeling today?" I ask.

He glances away, scrubbing at his neck. "Not . . . exactly."

"Huh. How's that little quid pro quo lecture feeling now?"

"Kate . . ." He sighs heavily. "Fine. My head fucking hurts. There, you happy?"

"Happy? No." I run a hand along his arm. "I hate that you hurt. That I can't do shit about it. But I'm grateful that you told me."

"Hmph."

I smile up at him, gently taking over rubbing his neck. A little groan leaks out of him. "Sharing your mess is easier said than done, isn't it?"

Christopher wraps his arms around me and sets his chin on my head. "Yes."

Hugging him back, I settle my head over his heart. "Tell me. Try."

He sighs heavily. "My neurologist thinks I need to try a new medication, but who the hell knows if it'll help or make things worse, so I'm holding off, dreading committing to that course of action. So, yeah, often lately and today, my head fucking hurts. I slept well with you when we slept, but I didn't sleep enough. I feel like I've got tiny woodland creatures scratching at the backs of my eyeballs and my neck hurts, and I hate it. Because I want to tell you to put on your Badazz Feminist playlist at full volume and head-bang to songs with you while we tackle this room's mess, then I want to lay you down on your freshly made bed and give you a couple orgasms, and I'm not sure I can do any of that right now."

"So we won't," I tell him, rubbing his back. "*I* will clear off my bed and put fresh sheets on it. And then you will get out of those fancy clothes and put on the comfy things you keep in your little Christopher drawer. You'll take whatever meds might help you get a lead on your migraine, and we'll nap or do whatever you need to ride it out. We'll take turns. You took care of me when I spiraled out this morning. I'll take care of you now. Deal?"

He swallows thickly, his cheek suddenly resting heavy on my head. "And here I thought I had a novice negotiator on my hands."

I smile against his chest, then kiss right over his heart. "You should know by now, I'm a very fast learner."

THIRTY-SIX

Christopher

For a moment after my eyes open, I have no idea where I am. Strangely, I'm not in my bed. Even more strange, I feel deeply rested. Strangest, loveliest yet, I'm wrapped around the slope of a familiar waist. A small, soft breast is my pillow. A steady heartbeat thuds beneath my ear.

My vision adjusts to the soft warm light coming from behind me, dimmed low. Now I see her, and everything makes sense.

Kate.

I stare at her as she comes into focus, lashes casting shadows on her cheeks, her mouth pursed in concentration. She wears her big headphones nestled in that bird's nest I love, knitting needles clicking in her hands, balls of yarn strewn across the other side of the bed.

She's the most beautiful thing I've ever seen.

As I watch her, my heart's door creaks wide open on rusty, unused hinges, heavy, slow, determined nonetheless.

And when she peers down at me, greets me with such a deep, sweet smile and those eyes like the ocean, peaceful and calm after a storm, I know with certainty I will never close that door again—for her, it's as good as gone, turned to ash, dissolved in the wind.

Because I love her.

"I love you," I tell her hoarsely, before I know what's come out of my mouth. My heart's an elevator, plummeting to its doom.

Until her knitting needles freeze as she nudges off her headphones and says, "Hmm?"

I exhale roughly, saved. "Hi," I tell her.

Her smile deepens. Back to knitting, needles clacking, she asks, "Comfortable?"

I nod and then feel water dripping down my temple. Bringing a hand to my head, I find cool plastic. A memory of frozen vegetables being piled on my head comes back to me. I remember Kate closing the curtains to her room, grumbling and pissed that I insisted on helping her make the bed. I remember the gentle way she shoved me back onto the mattress and tugged off my boots and jeans, then peeled off my sweater and kissed my forehead. I remember her sliding a clean, soft shirt over my head and how that felt impossibly more sensual, more intimate, than having my clothes taken off.

I remember her hands rubbing my shoulders and neck, soothing them as they tensed. I remember when the pain broke just enough to be bearable, tangling my legs with hers, dragging her close until our bodies clung to each other like vines, and sleep swallowed me up.

I should hate it. The mess I am. How fragile my body seems when it hurts like this, when it disobeys me, despite how hard I try to manage it. How naked I feel, even though I'm clothed.

But I don't hate it at all. I don't hate Kate for dragging me to bed in the middle of the day, for rubbing my neck and icing my head and holding me while I wrestled with pain until sleep and modern medicine mercifully won out.

Lying here, half-clothed, tangled with Kate, my mess just as known as hers, I feel stripped down and unburdened—a naked, wide-armed free fall into cool water on a hot summer day.

"How's it going?" she says, nodding her chin toward my head. No *Do you feel better?* No *Is it gone yet?* No expectation or pressure for the pain to have conveniently disappeared, though, thank God, it's faded drastically.

"Pain's better," I tell her. "Not gone, but much better. Thanks to the nap you forced on me and . . ." I lift the wet bag on my head to inspect it. "A bag of carrots and peas."

Kate sighs dramatically. "There goes my stir-fry tonight."

"Like you were going to cook a damn thing."

She smiles, and Christ, it's a sword and a sweet gift, cutting me deep and swift, reminding me how much, how uniquely, Kate makes me *feel*. "I had aspirations for dinner this evening," she says primly. "But *someone* had to be dramatic and get a headache."

My hands sink into her hips, then higher, beneath her shirt, because even when she's teasing me, I have to touch her and feel her like this, warm and whispering beneath the sheets, her legs tangled with mine. "What can I say?" I tell her. "I like the spotlight."

"Clearly." Lifting the bag of not-so-frozen vegetables from my head, she chucks it behind her on the bed. "And clearly you like to get headaches, too," she deadpans. "Otherwise, you'd do more to stop them, Christopher. Have you tried eating gluten-free? Dairy-free? Drinking more caffeine right when a headache comes on? Drinking less caffeine so you don't trigger them? Eliminating stress? Quitting your job? Relaxing more? Exercising more? Avoiding MSG? Getting acupuncture? Taking cryogenic baths?"

"It would be funnier if I hadn't heard every single one of those unsolicited pieces of advice before, countless times."

"People really think someone who gets migraines wouldn't have done everything they possibly could to avoid them," she grumbles. "I want to knuckle sandwich every one of them for you, but I don't think I'd do so well in jail, so I guess I'll restrain myself."

"I like you out of jail," I mutter against her neck, then press a hot, slow kiss there.

"Hey now," she says, tapping my shoulder with her knitting needles. "No funny business. We're still convalescing."

"The fuck we are." I nuzzle her breast, then kiss it through her T-shirt. "Unless you need to. If you're sore, we can do other things, instead."

"I'm not too sore, but—*ah*!" She draws in a harsh breath as I suck at her nipple. "Christopher, don't push yourself."

"Please," I whisper over her heart, kissing her there. "Trust me to make that choice. Let me love you. Besides," I tell her, sliding my hand beneath the covers, feeling her leg shift restlessly across the bed, her hips move toward my touch. "After all that pain, I think I deserve a little pleasure, don't you?"

Knitting needles and balls of yarn, a half-thawed bag of vegetables, soar off the bed. Kate burrows down in the sheets with me and whispers, "Yes, I do."

THIRTY-SEVEN

Kate

For once, I'm the one who can't sleep. My mind is flying, my limbs restless, and so I slip out of bed the next morning just as dawn starts to fill the main living space of our apartment. Part of me wants to lie there, watching Christopher sleep as sunlight warms his skin, burnishes the curling ends of his hair and sparkles off the scruff that showed up last night—scruff that I thoroughly enjoyed abrading my breasts and stomach and thighs while he brought me one stunning orgasm after another.

I could lie there all morning, staring at him, replaying those beautiful moments, wondering what beautiful moments lie ahead. But I know if I stay, watching him sleep, my wiggles will wake him up, and after years of such poor sleep, Christopher needs his rest so badly.

Quietly shutting my bedroom door behind me, laptop and headphones under my arm, I tiptoe over to the kitchen and turn on the coffee maker, which Bea or Jamie must have set up, because I know Christopher and I didn't.

While I wait for the coffee to brew, I wander into Bea's tiny studio at the back of the apartment, with its faded gold velvet armchair next to the window, facing the sunrise.

Settling into it, I power on my laptop, tug on my headphones, and start some mellow music, prepared to work on editing the rest of the nonprofit's photos. A reminder pops up on my calendar:

Jules's flight home tonight.

I blink at the screen, stunned, my heart thudding. I've been so consumed with Christopher, so fixated on work, I completely blanked on the dwindling countdown to Jules coming home. She'll be here *tonight*. Which means I need to figure out what I'm doing next. And I need to deep clean her room.

I shouldn't be so panicked. I knew this was coming. But like my classic self, I haven't done much—anything, really—to prepare for it. My suitcase still sits open, where I've kept my clothes. I haven't thought about where I'll go or what I'll do after this.

But maybe that's okay.

Maybe I haven't had to *think* about it—I've *chosen* it, little by little, along the way. I've chosen working at the Edgy Envelope, chosen new paths for my photography to connect me to people and capture their stories. I've chosen to cultivate friendships, spend time with my family, make myself a part of what I'd missed.

Maybe I've been choosing what I want all this time, since I came home and ran right into Christopher, and now that it's here before me—the life that reflects those choices—I'm already where I was worried I would never get to.

My gears turn as I think about what comes next. I could spend a month at Mom and Dad's, save up for a deposit on a tiny studio somewhere. Or I could stay with Christopher.

No. That would be too fast. Too soon.

Even though I know I'd love it. Even though I know we'd give each other a disgusting amount of pleasure and comfort. We'd laugh and argue and tease and make love—

Love.

That's what it comes down to. What I want, what I've chosen, is what I *love*—who I love. And one of those people is right down the hall, sleeping.

At least, he was.

I catch movement in the kitchen that I know is Christopher, broad and solid, dark bedhead waves sticking up. I smile, tugging off my headphones, prepared to call his name and say good morning.

But before I can, Christopher says to someone I can't see, "Why are you looking at me like that?"

I frown. He's speaking quietly, but his voice echoes down the hall from the kitchen to the studio. Who is he talking to?

Jamie's voice answers him. "I'm not looking at you like anything. I'm . . . surprised to see you. I didn't think . . ." A heavy sigh. "I don't know what I thought, and I don't know what to make of you being here. I thought you were going to fix things with her, to make peace. That's all we asked for."

That's all we asked for?

My ears start to ring. I know I should make my presence known. I know I'm eavesdropping. But I'm like an animal in the field, staring down the barrel of a hunter's gun, frozen, stunned.

Someone *asked* Christopher to "fix things"? Why did he never say? Why does it sound like some grand arrangement was made to deal with me and the complications I apparently presented?

And why does it feel like I'm going to throw up?

I whimper, a sob climbing up my throat, tears stinging my eyes, but then I stop myself, shaking my head.

No. I won't do this. I won't skip ten steps and assume the worst. I won't take a fragment of a conversation and fill it in with all my fears and insecurities.

I'm going to do what hasn't been easy but has made a way for

Christopher and me, cleared a path for us to finally live in the present, not twisted up in our past.

I'm going to communicate like a goddamn adult.

Once my ears stop ringing. And I can breathe properly.

I'm so focused on calming myself, I don't hear what they continue saying down the hall, but I don't want to.

I don't want to hear Christopher explain and defend himself.

I don't need proof of my belief that he cares for me deeply, that it wasn't whatever plea my family, maybe even our friends, brought to him, that made Christopher's heart see my hurt—it was *my* honesty, *my* truth, and his, too, that allowed us to truly see and choose each other.

We're the ones who chose this.

And I choose to trust him. Which is why, now that my lungs work properly and my ears don't sound like tiny foghorns are blasting inside them, I toss aside my laptop and headphones, wrench open the studio door, and march straight down the hallway toward the person who needs to hear that.

THIRTY-EIGHT

Christopher

Jamie and I stand at odds for the first time in our friendship, and I hate nearly everything about it. It's too damn early. I woke up to an empty bed without Kate. I'm starving for her and for a solid meal after having had no appetite last night after my migraine and not enough time with my hands and mouth on her, making her come.

The one redeeming part of this highly unpleasant moment is that Jamie's grilling me because he feels responsible for how his request to sort things out with Kate could hurt the woman I love, and for that, I can't fault him.

I just really want him to believe me and trust me.

"Jamie." I take a slow deep breath. "I acknowledge that I made a commitment to smooth things over with Kate at your and Bill's request, hell, even for poor lovesick Nick's sake, but the farthest that got me was a few bruised toes at Tacos and Tangos, and a decision to keep my distance from her, which I clearly sucked at, given I lasted a week before I came around for game night and couldn't leave her alone. That's what led to ... everything changing.

"Things changed when *Kate* told me how I'd hurt her. What she said wrecked me, and I swore to myself and her that I'd fix that. What came from that, where I am now, that's the result. What you're seeing, my being here, is born out of something that—no offense—has *nothing* to do with anyone but the two of us. Just please believe me when I say I would sooner die than ever willfully hurt Kate. She's safe with me."

Jamie exhales heavily and rubs the bridge of his nose. "God, I'm glad to hear that."

"Do you believe me?"

He looks at me like I just asked if bananas are grown on Mars. "Of course I do. I just couldn't not say *something*. If, even indirectly, accidentally, what I asked of you led to Bea's sister being hurt—"

"You don't need to explain. It means a lot to me that you care so much about her, that you'd come to me and make sure she's safe."

I offer my hand. Jamie takes it. And like always, we offer each other a bracing, backslapping hug.

"Petruchio."

My head whips toward the sound of Kate's voice calling my name as she storms down the hall. My gaze skips past her to the open studio door, and the blood in my veins turns to ice. What did she hear? What has she made of it?

Kate tips her head to Jamie, says, "Morning," then grabs my hand, hard and tight, and just keeps walking. I spin, following her as she tugs me down the hallway toward her room.

"Kate, I don't know what you heard—"

"Hush." She shoves open her bedroom door, rounds on me, gets a good fistful of my shirt, and yanks me down for a hard, bruising kiss. "I don't need a word of explanation," she says against my mouth. "I trust you, whatever it is. I believe you."

They're words I didn't know how badly I needed to hear, how desperately I needed to know she meant.

"Kate," I whisper brokenly, lifting her up, wrapping her legs around my waist, holding her so tight. "Listen to me."

She kisses my cheek, my temple. "I'm listening."

"Your family loves you. So much that they called me on my bullshit after I was an ass at Thanksgiving and told me to knock it off. As you can imagine, I didn't take that particularly well."

"Christopher, I told you, I don't need—"

"I know you don't. But *I* need." Searching her eyes, I tell her, "I decided I'd keep my distance, let us cool off, wait you out until you left. But then you didn't leave, and you broke my heart when you showed me how much I'd hurt you. I have never been so glad that I bought a bottle of Irish whiskey and that you drank a quarter of it, that I held you and put you to bed and you told me the drunken truth. But I'm even more grateful that now we don't need outside forces or liquid courage to help us face our truth and be honest. Because, yes, it's been messy, but this is what we have done since that night—we have been trying so damn hard to talk to each other, to see and understand each other, and I don't want that to stop."

I draw in a breath, brushing back a strand of her wild hair as I stare up at her, the woman I love so deeply. "And I want to do that because I love you, Kate."

Her eyes flicker, filling with tears that spill down her cheeks. I lean in and kiss them away, before I meet her eyes once more. "Because I have loved you a hundred different ways for so long I don't know when loving you began, just that I haven't spent nearly enough of my life making sure you know it. I don't expect you to love me yet, Kate. I know I don't deserve it. But one day, I hope you'll believe I'm worthy of your heart."

She shakes her head, a smile breaking across her face like the sunrise filling the room around us. Fresh tears track down her cheeks and she wipes them away. "You won't be waiting long."

My eyes desperately search hers. "I won't?"

"No," she whispers.

Air rushes out of my lungs as I hold her tight and bury my face in her neck, breathing her in, barely able to believe this is my existence, that this isn't some dream I'm about to wake up from.

Drawing in an unsteady breath, she lifts my chin until my eyes meet hers. And then she gifts me with the tenderest kiss. "I love you, Christopher Petruchio. With my whole wild heart. I love you so much, there aren't words to explain it."

Reaching behind me for the door, I push it shut, then walk her back toward the bed. "I can think of other ways you could explain how much you love me."

Her laugh is smoky and bright. "Oh, is that right? Well, I can think of a few ways you could return the favor."

"Katerina," I murmur, dropping over her onto the bed. "We both know I will more than double the favors you give me."

She lifts an eyebrow. "Is that a challenge, Petruchio?"

"Hell yes."

Hands fumbling for each other's clothes, we tug them off, laughing when arms get stuck, ankles twisted, as we rush to get naked.

Without preamble, Kate presses me onto my back, swinging one long leg over me until she straddles my lap. Holding my eyes, she smiles, then bends, kissing me tenderly. I sink my hands into her hair and tug it loose from its confines, until it spills down her back, over us, into a curtain blocking out the world.

"Now," she whispers, kissing me. "Please, Christopher, now."

As she lifts her hips, I guide the head of my cock inside her, stopping her from lowering down on me. "Not too fast, Kate. You'll hurt yourself—"

"Please," she says, cupping my face, her mouth brushing mine in the faintest, sweetest kiss. And then she gives me my words right back: "Trust me to make that choice."

I stare up at her as she splays her hands across my waist for leverage, as she sinks down on me inch by inch, her eyes holding mine.

Then she leans in, chests brushing, her mouth finding mine. I groan with relief as she moves, her body silken hot, wrapped around me like a vise, her hips moving fast and sure.

"Touch me," she whispers. "Make me come."

I crush her to me, pinning her hips against mine, taking over our rhythm, so it rubs her right where she needs. Her gasp fills my mouth as I stroke into her, as I feel her start to come in soft, tight waves around me.

"Yes," she cries against my mouth, sinking her nails like claws into my chest. I pant into her mouth as she comes and comes, and when her tongue grazes mine, a hot, sensual stroke, I arch up into her and spill so long and hard, my legs tingle with faint numbness, the fierce pleasure of being absolutely spent.

"Christ, Kate," I wheeze, drawing her in for a slow, savoring kiss.

She clenches her body around mine and laughs against my mouth as I groan helplessly. "And to think," she whispers, "I'm just getting started."

THIRTY-NINE

Kate

Six months later

"Katerina!"

I smile to myself because I can't help it. Every time I hear Christopher call my name that way, goose bumps still dance across my skin, and those absurd butterflies flutter in my belly.

"What do you want, Petruchio?"

His deep laugh echoes in the kitchen. "Well, when you put it that way."

The door from the kitchen to the dining room swings open. Christopher walks in and doesn't stop until he's bent over me as I hunch to catch the perfect photo of the luscious flowers and platters of delicious food that are set out for Jules and Bea's joint birthday party.

His mouth nuzzles my hair before he gently lifts it, setting my braid to one side so he can kiss my neck.

"Christopher." I snap a photo. "You're messing up my focus."

"I'm feeling needy, Katerina. Give a man a kiss when he's gone without for a week, while you gallivanted around the world."

Rolling my eyes, I set down my camera. "I was gone for five days."

"Felt like five years." He turns me in his arms, dragging me close.

"Yeah," I whisper, pressing on tiptoe, kissing him. "It did."

He peers down at me pensively, swaying me in his arms. "And you're leaving me again." He sighs. "You're lucky you're so fantastic in bed when you're here. And that I have such a great therapist when you're not."

I snort. "When I'm not fantastic in bed?"

"You're always fantastic in bed. When you're *not here*, smartass."

Laughing, I kiss him. "I love you."

He tips his head, tucking a strand of hair behind my ear. "I love you, too. So much, I am willing to host a Christmas in July birthday party with the most obnoxiously festive people I know, all because you asked."

"Hey, give me credit, I agreed to matching sweaters."

He grins. "Yeah you did."

My snowflake-stitched red sweater says, I DON'T DO MATCHING SWEATERS. His identical one says, BUT I DO.

I smile, glancing over my shoulder, drinking in his home. "Everything looks perfect."

While I was gone, Christopher threw himself into decorating for the Christmas in July party to celebrate my sisters' birthday and torture each other with bizarre holiday sweaters while the updated AC blasts through the house.

The place is covered in vintage Christmas decorations from Christopher's childhood and my own thrifting efforts. A record player spins, filling the air with holiday classics.

As our friends and family start to show up in goofy holiday sweaters, boozy eggnog (pasteurized, for Jamie's sake) and Margo's mulled wine are passed around, until folks are seated around the living room, plates filled with Christopher's rich Italian cooking along with Toni's homemade doughnuts, cakes, and cookies.

Jules sits beside me on the couch, almost as glowing and joyful as I remember my oldest sister used to be—dark, pretty hair combed out into soft silver-screen-starlet waves, deep dimples, that infectious smile that wins the heart of anyone she bestows it on.

As she laughs at something Sula says from the other side of the room, her cheeks turn nearly as pink as the sweatshirt she wears that says, IN A WORLD OF GRINCHES, BE THE CINDY LOU WHO.

I glance toward Bea, who sits on Jules's other side in a sweater that features Santa sucking provocatively on a candy cane and says SOMETIMES A PEPPERMINT STICK IS JUST A PEPPERMINT STICK. I find her eyes, sharing a small moment of gratitude that Jules is slowly coming back, from the trying-hard-to-smile, quiet woman who showed up last Christmas, now laughing loudly, tipsy on Margo's mulled wine, a bright smile on her face.

"Okay, but what *is* the science behind this?" Jamie asks, his cheeks a little rosy, eggnog in his hand. His sweater features a Christmas tree that's a pyramid of green cats with eyes whose bright colors look like ornaments, and says below, HAVE A MEOWY CATMAS. "How are zodiac signs so accurate?"

"Not to mention zodiac sign *pairings*," Sula says, her holiday sweater a lime-green sequined number that reads in cherry-red letters, I'VE BEEN NAUGHTY while Margo's red one says in green letters, I'VE BEEN ~~NICE~~, then written below it, NAUGHTIER. "The accuracy of compatibility in pairings, that's what blows my mind."

Toni sits up from resting inside Hamza's arm, the newlyweds wearing the only exception to the weird holiday sweaters theme. Theirs are silvery white and simply say in pretty cursive, MR., with jaunty Santa hats hanging on the *M*'s. Pulling out his phone, Toni says, "Let's check this. Are everyone's partner signs highly compatible?"

While he searches some website on his phone devoted to the subject, I slip my hand across the sofa and brush pinkies with Jules, the only one here who isn't partnered.

I know what it's like to feel as if you're the odd one out, and I never want her to. I never want any of us to, ever again.

Glancing my way, Jules says, "Thanks for planning all this, Kit-Kat. It's really special."

I smile. "Course, JuJu. I did have help, though." I tip my head toward Christopher, who sits at my feet, his hand idly curled around my calf, rubbing up and down. "Thanks for holding off on celebrating until I could come back from my work trip."

"Always." She slips her hand around mine and squeezes. "I do have one complaint about your work travels, though," she says, a sparkle in her eyes. "You hardly go on them anymore, and I feel like I'm due for another life swap. Now what am I supposed to do?"

"I don't know what to tell you. It seems I've become a domesticated Kat." That makes her laugh. "Maybe it's time for you to give in to the pull of our family's wanderlust gene, strike out on your own."

She smiles to herself, sipping her mulled wine. "Maybe I will. Try somewhere quieter for a while. Maybe upstate. Maybe halfway across the world. We'll see."

"To no one's surprise . . ." Toni calls, drawing us back into the group's conversation. "Nick's and Bianca's signs share *extremely* high compatibility." He peers over at the lovebirds, who wear matching powder-blue sweaters covered in fluffy white snowfall appliqués. With a snowperson on each sweater stitched to lean toward the edge, lips poised for a smooch, as Nick and Bianca sit beside each other, it looks like they're kissing. "Of course," he adds sweetly.

"Of course," we all singsong, with a few extra *awww*s, making Nick grin and Bianca laugh happily as he kisses her cheek.

"Next!" Toni says dramatically. "Kate, our Aquarius queen." I give a regal wave. "And then Christopher! A Taurus, if ever there was one."

Hoots go up. Christopher rolls his eyes from his seat at my feet. His hand slips down my leg and hooks around my ankle, squeezing gently.

Toni squints, reading the screen. "So let's see the Taurus and Aquarius sign compatibility."

"It's abysmal," Christopher says.

The whole room dims to a hush.

Christopher peers my way. "You're all obsessed with this astrological stuff, so I looked it up months ago, and when I saw in the summary that by all zodiac wisdom, an Aquarius and a Taurus are a terrible match, I decided it was bullshit."

Slowly, he turns, stretching an arm across my lap and threading his hand with mine. "But then I kept reading, and I came across a little paragraph that said there's a sliver of a chance that two people of these signs can be the exception that proves the rule. It said, if they're willing to do the work to get to a place of trust and understanding, they're rewarded with a passionate, electric connection— the kind of love that feels new every day." He smiles wide, his gaze warm and tender, only for me. "So I decided it wasn't absolute bullshit, after all."

I'm still shy about being affectionate in front of everyone else, but this time I don't hesitate to lean in and kiss Christopher, long and slow, for everyone to see.

"All right!" Sula says, springing up from her chair toward the vintage record player behind her. "Time to dance. Not only is it Jules's and Bea's fortieth birthdays—"

"Hey!" they call, offended.

"Okay, fine, thirtieth," Sula concedes, sifting through the records, "but it's a celebration of love!"

"Ooh, wait," I tell her, breaking away reluctantly from Christopher, then rushing over to the record player. "Let me."

I find just the record I wanted and lift the needle. As it drops with a crackle, followed by a burst of the tango's opening bars, I turn and stroll his way.

"Christopher."

He grins up at me from his seat on the floor, a flash of excitement in his handsome eyes. "Katerina."

I offer a hand, smiling at the man I love with all my heart. "May I have this dance?"

Christopher takes it and stands, then pulls me tight against him. One slow step, then another, a quick, breathless turn. Finally, a weightless, thrilling dip that I knew was coming.

He presses a kiss beneath my ear and whispers, "I thought you'd never ask."

———

Each time I leave home, it's harder. Of course, I still love experiencing new places for assignments, meeting new people, telling new stories. But the ache gets a little sharper, the longing lingers a little more, every time I'm gone from home.

I should be soaking up the white-hot beauty of Croatia in July, proud and happy that my work for this long-form piece on female entrepreneurship and growing economies is coming together so well, but as I sit, eating my meal and staring at the glorious view of the Adriatic Sea at sunset, all I can think about is how much damn fun we had at my sisters' birthday party last week, how Mom and Dad came over and joined in on the dance party, how I talked so much and laughed so hard my voice was hoarse by the time I saw people off, and then after everyone was gone, and Christopher made love to me over and over, I screamed in pleasure so much I lost my voice completely.

Turning back to my food, I poke an olive listlessly.

But then a shadow cuts across my little table, swallowing up the sun and turning the world as bleak as I feel inside.

I frown up from my plate, prepared to tell whoever's standing over me to move along, when I freeze.

Christopher stands there, breathtaking—sandstone slacks draping down his long, solid legs, a linen shirt rolled up to his elbows, golden sunlight spilling around his windblown dark hair. His amber eyes glow, warm and soft, as he stares down at me. "Hi, Katydid."

My fork drops to the plate. Tears blur my vision. "What the hell?" I croak.

Then I launch myself at him, knocking a shocked, deep laugh out of Christopher as he wraps his arms around me, swinging me around. "What are you doing here?" I shriek.

"Following you like a lovesick fool, of course," he says, before kissing me, slow and sweet. "I've been practicing while you've traveled for work, taking domestic flights and using those chances to do some more widespread networking. Once I could fly coast to coast, my therapist and I agreed I could probably survive a transatlantic flight."

My heart clutches. I set my hand over his chest, soothing it gently. "And did you?"

He tips his head side to side. "Eh, it was touch and go. I have a hunch being with you on my flight home will help. And that means I'll just have to fly with you everywhere from now on."

Fresh tears spill down my cheeks as I laugh. "And here I was, moping, being homesick, and deciding that my traveling-for-work days were over."

"Well now, I won't complain if you want to stay home more," he says, before he presses a kiss to my lips. "But I'm not giving up travel with you either. I think there's a happy balance there for us, waiting to be found."

"I think so, too." I kiss him, hungry and deep, drawing him close. "Let's go to bed."

"Katerina," he says, feigning offense, as my hands start to wander down his back, lower, over his backside. "I just got here, and you're objectifying me already."

"Damn right, I am."

He laughs into my hair as he hoists me higher, wrapping my legs around his waist. A hefty wad of local cash lands on the table before he starts to walk us down the road. "Where's your place?" he asks, kissing me as he speaks. "Please tell me it's close."

"It's close." I point toward the small apartment building to my left, and Christopher turns sharply for its entrance. Not for the first time, we fumble with locks and door handles to an apartment, then tumble across its threshold, slamming the door shut, tugging at each other's clothes.

On a particularly enthusiastic tug on my part, Christopher and I crash noisily into the wall.

We both burst into laughter as he kisses me, his hands cupping my breasts, mine raking down over his naked backside, pulling him close.

"These walls are paper thin," I whisper. "I have to try to be quiet."

"Yikes, Katerina. You? Quiet? Your poor neighbors are in for an earful."

I laugh against his kiss as he picks me up and walks me toward the small bed we're definitely about to break. "I'd say I feel bad for them," I whisper, "but then again, the alternative is them listening to me cry-sing to emo music because I miss you so badly. So, really, of all the things they could hear, us making wild, loud love is hardly the worst."

"The worst?" Christopher says, love in his eyes as he lays me down on the bed. "Katerina, we're in each other's arms, with all our lives before us—nothing could be better."

· ACKNOWLEDGMENTS ·

Second books are notoriously hard to write, but I told myself, since this wasn't my second book *ever* (just the second book in this series), that wouldn't be the case.

Oopsie. I was very wrong.

Thankfully, I had the best people in my corner while I wrestled my way through drafting, revising, and finally falling in love with this story. My friends whose empathy, support, and humor made me feel so much less alone—they're my people who see and love me as I am, who let me see and love them as they are, too, and that means so very much. Becs and Sarah, who get what a sometimes draining, self-doubt rollercoaster this writing life can be, whose GIFs, texts, and early-morning Marco Polos kept me going—thank you for reading this story with hearts in your eyes and encouraging me as I wrote it. Thank you, Sarah, Ellie, and Amanda for authenticity reading and for your invaluable feedback on the representation in this story. Kristine, my superstar editor, always patient with my endless questions and so very supportive of the heart of my work—thank you for helping me shape this story into its best self, especially that second act that now truly shines because of your wise insight. Samantha, world's best agent, who believes so deeply in what I do and is always excited about how I do it—I cannot thank you enough for being on this path with me, for all your guidance and support.

And last but not least, my two (not so little anymore—please stop growing up so fast, okay?) firecrackers, you are my greatest joys and my magnum opus. With every book I write, I want to make you proud. If you read this one day, I hope you'll recognize in this story the love I aspire to as your mother and what I believe you deserve from your friends, family, and (if you want this one day) partner—love that doesn't dim your fire but fans its flames.

I will never stop pinching myself that I get to write these stories as my job, that I get to dig into the daunting, beautiful, tender corners of existence and write about people who love each other not in spite of but *because* of those daunting, beautiful, tender places. I am profoundly grateful for my readers, who make it possible for me to write and publish romances reflecting my belief that *everyone* deserves a love story, and for my publisher, Berkley, and all the incredible talents there who work tirelessly in editing, design, publicity, and marketing. I can't thank you enough.

Finally, to anyone out there who has felt like a stranger in their own family or who's loved and lost the family they had; to anyone who, as I have, has struggled with trusting someone else with the truth of their brain and body, for fear it might not be something someone could see fully and love just as much: I'm sorry for how badly it can hurt sometimes, and I hope you are gentle with yourself, that you are proud of yourself for every tiny step you take as you open your heart again, as you find the courage to tell your truth, as you pick yourself up after the hurt or disappointment or grief. It might not always feel like it, but love—in its many unique, powerful iterations, for yourself, between others—is always worth it, and you are always worthy of it. I believe that with my whole heart, and I hope this story has helped you, even if only a little, believe that, too.

Better Hate
than Never

CHLOE LIESE

READERS GUIDE

1. If you're familiar with Shakespeare's *The Taming of the Shrew*, what are some parallels and departures that you noticed between the original text and this modern reimagining, in plot, themes, character names, and relationships? If you aren't familiar with *The Taming of the Shrew*, do you now find yourself curious to read it or watch a film adaptation?

2. Speaking of film adaptations, the iconic late-90s rom-com starring Julia Stiles and Heath Ledger, *10 Things I Hate About You*, is a clever, swoony reimagining of *The Taming of the Shrew*. If you've watched the film, did you spot any references to it in *Better Hate than Never*?

3. *Better Hate than Never* features a neurodivergent heroine who has ADHD and a hero who lives with chronic migraines. What was it like for you to see the world through their eyes? For those who aren't neurodivergent or don't have a chronic condition, do you think reading from this perspective impacted how you might perceive and engage people who identify as such? Are there some ways you relate to Kate's and Christopher's experiences?

4. Shakespeare's *The Taming of the Shrew* can be a difficult play for the modern reader to engage with, given its misogynistic language and treatment of women. Critics have long wondered what Shakespeare, who penned so many strong, empowered heroines, was up

to, writing a play whose title says it all. Was it a parody of sexism in Renaissance society, meant to unsettle and provoke? We can't be sure. How do we see the "taming of the shrew" idea subverted in this book, in the manner in which Christopher views and treats Kate? In Kate and Christopher's relationship arc? In how Kate is viewed and treated by those around her?

5. The term *shrew* has been used for centuries to mean an "argumentative" or "angry" woman, contrasted to a woman who is obedient, compliant, and subservient to men within the patriarchal power system. While we have evolved societally from Shakespeare's time, do you think we still cast women as shrews when they speak out, disagree with, and challenge cultural norms and ideologies? Why or why not? How do we see that borne out in representation of "strong" or "feisty" women in media coverage, books, film/TV, and other art forms?

6. Themes of found family and family belonging are prevalent in this story. What do you make of Christopher, who isn't a Wilmot, feeling a greater sense of family belonging in his found family of the Wilmots than Kate, who *is* a Wilmot, yet who doesn't feel like she belongs to her own family much at all? What do you make of the journey these two undergo in their relationship to the Wilmots and to the friend group, which is another found family system? How does this shift reflect Kate's and Christopher's character growth arcs and relationship arc throughout the story?

7. Kate and Christopher have a lot of unlearning to do about each other after years of misunderstandings and resentment. In that process of unlearning, they realize that while their approaches to life have looked quite different, they actually share some similar fears and vulnerabilities, as well as values and hopes for the world. Have

you ever built a positive relationship with someone—platonic, romantic, or otherwise—after it began with misunderstanding or acrimony? What allowed you to discover common ground and build a connection?

8. At the end of *Better Hate than Never*, some time has passed since Kate and Christopher began their exclusive relationship, and we see how these two are growing as individuals and also growing into their relationship with each other. What did you think of the ending in terms of how it reflected that? Was it what you expected, or did you think it might end differently?

Turn the page for a preview of

Once Smitten, Twice Shy

Juliet

I have never in my life been more drenched than I am right now. Hair plastered to my temples, sundress stuck to my skin, I stumble into the greenhouse behind my childhood home and shove the door shut against the sideways wind that carries sweeping sheets of rain. As I slump against the door and sigh with relief to have made it to shelter, my reflection greets me in a tall pane of greenhouse glass.

Irises wide as blue-green china saucers, my hair a sopping, tangled sable mess, I blink away water and try to catch my breath. There's a tear in my sundress straight up my left thigh from a branch that sunk its sharp end into the fabric, then ripped a hole when I tugged myself free. My pulse is flying after my run from the small woods behind my parents' house toward the nearest shelter (my physical fitness is currently shit). In short: I look like I barely survived a shipwreck rather than a summer evening rainstorm.

I knew I should have stayed inside where I was minding my business in my parents' house, with only *New Girl* reruns and a hefty pour of whiskey for company. But no, I had to go and chase the damn cat, who snuck out *again*, and then get myself stuck in a microburst.

Meow. Puck, the ancient family cat, and the sole reason for my current misery, crawls out from under Mom's potting table, his typical fluffy white fur and matching bottlebrush tail waterlogged and dripping. He looks like a mop.

I snort a laugh, wiping water from my forehead before more can drip into my eyes. "Serves you right for running out of the house before the whole damn sky opened up."

Meow, he grumbles, shaking himself to lose some of the water matting down his fur.

"Well, at least you made it to safety, too." Puck twines around my legs, tickling me with his half-wet, once-again-fluffy fur. "Wonder if we can make a break for it yet."

I turn to peer out of the greenhouse as the wind's howl slides up an octave, only to see a wall of rainwater rolling down it. Looks like we'll be waiting out the storm here, then.

Now that the adrenaline is wearing off and I know I'm not about to be swept away by a storm, my body's usual aches (thanks for nothing, mixed connective tissue disease) make themselves known. My elbows and wrists, hips, knees, and ankles pulse with pain. Sitting isn't going to make it go away, but standing isn't going to make it better, either, so, on a groan, I ease to the floor. A shiver racks me as the backs of my wet legs connect with the tiles. The greenhouse is, as you'd expect, quite warm, but its floor tiles are still cool.

I slump back onto a bag of potting soil and sigh. Per usual, the cat takes my reclined position as an invitation to help himself to my lap.

"Puck"—a grunt leaves me when a paw hits my ovary—"is it too much to ask that you sit on my lap without squishing my internal organs?" His front paw smashes my boob as he crawls up my chest. I wince reflexively. "This is all your fault, you cantankerous animal. You just had to make an escape and harsh my fun Saturday night vibes."

The cat plops onto my chest and lazily blinks his mint green eyes, as if to say, *What "fun Saturday night vibes"?*

"Listen here, you," I mutter, scratching behind his wet ears because I'm a sucker for this furball, even when he's a giant pain in my ass, "*New Girl* reruns and whiskey is the definition of a roaring good time."

Meow, he says, swishing his tail.

"You've got a lot of nerve, throwing that in my face. It's a *monthly* horoscope, Puck, and I reserve the right to act on its advice when and how I see fit within the *month* of July."

It's pathetic that I'm arguing with my cat, since really I'm just arguing with myself, but I've got no one else to verbally process with right now. My parents are off on one of their postretirement adventures on the other side of the world, which is why I'm house- and cat-sitting. Kate, my little sister, is traveling for work this week, and Bea, my twin, has been holed up in her studio the past few days thanks to a burst of inspiration for her next series of paintings. All my family members have their lives together; they're happily paired off. Same with my friends. When I'm feeling bad for myself, the last people I want to go to—even though I could go to them for anything—are people whose lives are all wrapped up in the beautiful bow of happily-ever-after.

So it's just me and the cat left to muddle over what to do with my monthly horoscope:

Time to leave behind the season that left you wrecked and stranded. You aren't helpless or hopeless anymore. Now, you prove that to yourself. Now you wade into new waters, not knowing what's on the horizon but trusting the course. Trust yourself to find your way again.

It's not bad advice. It's just . . . scary advice. The old Juliet never even needed astrological ordinances to kick her butt into gear. But this new Juliet does. And this new Juliet is also thoroughly afraid to act on them.

Meow, Puck drawls.

I narrow my eyes at him. "You have the audacity to call *me* a 'scaredy cat'? You were hiding under a potting table because you got a little wet!"

Puck opens his mouth, and while I'm thoroughly prepared for another sassy *meow*, the last thing I expect is the loud, deep snore that I hear instead.

The cat's eyes and mine widen in tandem. Whereas Puck's survival instincts wisely kick in, sending him leaping off me and under the potting table for cover, I'm frozen, a sopping, sitting—well, slouching—duck.

Another deep, long snore punctures the quiet inside the greenhouse, snapping me out of my stunned state. Slowly, I ease upright, then onto all fours, crawling only far enough to peer around the edge of the long table that runs down the center of the greenhouse.

There's no one there.

And yet another snore rumbles from the far end of the greenhouse. Even if I can't see them, there's obviously someone in here, and while I want to tell myself that they're not a threat, seeing as they're fast asleep, I can't assume they're going to stay asleep or that I'll be safe with them when they wake up. I've learned the hard way that assuming the best of people can epically blow up in your face.

Glancing around, I scour the place for some kind of tool that I can use for self-defense. There aren't any big shovels or rakes in here—those are stored in the nearby shed—not that, with the state of my hands and wrists, I'd even be able to wield one with any particular control or accuracy. I spot a short handle shovel leaning against the potting table, which will be perfect. Not too long or heavy, with a short but solid wood handle that leads to a wide, sturdy metal base.

Carefully, I ease up to a squat and awkwardly crouch-walk my way over to the potting table, then grab the shovel. My knees hate this position, so I risk standing until I'm bent at the waist, peering through the tidy rows of flowers in various stages of growth on the center table.

Another snore rumbles through the air.

Quietly, I stand until I'm fully straightened and peek over the flowers. I still don't see anyone, so I start to walk the length of the table, shovel raised in my hands. My heart pounds, faster and faster.

When I finally get to the table's end, another snore rends the quiet, and I come to a dead stop.

First, I see brown boots leading to legs crossed at the ankle. Not boots like the city guys around here wear, polished and fancy, worn purely for style. These boots are scuffed and creased, the laces weathered and tugged tight, clearly worn for practicality. The jeans stemming from them follow suit, roughed up and threadbare at the knee, as if they've been bent in and worn countless times—working jeans. My eyes trail up the weathered denim—long calves, longer, thicker thighs. A sun-bleached olive green tee, two arms folded across it.

I gulp.

This dude's body is entirely relaxed in sleep and yet his arms are *ripped*. His muscles have muscles. Veins and ropy tendons weave up his arms. Two bulky biceps peek out from the edge of his T-shirt sleeves. All across his skin are freckles.

Swallowing roughly, I clutch the shovel tighter. I'm such a sucker for freckles.

I shake my head to snap out of it. I am *not* eroticizing this intruder who, for all I know, could be an axe murderer.

Albeit a sleepy axe murderer. So probably not a very good one, but still.

I tip my head, trying to see his face, but his head's bent, as if his chin's tucked to his chest. I can't see past the ripped brim of his ball cap that looks like it might have once been white but has faded to dingy oatmeal.

His leg twitches as another snore leaves him, and he's either a hell of an actor or he's out cold. I'm mid mental debate about which is the case when my quandary is solved for me.

A loud *boom* of thunder shakes the greenhouse and he jolts, as if startling awake. So he was asleep. Which means, most likely, he's not an actual threat. Maybe he's just some down-on-his-luck guy who crashed here to catch a few winks and ride out the storm before he goes on his way.

We don't do that anymore, Juliet. We don't give people the benefit of the doubt. We don't assume the best of them. That's what bit us in the ass last time. That's what broke our heart.

Right. Time to brace for an attack. I lift the shovel higher, standing out of his reach but not so far that I can't swing and hit him with the shovel, if needed.

I watch his ankles uncross, his ball cap shift as he sits straighter, then he freezes. The ball cap lifts a little, then a little more, as if his gaze is trailing upward. Up *me*.

Finally, his ball cap's brim lifts enough to reveal his face, for his eyes to meet mine. A face that I recognize, eyes that I've seen before. Just once, across a bar in a small Scottish pub, seven and a half months ago.

Wide, catlike green eyes—sage, flecked with silver, fringed by auburn lashes. Long, straight nose. Two sharp cheekbones. The rest of his face hides beneath a thick, unkempt beard and similarly unkempt hair that peeks out beneath the ball cap.

It can't be him.

But it could only be him.

I remember those striking eyes and that unforgettable hair, its color like nothing I have ever seen before or since—burnished penny copper, cinnamon fire. When I saw him that night at the pub, all I could think was he looked like a Highlander romance hero ripped out of the past, wrapped in modern clothes.

Highlander romances are my weakness.

As are redheads.

And I was not in Scotland to fall head over heels for a hot Scot. I was there to lick my wounds and heal from a horrible breakup. So I tore my gaze away, ordered a double pour of whiskey, knocked it back, then turned right around, headed for my Airbnb cottage, before I could act on the tug I felt right beneath my ribs, like a hook had sunk in, reeling me toward him.

What the hell is the hot Scottish stranger from the pub doing *here*? In my mom's greenhouse?

There is no good explanation. So much for him being some innocent, sleeping guy. This man followed me from Scotland! He's been here, biding his time, pretending to be asleep—

That's when it hits me, the danger I'm in. And that's when I lift the shovel over my head and scream.

The man ducks my swing, then rolls away and springs upright in a display of athleticism that has me deeply concerned for my odds against him. "Wait!" he yells. "Hold on!"

I'm just processing that his accent is American, not Scottish, as I swing at him again and miss, knocking over a damask rosebush. He lunges and successfully catches the rosebush, which, come to think of it, is odd for an assailant to do, but I'm already swinging at him again as I process that thought, too. I miss him entirely, losing my balance as the shovel whips out of my hands, then crashes into the table. Thrown off by the momentum of my forceful swing, I stumble back, straight into potted gardenia that wobble, then start to tip off the table's edge behind me.

The man lunges again, catches my hand before I fall, and yanks me toward him, almost like a swing dance move that swaps our places, before he somehow also catches the gardenia plant and rights it on the table. When I try to yank my hand away, he turns suddenly, which pulls me with him, and, in a chaotic tangle of feet and pinwheeling hands, we crash to the floor, him on his back, me sprawled on top of him.

In an uncharacteristic feat of agility and speed that I can only attribute to the power of adrenaline, I lunge for a trowel that's resting on the table beside me, then bring it to his throat, staring down at him, breathing heavily. "What," I gasp, "the *hell* are you doing here?"

The man's breathing heavily, too, eyes wide, hands back in surrender. "I . . ." He shakes his head. "What are *you* doing here?"

"Nuh-uh, you don't get to ask questions." With my free hand, I shove back the drenched hair that's fallen into my face, trowel still at his throat. "You're in my mom's greenhouse—"

"Your *mom's?*" he croaks.

"—and the last time I saw you, you were in the same Scottish pub as me seven and a half months ago, sitting at the bar, so *you're* the one who's going to do the explaining. Now tell me why you're here."

He swallows. I watch his Adam's apple roll beneath the trowel's tip. His mouth parts, working silently, until finally, he says, "I'm staying next door, with Christopher. I went for a walk and stopped in here."

I narrow my eyes at him. "Prove it."

"Call Christopher right now; he'll vouch for me."

The man reaches for his phone in his pocket. I slap my free hand down on his wrist and pin it there, searching his eyes. "*I'll* get your phone, thank you."

I tug his phone from his pocket, swipe it to open, then spin it so it uses facial recognition to unlock. Straight to his contacts, I scroll down and find . . . Christopher's name, and his cell phone number.

My jaw drops. Then the trowel follows suit, landing with a clatter on the tiles. Oh my god. The pieces fall into place. He's here for the party, the one that I now remember Christopher saying was a birthday bash slash reunion for his friends from college—friends I've never met because Christopher kept to himself in his college years, while he was in the city. Christopher is my next door neighbor, has been my whole life; he's like a brother to me. And I just tried to bludgeon his college friend with a short handle shovel.

Then I held him at trowel point.

Heat floods my face as I stare down at the man beneath me. I am mortified. And confused. Why, when he's here for a party at Christopher's, is he in the greenhouse?

"What are you doing in here, then?" I ask.

He swallows again and his hands start to lower to his sides. "Would you mind . . . if I answered you . . . while you're not on my lap?"

If my face was hot before, it's incinerating now. I glance down to where I sit, straddling his waist. My thighs are pinned against his ribs. My pelvis rests on his pelvis, where I feel a solid, thick weight—oh my *god*, I have to get off him.

I list sideways and scramble off the man in a very ungainly tumble of limbs, thanks to my embarrassment making me clumsy, my stiff joints resisting sudden movement. "Sorry," I mutter, trying to arrange myself in a dignified seated position on the floor. I'm not even going to try to stand yet, not when I'm this turned around and discombobulated.

Slowly, he eases up, then leans against the table's end, how he was when he was asleep. He draws up his knees and rests his elbows on them, rubbing his hands down his face.

"So," I offer, trying to move past the tension, "you were saying what, uh, brought you to the greenhouse."

He drops his hands, and his eyes meet mine. I bite my lip reflexively. Those eyes. They had no business being so beautiful back when I saw them across a pub in Scotland, and they have no business being this beautiful now, either.

But they are. They're as rare and striking as his copper hair—pale green, slivered by shards of silver, like frost-streaked leaves. I tell myself to stop staring at them, but dammit, I can't.

"The party was . . . a lot," he finally says. For the first time, I register the quality of his voice—warm, yet edged with a smoky roughness, like whiskey that hits your tongue rich and smooth and finishes with a peat-tinged complexity that makes it taste infinitely better. "I needed a break."

I tip my head. "So . . . you came in here, and then you fell asleep?"

Pink creeps up his cheeks, past the edge of his thick beard. "Passed out might be more accurate."

"Ah." I peer down at my soaked dress and pluck at the fabric to unstick it from my thighs. When I glance up, his gaze jumps up, too, as if it was lower, as if he was following my movement.

Our eyes meet. He blinks, then looks away, his focus traveling the flowers lined up along the far wall. He tugs down the brim of his ball cap, until his eyes are in shadow and his profile is distilled to the brim of his hat, his long, straight nose, and thick beard.

"You have to admit"—I set the trowel back on the table where I found it—"that this is pretty strange, that I randomly saw you in Scotland, and now you're here. It's a very weird coincidence."

Serendipitous, even.

I ignore that voice. Because that's a voice that belongs to someone I'm not anymore. Someone who always used to see romantic possibilities—meet-cutes and kismet and love at first sight—so much so, it led me right out of reality into the kind of fantasy that started off a dream and ended a nightmare.

I don't do that anymore—romanticize moments and people and see the world through rose-colored glasses. I *used* to. All the time.

But eight months ago, I stopped. Because eight months ago I realized where it had gotten me—in love with a manipulator who I didn't understand was a manipulator until he'd twisted me up so badly, I didn't recognize myself. I ended our relationship, quit my PR consultancy work, and hid away in a Scottish Airbnb for a month, licking my wounds, pickling my liver with whiskey, pounding shortbread, and bingeing *Fleabag*.

And then I told myself it was time to pick myself up and come home and get my shit together. Deal with the nagging health issues I'd been ignoring and couldn't afford to ignore anymore. Focus on facing my future head-on, rather than numbing myself to the pain of my past. I decided I was going to heal, grow, and move on.

Since then, I've built a new routine that's gotten me into a better place: I take care of my body and take my meds; I write freelance on a flexible work schedule; I don't date. I'm still scared to trust myself to accurately read people, and until I can, I'm not giving romance a chance or giving my heart to someone new only to risk getting hurt all over again.

Generally, that's been going well. My body doesn't feel *amazing* yet, but these things take time. My work doesn't pay what I'd like, but it's enough to scrape by. And I haven't missed romance, because I get plenty from the novels I've been reading voraciously since age twelve, when I found Mom's bodice rippers in the family library.

Well, I haven't missed it *too* much.

Except, in this moment, maybe I do. Just a little. Because this is a moment the old Juliet would have thoroughly enjoyed—a chaotic meet-cute with an enigmatic, hot stranger who I saw across a room once before. The old Juliet would toss her hair over her shoulder and say something witty right now, offer this guy a hand up and flirt her way out of the awkward.

Which is why the new Juliet needs to get the hell out of here, before she reverts to the very kind of behavior she's sworn off for damn good reason.

I try to stand, which, between my stiff body and my waterlogged dress, doesn't go so well. The man springs up and grips my elbow when I teeter sideways, lifting me gently, firmly, until I'm standing upright.

And then he drops my elbow the second I'm steady.

I should be glad about that, but I'm a little sad to have lost what's now only an echo of the feeling of his hand, warm and rough, callused palm and fingertips.

The guy tugs at the brim of his ball cap, lowering it so the shadows over his eyes deepen as he stares down at the ground. "This is definitely very weird," he confirms. "Seeing you here, after seeing you in Scotland."

"So you saw me, too." I tip my head, peering up at him. A smile wins out that shouldn't, but I can't help but be pleased: I didn't just notice him that night; he noticed me.

He peers up from beneath his ball cap and catches me smiling at him. His mouth is mostly hidden by the thick beard, but I think it tugs down in a frown. He clears his throat as he shoves his hands in his pockets. "It wasn't busy that night. 'Course I saw you."

I lift my eyebrows. "It was *very* busy that night. I had to shoulder my way to the bar."

Oh, now he's definitely frowning. And I'm enjoying it. I have no business enjoying it, but I am. "Not how I remember it," he says.

"But you *do* remember it." My smile deepens.

His eyes narrow.

I bite my lip so I won't laugh.

This is bad. Bad, bad, bad. I'm flirting for the first time in over half a year with the last person I should—someone whose life is entwined with Christopher's, which means indirectly, it's entwined with mine.

I want to ask him why he was in Scotland that night, as much as I want him to ask me what I was doing there, too. I want to invite him in for a whiskey, like I saw him drinking back at the pub last December, and learn someone new and feel those butterflies, the thrill of a fresh start.

But as my heart starts to pound, and not in the good way, I'm reminded that I'm not ready. And even if I was, he'd be the last person I'd try again with. If I acted on this with him, if he was as interested as I think he might be—judging by the way he keeps trying not to look at everywhere my wet dress clings to my curves—and if it went sideways with someone who matters to Christopher, who's an important part of his life, that would be a disaster.

I need to go. I need distance from this man. *Now.*

As if the universe is smiling down on my resolve, the rain stops, leaving us in sudden quiet and soft, nighttime darkness closing in around the lights that brighten the greenhouse.

"Well," I finally say, reaching back for my hair and squeezing the water out of it. "Now that the rain's done, I'll be going. But feel free to stay here and regroup from the party chaos for as long as you like." I wait a moment, thinking maybe he'll respond, but he doesn't. He just clears his throat and tugs his ball cap lower again.

I offer my hand. "It was nice to see you again . . ."

It takes him a moment before he finally extends his hand and wraps it around mine. I bite my lip, resisting the urge to melt into how good his touch feels.

He doesn't offer his name. So I don't offer mine. I suppose, when all's said and done, that's for the best. It's easier to leave someone in the past without a name to knit them to your memory.